PRAISE FOR *WITH EX...........JUDICE*

"At the center of Fredrick Barton's fascinating tale of corruption and greed there gleams a rare and valuable gem, one which we seldom see in contemporary literature: a happy marriage."

—Valerie Martin

"Fredrick Barton gets an early hammer lock on the reader and leaves him, at the end, quivering like a broken hairspring."

—Will D. Campbell

"Fredrick Barton spins more than a yarn – there's steel in his fabric and a love of New Orleans that will tell you odd things about that exotic city."

—Vance Bourjaily

"Chocked full of all the great things: undying love, the movies, corruption and New Orleans. Rick Barton peels the onion better than any chef in the French Quarter."

—Brandon Tartikoff

"Honestly written and well-conceived, this is a book that supplies pleasure on a number of levels."

—*Publisher's Weekly*

"This book deserves your attention because of its stunning intelligence."

—*Book Page*

"A thrilling read."

—*The Middlebrough Evening Gazette*

"This very well-written novel is unusual and revealing as well as exciting."

—*The Morning Star*

"A believability that an ordinary writer could never match"

—*The Sanford Herald*

"From the Big Easy's meanest back streets to the antebellum mansions of the Garden District, Barton weaves a suspenseful tale of deceit, violence and murder."

—*The Geneva Republican, The West Chicago Press*

"Fredrick Barton's book will hook you."

—The Biloxi-Gulfport Sun Herald

"It's quite a wonderful book."

—The Cleveland Plain Dealer

"At last! A novel about New Orleans that gets it all exactly right. Thank you, Rick Barton for a writing a smart, sexy novel about real people."

—The Sea Coast Echo

"Pick of the list"

—Cover Pages

"An ambitious tale of bribery, homicide, racism and personal salvation"

—The Times-Picayune

"All the spice of a New Orleans shrimp dish and the exquisite sweetness of Commander's Palace bread pudding."

—Book Page

"A thoughtful and troubling look at racial attitudes"

—Pasadena Star-News

"A well-conceived book – fine and well-written"

—Woodbridge News Tribune

"A stunning resolution in which prejudice reaches beyond the racial and into an unexpected realm"

—The Pilot

"Fredrick Barton's novel delivers a knockout punch on several levels. Like a fine French chef cooking a delicate soufflé, Barton has prepared a delicious literary meal."

—The Columbia State

"An insightful commentary on a unique city"

—Bibliomaniac

WITH EXTREME PREJUDICE

Also by Fredrick Barton

The El Cholo Feeling Passes
Courting Pandemonium
With Extreme Prejudice
Ash Wednesday
A House Divided
In the Wake of the Flagship
Rowing to Sweden
Monday Nights

WITH EXTREME PREJUDICE

A NOVEL

FREDRICK BARTON

Printed in the USA.
Library of Congress Control Number:
ISBN: 9781608011001
Copyright © 2013 by Fredrick Barton
University of New Orleans Press.

UNIVERSITY OF NEW ORLEANS PRESS
University of New Orleans Press
unopress.org

For
Joyce Markrid Dombourian, as always, of course

and
In Loving Memory of
Peter Mampreh Dombourian, 1920 1992
Joyce Boyle Dombourian, 1919-2004
V. Wayne Barton, 1925-1997

And for my beloved friend Will Campbell, 1924-2013
Who is always on my mind

—To be aware of the possibility of the search is to be onto something. Not to be onto something is to be in despair.

—As always we take up again where we left off.

Walker Percy
The Moviegoer

ACKNOWLEDGMENTS

I am indebted to the Louisiana Division of the Arts for financial assistance during a critical period in the writing of this book.

I am very grateful to the University of New Orleans Press and its leadership, Abram Himelstein and G.K. Darby. Your support is deeply appreciated.

Special thanks to my first readers, Joanna Leake, Dennis McSeveney, John Gery, Chris Wiltz, and my two dearly missed late colleagues, Jim Knudsen and John Cooke. Your advice was invaluable.

Thanks to my mentors Will Campbell, Gary Nash, and Richard Ford.

Thanks to my colleagues in the UNO Creative Writing Workshop and English Department.

Thanks to so many who have blessed me with their friendship and support.

Shoutouts to David, Rebeca, Libby, Scott, Tricia, Merrill, Carol, Charlie, Peg, Mark, Dorothy, Ed, Marilynn, John, Rene, Miles, Sharon, Mel, Les, Neal, Joseph, Fred, Joe, Lenore, Steve, Billy, Beth, Brandon, Kim, Amanda, Rade, April, Robin, Dan and Becky.

Thanks to my incredibly fine students at the University of New Orleans. You have taught me so much.

Thanks to my family, my sister Dana, my mother Joeddie and my father Wayne.

And, of course and most of all, thanks to Joyce Markrid Dombourian, my partner of 42 years, my chief consultant, my fellow traveler, my infallible proofreader and stern grammarian, my boon companion. My love.

PART ONE

CHAPTER ONE

It was an act of impregnation. And the nausea it induced began when I returned from Los Angeles.

It was late Sunday night, and I was beat. I was also legally drunk. But I knew something wasn't right from the moment I opened the front door to my little shotgun cottage on Dante Street in the River Bend. The doors to the armoire in the dining room were standing open, and the drawers of both the chest and the writing desk in the living room were pulled out. Joan always griped that I was forever leaving things ajar, but it had been months since I'd opened a drawer or an armoire door in the front of the house. Besides, the envelopes which my neighbor Larwood Dupre had fetched from the mailbox and usually placed on the desktop were lying scattered on the floor. It was as if a whirlwind had blown through my house. Then, when I saw the chaos in my study, I knew I'd been hit.

And I'd had too many Scotches on the airplane to feel like dealing with it.

*   *   *

As the film critic for our daily New Orleans newspaper, *The States-Tribune*, I had been out to L.A. for the *Cocktail/Rescue* junket, to interview those pictures' stars, directors and producers. And on the way home I had fallen off the wagon yet again—the irresistible temptation of flying first class, this time courtesy of Touchstone Pictures. I hadn't touched a drink for nearly a week before the junket and had somehow settled for Diet Cokes on the flight out. But I was tired coming home. The movies were shit, and the interviews were stupid. And this was the way I spent a substantial portion of my life, and that was so aggravating, so enervatingly claustrophobic, sometimes I felt like a Cadillac had parked on my chest. Now was one of those times. I was existentially discontent, I wasn't going to get into New Orleans until one a.m., and I had to file my pieces for Friday's paper by the end of the day on Monday.

And I can make up excuses at least twice as fast as anyone can dismiss them.

So I wavered as I was buckling down in LAX when the stewardess said to me, "Mr. Barnett, can I get you something to drink before departure?"

I had been debating whether to write or sleep on the ride home. I don't know why. I can never manage either. But sleep sounded good, given the work load that always faced me on Monday. A drink might help me doze off. Just one before departure, of course. But suddenly I found an unsuspected reserve of will. "No thanks," I replied.

That's when she looked at my haggard face with its puffy undereyelids, at my unkempt shank of dark brown hair and said, smiling, "You look like you've had a rough day."

I nodded, vainly tried to think of something witty to say and settled for, "I've had a rough weekend."

"Going home?"

"Yeah," I said.

"Out here on business?" she asked. And since she was being friendly, I looked at her for the first time. I had gotten out of the habit of looking at women. She was attractive. In her thirties. Early middle, I guessed. Short blond hair, pretty face, nice smile. I wondered if she was married and almost dared a glance at her fingers for a clue

Joan always told me she knew whether people were married or not by looking at their fingers. "Women *wear* their rings," she said. "And even if men don't, there's always a circle of pale skin that might as well have a tattoo reading, 'On the prowl!'" I regularly argued with her that some people (particularly women) might wear rings to avoid getting hassled and that some perfectly decent men might *not* wear their rings because they played sports or worked with their hands.

But she always said, "Sez you. I look at their hands, and I can tell if they're married."

And then I'd say, "Y'can not."

And she'd say, "Can too."

And we'd go on like five-year-olds until one of us could think of a clever way to shift the exchange onto some other dumb topic.

But I never quite summoned the energy to look at the stewardess's hands. About halfway into the impulse to do so, I realized, what did I care if she was married. I was on a four-hour plane ride from Los Angeles to New Orleans. And when I got off the plane, I'd likely never lay eyes on her again. Besides, I couldn't have stayed up all night to do it with this stewardess, even if I thought there was the slightest chance that she'd find me attractive enough to want to do *it* with. So after she asked if I'd gone to L.A. for business, I just worked up a weary smile and said, "Yeah."

I'm a wicked conversationalist when I put my mind to it.

"You worked all weekend, huh?" she inquired, side-stepping from the galley toward me through the stream of coach passengers making their way on board.

"Yep," I said, flaunting my vocabulary.

"You need to work on the way home?"

I puffed up my chunky cheeks and blew out a breathy burst of air. "I need to," I said. "But then I *need* to do a lot of things. Maybe I'll try to catch a nap."

"Then let me bring you a drink," she offered. "There's still time before we push back from the gate."

"All right," I said, smothering the contempt I felt for myself under silent promises that one drink could hardly hurt me. "Scotch. On the rocks."

She beamed as if she'd just converted an infidel from his sinful ways. If only she knew the extent to which convincing me to have a drink was an act of preaching to the devoutly converted. "Chivas?" she asked.

I shook my head. "Dewars," I said with some resignation. I drink

Black and White usually. Johnny Walker Red if Black and White isn't available, which on airplanes it usually isn't. I'd long since learned that Delta carried three brands of Scotch only: Chivas, which I didn't much like, J & B, which I actively disliked (though hardly so much as to do without if there were no other choice) and Dewars, which I thought was pretty good if neither Black and White nor Johnny Walker was available.

"Most people prefer Chivas," the stewardess said, stepping back through the flow of passengers to the galley.

I smiled, not knowing how to respond, thinking nastily, *but most people, of course, are idiots*. I'd always teased Joan I'd gotten such misanthropy from her.

In a couple of minutes the stewardess set two little bottles of Dewars in front of me, along with two tumblers of ice, as always (mysteriously), one plastic, one glass. I'd conveniently managed to forget that in first class drinks are always served in pairs.

I finished them both before we took off.

Then came my standard contest to see just how many I could consume before we landed. I managed another two after takeoff and before dinner, two with dinner, and three after. This was madness, of course, and I knew it even as I kept ordering drinks. My guzzling on airplanes was born, I think, of some primordial sense of deprivation, some cellular memory of the time in graduate school when cheap wine was all that Joan and I could afford, when a brand like Sebastiani was a special treat, when we seldom even had a bottle of liquor in the house, when a Scotch and water at a restaurant or in a pub was an unusual and treasured luxury, when a wedding was a special, eagerly anticipated event because somebody's daddy was going to pay for an open bar that meant I could have as many drinks as I could conceivably want. I was years past the kind of financial need that meant I couldn't afford to buy a drink any damn time I wanted it. But I sat myself down in first class where the drinks were free and somehow felt I wasn't getting my money's worth if a single second were to pass with my fingers wrapped around an empty glass.

So I was just about to ask for a tenth Scotch when the pilot announced that we were making our final approach into Moisant

Airport. The stewardess would have brought it to me, I'm sure, and without a doubt, I could have sucked it down in the required time. But I was finally too embarrassed to ask.

I'm sure the stewardess would have accommodated me because along around drinks three and four we started to get chummy, and I could tell she was the sort who measured her success by the amount of service she could render. We really chatted up a storm once dinner was out of the way. I called her, "Gail," and she called me, "Mike," and everything was just as cordial as Courvoisier. There was only one other passenger in first class, so Gail didn't have much to do, other than bring us drinks and make conversation. She was married. Her husband sold real estate. They had no children. She was based in Atlanta. She had been flying twelve years. And so, in the final analysis, who in the hell cared?

But that was wrong, really. That was my ugly, bitter underside talking. Gail was nice. And I was flattered (as I always am) that she thought my jet-setting job was so exciting.

"Gee," she said, "you get paid to go to the movies? And you get to talk to guys like Tom Cruise?"

She added with a naughty giggle, "I'm a little too old for him, I guess, but if he stumbled over on top of me, I sure wouldn't push him off. If you know what I mean."

If I stumbled over on top of you with my bear-like girth, I thought, *you wouldn't be able to push me off, and you'd be squashed as thin as a communion wafer.*

"Who else have you interviewed?" she asked.

I trotted out some names I figured were pretty sure to impress her: Nick Nolte, Harrison Ford, Robert De Niro, Albert Finney, Michael Caine, Woody Allen (for male listeners, I always drop Jane Fonda, Meryl Streep, Diane Keaton, Jessica Lange, Sissy Spacek, Michelle Pfeiffer). And she responded with the expected ejaculations of envy.

I haven't really seen my job as all that glamorous for years, of course, though I like the pure writing of it, the daily reviews, even the feature pieces that I wouldn't do if they weren't a part of my job description. And I'm damn proud of the column of open-ended commentary I write for the Sunday edition.

Gail wanted to know if I was "famous" in New Orleans, and I

protested that the primary famous people in New Orleans were the Neville Brothers and Ellis, Wynton, and Branford Marsallis. But she wasn't much of a music fan, and in the end I admitted that yes, a lot people in the city knew my name. "Everyone goes to the movies," I pointed out, "and everyone reads movie reviews. And I've been writing my movie column for years now."

At some point Gail asked me if I'd seen such and such movie—I no longer remember which one—and I was momentarily flummoxed, as always when I got this question. I had to see *every* movie. So, of course, I saw such and such. That's what I did for a living. I saw such and such today. Tomorrow I saw *Such and Such II*. Still, it wasn't fair to wax irritable toward Gail or anyone else who asked me this question. Even my colleagues at the paper would frequently ask me, "Hey Mike, have you seen such and such?"

Sometimes my colleagues even made statements like, "What are you reviewing today, Mike?" And when I told them, they'd respond, "Oh really, have you seen it?"

What was I to say? I sometimes said, "No, I find I do a better job of criticism if I avoid polluting myself with the actual work itself."

But they seldom took kindly to this, I found. So mostly I restricted such sarcasm to friends and people I really hated.

I told Gail sure I'd seen such and such. Whatever it was. And we talked. About movies and whatever else. And I found myself liking her. Gradually the conversation became more personal, and when I didn't volunteer the information, she eventually asked. Afterwards the conversation didn't last much longer. Funny that she'd ask, isn't it? According to Joan women check your fingers, in my case, finally, ringless.

"I *was* married," I told Gail. "My wife died in an accident about a year ago."

Then Gail mumbled the expected oh gosh that she was sorry. And I shrugged my shoulders in a gesture of silent acknowledgment that didn't mean one damn thing. She went to freshen my first-class companion's drink and, save for keeping a midget bottle of Dewars and a fresh set-up in front of me, busied herself in the galley for the remainder of the flight.

That's the way it was, you see. Joan was dead, and there was nothing to say about it. Gail didn't know what to say. My friends didn't know what to say. No one knew what to say. That's what this whole thing was about. Joan was dead. And I didn't know what to say.

*   *   *

I asked myself, as I'd asked myself a thousand times in the last year, how could Joan *conceivably* be dead. One minute she was her whole complicated self, running and sweating and exhorting me with her incessant bullshit, and the next she was a broken bag of lifeless flesh. How could that be? What if she'd stopped? Or hadn't turned her head? What if I hadn't fallen behind, and we could have been together, both properly wary-eyed, both, as we should have been, looking ahead.

I know it's gratingly trite to speak such a notion, but it seems like goddamn yesterday when she was my childhood sweetheart, when we used to go bowling at Fazio's and roller skating at Causeway Roller Rink with our church youth group, and later to junior high dances, and later still when we used to ride the streetcar together down to Canal Street for movies at the Saenger or the Loew's or the Orpheum. Then in high school, when I was still skinny and thought scoring twenty points in a basketball game was more important than World Peace and that victory in any athletic contest was certainly more important than François Truffaut, she was the school brain who *had heard* of Truffaut and even dragged me off to see *Jules and Jim* during its belated, one-week engagement at the Center. It was she who first read *Cat's Cradle* and *Catch-22* and who worried about nuclear disarmament. She also worried about teenage pregnancy and therefore would never let me stray beyond third base when we went parking out on Lakeshore Drive. But even though I was a classic dumb jock, she insisted on being my best friend. So she never told me how stupid I looked wearing a flat-top.

In college at Tulane, she arrived first at the idea the Vietnam War was an atrocity. And to help me fight the draft after she'd turned me into a fellow war protester, she agreed to marry me shortly before our graduation in the Kent State/Cambodia spring of 1970. Or at least that's the first set of reasons she'd admit to. The real reason, I knew, though I could scarcely ever understand why, was that she loved me.

And wasn't that a kick in the pants?

We were married seventeen years, through my graduate school at UCLA where I majored in film studies and she worked as a legal secretary, through her three years at Tulane Law when I was a cub reporter at the paper, through our years of rapid rise into respectable yuppiedom, through our first glimpses of life's downward slope at the dawn of middle age.

Since we'd gone to graduate school in shifts, we were in our early thirties and thus older than others when we began to taste the fruits of the comfortable middleclass. And we probably hurried too much to catch up. A lawyer and a newspaperperson can spend just about as much time working as they can create time to spend working. And we spent a lot of time working. We might as well, we always figured, for the other one wasn't waiting at home; he or she was at work. And so we were successful. We were promoted early and often. Joan was soon a partner at her firm of Herbst, Gilman, Roquevert and Ivy. And I was soon the *States-Tribune* film critic. And we were prosperous. And we hadn't yet peaked, we believed.

So when my gut began to balloon from too many wonderful meals at Galatoire's, which was our one deliberate sin, or from too much time sitting in darkened theaters or at a desk or in a first-class airplane cabin surrounded by a half-dozen or so 50 milliliter bottles of Dewars, then Joan got me out to jog on the streetcar track down the grassy meridian we natives call a neutral ground on Carrollton Avenue and around onto St. Charles. But then one day a driver turned a corner into the St. Charles Avenue neutral ground at Short Street and ran Joan down. He was in a hurry to get home for dinner, he said, and he was watching an approaching streetcar, trying to gauge whether he had space and time enough to cross the neutral ground before it passed. He saw Joan clearly, but since he was already pulling across the neutral ground, he presumed she'd stop. He looked away, and then when he looked back Joan was running in front of him. Joan, of course, was looking in the other direction, away from him and at me, urging me to keep up with her. We'd been talking about her favorite movie, Claude Lelouch's *And Now My Love*, which we'd watched on video the night before. But I'd fallen too far behind to make conversation easy. Then I'd heard her say the name Grieve, and I knew she'd switched to talking about the case, the *Grieve versus Retif* lawsuit on which she'd been working for years. She had been noticeably preoccupied for the last week, and I had suspected she'd been working on the case again. She'd learned something, she said, and she needed to talk to me about it. She said something about Judge Delacroix. But I was too far behind, studying the passing yardage of packed dirt globbed with grease, stomped grass, and rusted track. I heard her voice, breathy with exertion and two words that sounded like "suit" and "case."

"What," I yelled back, "What?" But then there was a shout, and a thump, and a crack like that of a snapping tree limb. And I was screaming at the top of my lungs, "Get the car off her you asshole! Get the car off her you asshole!" He panicked, of course, as I might have too. A bearded, working-class black man with a tattered tennis hat crushed down on his forehead, his dingy white T-shirt flecked with paint, he leapt from his car to see what he'd done, me screaming at him all the while. And when he realized, it took him agonizing seconds to get the car started again.

Eventually he got the car off her. But it didn't do her any good. Joan was still alive when we got her to Ochsner Hospital, but she never regained consciousness.

And then we'd peaked for sure. Cut short on fucking Short Street. God was operating at the zenith of his creative powers when he invented irony, wasn't he? Joan was dead. And the only consolation I could find was copper-colored and luminous and lay somewhere beyond the mid-point in a fifth of Black and White.

*   *   *

My friends Wilson Malt and Carl Shaney occasionally upbraided me now that she'd been gone a year. "You're allowing yourself to wallow in unbecoming self-pity," they'd say. As if I didn't recognize what I was doing. But I knew full goddamn well. I was drinking myself into oblivion. I was trying to kill the ache I could feel behind my eyes. Now and then, as in the week before the *Cocktail/Rescue* junket, I pulled myself together. And I was always sober at work, always clear-minded when I wrote my columns. But I didn't want to stay clear-minded once I got home from the paper. I couldn't stand to walk around my house, which used to seem so crowded with just the two of us and now seemed cavernous. Joan had been dead a year. But I could still smell her in the house, in her closet, in the mattress on our bed. Yeah, Wilson and Carl, I *was* wallowing in self-pity. I knew it. But I knew this, too: only Black and White let me sleep in that bed without her.

*   *   *

So in my own unbecoming, self-pitying way, I was optimistic when I arrived home from the *Cocktail/Rescue* junket. I had enough Dewars in my gut that it wouldn't have taken more than a couple of Black and White chasers and I could have gotten some sleep. Only my house had been burgled. And I had to call the cops and try to sober up before they arrived.

CHAPTER TWO

Cocktail *made me drunk with embarrassment.*

Shortly after it gets underway, the movie locates itself in a place called The Cell Block, obviously one of New York's current hot spots. A throng of Manhattan's young and chic set are mingling and drinking and having their eardrums blown out by a stereo surely installed and operated by enemies of the national future. Out of sight, in an entirely different movie, Michael J. Fox is in the restroom fortifying himself with Colombian Marching Powder. You get the picture. The Cell Block is the place to be, where everything is cool. Make that COOL! And there's more. There's entertainment. Poets sometimes climb the stairs (that lead to God only knows where) and scream their verse to an audience they improbably manage to calm long enough to listen.

But mostly there are the two bartenders, two ragingly virile guys who prepare their potions with such flourish. They juggle cocktail glasses between their legs and behind their backs. They slide into moonwalks to shake their martinis. They flip bottles of hootch over their shoulders into dizzying twirls and snatch them to the lips of snifters just an inch from smashing. They are Tom Cruise and Bryan Brown as Brian Flanagan and Doug Coughlin, the featured characters in this movie called Cocktail. *They are the world's greatest bartenders. They are the stars of the summer's dumbest picture.*

Brian Flanagan is an army veteran, recently discharged with the single-minded ambition to become as rich as possible as soon as possible.

He's got a book on self-improvement in his hip pocket and a determined look on his handsome face. He's got some problems, though, namely no education and no experience. So, what the hey, he becomes a bartender, and he and buddy Doug Coughlin are such a smash at The Cell Block they begin to nurture dreams of owning their own place and someday franchising that place into every suburban shopping mall in the USA.

But then the two pals have a falling out and Cocktail *lurches into a whole new plot. Brian heads off to ply his acrobatic mixology in Jamaica where he meets Jordan Mooney (Elizabeth Shue), a vacationing sweetie with whom he hops into a picturesque waterfall just as soon as the two of them can slide out of their designer swimming suits. But no more has post-coital glow begun to ebb into a serious relationship than does Doug appear on the wings of outrageous financial success. Doug has achieved matrimony with a rich blonde fond of swimming attire with no tops and no backs. Having thus learned the secret of success, Doug advises Brian to ditch Jordan, who's just a waitress, and scramble between the sheets with a woman of means. Being the ambitious type, Brian becomes a gigolo. And* Cocktail, *in its final third, becomes the story of whether Brian will enjoy the life of the pampered hunk or will wake up to embrace the iffy life with Jordan.*

There's so very much to squirm about in this flick. But I'll concede its incidental positive qualities. Brian has got a no-nonsense uncle (Ron Dean) with some down-home, stoical observations about the inevitable passages of life. Tom Cruise has got one meaningful speech about how the drumbeat of daily drudgery slowly extinguishes the embers of a man's dreams. Lisa Banes as Bonnie, Brian's rich bitch girlfriend, has a knockout squelch line that unfortunately cannot be repeated in this family publication. But most of all, the picture has Elizabeth Shue, who is so beautiful and exudes such evident intelligence that you delight in every moment she's on the screen, even if you can't fathom for a second why she accepted a part in this movie.

Beyond that, Cocktail *has a soundtrack that calls for earplugs, an MTV visual style that seems guilty of being instantly passe, and a plot so contrived it seems the cinematic equivalent of a paint-by-the-numbers picture. Nothing prepares us for Brian's dumping Jordan for Bonnie, and the best he can muster in explaining is an attempt to foist the blame off on Doug. "When a guy lays down a dare," he says, "you have to take it."*

Thank God Doug didn't dare Brian to go commit the F-word on himself.

Of course, this is a flick in which lots of things don't make sense. What in the world is Brian doing messing around with Doug's wife? He abhors such behavior. More important, he abhors Doug's wife. Such questions abound as the film careens towards its climax. Does Jordan have to get pregnant? Is it remotely credible that her character would get pregnant? Does she have to be unspeakably rich and involved in that old peekaboo game of, "I didn't tell you because I wanted to make sure it was me and not my money you were in love with." And does Doug have to commit suicide when his life in the fast lane starts to run out of gas? He cites as a reason that his wife has started cheating on him. I'm sorry Doug. I thought you only married her for access to her bank account.

So who's to blame for this debacle? Alas, I think we have to blame Cruise. Now on the whole I like Tom Cruise. I've written with considerable enthusiasm about his work in Taps, Risky Business *and* The Color of Money. *And, as a matter of fact, I don't find anything offensive about his performance in* Cocktail. *As is his habit, he prepared thoroughly for this role. He went to bartending school, even worked a couple of nights at a Manhattan tavern for first-hand experience. He taught himself all the juggling tricks that Brian does and performed them all in the film. But what he didn't do, evidently, was notice that* Cocktail *is a story that just doesn't work. Even the business of all the fancy drink mixing doesn't work. Cruise says, "We wanted a shorthand way to show that these guys were great bartenders." But he should surely realize that being a great bartender has absolutely nothing to do with how to handle a glass before you pour something into it. My main reaction was that Brian and Doug could sure serve up a lot more drinks if they'd knock off all the horseplay.*

But chiefly, Cruise must shoulder the blame for Cocktail *because he was the critical ingredient in its ever going before the cameras. Producer Robert Cort disagrees, of course (as naturally he would), claims the picture would have been made whether Cruise was its headliner or not. But Cort admits that he'd had the film in development since 1982 and it only became a "go" project when Cruise agreed to star. Cruise himself says, "It was a film a lot of people didn't want to make. But if I say I* want to do something, I'm at a point in my career where I can get it made." This is credit you'd think he'd not be so eager to take.

But director Roger Donaldson acknowledges Cruise as well. "I definitely would not have directed this picture had it not been for Tom's involvement," he asserts. Gee. When you think about it, that's not a terribly strong endorsement from the man who made the movie.

Donaldson and Cruise were the big snowballs that started the fatal Hollywood avalanche syndrome. They respected each other's work, and each, perhaps, trusted the other not to choose an unworthwhile project. With the two of them signed, the rest was easy. Swept up in this avalanche mentality, Elizabeth Shue, whose Harvard-trained consciousness should have been outraged by the picture's depiction of the irrelevance of a college education, "was delighted with the opportunity to work with Tom Cruise."

Bryan Brown expresses almost identical sentiments. "I'm always eager to work with the likes of Tom and Roger," he says. "Also, I was intrigued," he adds, "to play a guy who commits suicide." One is tempted to comment that after starring in Tai-Pan, Brown must be an expert about on-screen suicide. But I don't really have the heart to be nasty to a good-natured bloke like Bryan Brown. So I'll just say there's an affable resilience to the Aussie actor that makes you suspect, like Michael Caine, he'll survive any number of terrible films to show up later in something worthwhile.

So what did Cruise and Donaldson see in this material? Cruise says, "It was different. It's a character-oriented movie. And I was attracted by the fact that the character does a lot of things you don't like." Yes, but Tom, the character does a lot of things that don't make sense to his character.

Donaldson says, "I was drawn to the picture because of its moral that the materialism of the eighties is on the wane, that one finds direction not in money but in people." If those elements had been clear in this movie, Roger, I'd likely be filing a different piece of copy than the one in which this sentence appears.

In the final analysis director Donaldson expresses the real bottom line about the making of Cocktail by invoking a nautical image. "Tom and I had been looking for a chance to work together, and when he signed for the film, I came aboard too." To stay with that marine language, I *predict they'll sail* Cocktail *into a great big opening week, but then they'll be torn apart by the Scylla and Charybdis of hostile critical response and disappointed audience reaction.*

And they'll all go down with the ship.

*   *   *

I wrote the first draft of the above column on *Cocktail* (revised the next afternoon with a clearer head) in the three hours and forty-five minutes that I waited for the police to arrive at my house. I'm an astonishing box office prognosticator, huh? The flick only became the summer's biggest, stupidest hit. Thank God the rightness of my judgment is neither affirmed nor denied by ticket sales. In my view, that is. Some of the people who read my work would no doubt contend otherwise.

I am by no means always as hard on movies as I was on *Cocktail*. But the picture pissed me off. It was so pointless, so formulaic, so calculated to make money. That was the only real agenda I could find in its having been made.

In hindsight, to be honest, perhaps I was rough on *Cocktail* because my house had been turned into a trash heap. And because I started writing just after a most unpleasant experience trying to report the break-in. Or maybe it was because I wrote it on a wave of nausea that threatened to send me dashing to the bathroom in the very next minute.

Anyway, after I got off the phone with a Ms. Fisher at the Police Department, I figured I didn't have any choice but to go to work—or suffer very deep shit trying to make my deadlines the next day. And given my condition, that fact, as you can imagine, put me in a pretty foul mood. I still think *Cocktail* deserved the treatment I gave it. But I concede that movies just as bad have elicited less of my indignation. Sometimes I worry over all the implications of the judgments I render. But not often. I do the best I can. I state what I think. I meet my deadlines. I admit, though, I am always comforted by the fact that in most significant ways I don't have to take responsibility for the verdicts I render. As most studio executives will tell you, the nation's film critics affect the success or failure of very few motion pictures. And I'm glad about that. I would abhor being saddled with the influence over a film's financial success that a New York theater critic exercises over plays that open on Broadway and off.

Before I composed the *Cocktail* piece, though, I had to deal with my home as crime scene. I dialed 911 and was immediately asked whether I was calling about a life-threatening situation. When I admitted I wasn't, I was put on hold. Then, after some considerable waiting and transferring, I got a woman at the Police Department named Ms. Fisher who communicated through her bored and irritated tone that she held me and all other crime victims personally responsible for making the lives of our local police officers so utterly miserable.

"I'd like to report a robbery," I told her, getting off to a most confusing and misleading start to our relationship.

"Just a minute, please," Ms. Fisher said. When she returned to the phone she began abruptly, presumably reading off some form, "Name of victim?"

"Michael Barnett," I said. The top of my forehead, just under my thinning hairline, was starting to throb.

"Victim's address?" she said. I gave her my address, and she then requested, "Exact location of robbery."

"Same as above," I said, adopting her formese. "Victim's residence."

"Was perpetrator known to victim?"

"No."

"Description of perpetrator or perpetrators?"

"Unknown," I said.

"Unknown?" Ms. Fisher challenged.

"Unknown," I repeated with a sigh. I am sometimes convinced that the world's bureaucracies have all been designed to inflict me with headaches.

"Mr. Barnett . . ." she said, "I am speaking to the robbery victim?"

"Yes, you are," I assured her. Mike Barnett, the victim.

"Mr. Barnett," she said, biting off her words in obvious annoyance. "If you are the victim, how is it that you state the description of the perpetrator or perpetrators is 'unknown?'"

"Miss," I said, as irked as she, "I didn't see them. I wasn't at home. I doubt that I'd have been robbed if I had been at home." I needed a drink. I stepped to the refrigerator, squeezed the phone receiver between my ear and shoulder, and began trying to pull an ice tray from the freezer compartment.

"Mr. Barnett," Ms. Fisher said, "have you called to report a burglary?"

"Yes ma'am," I responded with exaggerated sweetness, "that's exactly what I've called to report."

"Mr. Barnett," Ms. Fisher said, sounding just as sweetly nasty, "you distinctly said that you had called to report a robbery."

"Yay-us may-om," I said—once I switched into an exaggerated Southern accent, it was usually only moments before I began screaming "fucking this" and "fucking that" at the top of my lungs—"Mah how-us was robbed."

"You were not personally robbed?"

"Way-ell, may-om, I own most evathang in this how-us."

"You're telling me your home was burglarized while you were out."

"Yassum, thass about it. Ah was gone an ah got robbed."

"Burglarized, Mr. Barnett. I gather now that your home was burglarized."

"Jesus. Yes. Robbed, burglarized. What's the goddamn difference?"

"The difference, Mr. Barnett, is that you reported having been robbed. Consequently, I have been filling out a robbery report. Now we will have to begin again and fill out a burglary report. That's the goddamn difference."

Well, you learn something new every day.

My head was pounding, and I abruptly opted for four aspirin tablets instead of my nth Scotch of the evening. Ms. Fisher and I completed the repetitive process of filling out the burglary report. At the end, I asked her how long it would be before the investigating officers would arrive.

"As soon as they can get there," Ms. Fisher assured me.

"Are we talking days or weeks?" I asked.

She then gave me a lecture about the undermanned and underpaid nature of the New Orleans Police Department. I responded that, unlike a majority of the citizens of our neglected city, I had voted for every new tax initiative, either city or state, that had been placed on the ballot since I became old enough to vote. So I didn't exactly take kindly to being blamed for the town's desperate fiscal circumstances.

"But you understand," she countered, "that your situation cannot be considered an emergency." This ultimately translated into a prediction that officers would arrive in three or four hours.

That's when I began working on the *Cocktail* piece. I clearly wasn't going to get any sleep. I was going to be in very bad shape the next day. And my Monday deadline wasn't likely to begin receding unexpectedly. My office was a mess. So I set up my Zenith laptop on my kitchen table and had at it. I find that when I've been drinking, I can type about as well as I can guard Michael Jordan. Thank God for the invention of my word processing program's spell check.

The cops showed up just about the time I finished my *Cocktail* column. The *Rescue* review would have to wait until another day. But that was okay. *Cocktail* was slated for national release that weekend. *Rescue* wouldn't open in New Orleans for several weeks.

My verdict on *Cocktail* ran in Friday's entertainment tabloid almost exactly as it appears above. My editor changed only one thing. Where I wrote, "Thank God Doug didn't dare Brian to go commit the F-word on himself," Carl (my friend, entertainment editor Carl Shaney) changed it to read, "Thank God Doug didn't dare Brian to jump off the Empire State Building."

Later Carl said to me, "You know, Mike, one of these days I'm gonna go on vacation, and you're gonna pull some shit that makes it into the paper. Then the Old Man is gonna pull your tallywhacker off. What do you have to say to that?"

"I'd have to say you're incredibly old to still be using a word like *tallywhacker*."

Carl laughed. And when he did, I smiled.

It was the first time I'd smiled in a week.

CHAPTER THREE

It was already light by the time the police officers arrived at my house. Early morning is usually the best time in New Orleans. Three seasons a year, dawn finds this city at its most beautiful, quiet, damp with dew, fresh as if after a cleansing, alive with a potential that may be more craved than real. I gave up jogging after Joannie died. But I still sometimes liked to take walks before work along our old jogging route: down the streetcar tracks to Audubon Park, a quarter way around the park's two-mile asphalt oval, and across the shell path that bifurcates the golf course, underneath the canopy of stately oaks with their hoary wigs of Spanish moss. On those serene, early-morning excursions I could almost conquer the feeling of pointlessness that had suffocated me since her death. The city was so lush with bloom, so rich with the redolence of renewing life. But now it was July again. And the air hung heavy in the unwanted summer, like a mildewed blanket someone malicious had draped about our heads while we were sleeping. Even early morning in the summer brought little hope. The city failed to cool at night and produced a dusty, dewless dawn. And rather than provide an even fleeting freshness, its day-long aroma wafted with decay.

On that morning in late July when I opened my door for the policemen, I was greeted by a blast of hot, sticky air from the furnace that our city becomes every summer. It wasn't quite six, but they stood sweating, a white officer on the Creole green porch, his black partner on the apron of sidewalk between the brick steps and the front gate. The latter was presumably providing backup to the former, in case, I guess, the resident of my house proved a crazed, weapon-wielding lunatic.

"Mr. Michael Barnett?" the porchman asked. He wiped with his fingertips just under the line of his charcoal black hair.

"Yes," I said.

They began to fish out their I.D.s, and I said, "Come in, I've been expecting you."

The porchman was Lieutenant Frank Giannetti. His sidewalk partner was Sergeant Robert Rideau. They stepped into my living room and informed me they would need to look around.

"Nice place you got here, Mr. Barnett," Giannetti said, though not with much enthusiasm, I thought. I pigeonholed him in my mind: third generation policeman, Irish Channel Italian. No doubt his idea of the proper middle-class home was suburban, brick, one-story ranch-style or two-story French provincial. I gouged my own unearned and unbecoming superiority with the memory that such was exactly my own idea of a proper house until Joan shaped my appreciation for historic architecture.

My frazzled mind raced with a hundred different thoughts. It had been suggested to me since Joan died that perhaps I ought to sell this house to free myself from so many daily reminders of her. I couldn't bring myself to do it. But sometimes I was tempted. I remembered how in the year before her death we had talked of moving to a bigger, fancier place and how we'd begun saving toward that end. As if such saving were necessary. For reasons, I suppose, dating to our marriage at the height of the women's movement, Joan and I always kept our finances separate, two career couple that we were. And when she died, she left me $200,000 in savings, $100,000 more than she'd ever admitted to. I suspect that she planned to surprise me at some point, to find the perfect larger house, show it to me, and when I complained about what it cost, reveal with a delicious giggle that she already had the cash in the bank. If I were to buy a different place now, though, it wouldn't be the kind of house Joan and I would have bought together. It would have to be an edifice requiring far less attention than the Victorian places Joan loved. So though I could have, I didn't move because to have moved would have been to lose something else in my life that uniquely represented Joan and her taste.

Sergeant Rideau jerked me back from this bleary reverie. "These old houses are sure something," he said. "High ceilings and all, fireplaces." He began to rub his hand appreciatively over the surface of Joan's antique writing desk which stood mostly as an ornamental piece against the front wall of the living-room, directly across from the free-standing fireplace. Like most of every comparable piece of furniture in the house, its drawers were standing open over their former contents which were strewn about on the floor underneath. "You got some very nice pieces here, Mr. Barnett."

I thanked them for their compliments, and as we slowly moved from one room to the next, Rideau scribbling notes into a black police notebook, his own observations and Giannetti's, I answered their routine questions about how long I'd been away from the house, when I thought the break-in might have occurred, what in particular I thought they might have hoped to find, and so forth.

When we got to the kitchen, I asked, "Can I fix you fellas a cup of coffee?"

Giannetti responded with a short laugh and said, "No thanks."

Rideau looked up from his notebook. "We're pulling the graveyard shift." He grinned as he added, "We do a proper thorough job here, and we can call it a day. Last thing either of us needs is something to delay some needed shut-eye, which I myself am planning on commencing in just about"—he looked at his watch—"one hour and fifteen minutes."

In our bedroom, Giannetti noted, "Bed ain't been slept in." And I briefly explained what I did for a living and that I'd been writing while waiting for them to come.

"Movie reviewer, huh," Rideau said. "Yeah, I think I've seen your stuff in the paper. Mike Barnett, yeah." He stuck his pencil behind his ear and ran his hand along the cool foot rail of our brass bed and peered into the open, shuttered closets which stretched across one whole wall. The clothes in the closets had been pushed away from the center; items on the shelves behind had been dislodged. And all the shoes, Joan's and mine, had been raked from the closet floors into the room. "Say," Rideau said, "Whadja thinka that movie, *Die Hard*? That was a kick wudnit? Cop without his shoes. Shit!"

I have learned that when most people, particularly strangers, ask me for my opinion about a movie, they really want only an excuse to tell me theirs. So I have learned to mumble something noncommittally assentive, and that's what I did now.

When we got to the back room, the police officers stepped gingerly around the piles of papers, manila folders, and eight-by-eleven-inch glossy photographs, which seemed to cover the heart-of-pine floor like a lumpy, badly installed, checkered carpet, and began to inspect the door where the burglars had obviously made their entrance.

"This is where they got in," Giannetti said to no one in particular. He pulled the door open into the room and the two detectives examined the splintered wood around the dead-bolt lock.

Rideau began writing in his notebook again and said as he made his notations, "Fairly standard M.O."

Giannetti explained to me, "Sledgehammer. One good blow right on the outside lock face and they're in." He looked at me, and, as if to assure me that he wasn't critical of my security precautions, said, "Dead bolts are OK to keep out kids, amateurs, people robbing houses as a lark, you know, on the way home from the grocery. But if somebody wants in your house bad enough, nothing's gonna keep 'em out."

Rideau said, "We got another case, raised house like this one, guy crawled underneath with a buzz saw, cut a hole right through the floor. What you gonna do?"

"There a gate to the back yard?" Giannetti asked.

"Yeah," I replied, feeling a wave of fatigue sweep behind my eyelids. "Around on the side."

The policemen stepped out on the deck, looked briefly at the seven-foot "privacy" cedar fence and the towering silver maple which stood in the center of the yard. Then they made their way down onto the washed pebble sidewalk which curved around the side of the house to the backyard gate. I looked at my ruined room and wondered just how long it was going to take me to put everything back in order.

The people from whom Joan and I bought our house had used this back room as a den. It was painted a pastel blue to enhance the brightness, and its entire rear wall was glass, two shelved picture windows on either side of a wood-framed door with fifteen rectangular glass panels. But aesthetically sensitive as Joan was, she was equally as practical. Why have a living room, she believed, if you didn't live in it. Thus, a den we didn't need. And the back room became our home office, neatly outfitted with full-sized his and her desks and a five-drawer filing cabinet for each of us.

In the years we lived in the house, however, I don't think Joan ever did a single day's work at the desk we designated hers. She was normally in her fifty-fifth floor Place St. Charles office by eight-thirty in the morning, seldom home before eight o'clock at night. And there were few weekends when she didn't spend at least one whole day downtown. She kept some personal papers in a desk drawer or two, but she never filled but one of the drawers in her file cabinet. She said that she sat at a desk for so much of her life at work she would be damned if she'd sit at one at home. So on those too frequent occasions when she brought work home with her, she did it while sitting cross-legged, Buddha-like, in the center of our king-sized bed, the bulging canvas satchel she used as a briefcase sitting against the headboard, stacked papers surrounding her in a semicircle.

I, on the other hand, as my tenure at the paper increased, came to do more and more of my work at home. I was frequently out of the office at the movies anyway. I couldn't do my work on anything approaching a regular nine-to-five basis, so, though I almost always made at least a token daily appearance at my office, I did a great deal of my writing at home. Both my IBM-PC desktop, which three years ago was shifted to a permanent position on Joan's desk, and my Zenith laptop, on which I now did practically all my work, were equipped with modems, so I didn't even have to leave home to file my copy. Save for Joan's lone drawer, the filing cabinets (all three—much to Joan's outspoken dismay I insisted on wedging in a third) were crammed with folders containing press kits and photographs from the last decade's movie releases. The book shelves were lined with my various film books, research volumes, biographies of assorted directors, screenplay paperbacks and hardback anthologies, the last ten years' issues of *Film Quarterly*, and countless novels that had enjoyed cinematic adaptations.

Most of the books, now, remained on the shelves. But the contents of all the desk drawers had been thrown on the floor. Two of the filing cabinets were similarly emptied. The third was intact except for its top drawer, whose contents, like all the rest, lay strewn around the room as if they'd been deposited there in the aftermath of a tornado.

Giannetti and Rideau came back in through the rear door. "Probably just kicked in the back gate," Giannetti said. "You could probably do something better back there. But with a raised house, as I said . . ." He broke off without finishing. It was no use, he no doubt presumed, to chastise the victim for his carelessness.

The two detectives questioned me more thoroughly now about what was missing. I told them I didn't know for sure. I reminded them that I'd been told by Ms. Fisher not to touch anything. "All three TV sets were left alone," I said, and as I spoke I flashed abruptly on myself as a college student and how ridiculous I would have thought it to possess three TVs. "So were the Beta, the VHS and the stereo. Although the stereo is so antiquated they probably wouldn't have bothered. They clearly stirred through the jewelry box in Joan's bathroom. I wouldn't know if anything is missing. Nothing of much value was in there. Her nice stuff, I gave to her sister."

"Joan is your wife?" Giannetti asked.

"Yes," I responded. "She was. She died a year ago."

"I'm sorry," Rideau said.

I shrugged, took a deep breath. "I think our camera is missing from the bedroom wardrobe. I mean, it's certainly not there. But I haven't seen it since my wife and I got back from an Alaskan cruise shortly before her death. So, frankly, God only knows if it was in the chest or not. Probably it was, and if so it's missing."

"Expensive camera?" Giannetti asked.

"I guess. A Nikon. Christ I can't even tell you what model or anything. We paid about $400 for it. Which was expensive to us."

"Anything else?" Rideau asked.

I hunched my shoulders and shook my head. "Not that I can determine without cleaning this place up. What I can't figure out is why they left the TV sets. The JVC in the bedroom is almost brand new."

"Who knows, Mr. Barnett," Rideau said. "They could have been looking just for money or the jewelry you mentioned. Or a firearm."

"Or drugs," Giannetti added.

Had I been less tired, I might have bristled at the conceivable insinuations of this last comment, but at the time such implications didn't even occur to me.

"From the looks of things," I said, "they ransacked this back room a lot more thoroughly than they did the rest of the house. And there's certainly nothing back here worth stealing. They left the computer, for Christ's sake. They didn't even take the floppy disks. They're worth money. They sure cost me every time . . . " I suddenly felt utterly stupid for ranting about computer diskettes.

Rideau smiled. "I don't think your average burglar is into computers, Mr. Barnett."

"Of course," I said, shrugging my instant concession. "But why not the TVs or the VCRs? I thought there was always a black market on that kind of consumer electronics."

"Fence doesn't pay but about five percent on the dollar for that kind of stuff," Giannetti said. "But that doesn't mean they wouldn'ta taken it. Way I figure it is they gave the back room a thorough going over because that's the first one they got into. Maybe they never planned to try to lug out any of the heavy stuff. Maybe they got spooked by something and got the hell out without taking, say the bedroom TV, which they'd planned to. Who knows?"

Rideau said, "Coulda been you coming home they heard. Bolted out the back and around the side without you ever knowing they were here."

Giannetti added, "You can't tell a thing what these ni..., what these . . ." He abruptly cleared his throat and coughed into his fist. "Nobody can figure a pattern M.O. for burglary nowadays. 'Bout all that's predictable is that it's drug related. Project crackhead trying to finance his habit."

There was a barely perceptible little pause after that, and then Rideau asked me if there was anyone else who had access to my house. "Only the Dupres," I told him.

"And who are the Dupres?" Giannetti inquired.

"Older couple," I said. "Neighbors. Live just around the block there on Freret corner of Cambronne. Delinda cleans house for me. Started working for me and Joan when we first bought this place.

Larwood does the yard, brings in the mail when I'm out of town. He does odd jobs for most everybody in the River Bend."

Rideau was writing in his notebook. "And how do the Dupres have access," he asked.

I shrugged. "They have their own set of keys."

"And why would that be?" Giannetti asked.

"I keep sort of irregular hours," I responded. "I'm here a lot, but I'm out a lot, too, day and night. Delinda comes over once a week to clean. She can just let herself in. Same with Larwood. I like to keep the back gate locked." I laughed. "For security purposes. Larwood comes through the house to open the back gate so he can mow back there. And they keep an eye on the place when I'm out of town. Larwood mostly. Comes over, takes the mail and the paper inside. That sort of thing."

"These Dupres black or white?" Giannetti wanted to know.

"Black," I said.

"Uh huh," Giannetti responded. Then he added, "And they'd know just about everything in the house here. Everything of value. The camera. Your wife's jewelry and so forth."

I felt incredibly tired.

"Larwood and Delinda Dupre didn't rob my house," I said.

"You never know," Giannetti said.

"They have keys," I pointed out. "Why would they bust open the back door when they have keys."

"So you'd never suspect it was them," Giannetti replied.

"Well you can take my word for it," I said. "The Dupres didn't do this. You said yourself it was probably drug related. Probably kids. This is an older couple. In their sixties."

"I don't remember saying anything about kids," Giannetti said. "But I'm sure Sergeant Rideau has noted your testimony on the Dupres' behalf. And I'm sure if they're the good neighbors you contend, they won't mind answering a few questions for us."

"I don't think you even ought to bother them," I said.

"Yeah," Giannetti said. "Well I doubt they'll think it's such a bother. And seeing as we're about wrapped up here, maybe we can catch Mr. Dupre before he heads off this morning to cut somebody's grass."

As the policemen were leaving, Sergeant Rideau said that he was sorry about what had happened and was glad it appeared I hadn't anything more than a big mess to clean up. I agreed, and remarked that I had theft insurance and would be compensated, I guessed, for whatever I finally determined was missing. Giannetti told me that once I had a fairly final list of the missing items to call it in and it would be placed in the file on this incident.

Rideau said, "I'm glad to hear you've got insurance. Because I'm afraid there's little likelihood the burglars will be apprehended."

"Unless Mr. or Mrs. Dupre are able to shed any light on what happened here," Giannetti said.

"Which, of course, isn't very likely," Rideau added.

*   *   *

After they were gone, I thought about calling Larwood to warn him that cops were on their way to his house. But I didn't want to unduly frighten or confuse him. And I figured Giannetti and Rideau would be there before I could get the situation adequately explained.

I modemed in my *Cocktail* piece, left a message for Carl that I would not be in until late afternoon, and set my radio alarm for one o'clock. It was just after seven. If I went right to sleep, I could get nearly six hours before I had to make the minimum gestures to keep my job.

The phone rang before I could get into the shower. It was Larwood Dupre.

"Mr. Mike?" he said.

"Hi, Larwood," I said.

"Mr. Mike, me and the Mrs. just had some policemens here. Somethin' about somebody bustin' into your house. You knows about that?"

I explained that my house had been burgled and apologized to Larwood for getting him involved.

"What's this business with my ball-peen?" Larwood asked. "Them policemens want to know what kinda tools I had. I tooks 'em out to the truck and shows 'em what all I got. And they was might interested in my ball-peen. Ax me if I ever used it over by your house. I told 'em sure. I used it at your house when I broke up that ole patio when you an Miss Joan put in that new back poach."

"The cops think someone used a sledge hammer to break into the back of my house," I said.

"But now Mr. Mike," Larwood said, obvious concern in his voice. "You don't think I had nothin' to do with that, now do you? I been woikin' for you an Miss Joan fore she died, God bless her, for a lotta years."

I wasn't very successful at setting Larwood's mind at rest. But I assured him repeatedly that I didn't suspect him in the least and that I was sorry as I could be that the policemen had even bothered him. I felt fairly confident, though, that Larwood and Delinda had nothing more serious than bruised feelings to worry about. And I promised myself I'd think up some way to make it up to them. They were good people, and I was quite fond of them both.

When I finally got off the phone with Larwood, I showered quickly and got into bed. At first I was unable to sleep. I'd screwed my mind around with too many different kinds of substances, Dewars from Los Angeles to New Orleans, Community Dark Roast Instant Coffee from two o'clock until nearly six. My brain was buzzing. And I felt creepy in my house in a way I'd never felt before. Someone uninvited and unfriendly had been in this very room. Somebody I didn't know had put his hands on things that were mine. Somebody careless, indifferent, and even hostile to the kind of order I always tried to maintain in my life had defiled the space in which I lived and worked.

Finally, exhausted, I fell into a brief, uneasy doze which was marred by the dream that had been plaguing me since Joan died. In the dream, I was in high school again, lean and fast and playing baseball at a practice diamond in City Park. The dream always started in the middle: I am steaming toward third at full gallop; the third base coach is windmilling his arm for me to try to score. I fly past third and turn for home. The tiny catcher comes out to block the plate. I lower my head, drop my shoulder. I hit him just below the center of his chest and knock him sprawling into the dirt.

But today for the first time there was a different element in the dream. Today the catcher is black.

Waking, I lay in clammy sheets, and this new element of my dream seeped into my conscious imagination. I pictured the burglars:

there were always two and they were always male. I saw them going through my filing cabinet drawers, throwing file after file, fistfuls at a time over their shoulders and onto the floor behind them. What in the hell were they looking for?

And this was the disturbing part, this was the key to my dream's metamorphosis: in my mind the burglars were always black. That was the unfinished presumption in Lieutenant Giannetti's sentence, too. He was about to say, "You can't tell a thing what these *niggers* are gonna do." Or something like that. Whatever, you can bet he caught himself just about to use the word *nigger*, and you can probably bet he wouldn't have hesitated to use it had his partner not been a black man. I felt certain that Giannetti had seized upon the Dupres as suspects, however tepid, exclusively because they were black.

I felt guilty sharing Lieutenant Giannetti's fundamental presumption. It was one thing for a New Orleans cop to be racist, but it was something entirely else for me suddenly to run headlong into my own prejudices. I was a New Orleans boy, born and bred. I'd lived here all my life except for the three years I was in graduate school at U.C.L.A. But I'd grown up with the myth of my home town as The Big Easy, the Southern haven where blacks and whites loved the same music and the same spicy food and related to each other, if not as equals—you couldn't deny the segregated schools, after all, or Jim Crow's "Colored Only" signs on water fountains and bus-seat backs—then at least in an atmosphere of widespread acceptance and benevolence. Eventually, of course, I managed to grow up and out of such naïveté. As an adult I saw rather more clearly the deep and longstanding racial divisions that New Orleans tried to mask behind its good-time, party-town image. But I hadn't lost my values. I was widely known in local media circles as the town liberal. I'd voted for George McGovern for Christ's sake. And for Jimmy Carter (twice) and for Walter Mondale. I was going to vote for Michael Dukakis in November. I even voted twice for Napoleon Beaumont, a black man I didn't like, but grudgingly respected, in his races against white opponents for mayor of our city.

I wasn't even a late blooming liberal. My parents made me that way. Like Joan's parents, they were school teachers, and for reasons I never quite put together, given the circumstances of their own families and upbringings, they believed in human equality. I was raised believing that Martin Luther King was a hero. My father had taught me that the word *nigger*, not the word *fuck*, was the dirtiest word in the English language. So I would never have said that the men who robbed (make that burgled) my house were "niggers." But all the same, I *presumed* they were black. And that was a notion that ate at the sills of my consciousness like a pesky swarm of termites. It was a notion I couldn't rationalize as anything other than prejudice.

*   *   *

Like absolutely anything, of course, it is hard to ascertain the truth of one's memories. But New Orleans seemed a town that was going somewhere when I was growing up in the fifties and early sixties. We were still a minor league town. But we were chafing under that fact. The crowds at Pelican Stadium, the home of our Double A baseball franchise, dwindled until the park was bulldozed for a fancy new hotel. We didn't need a minor league team hovering around to remind us that we lacked a team in the majors. We were the fifteenth largest city in the nation in those days, and we were damn proud of that fact. We were moving. Denoux Leblanc was mayor, and he was so progressive that the rednecks from the rest of the state wouldn't let him become governor. But that was okay because he was a friend of John Kennedy's, and our town was Kennedy territory, and like the whole country in JFK's fleeting Camelot, we were going somewhere. We were going to get a football team (which we have) and a baseball team (which we haven't). And we were going to ride the post World War II prosperity into a second Golden Age, the first of which, when cotton was king and New Orleans was king of cotton, had made us the richest city in the world. We, not Atlanta or Dallas, and certainly not that cow town Houston, were going to be the shining light of the long heralded New South. And we were going to integrate our schools without embarrassing ourselves the way the folks in Norfolk and Little Rock had.

But it wasn't to be, of course. Our schools were "integrated" with less trauma than happened elsewhere. But that was because we tried to fool the feds into buying the idea that a handful of black kids in a handful of classrooms was sufficient. LBJ's Great Society didn't buy it, of course. And pretty soon we were forced to integrate for real.

But by that time something awful had gone wrong with our economy. The rest of the country was in boom, and we were sinking backwards. The city got some dynamic political leadership in the early and mid-seventies. The Superdome was built on Poydras Street, and the slide of the Central Business District was reversed. Downtown was saved, though its epicenter has gradually shifted to Poydras and away from historic Canal Street. But New Orleans changed in a way that may prohibit its full recovery for a very long time. The primacy of the port declined. Many small industries providing reputable work for blue collar people collapsed and died. And our city suffered a panic of white flight that has changed its face forever.

Through the first few years of the seventies, whites still composed a sizable portion of our public school student body. Today, only five percent of public school students are white. Don't get me wrong. Jim Crow's dual school system, separate and indisputably unequal, was an abomination. It had to be destroyed. But today, the same public high school from which Joan and I graduated can muster a satisfactory ranking in English for fewer than a third of its graduates. I can barely even contemplate the vast implications of this fact, but among them, I know, is fuel for the racist proclamations of men like David Duke.

When New Orleans whites rushed beyond the city limits to neighboring Jefferson and St. Tammany Parishes, they took our town's tax base with them. The parish schools are new and flush with up-to-date facilities. And the city still doesn't have integrated schools. *Brown versus The Board* promised blacks educational equality and it gave them, in our city anyway, the same old screw job.

And we all, whites and blacks alike, pay the price. White people who have stayed in New Orleans, and whites have been a minority now throughout the eighties, feel that they can't send their kids to any public school other than James Madison, an Uptown magnet high school for students with I.Q. scores over 120. Middle-class black parents feel basically the same. Our public schools are now among the worst in the nation. As a result, middle-class people from elsewhere, and the businesses who employ them, are reluctant to locate here. High tech industries, computer firms and the like, and white collar companies, insurance companies for instance, bypass New Orleans because they feel the pool of potential employees is too small.

For a time, of course, big oil sustained us. But the oil surplus, which saved Reagan's ass and let him claim credit for whipping Arab-oil-fueled inflation, did us in. All those oil company geologists and engineers and management types of various sorts didn't live inside Orleans Parish and thus didn't send their kids to Orleans Parish schools. But they did pump a huge amount of cash into the local economy. And that had its benefits for everyone who lived here. But then oil went from thirty-four dollars a barrel to twelve dollars a barrel. The oil companies pared their operations and relocated their people to Houston. And huge brick ranch-style and French provincial housing developments on the West Bank became ghost towns.

I give credit to aspects of the political leadership our city has enjoyed during these tough times. Mayor Beaumont was saddled with an unfortunate personality, but he did what he could for the city. Beaumont's successor, Charles Fredericks, has faced even worse circumstances. That great courtroom performer and sometime state governor, Frank Falcone, often indicted but never convicted, he who immortalized the defense against the charge of influence peddling, "It may have been a crime for him to pay me that money, but it was certainly no crime for me to accept it," that same Frank Falcone at the height of the oil boom tied state revenues to a tax on oil depletion— as measured by the barrelhead price, not by the volume itself. So when oil dropped over $20 a barrel, the state lost $600 million. Try running state education with that kind of drop in revenue. Louisiana, which has practically no property tax and only a piddling income tax, *has* been trying. Teachers, for example, haven't had a measurable raise in almost a decade. And they are fleeing the state in droves.

Fredericks' response, like that of Beaumont before him, has been to try to bolster the only industry that has remained healthy through this long, dark passage, namely tourism. New Orleans is booming as a convention town. Everybody loves the city's beauty, its grand parks, its historic and, as a result of the tourism boom, revitalized riverfront, its streetcars and, of course, its great restaurants. The National Football League loves to stage the Super Bowl at the Superdome. And now the NCAA feels likewise about the Final Four. Civic leaders have worked hard to bring these events here, as well as the huge American Booksellers Association annual convention and a host of similar events. And they should be commended for their diligence and salesmanship. But there's an unhappy bottom line to their labors. The kinds of jobs that tourism creates, waiters and waitresses, hotel janitors and maids, short order cooks and fast food counter workers, these are minimum wage jobs of the most dead-end variety. Tourism may bring jobs to a city that badly needs them, but it doesn't bring good jobs; it doesn't bring genuine, lasting, sustaining hope for the future.

The civil rights victories of the mid-sixties, particularly the great civil rights legislation of 1964 and 1965, were supposed to provide black people with a way out of their second class citizenship. It hasn't happened in New Orleans. There *is* a sizable black middle class here. And though there has always been a class of influential and talented black leadership, it is larger today than it was twenty years ago. But the so-called black underclass is larger today, too, and arguably more hopelessly rooted in poverty than ever before.

In his opening stage directions for *A Streetcar Named Desire*, Tennessee Williams describes New Orleans as a "city where there is a relatively warm and easy intermingling of the races." The truth of Williams's assertion, even in the 1940s, is, I'm sure, a subject endlessly debatable. But it's part of the myth of The Big Easy. And it's one of the virtues New Orleanians like to believe about themselves. But however much such intermingling was true at a time in the past, it is certainly less so today. Historically, New Orleans was residentially segregated only on a block-by-block, or, if such a distinction has any meaning, a house-by-house basis. Blacks and whites were, therefore, necessarily in frequent contact with one another, shopping at the local grocery, waiting for the same bus, getting food or drink at the same local restaurant and tavern. I'm not for a second maintaining that these connections were made in anything approaching an atmosphere of equality. Blacks weren't allowed to sit down at the restaurants; they could only sit down on the back seats of the bus. But at least there *were* connections. And that probably *did* distinguish New Orleans from other cities where blacks and whites resided in separate neighborhoods. Today, though, so many of the whites are gone that houses and blocks that were occupied by white families when Joan and I were growing up are now occupied by blacks. The races are growing more distant from one another. I don't claim to be altogether comfortable with my relationship to Larwood and Delinda Dupre, for instance. They work for me. And they approach me with a kind of deference that I neither insist upon nor even like. But I think it's valuable for both me and the Dupres that we have a relationship, that we know each other on a personal basis, that we actively care about each other.

My racist upstate redneck grandfather used to like to fish with an old black man I knew only as M.F. (my father insisted, properly, that I address him as Mr. M.F.) After listening to one of Pawpaw's diatribes on the inferiority of the black race when I was about ten, a speech that claimed a white man would "vomit his guts out if he had to eat with a stinking nigger," I asked how come he didn't get sick when he ate lunch out on the fishing boat with Mr. M.F. My question, actually, was genuinely inquisitive, a matter of a child's insistent logic rather than purposely inflammatory. But you can imagine my father's liberal delight at hearing me ask it. Pawpaw's response remains instructive, I think, to this day. "Goddamnit, I ain't talking about Uncle M.F.," he said, flushing red. "I'm talking about goddamn niggers."

What's happening in the New Orleans of my adult years is that white people and black people fear and resent each other as "types," as *nigger* and *whitey*. I should know. My best friend is black. And there wasn't a single clue to suggest that those who burgled my home were black. But I assumed that they were anyway. And in so doing I committed a grievous sin.

CHAPTER FOUR

Beware!

Some movie studio executive has been watching bad movies again. And one of them just had to have seen that dreadful exercise in American jingoism called Iron Eagle, *a 1986 travesty of a motion picture about an Air Force brat who commandeers a plane and flies off to North Africa to save his daddy who's being held hostage by an Arab meanie, who isn't Khaddafy, of course, or Qaddafi or however we're supposed to spell his name this week, but just looks like Khaddafy or Qaddafi or however we're supposed to spell his name this week.*

Anyway, sailing headlong toward Iron Eagle's *bottom ten spot this year is* The Rescue. *Because, hey, if one bratty kid saving one dad can make X amount of money, shouldn't five bratty kids saving four dads make 4½ X amount of money?*

Damn, but I hope not.

How original is The Rescue? *Well the dads are in the Navy rather than the Air Force. That's an imaginative difference. And they're captured by North Korean meanies rather than Arab meanies. And not a single one of the North Korean meanies looks even remotely like Khaddafy or Qaddafi or however we're supposed to spell his name this week.*

In addition . . . well, you don't want too *much variety.*

The Touchstone Studio flew me all the way out to Beverly Hills to interview everybody important in this movie. So I don't want to be too critical. You understand. But, just for fun, let's consider the improbables in The Rescue. *In order to pull off their feat of derring-do, our four teenaged heroes—if you're keeping a scorecard, sullen bad boy J.J. (Kevin Dillon), cute tomboy Adrian (Christina Harnos), electronics whiz Max (Marc Price), and Eagle Scout straight arrow Shawn (Ned Vaughn—do you think actors who rhyme with their characters possess a special cinematic karma?), along with, for the pre-pubescent viewer, of course, Shawn's pain-in-the-ass little brother Bobby (Ian Giatti)—have to sink a North Korean naval riverboat without having the country's entire military force put on alert; have to steal a North Korean sailboat without irritating its owner and his friends and neighbors; have to possess graduate degrees in explosives and weaponry; have to, evidently, be able to hide huge spools of cables in their socks or undershorts; have to be able to locate that unguarded tunnel that always leads to the very center of movie prison camps; and, critically, have to benefit from the fact that movie North Koreans are worse shots than blind people. Given the number of shots these movie North Koreans squeeze off, a normal blind person would have hit something just by accident.*

To say that this movie is preposterous is an understatement. At the screening for the film I attended in Los Angeles, when the brats announced their intentions to invade North Korea in order to rescue their dads, the audience laughed out loud. And the guffaws emerged from people who presumably knew just exactly what they were in for.

But hey, don't take my lefto pinkword for it. Consider what those who were involved with the project have to say about it. "It's an outlandish concept," says writer Jim Thomas, who must wonder just what lucky star he woke up under when this script went into production. I identify with writers. So I hope Jim got all his money up front. (I don't think there's gonna be all that much back end dough to spread around. If you know what I mean.)

Kevin Dillon says he originally passed on the film, but later agreed to participate when he discovered a rewrite which "was so much better than the first draft." Were the brats accompanied by E.T. in the first version?

Charles Haid, who plays Shawn's daddy and thus gets to sit out the middle part of the movie in a nasty prison camp, admits that "There's nothing very profound in this movie," but goes on to assert, "But I had a great time in New Zealand." Yes Charles, that's a telling endorsement.

If Touchstone had flown me to New Zealand to interview you, my attitude toward this movie might soften somewhat, too.

Director Ferdinand Fairfax says he was drawn to the project because, "I was attracted to the idea of Americans abroad." Scratching my head as he said this, I kept wondering if he thought this film somehow placed him right in there with Henry James. Thanks anyway Ferdie, but I've got to publish my commentary on this film back on Earth.

My favorite comment comes from Edward Albert, who plays J.J.'s pop. Extolling the flick's finale, Albert says, "It's like someone grabbing you by the collar and slapping you in the face for twenty minutes."

You know, Eddie, I couldn't have put it any better myself.

*　　　*　　　*

I wrote the above review in about two hours when I got to the office at three p.m. the day after I discovered my house had been broken into. I hadn't really slept. I hadn't shaved. I hadn't eaten. I had a pounding hangover. All right, I was in a damn bad mood. But *The Rescue* deserved every scathing thing I had to say about it.

Carl had to do his usual tampering with the review, of course. Three weeks later when the movie opened, it ran in Friday's tabloid, and I discovered that he'd made several changes. Where I wrote, "Damn I hope not," he edited it to read, "Goodness I hope not." Where I wrote of Shawn's "pain-in-the-ass little brother" he substituted "pain-in-the-rear." And where I challenged, "hey, don't take my lefto pinkword for it," he conservatively blue-penciled *lefto pink*.

I love Carl, you know. Shitty as I like to pretend it is, somebody's got to do my job. And if it weren't for Carl, that person probably wouldn't any longer be me. What I'm afraid of is that one of these days I'm going to pull some shit when Carl goes on vacation. And the Old Man is going to pull my tallywhacker off.

*　　　*　　　*

When I finished *The Rescue* piece, I saved it off and placed hard copy in Carl's in-basket. I was so agitated by the fact that my house had been burgled I wasn't able to think about much else and decided to sort through my mail as a way of retaining at least the semblance of productivity. I threw away without reading all the studio puff pieces about who had been promoted to what, and what movie had just started principal photography on location where, and what best selling novel had just been purchased for what outrageous amount of money. I sometimes rewrote those news releases, or turned them over to an intern to rewrite as filler, but usually I just threw them away. It always astonished me that every studio had somebody writing this publicity material and no doubt paid them good money to do it, probably more than I made, in fact. When I had concluded throwing away my pointless mail, I opened my large manila envelopes of press kits, selected those on movies I would be writing about soon and loaded them in my briefcase to take home. The others I filed in the In drawer of my filing cabinet which contained, among other things, press kits on movies that hadn't yet opened in New Orleans.

All that routine desk organizing completed, I did a rewrite on my *Cocktail* column and then began my editing work for Friday's tabloid on the list of movies that would be in town the coming weekend. By seven p.m. I was finished and ready to go home. I could have stayed longer, of course. There was always more work to do. But I had met all my deadlines. I could see out the door of my office that Carl Shaney was still at his desk. I thought maybe I could get him to join me for a drink somewhere. After that, if I was lucky, maybe a couple of stiff glasses of Black and White right before I crawled into the sack would give me a shot at some sleep. I loaded my Zenith laptop into its backpack, closed my briefcase and headed out of the office. As I did so, I thought again of the burglary and suddenly felt a surge of anger so intense that I thought I might abruptly slam the door to my office. I breathed deeply in an effort to control myself and managed to get out into Editorial without smashing anything. But around the handle of my briefcase my fingernails were biting into my palm.

In Carl's office I set down my gear against his desk and slumped into a hard wooden chair facing him. "Let's go bend an elbow," I said, my voice thick.

Carl didn't even acknowledge me. He was staring intently at his computer terminal, its screen split between his computer-preserved notes and the story he was writing.

I wrestled with myself to find the affectionate flippancy with which Carl and I usually related. "Paraphrasing Jack Nicholson in *One Flew Over the Cuckoo's Nest*," I said, "contrary to your deepest wish, I am not a figment of your nightmarish, paranoid imagination. I am a real live thirsty person here."

"I presume you can't see that I am writing," Carl said, still not looking at me. "I presume you fail to notice that I am in the process of saving the world again. Saving it as I am called to do over and over again. At the moment, if you must know and promise not to tell, I am saving the world from sales tax fraud. How could mending an elbow, whatever the fuck that means, possibly be as important as what I'm doing."

"People always complain that you ignore them," I said. "I think maybe you're just deaf. I'd say stupid, but I don't know that I could bear up later under the psycho-socio-racial implications of such a judgment."

Carl responded with a riff of furious typing, followed by a snap of the fingers on his right hand and a triumphantly flourished fist. "Damn but I'm good," he said to his computer screen.

"Now that we've got that debatable fact established," I said, "why don't you get your barely black ass up from that drudgery, and let's go wet our whistles."

Carl still didn't so much as glance in my direction. "I can do without your comments about the shade of my ass," he said, "which, as a matter of fact, I find sort of perturbing you've even taken notice of. Next time after I kick your lily white ass at racquetball, remind me not to bend over for the soap in the shower. But since you brought the topic up, it's my view, though I've admittedly never had the opportunity to confront the situation head on, so to speak, that my ass is as white as yours and a good deal less dimpled. I'll grant, of course, that it's plenty black enough that your ancestors would have been happy to call me 'nigger.'"

"Christ," I said. "Always the same. I want to have a drink. And you want to talk about asses. I think you must not be getting enough ass, or the topic wouldn't occupy your mind so much."

"You're one to talk about ass, now aren't you. You haven't had any in so long you're mistaking mine for one you might take interest in. But it seems to me you stopped by here to introduce the topic of drinking, a subject with which you are altogether too familiar, I fear."

"I'm an expert," I asserted sadly.

"Yes," Carl said. He looked at me now, his dark eyes gone serious. His large head with its short nap of graying hair, thinning to reveal a freckled scalp, nodded at me slightly. He pulled his hands from the computer terminal keyboard. "How you doing, anyway, Mike. You look like shit."

"I didn't get back from L.A. last night until one. Then had me a little adventure when I got home. Anyway, I'm bushed. Thought I'd walk over to Napoleon House, have a drink or two and a sandwich. Get to bed early. But I got something I need to talk to you about."

"What kind of adventure'd you have at one a.m. last night? That new blonde intern didn't sneak in and handcuff herself to your bed, I hope?"

Suddenly I was sick of the banter. "Damn it, this is serious, Carl."

He turned in his chair to face me. "What's going on, Mike?" he inquired.

"I'll tell you at Napoleon House."

"Can it wait just a bit," Carl said softly. "I'm on deadline."

I took a deep breath. "Sure," I replied with a shrug.

Carl rubbed his eyes with the fingertips of both hands. "Tell you what," he said. "Let me try to bang out the rest of this paragraph or whatever. And I'll meet you over there in twenty minutes." He must've thought he spotted disappointment on my tired face because he added, "Why don't you ask Wilson if she wants to keep you company till I get there. She's still around here somewhere. Or maybe that crazy Preacher Martin. I've never known him to turn down an invitation for a drink."

Wilson Malt was our police reporter. A former cop, she was twenty-seven years old and the best looking woman on the editorial staff, though her looks were all-American-girl-next-door rather than the fashion-model variety. Tall and solidly built, her features were soft and inviting rather than chiseled and forbidding, and the fresh openness of her personality no doubt accounted for as much of her attractiveness as any physical quality. Carl and I idly teased each other about Wilson all the time. And once in a while one of us would invite her to meet us for a drink after work, an invitation she usually accepted. Though she was significantly younger than we were, it seemed pretty obvious that she liked us and enjoyed our company.

Preacher Martin was a local novelist and self-described "outside agitator" who earned a piece of his living as our religious editor, a part-time position that required only one day in the office a week to write or rewrite or edit a series of stories for Saturday's religious section.

"I'll give Preacher a call," I said, hoisting the backpack over my shoulder and picking up my briefcase. "But you know he's always out somewhere doing some mysterious good. And I think Wilson's already gone. So it's probably gonna be either you or me by my lonesome. Besides it's you I want to talk to."

"I saw Wilson go over to Layout about ten minutes ago," Carl said. "Stop over there and look for her on your way out."

"Right," I said. But when I passed by the Layout Department Wilson was nowhere to be seen.

*   *   *

Waiting for Carl, I sat in the front room at the Napoleon House, consciously grateful that, at some point in the eighties, management had installed an air conditioning system. I liked the place so much I might have gone there anyway. There were plenty of sweltering summer nights in the past I'd sat at a sidewalk-side table and felt as if the beer I was drinking went from the glass, through my mouth and directly into my shirt. The managers were still awfully late in the spring turning the system on. But tonight it was running. And it was nice to be cool as I waited alone. Preacher, predictably, wasn't home when I called him. And Carl was forty-five minutes rather than twenty in arriving.

Carl Shaney was probably the most distinguished writer at *The States-Tribune*. He'd won countless awards on the state and local levels for his investigative reporting. His work was good enough that most of us thought he'd someday win a Pulitzer. He was forty-three years old, a native of our city, a graduate of St. Francis High School and Xavier University, and one of the major non-politician black figures in the city. He was also one of the most hated. Nobody likes a gadfly, and Carl was a gadfly of the most tenacious variety. He was loyal to nothing save his own rarefied sense of right and wrong. He was politically left, but it seemed he would go after a liberal Democrat just as quickly as a conservative Republican.

At the paper Carl's reporting was allowed a freedom granted to no other staff writer. He answered only to the Old Man himself. He published when his stories were ready, not before, and no one, other than the Old Man, had the authority to ask him how a piece was going. This autonomy made Carl the envy of most of his colleagues in News. For years, many thought he wasn't a team player because he couldn't be called upon, even in a crunch, to do the kind of routine stories that sometimes needed hammering out at the last minute. And Carl almost willfully aggravated the resentment many of his co-workers felt for him. As he said about himself, "My best trait is my arrogance. After that, the best you can say is I'm a real son-of-a-bitch. I'm opinionated, irritable, rude and cold. I don't give a shit about you and your problems, and I don't give a shit that you think I'm an asshole."

But in truth, of course, Carl did give a shit. And to illustrate that he did, when our entertainment editor retired in 1985, Carl asked to be assigned to the position. He didn't want to write entertainment stories, and, in fact, he never did. But he thought that if he shouldered some managerial responsibilities, he'd dampen the resentment the other reporters in News felt toward him. That ploy only partially worked, of course. It was true that people could no longer complain he didn't carry his fair share of the load. But he was widely slammed for being so arrogant as to think editing a whole section of the paper was something he could do in his spare time. What folks didn't realize about Carl, though, was that he had no concept of spare time. There was working. And there was sleeping. There wasn't anything else.

He was capable of such phenomenal concentration that he sometimes walked past people as if they weren't there, not because he regarded them as not worth speaking to, but because he didn't see them. But on those infrequent occasions when Carl wasn't working, he was as lively and companionable a man as you'd ever want to have a drink with, widely knowledgeable and interested in topics ranging from baseball to Beethoven. His passion, though, was local politics and the capacity of the Louisiana populace to tolerate corruption among its elected officials. "In what other state," Carl liked to ask, "could someone like Frank Falcone not only get elected, but get elected to a second and a third term? In what other state is there an office like the Orleans Parish Custodian of Notarial Archives where the top guy, an appointee of the governor, is perfectly within his legal rights to pay himself a $250,000 annual salary?"

Carl grew up in the Jim Crow South, the only child of a middle-class family. His parents were prosperous New Orleans "Creoles of color," the same class of light-skinned blacks that produced Mayors Beaumont and Fredericks. Carl's mother was a school teacher. His father was a prominent black businessman who owned a couple of small grocery stores, a small chain of dry cleaners, and enough real estate to have left Carl thoroughly comfortable if he'd chosen merely to collect rent for the rest of his life. But a single story that Carl told me captured for me, in a way that I'll never forget, what it was like to have grown up black in the era of official American apartheid.

To grasp this story thoroughly, one has to picture Carl Shaney as he was (or, anyway, as I picture him) in 1963, his senior year at St. Francis, tall (nearly as tall as I am and almost as big), erect, handsome, bright and well-educated. It's easy for non-Southerners and Southern white people to forget that Jim Crow was very much alive in 1963. We had so many black heroes by the early sixties, even apart from Martin Luther King. Jackie Robinson had been *retired* from baseball for seven years by 1963. The great Bill Russell was already in the middle of his storied career, more years in Celtic green already behind him than lay in front. Jim Brown had only two seasons left to play before he would hang up his spikes as the greatest back ever to carry a football. And 1963, of course, was the year Sidney Poitier won his Best Actor Oscar for *Lilies of the Field*. But in New Orleans, as in all the other Southern cities of the time, young black men like Carl Shaney couldn't take a seat in the downstairs section of a downtown movie house. Joan and I began to date that year. We were in the ninth grade, and I used to take her to the movies practically every weekend. I took her to see *Tom Jones*, and *Irma La Douce*, *From*

Russia with Love and *Love with a Proper Stranger*. Carl Shaney, my friend and colleague, took his girlfriend to see those films as well. But he didn't sit by us. If he'd tried, he'd have been arrested. For the law said he was the wrong color. He didn't sit beside us when I took Joan to see *Lilies of the Field*, either. But on some of those nights he may have been sitting above us in the third balcony at the Loew's. He may have been forced to watch Sidney Poitier give his Oscar winning performance from "nigger heaven." That's how close the outrage of Jim Crow clings to our own day.

But I'd guess that the viciousness of legal segregation fueled only part of the engine that drove Carl Shaney. After he graduated from college in 1967, he was drafted to serve in Vietnam. He's not shared with me many of the details of his experiences in southeast Asia. And I've purposely never asked him to do so. Perhaps he killed somebody he later suspected wasn't a Viet Cong soldier. Perhaps he was witness to an atrocity.

Whatever, something clearly happened over there that subsequently haunted him. There's no doubt that before he left he came to be utterly ashamed to have lent himself, in whatever capacity, to the horror that America made of Vietnam. He explained this shame to me in especially powerful terms once when I was quizzing him about his work. We were fairly deep in our cups at one of our favorite watering holes, on the porch at The Columns, watching the streetcars and the traffic crawl down St. Charles Avenue. I had just offered the opinion that what he did was dangerous, and he said, "Yeah, man, but I've been in Vietnam, you know."

I thought at first he merely meant that after having been in a war that he wasn't so easy to scare, thought he was indulging in another instance of ironic macho posturing, which was one of the ways that we had taken to relating to each other. But he took a swallow of his drink and added so solemnly that I've never forgotten it, "And now I've got my soul to save."

*　　　*　　　*

I was on my third Black and White when Carl finally arrived. He ordered a gin and tonic, his drink, and we told the waiter we'd split a whole muffaletta (a local specialty sandwich of ham, salami, provolone cheese and olive salad on a loaf of round Italian bread). As we ate, he confided details of the most recent scandal he'd uncovered.

"I got sources in the city department of revenue," he said, quietly, checking about us to make sure no one could be listening to our conversation, then lowering his voice even more, "who claim that certain businesses in this town are given, shall we say, *breaks* on the payment of their sales taxes."

"Breaks?" I said. Impatient to tell my own story, I beat my swizzle stick against the rim of my glass.

"Penalty-free waivers of timely payments," Carl explained. "Reductions. Outright cancellation of their sales tax obligations. In other words, the usual New Orleans rip-off. Screw the poor by running government on sales taxes, the most regressive kind, then give 'em rotten, underfinanced government with piss-poor services and not collect the goddamn taxes they pay."

"Jesus," I said, for a moment forgetting my own troubles. "Who's gonna fall? The mayor?"

"Maybe. Though probably not. People close to the mayor though."

"Who?"

"Remains to be seen. And that's all I'm saying." He took a swallow of his drink and lifted his sandwich with both hands, then looked at me over the top of it.

"And you ain't sayin nuthin," he added, slipping deliberately into a tough street accent.

"Damn," I said. "And I was planning on putting it in my Sunday column, too."

Carl swallowed down a last bite of muffaletta and said, "Oh well that's okay. Nobody reads anything you write anyway."

"Thank goodness. I was worried they might and they'd discover that I don't have anything to say."

Carl looked at me sternly. "Goddamnit Mike, you're fucking impossible to insult."

"Just naturally humble, I guess."

"Humble my black butt. You're as prideful and as competitive as anybody I ever met. And as ambitious. You still working on that collection?"

I shrugged in reply. Before Joan died, I had gathered together some of the pieces I was proudest of, but a structure eluded me. I never hit upon a format I liked. I wanted, as Monty's Pythonians were wont to say, something completely different, something novel. And I could never quite find it. Then Joan died, and like most everything in my life, I let the project drop.

Thinking then of Joan, I said without transition, quite abruptly, "My house was robbed, Carl. Or, more properly, burgled. That's what I discovered when I got home from L.A. last night."

Carl grew instantly serious. "Jesus, I'm sorry, Mike. That's what you wanted to tell me, and I been goin' on about this other shit." He ran a hand through his hair. "Christ, I'm sorry, man. Did you lose a bunch of stuff?" He took a swallow of his drink and set the glass down with a sudden thump. "Goddamn city. In another decade we're going to be living in a fucking jungle. Every man for himself."

I explained to him that though the burglars had trashed the house pretty effectively, especially my study, they hadn't seemed to have taken anything more than a camera and perhaps some items of inexpensive jewelry.

And then with considerable self-recrimination, I went on to tell him that I was troubled because I presumed the thieves were black.

Carl fished in his shirt pocket for his pack of Camel Lights. He shook one out and offered it to me. I never bought cigarettes, but I sometimes smoked his, especially when we sat and talked over Scotch and gin. I shook my head no, and Carl pulled a cigarette from the pack with his lips, brought a disposable lighter from his pants pocket and lit up.

He inhaled and then exhaled his first puff before saying, "So why are you telling me this. Am I supposed to say it's okay, say 'Forget it, Mike; it's just a *little* racist.'?"

I didn't say anything. He dragged on his cigarette. I sipped my Scotch.

"So what?" he said after a moment.

"So I don't know, goddamnit. My house has been robbed. I feel violated. I can't stop seeing assholes messing up my things. And the assholes I see are always black. And that *is* racist. I know it.

But I can't stop it. So I want to talk to somebody. And Joan is dead. She'd have talked to me. But she can't. Preacher's off doing Godknowswhat. So that leaves you. My friend. Only you're black. And so . . . so fuck."

Carl took the cigarette from his lips, pinched it between the index and middle fingers of his left hand, and laid that hand lightly on my right forearm.

"Look, Mike," he said. "What can I tell you? You act like you want absolution. Only I'm not a priest." Carl removed his hand to smoke again, but my arm was slightly damp where he'd touched me, and as the perspiration of our contact cooled, I could feel the spot where his hand had lain.

"I want more than absolution," I said. "I want to be, I don't know . . . I want to be color blind."

"Ah," Carl said. "Then you are truly fucked." He held his arm up in the light. "See it," he said. "Black. Yours is white; mine is black. And there's no use pretending they're both chartreuse."

I started to say something, but Carl held up a finger to indicate he wasn't finished. He lit another cigarette and took a deep drag before he continued. "The way I see it, all men are prejudiced toward things and people of their own kind, and against things, to whatever slight degree, which aren't of their own kind. I know that I am. I'm not proud of it, but I know that I am. As I've told you before, when you first came on the paper, I was suspicious of you. I heard that cracker accent of yours. I learned you were a local boy, went to segregated schools in this town. I figured, shit, this boy and I won't ever have a thing to do with one another. That suspicion, of course, toward you or whomever, is prejudice. You can't help where you grew up any more than I can help my skin color. You can't help how you talk. But I pegged you as another one of *them* before we'd even spoken a word."

"So what do we do?" I asked, less to Carl than to heaven.

Carl replied, "We do what we're doing. We talk about it. And we fight it. You fight it in you. I fight it in me. Fight the society that nurtures it. Don't ever give those who accommodate it or benefit from it a moment's peace. Get the goods on 'em, and every chance you get pull them down."

*   *   *

Carl and I talked for another two drinks that night at the Napoleon House. He tried to get me to let him come over and help put my house back in order, but I assured him there was little he could do.

At about ten Carl noted that I was operating on a minimum of sleep and insisted that I go home. On the way I stopped at the Winn-Dixie Marketplace on Tchoupitoulas and bought a pot roast and a few other food items and household supplies. Before returning to my house, I passed by the Dupres'. The light was on in the living room, so I stopped. Delinda answered my knock on her door. A slight, dark-skinned woman, she was dressed in a plaid calico house dress and pink fuzzy slippers. She wore her gray hair pulled back tight against her scalp and gathered into a bun in the back.

"What you doin' out this late, Mr. Mike?" she asked. Before I could formulate a precise answer, she turned into the house and called out, "Larwood, Mr. Mike's come visitin' like he don't know it's the middle the night."

I laughed as I was supposed to, and bumped the plastic grocery bag I was carrying against my thigh. As I stepped into their tiny over-furnished living room, Larwood appeared, slipping the suspenders of his work britches up over the shoulders of his long-sleeved T-shirt. Larwood's skin color was more gray than black. He was a man of medium height, faintly stoop-shouldered and bony in build. His grip was strong when we shook hands, and he clapped me once on the back as I turned away from him to tell Delinda, "I just stopped by to let you know it doesn't make much sense for you to come over to clean tomorrow. The people who broke into my house have left it pretty much uncleanable until I get everything all sorted out again."

"You need some help with that, Mistuh Mike?" Larwood inquired. "Delinda and I could stop on by tomorrow evenin' and lends you a hand."

I told him no, that it was mostly a sorting-things-out job that I'd have to do myself. "Anyway," I said to Delinda, "I know you count on your work, so I wanted to drop your check by."

"You knows I don't like takin' no check when I don't do nothin' for it," Delinda said.

This was a ritual we had gone through before. She felt she ought to make such a statement, but she knew I wouldn't be dissuaded. And the unspoken understanding between us was that she deserved to be paid. The Dupres each only worked for me one day a week, but my attitude, and theirs too, was that they were salaried, rather than hourly wage earners. They always did things around my house in addition to their specific duties. The least I could do was honor their industry and loyalty by making sure they didn't lose income due to circumstances beyond their control. So after some ceremonial squabbling, Delinda accepted the check, folded it in half and slipped it into the waist pocket of her dress.

"I'll find you an extry day to make up," she said.

"I'll get the house extra dirty and let you make it up that way," I responded.

"I bet you do," she said, smiling and nodding her head.

"Larwood," I said, "I'm real sorry about the policemen bothering you this morning."

"Wudn't none a your doin'," he shrugged.

"Well, anyway," I said. "I wish you hadn't been bothered."

We stood looking at each other for a silent moment, and then I said, "Well, Delinda's right, it's the middle of the night, so I better be running on." I turned toward the door to leave, but then I stopped and said, "Oh, I almost forgot." I handed Delinda the grocery bag I'd been holding. "You know how bad I am about cooking for myself. I found this pot roast in the bottom of the ice box, and I figured I better bring it over to you before I let it go to waste."

"Thank you, Mr. Mike," Delinda said. "This'll make up some fine stew."

As I stepped onto the concrete stoop in front of their house, Larwood said, "I be by and do your grass on Thursday. Just like always."

The Dupres were not educated people, but they were far from stupid, and I suddenly realized that they would recognize a fresh piece of meat, and deduce exactly why I'd brought it to them. On the drive around the block to my house, I reflected on what pitiful offerings we bring to buy expiation for the sins of twenty generations.

*   *   *

Walking into my house in its still chaotic state was like enduring a
body blow. I knew, of course, what I was in for. But it was a shock
nonetheless. As best I could, I steeled myself to walk quickly through
the darkened living and dining rooms. But the mess in the bedroom
was as intolerable as it was unavoidable. The idea of strangers amuck
among Joan's possessions evoked a torrent of emotions that cascaded
in an instant from astonishment to fury to despair. I wanted to run,
and I wanted to break things, and I wanted to cry.

As I undressed, I listened to my phone answering machine. There
were two messages. The first was from Wilson, the other from
Preacher.

"Michael," Wilson said from the machine, her voice rich with
concern. "I was going over today's police reports late this afternoon,
and I learned that your house was broken into over the weekend. I'm
so sorry. Don't hesitate to call me if there's anything I can do. The
investigative detectives probably told you there's not much hope of
getting any of your stuff back. Whatever's missing. But please let me
know if I can help somehow. I've got friends in the department and . .
. and I've got a broom if they messed anything up. You know what
I'm saying?"

Preacher's message said, "Damn you Barnett. This is your redneck
shepherd. You gonna do something important like drink whiskey
you need to give better notice. How in the fuck can I lead you by the
still waters if I don't know when you're about to lie down in green
pastures."

I thought about calling my friends back, to thank Wilson for her
concern and to badger Preacher with something obscene. But I was
tired and let the idea slide away. It was late, and I would talk to
both of them tomorrow. I got into bed where I fell instantly into a
dreamless sleep. Unfortunately, I awoke with a headache about two-
thirty a.m., got up to take a handful of aspirin, and couldn't fall back
asleep. A summer lightning storm had started outside. It wasn't
raining, and there were no cracks of thunder, but the clouded sky
lit up repeatedly, as if God were trying to switch on a vast canopy
of illumination and somewhere his system was shorting out. The
strobe of flashes around the Levolor blinds that covered the window
across from my bed arrived like instant dawn, upon me now and just

as quickly gone. I pulled the slip off Joan's pillow and draped it across my face, but the flashes continued, if only in my mind.

After a half hour of squirming around, I got up and began to attend to the wreck the burglars had made of my house. The front rooms were relatively easy. I wasn't all that conscientious about putting things back neatly. The bedroom was harder because it required handling things that had distinctly belonged to Joan. I tried to be careful. Replacing her shoes on the shoe racks in the bottom of her closet was simple enough, as was hanging up the dresses the burglars had thrown to the floor. But Joan had had a special way of folding her slips and panties, and I couldn't match the precision she'd brought to this mundane task. I made an effort for a while, but finally I just folded things over a time or two in order to get them back in drawers and out of sight as quickly as possible. I reminded myself bitterly that Joan wouldn't be back to check up on me.

Sometime after three I was ready to tackle the disaster in my study. This was the labor that really needed doing. This was my work area and required order. The process was aggravating but actually went faster than I expected. Joan's few folders of material were obvious, each labeled with the name of a case she'd determined was important enough to maintain a file at home. I set the folders themselves in a stack with all the yellow sheafs of lined legal paper which belonged in them, each aswarm with inked notes in Joan's small, precise, unerringly legible handwriting.

My own folders were each marked with the name of a movie, and I placed them back in my filing cabinets as I came upon each one. Many had retained their contents as they'd been flung to the floor by the burglars. The materials in others had come dislodged. But since each press kit and each photograph bore the name of a movie, the process of rebuilding my files was largely mindless. I passed the three hours it took in a reverie about the glorious vacation Joan and I had taken to Alaska early in the month that she died.

*   *   *

We had sailed north out of Vancouver aboard the M.S. Noordam. Our first port of call was in the southern Alaska town of Ketchikan which seemed to be nailed like a rickety shelf to a mountainside rising almost vertically out of the cold Pacific. We took the tender ashore and exhausted seeing the places of interest within a couple of hours. There was a row of creaky clapboard buildings purporting to date to turn-of-the-century, gold-rush days. Elsewhere, a cannery had been converted to a museum about the fishing industry.

The day was uneventful, chilly and overcast. But I remember it with a vivid tenderness. In New Orleans Joan and I always had so much going on that our days felt crowded, our lives inadequately spacious. Our separate jobs kept us out nights frequently enough that "I feel like I haven't seen you all week," was an all too common Saturday morning greeting. A sleepy Alaska village, in contrast, was a treasure because it provided so little to do and allowed us to luxuriate in the undiluted pleasure of one another's company. We sat for a long afternoon before the fire in a Main Street bar, nursing steins of Bass Ale. We had been married 17 years, but like moonstruck teenagers on a third or fourth date, we held hands while talking. And when we emerged from the bar in late afternoon, it was like walking into a new day. The sun had finally broken through and burned a bright orange low in the western sky.

Waiting on the Ketchikan dock at sunset to catch a tender back to the Noordam, Joan put an arm up under my jacket and around my waist and laid her head against my shoulder. "I love you, Mr. Mickey," she said.

I squeezed her to me and kissed the top of her head.

"I'm a very lucky person," she said. "And don't you forget it."

I laughed as I was supposed to and asked, "And what makes you so lucky?"

"Good luck, I guess."

I laughed again.

"I'm a very lucky person," she said, "because I get to live with you for all the rest of my life."

The sun had just kissed the horizon, and its orange and yellow blaze obscured the ship on which we were shortly to sail. The glowing streaks of the setting sun seemed to reach toward us, golden fingers of a divine hand raised to bless the intensity of our loving.

That's the way we are, frozen in the snapshot of my agonized memory, standing there always, blissful, looking westward, our arms around each other, blinded by the glare.

*   *   *

When I finished reconstructing my own files, I turned my attention to those belonging to Joan. The work went more slowly now and required greater concentration. I couldn't always be certain which file the individual sheets of her folded legal paper belonged in. But I did the best I could. Joan had been such a dedicated and careful attorney, it seemed a desecration not to preserve her records as she would have maintained them herself.

I knew this was madness, by the way. I knew that these files were as useless now as all her other possessions which still filled the rooms of our house, the house she loved so much. Her closet still contained her clothes and her shoes, her bathroom her assortment of towels and washcloths, her wardrobe her stacks of slips and panties that caused me pain just to see and handle. But somehow, this file of papers was most thoroughly Joan, for she'd spent so much of her life working, preparing the legal cases that each of these folders represented. But they were unquestionably useless now, as useless as her ashes, which I'd scattered in the bathtub brown waters of the Mississippi Sound, across from the Gulfport motel we used as a hideaway when the thought of another weekend at the mercy of our telephone was more than either of us could bear. But since I'd scattered them, I'd wanted those ashes back. I knew how sick this was. I knew it. But if I'd only kept them, I would have brought them into bed with me. And they would have helped me sleep.

It was a comparable sickness, now, that made me pore over her files, to search the lined yellow pages, still alive with her handwriting, for the critical clue of words that would identify for me the folder to which each belonged. Finally, when I had filed as many as I could, I created a new folder for all the sheets I had been unable to place. Then I alphabetized the entire stack, fewer than twenty-five folders in all and filed them away.

I had already closed the file drawer, absently examined my reclaimed study and made my way into the kitchen, puzzling over what I might eat for breakfast, when I realized something that gradually turned my blood to ice. In an instant I thought I was going to hyperventilate. Reining myself in from running, I returned to the study and went through Joan's files once again, slowly, painstakingly, making sure that nothing was out of order or overlooked.

On the Saturday that she died, Joan had been at home, working once again on the *Retif* case. She had worked on the *Retif* case, it seemed, her entire career. It was a case with so many permutations that she used to joke she would probably be handling it on the day she died. Cruel fucking irony. She had won parts of it, and she had lost parts of it; finally, bowing to her client's wishes, she had settled what remained of it. But she had never stopped working on it. I used to chide her for not letting the case go. I used to get impatient that she let her obsession with the case continue even after she any longer had any official connection with it. So she'd stopped talking to me about whatever her further researches on *Retif* either revealed or fail to reveal. But I knew she continued to work on it until the very end. I'd see the papers spread out around her on our bed, and even when they weren't *Retif*, the names on those papers were telltale: *Delacroix* and *Moon* and *Thomas Jefferson Magnet.* As with all the cases on which Joan had worked, there was a folder for the *Retif* case. There was a fat, brown accordion folder with a fastening strap that she occasionally lugged home from the office. And full of copies of the case's essential documents, there was a slenderer manila folder which she kept at home. I had seen her poring over the latter many, many times.

After my labors that morning, there was once again in my study a lone file drawer for Joan. But in that file drawer, for reasons I couldn't fathom, there wasn't, as there should have been, a folder of any kind labeled *Retif.*

CHAPTER FIVE

After enduring the usual delay of being put on hold, I was connected with the phone of Lieutenant Giannetti at N.O.P.D. to report that a folder was missing from Joan's legal files.

"A file folder, huh?" Giannetti said. He sniffed loudly into the phone. "And what else?"

"Just the camera I told you about when you were here. And maybe the jewelry I mentioned. I can't be sure. But I think the file is significant."

"Yeah?" he said. "What was in it? Something embarrassing to somebody? Blackmail type stuff?"

"I don't think blackmail . . . My wife didn't handle the kind of cases that . . . I mean, I don't think there would have been any personal material in the file."

"What then?"

"Well, I don't know exactly. But it was something my wife . . ."

"If you don't know what was in it, what makes you think the fact it's missing is important?"

"Because it was a case my wife worked on for a very long time."

"Uh huh?"

I could hear Giannetti take three sharp breaths of an unstifled yawn.

"Look," I said. "If you think back a little ways you may remember the case. *Grieve versus Retif.* Had to do with the building of Jefferson High School. Big stink about where the school was going to be located and who was going to do the construction. Black guy, Tom Grieve, sued Sheldon Retif, you know the big real estate guy. Trial argued before Judge Delacroix, Leon Delacroix."

"Okay."

"You remember?"

"Yeah. Sort of."

"Ended up in a big trial. Went all the way to the Supreme Court."

"Okay," Giannetti said. I could hear a tinkling sound, as if he were drumming his pencil, against a coffee mug perhaps. "So why would someone want to steal a file on a case about building a school?

"I don't know," I admitted. "Joan always felt there was something rotten at work in the case. You know, like the judge was bought or something."

"I gather she lost the case," Giannetti said. "So what are you telling me? You want to bring charges against a federal judge for breaking and entering?"

"Well, of course not. Not at this . . ."

"Right," Giannetti interrupted. "Let's see if we can make some progress here. How exactly do you know this folder is missing?"

"It's not in the file drawer where she kept it?"

"And you're sure it was there before the burglary?"

I had to admit, of course, that I wasn't. I presumed it had been there. I had no reason to believe it *hadn't* been there. But, no, I wasn't sure it was actually there before the break-in.

And with that my conversation with the lieutenant wound its way to a close. He made little effort to conceal his contempt for my having wasted his time, but he patronizingly assured me his report would reflect that I thought a legal file was missing from among my possessions. He didn't even bother to suggest he thought my calling him was of the slightest interest or to offer me the slimmest hope that he would pursue the missing file as any kind of lead.

*   *   *

That's when the sickness began in earnest. I felt a nagging nausea that stopped just short of making me throw up. I hadn't really had all that much to drink the night before, six glasses of Black and

White, I think, though I didn't count, enough to make an average person rip roaring drunk, in other words, but barely enough to give me a decent buzz. I hadn't slept, of course. And that was no doubt a factor in my morning sickness malaise. Perhaps I was just hungover. But I didn't feel I'd drunk enough the night before to have deserved it.

And I'm expert on hangovers, of course. I grew up in Mardi Gras City, and I learned to drink and hold my liquor young. New Orleanians have such a tolerance for alcoholic consumption we used to joke that local tavern owners would sell you something to drink just as soon as you were tall enough to place the money on the bar. And we weren't far wrong. By ninth grade my friends and I we were consuming bottles of Thunderbird and Ripple which we bought at a nearby Time Saver. We weren't yet sixteen.

In high school we took to going to bars, especially the famous Pat O'Brien's where we had to display fake I.D.s. Even Joannie had her fake I.D. and was a regular on our illicit jaunts to Pat O's. Drinking was legal by the time we were in college, of course, and I indulged both more often and more heavily, though my consumption remained, I think, quite controlled. I drank on social occasions, sometimes to drunkenness, but I didn't drink on a daily basis and would sometimes go several weeks without drinking at all.

That gradually changed after Joan and I married. Particularly after graduate school and law school were behind us, and we became flush with incipient yuppiedom, we took to maintaining a bar in the house. And I took to finishing almost every long day with a Scotch or two, sometimes more. Joan, on the other hand, remained constant in her relationship to alcohol. She used it before I did, actually. She and her girlfriends used to sneak nips of Southern Comfort from her daddy's liquor cabinet as early as sixth grade. But she never became as regular or heavy a drinker as I did. There'd be times she'd get rip-roaring drunk. Once in a hilarious scene at Pat O'Brien's—it was after my thirtieth birthday dinner at Galatoire's as a matter of fact—she got so blasted on hurricanes that she tried to challenge a tall blonde to fight because I joked that the woman was making eyes at me. But as we got older, she drank rather less, I think, though this choice was by appetite rather than philosophy. She never said a word to me about my drinking, and, in fact, until she died, I didn't realize I had a problem.

Even after Joan died, I prided myself on keeping my drinking under control. Aside from a few close friends, no one at work had any suspicion that I killed about five fifths of Black and White a week. That consumption showed on my face. But people no doubt just thought I was getting old.

And I had that problem, too.

I'd like to blame this culture I grew up in for planting the seeds of my reliance on alcohol and the respite it provided the weary psyche. Our Carnival mentality resulted in a different attitude toward alcohol than I suspect adhered in other, more uptight and Anglo parts of the country. Public drunkenness wasn't just routine at Mardi Gras; it was practically required.

To some degree, this Carnival mentality persisted in our city all year long. Lawyers and businessmen thought nothing of consuming a drink or two at lunch. University professors didn't give a second thought to heading for class with several beers in their bellies. There is perhaps something salutary about surrendering all your inhibitions once in a while. But a drinker like me had very serious problems. And knowing that fact didn't mean one damn thing. The kind of drunkenness I practiced was insidious. I was always under control, or at least apparently so. But my apparent control was a false mastery over something that was really mastering me.

So far, though, I hadn't found the will to stop. Black and White was my friend. It provided what I craved most. Oblivion. Sweet oblivion. It bathed my brain with an anesthetizing balm. It provided a treasured dullness that allowed me to watch TV when I couldn't read, to sleep when I was terrified to think. Black and White tricked me into thinking that I no longer cared, that I was finally at one with this place that billed itself as "The City That Care Forgot." Black and White was my key to the door of my homeplace, my entree to The Big Easy. And when I was done with another day's writing, when I'd seen another day's list of rotten movies, then I sought the ease of Black and White. It beckoned me with all the brashness of a hooker on Bourbon Street, and it was as accessible as a broken seal and a tilted bottle. All I needed to add was ice, perhaps a dash of water and the proper persistence.

And when I lost feeling in my gums—that was the test—then I was home. Home to the satiny enclave of my private Big Easy.

It stood there waiting for me, ready. There, just beyond the golden brown mid-point. There, where Joan's name was never spoken and never heard. There, where love wasn't known and thus couldn't be missed.

*　　*　　*

So on that cloudy, rainy morning in July of 1988, a morning in which a lightning storm had delivered repeated bursts of false dawn, I resolved to put away my bottle of Black and White, if not for always, then for a time. Joan's file on the *Retif* case had seemingly disappeared. I had to understand why. And if the police weren't interested, I'd have to try to figure out why on my own. To do so, I couldn't afford the luxury of Black and White's fuzzy headedness.

I started by searching still again through the dozen drawers and hundreds of folders in my own movie files. I had to make certain that in the early hours of a bleary morning I hadn't created my own mystery. It took me two hours when I got home from work that afternoon. But by the time I headed off for that evening's screening of Martin Brest's *Midnight Run*, I felt sure of one thing at least, the manila folder on the *Retif* case was definitely missing from the files Joan maintained at home.

My next move was to discover whether Joan might have taken the file to her office at Herbst, Gilman, Roquevert and Ivy. This seemed unlikely to me since the file she kept at home was only a folder of the *Retif* case's more salient documents, and just photocopies at that, a set of handy references available for when she labored on the case at night after dinner or on weekends. The complete file of briefs and countless original items of correspondence no doubt filled several drawers in her firm's storage room. A rough accumulation of the case's most important documents I knew she kept gathered in a large brown accordion working file. But perhaps she had indeed stuck the home folder in the accordion file and returned it to the office for some reason. In order to find out I made a lunch date with Jason Roux, Joan's closest friend among her law partners.

Jason and I met at Mr. B's, he in his lawyer's eight-hundred-dollar suit, me in khaki pants and a blue blazer, my uniform. He was a good deal shorter than I, but in perfect trim. Jason was an especially good looking man, a few years younger than we were, always well-tanned and immaculately groomed. Before Joan died I sometimes fretted that I could never manage the polished look of a Jason Roux.

Joan once told me, "You want to look like Jason, do four things: buy a truly expensive suit, get your hair cut every week, and wear starched shirts."

I said, "But I don't want to spend a lot of money on a suit. I don't even like wearing a suit. And I don't have time to get a haircut every week." Aping Rodney Dangerfield, I ran a finger inside my collar. "And I hate starched shirts."

"And that's why you look like you, and not like Jason Roux," she said.

"But not entirely," I said. She looked at me wide-eyed. "You said there were four things I could do and you've only listed three."

"Ah yes, the fourth," she said.

"That's right, the fourth," I pointed out. First, second, third, fourth. Like that. *Uno, dos, tres, quatro. Ein, zwei, drei . . .*"

"Oh shut up," she said, laughing. "Jesus, you got a mouth on you."

"*Vier*," I said.

"I'm gonna give you something to fear," she said, shaking her fist at me. "Right upside your head."

"My unkempt head," I asserted. "Never forget, I don't have the time to get the proper number of haircuts. But speaking of forgetting. Or should I say four getting. I don't believe you've been getting—on to number four."

"Four," she said, "I'm afraid you'd have to change your sexual preference."

"You are referring to the fact that our friend Jason prefers men to women."

"Only as sexual partners, I'm sure," she said.

"To look like Jason Roux, I've got to switch from A.C. to D.C.?"

"To look like Jason Roux, I'm afraid you have no other choice."

"I don't want to look like Jason Roux," I said.

"Why not?" she inquired.

"I don't think you're capable of growing a dick."

"Well that settles it then, I guess."

"I'm afraid that looking like Jason Roux is out of the question," I said. "Given the alternatives at hand."

"Given the alternatives at hand," she replied, "and several other locations about the male anatomy, I suspect. I don't, of course, speak from experience."

"I'd say you've a certain applicable experience in this area. A limited hand-to-mouth kind of experience I might term it."

"You are a disgusting, filthy-minded person."

"I try to be the most disgusting, filthy-minded person you know. You know."

Flashing her eyebrows like Groucho she said, "I *know*."

And I knew that living in this world without her was like trying to breathe in a vacuum.

*   *   *

At Mr. B's now, Jason Roux ordered a vodka martini; I had iced tea. So that he wouldn't be tempted to put me off on the phone, I hadn't told Jason what I wanted to see him about. He no doubt suspected he'd joined me for a purely social occasion. He must have thought that fact peculiar, though, given that we hadn't visited since Joan's funeral. I was edgy as we made small talk at the beginning of lunch. Part of me wanted to get right to it, but the calculating Southern part wanted to take the slow, genial, polite route.

So first Jason and I talked about old times, the annual firm Christmas party, a swank black-tie affair in the vaulted marble lobby of the New Orleans Museum of Art; the long weekend at firm expense in Biloxi, Mississippi, every year for the Louisiana State Bar Association; the seafood jamboree each summer in Audubon Park; the annual fall retreat to Point Clear, Alabama, for partners and their spouses.

A short silence followed our volley of shared reminiscences and then Jason said, "We miss her, Mike. We really miss her."

"Yeah," I said. "Me too."

"I know what you're going through," Jason said softly, "and I'm so very sorry."

"Yeah," I said, sighing, "I know you do." And he did know, of course, because three years earlier Jason's housemate Preston Parkerson had been one of the earlier victims to die of AIDS. I never knew Preston very well. We had met him on very rare occasions when he'd accompanied Jason to private dinner parties hosted by one or another of the younger attorneys at Herbst, Gilman. But I knew that Preston and Jason had been together for several years before Preston got sick. And I knew that Jason was extremely slow to recover from Preston's death.

Jason reached out a hand and squeezed my forearm a second. "So," he said. "Seen any good movies lately?"

I smiled at his well-meaning if artless determination to change the subject. And, of course, I had long since grown accustomed to people laying this line on me. It was a natural way for them to get over any spot of discomfort they might feel. I had always spent the bulk of my time with Joan's colleagues at Herbst, Gilman talking movies. And that's what Jason and I did now. We talked about *Cocktail* and a handful of other movies currently in town.

As we talked we ate from our bowls of Mr. B's wonderful gumbo ya-ya. We'd each ordered the soup and appetizer luncheon special, a selection not appearing on the menu but that the waiters would bring if you asked.

Finally, I brought up the reason for our meeting.

"What's the latest on *Retif*?" I asked.

"The *Retif* case?" Jason said. "Thomas Jefferson Magnet School suit?"

"Yeah. You know, Joan's life-long undertaking."

Jason wiped his mouth with his white linen napkin. "That was settled two years ago, Mike."

I smiled. "Well, I know *that*. But surely you know that Joan was still working on *Retif* when she died. I mean, I used to gouge her so for working on something settled that she wasn't talking to me about it anymore. But she was still working on it. I used to catch her at it and then have to ignore it so we wouldn't get into a dumb argument. Anyway, she was doing something on the case the weekend she . . . you know."

"She was?" Jason said, puzzled, a forkful of beer-battered shrimp poised halfway between his plate and his mouth. "No, of course, I didn't know that. I don't even see how that's possible."

"She could never understand Judge Delacroix's initial ruling in Retif's favor. She always thought something was tainted in his decision."

"Well, of course, we proved Judge Delacroix had a conflict of interest. We won that round."

"But Joan was never satisfied by the issue the Supreme Court agreed to hear."

Jason laughed. "Well, the Supreme Court was adequately satisfied. That's what counted."

"Not with Joan, though. She got Delacroix reversed with her 'appearance of impropriety' argument, but she always believed that the judge had some real and personal motive for ruling as he did. She believed maybe Retif had something on Delacroix."

Jason laughed quietly and without mirth, then coughed and cleared his throat. "Let me just say that she was not exactly alone in her suspicions. Delacroix's ruling knocked us absolutely flat. We thought we had won the case cold."

Jason pushed his elliptical plate toward the center of the table. He'd eaten only about half of what he'd been served. I tried to remember the last time I'd abandoned food like that. Unlike me, of course, Jason Roux wasn't a fucking pig.

"But whatever we all thought," Jason said, "Retif built the school. And after the Supreme Court remanded the case for retrial, Tom Grieve settled."

"Against Joan's advice."

"True. But that's the client's prerogative."

"Yeah. Tom Grieve was out of it. And therefore Joan and Herbst, Gilman were technically out of it. But she never quit asking herself why. Why did Delacroix rule as he did?"

"Is that what you mean by she was still working on it when she died, which was what, a year after the settlement?"

The waiter cleared away our plates and began pouring coffee. When he left the table I said, "She was doing more than that. Just on a now-and-again basis, of course. She had plenty of paying clients to keep her busy. But in her spare time she was digging around on Delacroix and Retif. I had started telling her to stop. But she kept looking around, just to see what she could find."

"And what did she find?"

I puffed my cheeks and blew out a noisy breath. "I don't think she found anything."

Jason sipped his coffee and glanced at his watch. "So what's this all about, Mike?"

"Someone broke into our house on Sunday night. Whoever it was stole Joan's file folder of current notes on *Retif*."

"Are you sure?"

"Well, no, of course not. But I think I remember that Joan was fooling with that file right before we put on our jogging shoes . . ." I looked up at the bright white ceiling and then out the window at a tourist couple, their heads together over a map. "She could have been working on something else, I guess, and only started talking about *Retif*. The case really bugged her."

"So what can I do for you, Mike. I don't know what in the world to say about the burglary at your home."

"Well," I said, "I thought you might let me look at Joan's old files on the *Retif* case."

Jason began to stroke slowly at his chin. "Jesus," he said. "I don't think I can do that, Mike. I mean, I'm sorry. But there's a problem with legal ethics and all. You know what I mean?"

"Well let me just ask you this," I said. "Y'all still have the files, I presume."

"Yes," Jason said. "I guess so. I don't know where in the hell they are. But we don't throw anything away."

"So if the files are there, what's the problem with letting me have a look at them?"

"Why?"

"Mainly to try to put my mind at ease," I said. "Occasionally Joan brought home a big *Retif* working file in a brown accordion folder. Maybe for some reason she put her home packet of *Retif* materials in that and took it back to work. If so and we find it, then that's one fewer things I need to worry about."

"Sounds simple enough, Mike, but I don't know. There's a problem with client privilege and all."

"What client privilege?" I asked. "Tom Grieve is dead. And the case is settled."

He looked at me pensively, brushing his right index finger back and forth across his lips. Then he took a deep breath and said, "Okay, I tell you what, I shouldn't be doing this, but if you can you come up to my office at say six-thirty tonight . . ."

"No problem," I said. "I really appreciate your help, Jason. I really do."

"Shit," he said, confirming his decision. "Who the hell cares about files on a case that's been settled for two years."

Jason tried to pay the check which the waiter had placed on his side of the table. But I insisted on paying half. We left a wad of bills, then stood and made our way out of the restaurant to Royal Street where we were greeted by the relentless heat.

As we shook hands, Jason clasped my upper arm. "See you six-thirty," he said.

Then Jason turned and headed back toward Canal Street. I walked over toward the river. I had a two o'clock screening of Barbet Schroeder's *Barfly* at Canal Place. *Barfly* had opened elsewhere in the country earlier in the year, but it hadn't done well and was only now about to get a New Orleans release. Mickey Rourke starred, and whereas that once would have made me hopeful, I had lost my enthusiasm for his work. I'd interviewed him on a junket for *Angel Heart*, and he'd acted like such an arrogant asshole I no longer even rooted for him.

But hey, I told myself, somebody's got to be the movie critic.

*   *   *

After the screening of *Barfly*, I stopped in at the paper, opened mail, filed things away and knocked off half of my review of *Midnight Run*. At a quarter after six I packed up the stuff I was taking home, zipped the Zenith into its backpack and headed over to Place St. Charles. For such a big-time building with so many high-powered people working there, the lobby of Place St. Charles, save at lunch-time or precisely at five p.m., always felt eerily empty. At six-thirty it seemed abandoned.

I exited the elevator on the fifty-fifth floor only to find the huge doors to the law firm of Herbst, Gilman, Roquevert and Ivy shut and locked. I hammered, though, and Jason let me in. He steered me through the reception area with the name of the firm in gigantic gold letters high on the wall behind the receptionist's desk. We walked around a partition and the storage closets that stood behind them, and down an aisle with a half dozen secretarial stations on the left and a row of attorney's offices on the right.

When we came to Joan's old office, I couldn't help myself. I stopped and went in. It was occupied by a new partner now, one of the former associates who'd been promoted since Joan died. The furnishings were the ones Joan had picked out, though. And I suddenly felt the mad, perverted impulse to run around the desk and lay my head on the chair where she'd sat for so many years. I looked out the window at the dramatic view of the Mississippi's ninety-degree bend from north to east.

Back in the hall, Jason was waiting for me. He didn't say anything, but clapped me on the back as we turned to walk on toward the Common Street end of the building. At the corner, across from Arnold Herbst's elaborate office, Jason showed me into a huge room that cut through the center of the whole floor. It was filled with file cabinets, row upon row upon row of them. Finally we arrived before the ones we were seeking, one whole five-drawer file cabinet and two sections of a second, containing the firm's records on the Thomas Jefferson Magnet School case. Each drawer was labeled "*Thomas Grieve vs. The Retif Realty Company, Inc.*" followed by a year, a drawer each for the years 1981 through 1987.

"You just want to look in the stuff Joan was working on at the end," Jason said.

"Right," I replied.

"Should be in here," he said, pointing at the drawer for 1987. "Let's see what we've got."

He pulled the drawer open, and it rolled out easily, with a sickening, hollow thwang.

It was empty.

PART TWO

CHAPTER SIX

Joan spent the last six years of her life working on the *Retif* case. She was still an associate at Herbst, Gilman when she was engaged by Tom Grieve to file suit on his behalf against Sheldon Retif. It was 1981. We had entered our second decade of marriage. And we were still trying to have children.

By 1987, when she died, the *Retif* case had become Joan's child. We had resigned ourselves to barrenness and had tried to locate in our careers the kind of energy and satisfaction others might find in their offspring. Because our failed efforts at child bearing were coincident with the years she worked on *Retif*, the case came to have even more importance for her than it might have under other circumstances. But the case was so complicated and dragged on so long, it would have been plenty important to her without its associations with our private life. She took one of its issues all the way to the United States Supreme Court, weathered the relentless questioning of its members, held her ground, and won.

The actions giving rise to the suit had begun nearly two years before Grieve hired Joan to represent him. Or perhaps the facts really began in 1960 when the Orleans Parish School Board instituted its plan for desegregating the city's public schools. Or perhaps they began in 1619 when the first black slaves were imported into the fledgling British colonial outpost in Virginia.

However distant in the past one may choose to trace its roots, the case had to do with building a new high school, Thomas Jefferson

Magnet High School. By the mid-1970s, a decade of white flight to the suburbs, combined with rampant paranoia on the part of those white parents left inside the city limits, had conspired to turn our public school system more than ninety-five percent black. Only a couple of grammar schools on the Lakefront and one Uptown retained even a fifty percent white student body. The only high school with a white majority student body was James Madison High School for the gifted. Everybody understood what a devastating development this was for the city. But no one had a program for attracting whites back to the school system. You couldn't pass a law forbidding white residents from relocating to Jefferson and St. Tammany Parishes where their kids could go to white majority schools. And you couldn't pass a law prohibiting those white parents still residing in the city from sending their kids to white majority private and parochial schools.

So what the school board did was launch a program of magnet schools designed, of course, to upgrade the quality of public primary and secondary education in our city, but designed as well to create environments attractive enough that white parents might once again send their children to public school. The term *magnet* was employed to designate any school which drew its student population from across regular school district boundaries. Any Orleans Parish student who met the entrance requirements could attend a magnet school whether that student lived next door to the magnet school or clear across town. A number of existing schools were incorporated into this magnet program. But the flagship of the new magnet system was to be a brand new school with all the latest facilities in both its educational and extra-curricular areas. The design of Thomas Jefferson Magnet was produced with great fanfare in New Orleans. The school was hailed as the beacon of a new beginning. And in August of 1980, the Orleans Parish School Board voted to grant its Certificate 34 or "Builders Prerogative" to Sheldon Retif's Retif Realty Company.

The location of the school, as one might imagine, was a matter of considerable debate, both among the members of the school board and in the community at large. Parents on the predominantly white West Bank hoped the school would be housed on their side of the river. But the part of Orleans Parish located on the West Bank was small enough that building the school there was never a serious possibility.

Uptown parents lobbied for housing the school on the riverfront site of the old Public Health Service Hospital on Tchoupitoulas between State Street and Henry Clay. The advantage of choosing the handsome old hospital complex lay in the cloistered beauty of its walled courtyards and historic red brick buildings. But renovation costs might easily have proved more expensive than new construction, particularly given the kind of equipment and facilities the new school was designed to enjoy. And besides, the Uptown location was the least central of the various options the school board placed under consideration.

Eventually the school board decided not to decide. That was the Big Easy for you. Under the terms of the Certificate 34 agreement, the board required a minimum acreage for the school grounds and restricted the future site of the school to "locations in the Lakefront, Gentilly or East New Orleans areas of the city," a site the board specified, "conveniently accessible to the Interstate Highway System." In other words, rather than choose the location for Thomas Jefferson Magnet High School itself, the school board surrendered that choice to the Retif Realty Company. To have done otherwise would have required a vote for the public record, and a vote for the public record might well have been used against board members when they next ran for reelection.

It is also important to note that the Certificate 34 was a transferable document. Sheldon Retif had been granted the "Builder's Prerogative," but he didn't have to exercise the prerogative to build Jefferson High himself. He was perfectly within his rights to assign that option to some other party. And that's exactly what he did. Or what Joan contended that he did, I should say. For Tom Grieve alleged in his suit that Retif assigned the Certificate 34 to Grieve General Contracting.

Orleans Parish and its school board had learned their lessons well. For this was a state, remember, where a governor could appoint a local notary who was free to pay himself $250,000 annual salary.

Which was a very convenient way to reward a campaign ally, now wasn't it?

For the school board in Orleans Parish the reward was called the Certificate 34 or Certificate of Builder's Prerogative. And in 1980, to build Thomas Jefferson Magnet High School, it was awarded to the Retif Realty Company which was owned by Sheldon Retif. Who just coincidentally happened to be a campaign ally of Dr. Hastings Robert Moon.

Who just coincidentally happened to be president of the Orleans Parish School Board.

Calvin Coolidge was on to something when he said, "The business of government is business." In Louisiana, though, Coolidge's slogan has mutated to read: "The business of government is the business of those I'm in business with."

The States-Tribune covered the ceremony at which the Certificate 34 was awarded, and one of our photographers snapped a picture of Moon and Retif, wide smiles on their faces, holding up the artist's rendering of the still siteless Thomas Jefferson Magnet High School. The drawing was covered for protection with a sheet of slick plastic. And the plastic reflected the flash of the photographer's camera, thereby completely obscuring the school in a huge circle of dazzling gold. But with their arms around one another's shoulders, sharing the weight of the large drawing between them, together they made a perfect symbol for the new city they said they hoped their magnet school project would help usher into being. For Retif was a white man, and Dr. Moon was black.

*   *   *

In 1980 Sheldon Retif was fifty-nine years old. He was gray and balding, round-faced and red-nosed. He was a large man, over six feet tall and weighing, no doubt, close to 260 pounds. He had made his fortune in the early sixties building whole blocks of houses in the fast-developing Lakefront area of the city. Moving his construction crews from one house to the next in sequence, he was able to minimize his costs and maximize his profits. The city was still enjoying its post-World War II boom, and the houses he built on spec sold quickly to a rising upper middle class in thrall to the dream home of the day— brick, ranch-style, four bedrooms, two and a half baths.

Retif's connections with the black community dated to this same early sixties era. For there was a rising black middle class, too. And Retif saw the potential money he might transfer from their pockets to his. He built for these local black businessmen their own blocks of four-bedroom, two-and-half-bath, ranch-style brick homes in a Gentilly neighborhood called Pontchartrain Park.

One of the homes that Retif built in Pontchartrain Park, he sold to Dr. Hastings Moon, a one-time high school guidance counselor who had put himself through chiropractor school and thereafter made a fortune giving "adjustments" to the city's black population. Dr. Moon was a good chiropractor, and he had a reputation for kindness. If you couldn't settle your bill all at once, he was happy to let you pay him off month-to-month. And he didn't charge any more interest on the unpaid balance than you'd pay for a refrigerator bought on installment from Sears.

In the seventies, Retif's ties to certain elements in the black community strengthened. There was no more money to be made building houses for white people inside the city limits. All those white people in the market for four-bedroom, two-and-a-half-bath, ranch-style, brick homes were looking to buy them in some other parish where their kids wouldn't have to go to school with black children. So if Retif was going to do his stock construction in the city, he was going to have to concentrate his building on homes for black people. And since cash is color blind, he did just that, becoming a leading developer of New Orleans East as middle-class blacks flocked to that newest area of the city.

Interestingly, Retif shared with Moon a background in education. He'd been a high school mathematics teacher until he got sick of living on a teacher's meager income and transferred his talent for figures to the construction trade. Sadly, neither man likely saw himself as having a thing in common with Tom Grieve. Like Retif, Moon was a large person. He wasn't as tall as Retif, but he was as heavy. He had an enormous head and, in 1980 when he was fifty-six, wore his shiny black hair in a bushy Afro that was already several years out of style.

Unlike either, Tom Grieve was short and thin, sinewy with the signature physique of a man who had worked a lifetime at physical jobs. Retif and Moon may have belonged to different races, but they shared the privilege of having grown up in educated homes. They both graduated from high school and both went on to earn college degrees. Grieve, in contrast, shared only his race with Moon. Grieve's father was a railroad porter who disappeared when Tom was a boy. His mother cleaned houses for a living, brought her two daughters into her cleaning "business" when they were in their early teens, and put her four sons into the labor market at the same age.

Tom dropped out of Dubois High School after the tenth grade. But he discovered a talent for carpentry and earned a decent living for himself in the boom years of the fifties and the early sixties doing construction carpentry for white builders. But then, at the height of the civil rights movement, Tom found himself short of work. Times were tense, and he started his own company so that he'd never again have to miss a paycheck while a less skilled white man was kept on the payroll.

Tom had his ups and downs as a building contractor, but by 1980, in his forty-eighth year, he was in the position to have bid against Sheldon Retif for the Certificate 34 to build Thomas Jefferson Magnet High School. His bid was lower than Retif's. But under state law, the school board had no obligation to accept the lowest bid.

So Tom Grieve, of course, who wasn't an old ally of anybody, wasn't picked from the bid pool to do the job.

*   *   *

In the aftermath of the awarding of the Certificate 34, Sheldon Retif issued a statement promising a quick decision on a location for the new school. He said several sites were still under consideration and that he would choose the best one for the school children and parents of our city. Despite his contention that no decision had been made, however, it was widely assumed that he would build on a plot of land in New Orleans East off Morrison Road near Lake Kenilworth. The property was easily big enough to satisfy the minimum acreage specifications and met the requirement of being convenient to I-10. A further convenience could be found in the fact that the land was owned by the Retif Development Corporation, another of Sheldon Retif's several companies.

Wasn't there some prohibition against this? Well, no, there wasn't.

It may have been widely presumed that Retif would have to purchase land for the school from someone else. But that presumption wasn't a requirement. And why should it have been? "Share-Our-Wealth" was a program of Huey Long's, not the Orleans Parish School Board. So what was wrong with Retif using his own land for the project? Well, nothing, perhaps. The cost of the land was included in the six million dollars the school board would pay Retif for the completed school, after all. Somebody was going to make a profit off the land. Why not the Retif Development Corporation? After all, "The business of government in Louisiana is the business of people I'm in business with."

And the Retif Development Corporation was most certainly in business with Retif Realty.

After the hoopla over the awarding of the Certificate 34, our education writer, Amy Stuart, covered further developments with Retif Realty only intermittently. So some of Retif's maneuvers in the days before Grieve sued him weren't included in Amy's reporting and, as a result, did not come to wide public attention. In Joan's trial preparations, of course, she was able to build a precise chronology of what took place.

A provision of the Certificate 34 agreement stipulated that the builder of Jefferson High would encounter a $10,000 per week penalty for every week he missed a completion date in time for the beginning of the school year in September, 1983. One would have presumed, therefore, that Retif would move with all due speed. But he didn't, it seemed. Shortly after receiving the Certificate 34, he created the Thomas Jefferson Magnet School Corporation. But after that there was no word about Retif's plans for months.

In December of 1980, rumors began to circulate that Retif was about to announce plans for building Jefferson High on the wide neutral ground which separated West End from Pontchartrain Boulevard. Amy Stuart published a small squib in the paper which quoted an unnamed source as predicting that such an announcement would be forthcoming within a month. But no such plans were ever revealed to the public.

Instead, in late January of 1981, Retif announced that after a careful review of available locations, he was going to build Jefferson High on the Morrison Road site in New Orleans East. Despite the fact that canny students of local political practice and procedure had predicted this exact development for nearly six months, Retif's declaration nonetheless triggered a brief furor of protest. Parents on the West Bank, in Uptown and even in the Lakefront area decried the decision, complaining that the Morrison Road location was too far away from too many areas of the city. What good was a magnet school, they said, that was positioned in such a way it wouldn't attract students on a city-wide basis?

As is so often the case in our city's squabbles, the hidden agenda here was race. White parents in white areas of the city believed the school was being situated in New Orleans East to cater to the large population of middle-class blacks who lived in that area. They had not the slightest hesitation about saying such a thing in private. In public, however, the stated reason for opposing the Morrison Road location was not skin color but distance.

The school board did its duty with regard to those upset by Retif's choice of locations. The board held hearings and allowed people to come before them to wail and gnash their teeth. The local television stations sent out their film crews at the beginning of the hearings. And anguished parents were able to gather with friends in somebody's living room to watch themselves state their cases in thirty-second sound bites on the ten o'clock news.

But then at the end of the week of hearings, Dr. Hastings Moon rose to address his colleagues on the board. He spoke to the real issue at hand no more directly than had the parents before him. Instead, he delivered a rousing defense of the character of Sheldon Retif. It didn't matter that none of the protesting parents had attacked Retif, that there was, in fact, no record that anyone had even raised his name. In Moon's view, Retif's integrity had been called into question, his reputation had been besmirched.

Retif had shouldered an onerous burden on behalf of the parents and school children of our city, Moon declared. And he had carried that burden when the school board itself had shirked it.

Here Moon carefully neglected to mention that he was no more anxious than any other school board member to be saddled with the final decision about a location for Jefferson High. But by defending Retif, Moon could avoid the necessity of defending the Morrison Road choice. By defending Retif with enough flamboyant indignation, he could avoid even the inconvenience of addressing the Morrison Road choice.

Sheldon Retif was a selfless civic leader, Moon said, a man with a record of public-mindedness that reached back three decades to his days as a tenth and eleventh grade math teacher. The people of the city and the members of the Orleans Parish School Board could only trust that Retif had done his duty in this instance as he had always done it before. Moon was sickened, he said, to see such a man as Sheldon Retif dragged through the mud and muck of malicious insinuation and reckless innuendo. He wouldn't have it. He was disgusted by it.

Furthermore, Hastings Moon was the kind of man who believed in the sanctity of a contract. The board's Certificate 34 constituted a contract, Dr. Moon reminded his listeners. And that contract stipulated New Orleans East as a suitable venue for the long awaited Thomas Jefferson Magnet High School. If the board meant it when they awarded the certificate, how could they not mean it now? To abrogate a contract was to act in a way uncivilized, in a way un-American. And he, Dr. Hastings R. Moon, would not be a party to it.

When Moon finished his speech, some hour after he'd begun, the board voted immediately to table further discussion about the Morrison Road location for Jefferson High. Moon's chief ally on the board then introduced a motion of commendation for Sheldon Retif. Which passed by acclamation. Outside the meeting room, the few lingering protesters (most had not shown the staying power to endure Moon's oration) muttered solemn promises not to let this issue die.

But the next week marked the beginning of the Carnival season. And at Mardi Gras, our city regularly took off its costume as a city that was concerned with such issues as educating our children and revealed its naked nature as "The City That Care Forgot." By the time the Carnival revelry had left in the wake of its good times and good cheer, its tons of refuse from Napoleon Avenue clear to Canal Street, the controversy over building Thomas Jefferson Magnet School off Morrison Road in New Orleans East was a matter which no one could quite remember.

*   *   *

I likely never would have become acquainted with the complicated facts surrounding Jefferson High School had not Sheldon Retif decided that same Mardi Gras to sell his plot of ground on Morrison Road, along with his Thomas Jefferson Magnet School Corporation, to Tom Grieve. This was a purchase Tom Grieve would live to regret. He would have been far better off had he avoided doing business while the rest of the city filled itself with parades and his fellow citizens strained their vocal cords screaming to the maskers on every passing float, "Hey trow me sumpin, mistuh!"

But as Tom explained to Joan later, the deal meant taking his contracting operations into the big leagues of New Orleans business. And he was certain he could still make a profit, even after conceding the terms Retif demanded. In sum, Grieve paid the Retif Development Corporation two million dollars for the Morrison Road property, despite the fact that the property had an appraised value of only $1.9 million.

The contract Grieve and Retif negotiated stated that the Thomas Jefferson Magnet School Corporation was transferred to Grieve as well, but did not specify a price for this act of transference. This fact, or better, lack thereof, would cause problems for Tom later on.

The kicker in the agreement, though, was the clause that required the *buyer*, rather than the more standard *seller* to pay a five percent real estate commission, in this case another $100,000 dollars.

The commission was paid to the Retif Realty Company.

Of course.

Joan was dismayed just looking at the original contract. But again Grieve argued that he went into the deal eyes open. As far as he was concerned, he'd paid $200,000 for the right to build the school. That was a price, he figured, worth the benefits the job would bestow upon Grieve General Contracting. And he still figured to walk away from the enterprise with a profit of $400,000. The going rate for such work was a profit margin of ten to twelve percent. If he brought the project in so as to net $400,000, his profit would amount to only about half that. But as he stated to Joan, four hundred grand was still an awful lot of money for two and half years work.

Sheldon Retif obviously didn't think so. But then Sheldon Retif was able to make $200,000 for the mere effort of having friends in the right places.

I still would probably never have become acquainted with the details of *Grieve versus Retif*, had not the Chancellor of the University of

New Orleans called a news conference in April of 1981 to announce that he'd arranged with his Board of Trustees to donate a section of the local campus directly across from the intersection of St. Anthony and Leon C. Simon to house the city's new magnet school, Thomas Jefferson High. Standing by the chancellor's side as he read this announcement were Hastings Moon, president of Orleans Parish School Board and Sheldon Retif.

In his remarks at the news conference, the chancellor identified the latter as the man the city had chosen to build the school which would show the way to a bright and better future.

CHAPTER SEVEN

So here's the question. You're Faye Dunaway. You're over forty-five, but you still look great, even if your hair could use washing. You're still slim, and your legs have held their shape. You've been drinking too much, and your virtue has waxed toward the easy. But you're hardly a sloppy lush, and you're resolutely not a hooker. You haven't had to stoop that low. And you wouldn't. Your apartment isn't a penthouse at the Ritz, but it's spacious and clean. Your wardrobe is stylish and well-maintained. Take some aspirin and let the sun shine on your face and you look a whole lot like, well, Faye Dunaway.

One night you're in your local bar, contentedly alone with a glass of Scotch, when Mickey Rourke takes the next stool. As you well know, Mickey's a sleazebag even when he's rich in a picture like 9½ Weeks. *This time out Mickey's less attractive than he was as the arsonist in* Body Heat. *He lumbers about like a man with diaper rash. He hasn't bathed since* A Prayer for the Dying. *And speaking of* A Prayer for the Dying, *Mickey hasn't changed his underwear during the Reagan presidency. In sum, he is to utterly disgusting what the Grand Canyon is to ditches.*

So does your idea of a good time involve going to bed with this guy?

If your answer is yes, then you'll probably find much to admire in Barbet Schroeder's Barfly. *If your answer is anything from uncontrolled retching to you'd opt for a close encounter with Rodney Dangerfield, then you'd probably better choose some alternative form of entertainment.*

Barfly is surely the most viscerally repellent picture to play our city this year. And it's objectionable for reasons beyond the mere fact that scene after scene turns your stomach. Candidly based on the life-long gutter ramblings of writer Charles Bukowski, Barfly *is arrogant, pretentious, and self-righteous, in addition to nauseating. No greater feat of self-indulgent self-glorification has ever been perpetrated on celluloid.*

Rourke plays a character named Henry Chinaski, an iconoclastic fellow with the unquestioned courage to stink. He's taken society's measure, and he's got society's number. Henry is smart. He listens to Mozart and casually quotes Tolstoy. Henry is deep. He thinks. More important, Henry sometimes sidesteps through his own fumes and, ta da, writes. *Heavy. Henry is profound. "Hatred is the only thing that lasts," he asserts. "Endurance is more important than truth."*

Far out, man, I mean, like, like . . . like far out, man.

I dig it. That's the theme, man: endurance is more important than truth.

In other words, Henry Chinaski sees society's hypocrisy so clearly that he's not buying a single aspect of society's expectations. He isn't going to work. He isn't going to be responsible. He isn't going to bathe.

What he's going to do is stay as drunk as possible as long as possible and thereby stick it up society's bottom. And just to make sure you don't think he's a coward, just to show you he could do any damned thing he wanted, if he wanted, he's going to pick a fight with the biggest guy in the bar. And if that guy beats him senseless tonight, well he'll be right back to get beat senseless again tomorrow night.

Say, is this guy Norman Mailer's Existentialist Anti-Hero, or what?

Or, on the other hand, is Henry Chinaski emblematic of the mean little self-centered eddy off mainstream existentialism that Mailer and others have invented to send Albert Camus spinning in his grave? Viewed from this perspective maybe Henry Chinaski (and the Charles Bukowski who brought him into being) is just a bum so full of self-justifying bullshit that he thinks body odor is a philosophical statement and dereliction a moral crusade.

Examine the narrative's central conflict. Henry has decided he cares about Wanda Wilcox (Dunaway). But then a wealthy magazine publisher named Tully Sorenson (Alice Krige) arrives in her Mercedes sportscar to offer Henry both fame and fortune. Literary lionization *is just around the corner. If Henry will only agree to turn the corner and pass the bar always located there. Such a deal she's got for him. Including her perfumed and powdered body. He doesn't even have to shower. Henry teeters. And not just from the Scotch he guzzles with the $500 Tully gives him. But wait. It's a catfight. Wanda's got Tully by her cashmeres. And it doesn't even matter who wins. 'Cause if Wanda's willing to fight, Henry's got a drinking mate he can be faithless to for the rest of the picture. And that's all that really matters.*

There are countless reasons to hate this picture. Having to look at Mickey Rourke's bloated, smart-aleck face makes you sick to your stomach. Seeing his sarcastic gray smile makes you pledge a rigorous new program of proper dental hygiene.

As you squirm about in your seat, you ask yourself irritated questions. Why doesn't anybody in this film wash his or her hair? Because it would take two hands, requiring that one be removed from the cocktail glass.

Why would lookers like Wanda and Tully be attracted to the likes of Henry? Obviously a new order of masochism.

Why does Rourke sound like Leonardo Lion? It's the only lionizing Charles Bukowski could reasonably hope for.

Why would Faye Dunaway get involved in a project this repulsive? Given that her last two films never made it into wide release and given that her picture before that was *Mommie Dearest*, perhaps her career options were either playing Wanda Wilcox or *becoming* Wanda Wilcox.

In conclusion, let us never forget that Barfly *is a motion picture which takes itself altogether seriously. And if for no other reason (and there certainly aren't any other reasons), it deserves to be taken seriously. So, if only for a moment, let's do that. Henry says that hatred is the only thing that endures and that endurance is more important than truth. Hatred, therefore, is more important than truth.*

Yes, yes, Chinaski's ideas smell as bad as he does.

But there's more. Henry says that he doesn't hate people (he doesn't comment on whether that makes them, then, more or less important than truth). But he admits that he does like things better when people are not around.

Let me be just as frank. The hated truth about Barfly *is that I'll like things better when it's no longer around.*

*   *   *

I banged out the above review in a fit of agitation when I got home from Herbst, Gilman after discovering the empty 1987 file drawer where Joan's working materials on *Retif* should have been. What the hell was going on? First somebody broke into my house and there appeared to be a folder missing from my study. Now Joan's office files seemed to have been ripped off too. By whom? For what reason? Jason had said I shouldn't presume that the 1987 files had been stolen, that it was just as likely they'd been misplaced somehow. But he admitted the coincidental disappearance of both sets of Joan's *Retif* files was indeed perplexing. For me it was more than perplexing; it was unnerving. I called Carl to ask if he could conceivably imagine why somebody might want to steal these files, but he was neither at home nor in his office. My efforts to reach Preacher and Wilson proved similarly frustrating. In the absence of someone to talk to, I resorted to working. This *Barfly* piece was the result.

At least I pulled none of my usual shenanigans in the review. I almost wrote in response to Henry Chinaski's dictum that endurance is more important than truth, "Far effing out, man, I mean like, like . . . far effing out, man." I had the line like that on my laptop screen. But I deleted the *effings* out of it. I knew Carl would have to anyway. And, just now, I didn't feel like hassling him. He left the word *bullshit* in. That was certainly an unacceptable term twenty years ago. But it's routinely printed in *Newsweek* and other national publications nowadays. So I guess Carl figured that what was good enough for *Newsweek* was good enough for *The States-Tribune.*

Either that or he was confident the Old Man never read the stuff I wrote.

It was late when I finished writing, but I hazarded another call to Carl. When he still didn't answer, I went to bed and fell into a fitful sleep, tormented by my recurrent dream about hurting a friend in a baseball game.

*   *   *

The next morning I got to the office early. I wanted to talk to Carl, but he was in with the Old Man. I unpacked my Zenith and finished off the *Midnight Run* review I'd begun the day before. I printed the piece, modemed both the *Midnight Run* and *Barfly* reviews into the system, lettered the top of my hard copy with my access code and the file name for each review, and then, shortly before noon, dropped the hard copy into Carl's in-basket.

Carl was in his office by then. Staring through his open door, I could see that he was working on a story. He had the phone pinched between his shoulder and his left ear. And his fingers were moving on the keys of his computer. Carl hated to take handwritten notes, and when he was forced to, he always typed them into his computer as soon afterwards as possible. As a result, he liked to make all his contacts by phone so that he could save himself a step by typing his notes directly into our computer system. When he wrote, he used a split-screen procedure that displayed his notes on the bottom with the text of his story on the top.

From across editorial I waved my arms at Carl until I got his attention. I performed a crude pantomime about eating and pointed back and forth between the two of us. He responded with some sign language of his own by shooting me the finger. But a few minutes later he stopped by my office.

"So where we eating, Marcel Marceau?" he asked. "And why should I eat with you when I can piss off more people by dining in public with a blond cop all by myself?"

"You got a lunch date with Wilson?" I said.

"Better not be a date. Woman's got a hollow leg, and I don't have money enough to buy two lunches. She can eat almost as much as you. Christ, I'd have to hit up my savings."

*   *   *

On the way out of the building the three of us ran into Preacher Martin who agreed to join us for lunch. We walked up to Felix's at the corner of Iberville and Bourbon. Keeping the paper's office in the heart of the French Quarter—we were located on Royal Street between Toulouse and St. Louis—was frequently a major pain in the ass, primarily because parking was such a persistent hassle. But it did have the advantage of allowing us to eat lunch, any day we chose, at some of the world's great restaurants. Felix's wasn't exactly in the class with Mr. B's, which was such a favorite in the legal community, but frankly, a little pricey as a lunch outing for most in the newspaper business. Felix's also lacked the charm of the Napoleon House. But for inexpensive fried and boiled seafood, Felix's provided as solid a bet as there was in town.

I'd intended to talk about the missing files with Carl alone. But as we were walking to the restaurant, I recognized that Wilson's background in law enforcement and police reporting might prove valuable to me as well.

Wilson had held her position at *The States Tribune* for a little over a year and a half, so she wasn't really a rookie any longer, though she was enough younger than Carl and Preacher and I that we teased her in a way we might not have someone our own age. We'd needed someone in Wilson's crime-beat post for over twenty years. The position had been held by an old gentleman who just withered away on the job, hanging on until he neared age ninety. But the Old Man's one soft spot was that he hated to force people into retirement. So we were stuck until our octogenarian colleague passed away at his computer one day. Lore has it that he fell face forward onto the keys and typed out several pages of Zs with his deceased nose. But like so many colorful stories, this one just isn't true. The caps lock was on when he expired, and, actually, he typed out exactly seven pages and fourteen lines of question marks. ?????? An appropriately inquisitive way to take one's leave, don't you think?

Wilson landed the suddenly vacant job on the basis of her undergraduate degree in history from the University of New Orleans where she had written with some distinction for the school newspaper. After her college graduation, for a number of years she contributed occasional stories on police matters to *New Orleans Weekly*, our "alternative" news publication. So she was a natural to replace her predecessor when he finally showed the good grace to die.

Wilson's other major qualification for her current post, her career as a policewoman, was no doubt equally significant in helping her land the job. Explaining her years with N.O.P.D., she quipped that like many a loyal child before her, she had gotten her education and then gone into the family business. Here as elsewhere, law enforcement was frequently a family occupation. Wilson's father was a New Orleans police captain. Her uncle was a sergeant. So had been her grandfather.

Wilson's family name was originally Malinowski. Her immigrant grandfather had renamed himself for a milkshake he got at a Canal Street drugstore shortly after his arrival in New Orleans. Wilson was strikingly tall, nearly 5'11" and big boned. She was trim waisted, but her full bosom made her look heavier than she was. Her face, with its wide, ready smile, was very pretty, I thought, and so did Carl. He always referred to her as our blond cop. Her hair was really a sandy brown, though, and unusually thick. She wore it long, three or four inches below the shoulder, most often pulled back off her face with two large barrettes, sometimes gathered into a long ponytail with a brightly colored bow.

As far as I was concerned, Wilson came from an entirely different generation than I did. She was born when John Kennedy was president, and she graduated from college in the presidential administration of Ronald Reagan. For Wilson, The Beatles were that group with whom Paul McCartney played before he formed Wings. Ironically, though, Wilson reminded me a lot of women I knew in the sixties. She hadn't adopted the severe look of the eighties' professional woman. Her long hair wasn't fashionable any longer, and neither was the way she tended to dress, in full skirts and loose fitting cotton blouses. I had never seen her in a woman's business jacket. I doubt she owned one. Her personality recalled the kind of woman in the sixties we used to term "earth mothers." She loved dogs and cats and little children. She liked having friends over to her West Bank house for crawfish boils and barbecues. She seemed independent and self sufficient and yet quick with a word of instinctive concern for anybody suffering or in need.

Wilson had been with the paper only about eight months when Joan died, but we had gotten to know her a little. Joan liked her, and that encouraged me to like her, too. Joan really got to know her when Wilson invited us to her house to eat crawfish that first spring. On several subsequent social occasions in the few months Joan had to live, she and Wilson would always talk. It was Joan who got her to open up somewhat about why she'd made a career change. Carl and I had each asked her about that more than once, but about all we could determine was she evidently didn't like to talk about it.

A story Wilson told Joan one night provided our best understanding into why she left police work. The three of us had gathered for happy hour at Bailey's, a bar on the first floor of the Fairmont Hotel.

In the midst of chitchat about godknowswhat, Joan just asked her straight out, "Why'd you leave N.O.P.D., Wilson?"

I was allowed to listen to Wilson's reply, but she gave it, really, only to Joan. Wilson had done scores of strip searches during her years on the force. Standard operating procedure. Make a collar, a junkie, a drunk, a streetwalker. Cuff 'em. Drive the perp to Central Lockup. A round of questions, sullen answers, a typed report. Then the routine. Male officers did the male offenders; female officers did the women. Always in pairs, establishing the power, two on one. Get her stark naked. Goosebumps on her arms from the cold. A shiver maybe. Maybe another. This one was defiant; hatred burned like lasers from her eyes. She tried to turn her nudity into a mocking armor, to embarrass you for what you were ordered to do. That one was humiliated, biting back her tears, tried to cover herself with her hands. No matter, the steps for each were the same. Wilson hated it because the degradation was part of the object lesson. Stated purpose was the search might reveal a wrapped razor blade secreted in a vagina, a sheathed knife stuck up a rectum. Incredible, but demonstrably possible. Wilson's dad said he knew of cases, her uncle too. So the search might save a life, somebody inside, maybe your partner's. Maybe even yours. But Wilson never grew comfortable with it. She loved her dad; he was a good man, a good father. She loved her family. But what if the cases they knew where weapons were found inside body cavities weren't their own cases but cases they had heard about, the way she had heard about those cases from them. Her reality was in her experience. She had executed the searches and never found anything. But this she saw in every strip search she supervised: Naked and outnumbered, powerless, the prisoner was transformed from perpetrator to victim.

Then there was the last one, Lakeesha Johnson, a twenty year old black woman from the Iberville Housing Project. Wilson answered a squeal from store security and busted her coming out of the Maison

Blanche on Canal Street. Lakeesha had three children with her, twin four-year-old boys and a nine month old baby girl in a beat-up stroller. She had a pack of Pampers and three bargain-table dresses crammed in a cheap plastic diaper bag. Squeezed in her fist, she was carrying a pair of rhinestone earrings, still attached to the display square of white cardboard. On sale for three bucks. Two stuffed toys, a yellow and black tiger and a gray Pooh bear were tucked under the foot of the baby's blanket. A glass baking dish had been concealed under the baby's foam pad.

At Lockup Wilson had to wait with the woman until City Welfare could send a worker over to pick up the children. Then she ran the priors: no charges of violence, but three previous arrests for shoplifting, six for soliciting, two for crack possession. Lakeesha denied everything. The computer had her confused with some other party. She didn't know how the dresses and other goods got in her possession. Her kids must have put them there. She was going to pay for the earrings; she just forgot for a minute. She was on her way back into the store when Wilson arrested her.

Wilson took Lakeesha into strip search and uncuffed her. The matron was a young officer named Tracy Miller, just about the furthest thing from the stereotype of middle age, stout and coifed in a severe gray bun. Miller was young, trim, and blond. She was also vicious. Most cops hated strip search. Miller got off on it.

Miller and Wilson held their batons in both hands as they began the procedure. Miller told Lakeesha to get undressed. Lakeesha did so slowly, starting with her imitation leather sandals. Then she unbuttoned her blouse and stepped out of her elastic waisted print skirt. She wasn't wearing underpants. She was slim and chocolate brown. If she'd had the money to fix herself up, she could have been pretty. She reached behind herself to unhook her brassiere which was gray with age and yellow with sweat stain. When she had shrugged out of the bra, Wilson noted a purplish scar, thick and long as a forefinger which ran down from her left shoulder toward her breast, a knife wound, no doubt stitched back together by a doctor indifferent to the subsequent disfigurement.

"You know the routine," Miller said. "Turn around, grab your ankles."

Lakeesha mumbled something but slowly did as she was told.

"Reach back, spread your cheeks," Miller ordered. Lakeesha did so and Miller said to Wilson, "At least this one has bathed in the last month."

Wilson saw Lakeesha's eyes flash as she stood back up. Her mouth moved, but she smothered whatever words had formed in a grunt.

"Last station," Miller said as Lakeesha turned back to face her.

Lakeesha didn't move a muscle.

"Complete the routine," Miller said. "Hold yourself open and squat three times. Hard. Do it!"

"Fuck you," Lakeesha said.

"Just do it," Wilson said. "Do it and be done with it."

"Fuck you too," Lakeesha said.

Miller stepped closer to her and said in a voice so low she was almost whispering. "I want you to grab two handfuls of pussy and yank it open wide enough for Paul Bunyan." She laid her Billy against Lakeesha's collar bone and then flicked it away against her breast. "Now do it before I cram this stick so far up your ass you're gonna be beggin' me for my phone number."

That's when Lakeesha spit full in Miller's face. Miller instantly tried to draw back her baton, but Lakeesha grabbed the top end and began to wrestle for it. Wilson stepped forward and hit Lakeesha across her shoulder blades, but the prisoner managed to deliver a crushing right-handed punch to Miller's jaw and to wrench away Miller's club. Swinging wildly, Lakeesha hit Wilson a glancing blow across the chest. Before she could raise the baton again, though, Wilson cracked Lakeesha's right arm with such force her radius broke in two places.

A person in control of herself would have stopped then, but Lakeesha backed into a corner snarling "Fuck you, bitch, fuck you." Wilson ordered her to lie face down on the floor, but she refused. Crouched in the corner, waving Miller's night stick in her left hand, she shifted her weight back and forth from one foot to the other. Miller staggered to her feet, hit the alarm button for back up, and yelled, "Hit her in the head. Knock her fucking brains out."

"She's hurt," Wilson said. "Backup will be here in a second."

"Fuck backup," Miller said. She reached over and snatched Wilson's baton away, then swung once at Lakeesha's head, and when the prisoner raised her stick to try to protect her face, Miller swung at her midsection, aiming for the hip as she was trained, she later said in her report. But the blow caught Lakeesha flush in her stomach. She went down then, first on her knees and then curled into a ball on her side. By the time the ambulance arrived, she was bleeding profusely from the vagina.

Miller's blow ruptured Lakeesha's uterus and required the doctors at Charity to perform an emergency hysterectomy.

When the word came down near the end of the day, Tracy Miller sought out Wilson to joke that by ending Lakeesha Johnson's reproductive life, "I ought to be named crime buster of the year."

Wilson resigned from the force the next day.

"I didn't quit because I broke Lakeesha Johnson's arm," Wilson told us that night at Bailey's. "I didn't even quit because I detested working with the likes of Tracy Miller. Though I ought to have quit for either of those reasons." She combed her hair out of her eyes with her fingers. "I quit because I wondered how long it would be before Tracy Miller's attitude became mine, before some future Lakeesha Johnson fought back so hard I did indeed hit her in the head, and the next one after that I hit repeatedly until finally I beat a person's brains into custard." She looked up at the ceiling, cocked her jaw to the side and laughed a single expulsive breath. "I quit because I stood by while Tracy attacked a basically defenseless injured person. I quit because I was partner in inflicting the punishment of hysterectomy on a person guilty of shoplifting. A poor person, Jesus Christ, a poor person stealing toys for her children."

A moment passed in which none of us said anything more. Finally, Joan touched Wilson's arm and said softly, "So now you're doing something else."

Wilson took a deep breath and smiled without any light in her eyes. "So now I'm doing something else."

*   *   *

When Joan died, I think Wilson missed her as much as anybody. Joan had lots of friends in this town. Dozens of people sent flowers to her memorial service. Out of respect and love for Joan, many of the arrangements were lavish and expensive. The wreath that Wilson sent was the smallest at the funeral. But I could tell that she had made it herself, an oval of twisted twigs, adorned with orchids, and a magnolia, Joan's favorite flower, in the center. I was touched Wilson felt so much for Joan, that she wanted to spend her time, rather than merely her money, to make a gesture of remembrance.

My fondness for Wilson, however, and Carl's and Preacher's, too, for that matter, was in some ways utterly surprising. For despite her resignation from N.O.P.D., her politics remained very much those of a policeman's daughter. And in that respect she was an unlikely pal. Both of her votes for president she'd cast for Ronald Reagan. Her next would be for George Bush. She believed in capital punishment. She thought the Supreme Court decisions following Miranda-Escobedo were an outrage which bred in the criminal mind a heightened contempt for law and order and frustrated society's fully justifiable desire to make the guilty accountable for their crimes. She dismissed liberal counter arguments in these areas as so much bleeding heart nonsense, and she was plentifully enough armed with examples of the guilty going free to harm the innocent anew that she could sometimes reduce a bleeding heart like me into frustrated silence.

Wilson was by no means an orthodox right winger, though. Her Catholicism made her personally opposed to abortion. But she believed in a woman's right to choose all the same. And she thought the federal government in the Reagan years had exacerbated social and racial divisions by gutting social welfare programs and aid to education.

Joan's judgment of Wilson was simply that she'd grown up at a different time. The examples upon which she based her positions, mostly taken from her father and other family members, were true. She just lacked the set of experiences to put those examples in a different perspective. Preacher Martin made a similar point about Wilson. "I trust her heart," he said. "I may not agree with a lot of her abstract attitudes. But if I confront her with a specific situation about real human beings, I think she'll choose what's right."

That Preacher spoke up for Wilson was in certain ways even more remarkable than the fact that Joan and Carl liked her. I'm not sure that she and Preacher agreed on a single thing. A man fifteen years my senior, Preacher was a social and political radical before the sixties made such a stance chic. And he remained a radical long after most of his comrades in the "movement" of the sixties had begun to worry more about foreign automobiles and the right stock portfolios than about U.S. imperialism abroad and civil rights at home.

Edward J. "Preacher" Martin was a human anomaly. Raised a central Louisiana redneck, he became a civil rights activist. Educated at Yale, he made a point of seeming ignorant. Trained for the ministry at Union Theological Seminary, he had never held a pastorate. Nicknamed "Preacher," he had seldom stood in a pulpit to deliver a sermon. Thoroughly serious about his religious calling, his every other utterance took the Lord's name in vain. Identified with liberal causes throughout his career as a writer and an activist, he was adamantly "pro-life" on the abortion issue, going even so far as to embrace the "abortion is murder" rhetoric. An outcast from most institutions of organized religion, he edited the paper's religious section, regularly writing upbeat stories about the activities of groups whose social attitudes he found appalling.

The States-Tribune, of course, paid Preacher far too little money to live on. He made the bulk of his income from writing fiction and from speaking engagements his fiction generated. His novels ranged over many subjects from a bizarre tale of murder and mutilation set in the heart of Louisiana Cajun country, to a story of cowardice and betrayal set in Vietnam, to a trilogy of books about black/white relations set against the backdrop of the civil rights movement. Preacher's theme was always the same, the obligation human beings had to let their actions on this earth be governed not by an insistence on justice, but rather by a commitment to forgiveness.

*　　　*　　　*

We stopped at the oyster bar in the front of Felix's before we took a lunch table. The shucker opened a dozen for each of us. Carl, Preacher and Wilson each ordered a draft beer. I got a Diet Coke, wishing I didn't think I had to. When he heard my drink order, Carl glanced at me sideways, but he didn't say anything. Preacher and Wilson ate their oysters the same way Joan had, slurping them directly from the half shell. Carl and I both performed the ritual of making up the tangy sauce of ketchup, lemon juice, Tabasco, and horseradish. I loved the bite the horseradish gave me way up in my head, behind the tops of my nasal passages. And I loved to soothe that bite with a cold swallow of beer. Diet Coke didn't provide quite the same kick.

The oysters were cold and salty, but small. And the shucker opened another dozen among us to make up for their size. "Lagniappe, cap'ns," he said, pronouncing the first word *lanyop*. He was new and no doubt presumed we were from out of town. Felix's was especially popular with tourists. The shucker was a small, wiry black man with thick veins bulging violet against the dark skin of his forearms. He smiled at us broadly, showing the gold filling around one of his front teeth.

"Sumpin extra," he said. "That's lanyop. Sumpin extra. To be friendly."

We thanked him and ate the extra oysters gladly. When we headed back for a table, we each put a dollar bill in the mason jar he used to collect his tips.

At a table far in the back, in the part of the restaurant that Felix's took over when Tony's Italian Restaurant closed its French Quarter operations, we ordered three portions of boiled shrimp and one seafood platter to split. While we waited for the food to come, I said to Wilson, "Thanks for your call about my house being robbed."

"Your house was *robbed*?" she said, eyes flashing.

"You saw the report," I said, falling for her trap.

"You mean your house was *burgled*," she said.

"Cop," Carl said, looking at me and pointing at her with his thumb. "See what I told you. Fucking blond cop."

"Never fucked a blond cop in my life," Wilson said, turning toward him in mock indignation.

"Jesus," I said, impatient to tell my story. "Will you guys cut out the crap so I can tell you something important. My house was robbed goddammit. And I think I know what was stolen. Doesn't anybody care?"

"I don't care," Preacher said. "I didn't have any of my shit at your house."

"Jesus," I laughed.

"I care, Michael," Wilson said. "And so do these two assholes."

Carl added, "I've got to sit here to eat. I might as well hear you rattle on about a bunch of middle-class possessions black boys like me only get to see in catalogues. And if you keep banging your gums long enough, I might . . ." He looked at Wilson pointedly. "I repeat I *might* be able to get my share of the shrimp."

And so I told them.

And as I did, the banter from all of them abruptly dropped away.

*   *   *

I told them about the missing files and tried to bring them up to date on what I knew about the entire *Grieve versus Retif* law case. Carl knew some of the story, and he occasionally added a comment or two. He seemed unhappy about something, though, and his comments seemed to have an unaccounted for edge of testiness. I presumed he was preoccupied with his forthcoming story on the sales tax scandal.

Though I talked through most of our lunch at Felix's, I managed to relate only about half of the Tom Grieve/Sheldon Retif story when we had to go back work. Or at least Carl and Wilson did. Preacher was done with his *States-Tribune* work for the week. And my responsibilities at the paper were such that I seldom *had* to return to the office. As was frequently true, I had scheduled an afternoon screening, today of Glenn Gordon Caron's *Clean and Sober* at the Downtown Joy.

Since I had done most all the talking for the better part of an hour, Carl and Preacher had eaten most of the shrimp, though this was an accomplishment they vigorously denied.

"Bullshit," Carl said. "Blondie the Amazon here took care of her share."

"How would you know?" Wilson said. "You were far too busy stuffing your face to notice if I managed to eat a single shrimp."

"I sure as hell didn't get my share," Preacher said.

"Well I didn't get any," I said, stirring with a fork through the pile of shrimp peels in front of us.

"And you're just gonna dry up and blow away," Wilson said to me.

We each threw a stack of bills on top of the check.

Pointing to me, Carl said to the other two, "This man look to you like he ever missed a meal?"

We got up from the table and began walking back toward the restaurant entrance on Iberville Street.

"Hey," I said. "I wouldn't be talking if I were you. You look like you're ready to play tackle for the Saints."

"And you look like you're ready to play the entire backfield," Carl said. "But you're right you wouldn't be talking if you were me. Because if you were me, you wouldn't be able to get a word in edgewise."

"That's just as well," Wilson said to Carl. "Because you wouldn't be able to do anything but mumble."

"With your mouth so full of shrimp," she added after a beat.

Preacher and I both laughed.

Outside Felix's we turned left and walked a block to Royal where we stopped for a second on the street corner. Carl and Wilson were going back to the paper; Preacher and I were off in other directions. "You weren't interested in this business about the missing files?" I said to Carl before we went our several ways.

Carl shrugged. "I'm just distracted, I guess. Sorry."

"Why in the world would you think someone would steal Joan's *Retif* files?" I asked him.

"Well, now you don't know they've actually been stolen," he replied.

"Evidence sure suggests they've been stolen," I said. "And I'd sure as hell like to figure out who did it and why."

"Sounds to me like they've been stolen," Wilson interjected. "And I'd really like to hear the rest of the background on the case. Or what you know of it anyway."

I squeezed Wilson's shoulder. "I've got to go preview the new Michael Keaton picture, but when I'm done I'd be happy for the opportunity to tell you the rest of it. How about The Columns at six, six thirty?"

"I can make that," Wilson said. "Yeah. I'd like to."

"What about you Carl?" I said. "I could use your input."

"About what?"

"I don't know," I admitted. "I guess about whether I should try to figure out why somebody would want to steal Joan's files. She always believed there was something deeply rotten in this case, you remember. Maybe somebody wanted to see if she ever got close to figuring anything out."

"Presuming the files aren't just misplaced somewhere," Carl said.

"Both of them misplaced?" Wilson said. "How likely is that?"

"I'm thinking exactly like Wilson," I said.

"And the police?" Carl wanted to know.

"The police aren't gonna do shit. Guy I talked to at N.O.P.D. practically snored in my ear."

Carl said, "So now you want to go play detective?"

"Maybe I do," I said. "Maybe I do."

Carl shook his head. "I gotta tell you I don't advise this," he said. "I think you're looking at a big waste of time. And I can't see how stirring around in this mess could do you any good." He looked at me solemnly. "You know what I mean?"

I shrugged.

"Be a film critic, Mike," Carl advised. "That's what you're good at."

"I don't think I can just ignore the fact that my house has been burglarized, Carl."

Carl breathed deeply and glanced at his watch. "No, I don't guess you can," he said. "So since I haven't got any choice, I'll see you at six thirty."

"Thanks," I said and smiled. "You coming, too, Preacher?"

"Shit," he said. "I guess listening to you is marginally less boring than my other option for this evening."

"Which is what?" Wilson inquired.

"Listening to the termites eat out the inside of my walls," Preacher said.

CHAPTER EIGHT

I was struck by how much he seemed to have aged.

After my screening of *Clean and Sober*, I had some time to kill and abruptly decided to walk up to the Federal Court Building on Camp Street to see if I could get a copy of the decision Judge Delacroix had rendered in 1981 when Joan first argued the *Retif* case before him. It occurred to me that reading the ruling in the case might provide me some insight into who might want to steal Joan's files.

While I was at the courthouse waiting for a clerk to make me a copy of the decision, I saw him. Judge Leon Delacroix came out of his office and walked slowly down the hall toward the restroom. It had been five years since I'd seen him, but he seemed to have gone from late middle age to elderly during that half decade.

For moral support, I had attended Joan's closing arguments in the *Retif* case back in 1981. She thought she was about to win, of course. And we regarded Judge Delacroix as our ally in the pursuit of justice. I remember thinking how wise he seemed and how distinguished.

My attitude was a little different when I saw him the next and last time, at a 1984 Louisiana State Bar Association reception at the Fairmont. Joan was on the host committee, and thus she and I had to stand in a receiving line outside the banquet room and greet people as they arrived for the party. I'm sure the judge had no idea Joan was waiting in line, or he'd have chosen to skip all the formal how-do-you-do business. For at that very time, a federal appeals court was considering Joan's accusation that Delacroix had ruled in the *Retif* case despite a conflict of interest. But suddenly there we were face-to-face with the judge and Mrs. Delacroix.

Down from his courtroom perch, I remember thinking, shorn of his judicial robes, he was far less imposing a presence. A tiny, small-boned man, he was barely five feet five inches tall, olive-skinned, gray-haired and bespectacled. As he came through the line, he greeted me without any hint of recognition, and introduced me to Mrs. Delacroix with whom I shook hands as well. Physically, at least, they were an oddly matched pair. She was as tall as the judge was short, pushing six feet in her heels. She was impeccably dressed in a fashionable black silk cocktail dress and a triple strand of pearls. But no amount of taste in expensive clothes and jewelry could make up for the fact that she was a strikingly unattractive woman. Inside her precise black pageboy coiffure, her face looked like that of a mob arm-breaker. And that was appropriate, I guess, given the rumors that her father was once a key player in New Orleans crime circles. Her earlobes glittered with dangling diamond earrings, but her expression suggested that she'd just eaten ground glass. And this was such a contrast with the judge's face, which sported twinkling eyes and a quick smile. He had a courtliness of manner which suggested a humility about his station and privilege, if, at the same time, just a hint of patrician Southern decadence.

I spotted the dismay in the judge's eyes when he realized he was going to have to exchange pleasantries with Joan, whom he did recognize. But he carried it off well enough until he went through the ritual motions of introducing Joan to Mrs. Delacroix. After opening with the line, "Ms. Barnett, I'd like to introduce you to my wife," he turned to his right only to discover that Mrs. Delacroix had abruptly vanished. And then the judge reddened, shrugged his shoulders, stepped out of the line and distractedly walked toward the banquet room, mumbling something we couldn't hear.

Altogether, there must have been a thousand people at the reception, perhaps more. The huge Fairmont banquet room was jammed. And though I tried to stand at Joan's side for most of the evening, the fact is that we'd frequently get separated. I'd head off to the bar to freshen our drinks, get caught by some acquaintance and two-fist down both our Scotches before I could extricate myself. On one of my excursions to and from the bar, I remember talking to Jason Roux just outside a circle of late-middle-aged women that included Jessica Delacroix. I didn't intend to eavesdrop. But just as Jason was distracted away into another conversation and before I could head off again in search of Joan, I heard the name Barnett and thought for a moment that someone had addressed me. I turned toward the circle of women in their sleek black dresses and glittering jewelry, expecting to find in their number a movie fan or two. At first I didn't even notice Mrs. Delacroix, who had her back to me. But before I made the incredible *faux pas* of speaking to anyone, I realized that not only was no one talking *to* me, no one had even noticed my presence. They were talking, it turned out, about Joan and her allegations against Jessica's husband.

I didn't dare linger long, of course. And over the hum of noise in the hall I couldn't catch everything that was said. But I did hear one conversational exchange clearly enough to be shocked and then disgusted. A woman across from Mrs. Delacroix remarked that she admired the judge, of course, but hadn't exactly always agreed with his legal opinions.

Mrs. Delacroix rejoined "Well that's not so remarkable, dear. Like most decent people in New Orleans, neither have I."

That drew titters of approval from her listeners, and the first woman then offered that despite Leon's liberal attitudes, she strenuously objected to this Joan Barnett's attempts to besmirch his reputation for integrity.

To this Jessica lowered her voice to an artificial whisper and elicited outright guffaws by responding, "But what else can you expect of such a *person*. I've asked around about *Ms.* Barnett. We already know she takes clients with year-round tans. Think about the fact that she doesn't have any children. Her husband is a communist. And the majority of her law partners are circumsized."

I thought again of his wife's grape-shot snobbery as I watched Judge Delacroix shuffle down the hall toward me now at Federal Court. He looked so much older. His hair had turned almost totally white, and it had become thin enough I could see the gray shine of his scalp. He walked slowly past me without so much as a glance in my direction. But before he reached the restroom, one of his judicial colleagues joined him in the hall, and the two stopped a minute to talk. I was too far away to hear what they were saying, but I suspect the other judge told him a joke. Judge Delacroix threw back his head and laughed. And after he did so, he made a gesture toward the other man that was almost maternal in its affectation, a waving away of his colleague as if to scold him for being naughty.

Judge Delacroix seemed so likable, a colleague regarded with such fondness by his peers that I recalled again how much Joan had admired him. But then I recalled as well our subsequent astonishment when he ruled against Tom Grieve. Joan never quite got over her mystification and sense of betrayal by Judge Delacroix's decision. As I watched him laughing now I thought of Hamlet's observation, "that one may smile, and smile, and be a villain."

*   *   *

"The paper ran a page-one story on Chancellor Joseph McConnell's donation of a square of University of New Orleans land for Thomas Jefferson Magnet High School," I said that evening at The Columns.

We were sitting out on the porch with drinks. Wilson and Preacher had bottles of Lite Beer. Carl was sipping on a gin and tonic. I had an iced tea. I didn't think I was in as bad shape as Michael Keaton in *Clean and Sober,* but I didn't want to get there, either. It was hot, and we were sweating. The whole back of my shirt was sticking to the chair. Wilson had a fine bead of sweat over her upper lip, which she kept dabbing at with the damp napkin the waiter had set under her beer bottle.

"I remember that story," Preacher said. "Seemed like this little piece of good news. The city going to get something nice for once. And getting the land free and all."

"At the press conference with Chancellor McConnell," I said, "Sheldon Retif announced that because he had allotted two million dollars for land acquisition in his bid to the school board for the Jefferson Magnet project, he would now accept a payment of only four million when the school was completed. Paper ran an editorial that next Sunday's praising Retif. Cited his remarkable civic-mindedness. The whole publicity burst gave Retif such positive standing in the community that it really made Joan's situation difficult once she got involved in the case."

"I'll bet Tom Grieve didn't regard Sheldon Retif with nearly the same degree of admiration," Preacher remarked.

"Not hardly," I said, invoking a symbolic double negative. "Tom, too, saw *The States-Tribune* article. The next day he contacted the Orleans Parish School Board in an attempt to learn what was going on. No one at the school board could tell him. School Board President Hastings Moon was unavailable to speak with him. So was the school superintendent. The vice superintendent told Grieve that he was quite unfamiliar with the circumstances of Grieve's inquiry. As far as the vice superintendent understood, the 'Builder's Prerogative' had been granted to the Retif Realty Company. Beyond that, the vice superintendent could not say. He confirmed for Grieve that Retif Realty did indeed have the right to assign the Certificate 34 to a third party. But if such an assignment had been made to Grieve General Contractors or any other third party, the vice superintendent had not been so informed. Not that he necessarily would have been, he said."

"Not that he necessarily would have been, my ass," Preacher snorted.

"Right," I said and went on. "Grieve's attempts to gain an explanation of Chancellor McConnell's announcement at Retif's office were no more satisfactory. Less so, in fact. According to secretaries at Retif Realty, Mr. Retif was not in. For like a fucking week, Mr. Retif was simply not in. Furthermore, they did not know when, exactly, Mr. Retif was expected. They would be happy, they said, to give Mr. Retif any message Mr. Grieve would like to leave. Yes, they were certain any prior messages Mr. Grieve had left for Mr. Retif had been given to him. But no they wouldn't want to say Mr. Retif always returned calls on the very day he received them. And alas, no, they didn't know of anyone else at the company who might be able to help Mr. Grieve. They really thought that Mr. Grieve ought to speak with Mr. Retif himself."

"And so finally Grieve decided he was going to have to sue," Wilson interjected.

"Well, after about a week of the run-around, he went to see Joan," I responded. "Said Joan had been recommended by a friend of his whom Joan had opposed in a divorce case, of all things. Tom didn't even know that Joan had developed a specialty in education law, had defended U.N.O., for instance, in two cases where the school had denied tenure. Anyway, early in her career Joan did a good bit of domestic law. She had represented this man's wife and stuck him with hefty alimony payments. Grieve reported that his friend had called her 'a cold-hearted bitch with a mean streak as wide as Texas.'"

"Joan used to psyche up for her court appearances by reading Mike's movie reviews," Carl said to the other two. It was the first comment he'd made all night.

"Hey," I said to him. "I'm not always a cold-hearted bastard with a mean streak as wide as Texas."

"No," Carl responded. "You always give good reviews to foreign shit that has a lot of naked French women in it."

"Well, I do like pictures with a lot of naked French women in them. I'll admit that."

"French nudity always excites me," Preacher said. "Either that or depresses me. I can never quite remember which. For sure, though, it makes me thirsty. So I think I'll have another beer. Anybody else?"

"Just order a round," Carl directed. His testiness from lunch didn't seem to have abated.

When the drinks came, Wilson said, "Okay, now, this guy recommended Joan because she'd gotten big-time alimony for his wife."

"Right," I said. "According to Grieve, the guy told him, 'If I was ever going to court again, I'd sure want that woman on my side.'"

"Why didn't Grieve go back to the guy who handled the contract with Retif in the first place?" Wilson asked.

"On the day that Grieve came to Joan's office," I said, "she asked him that exact question. He explained that the attorney who had worked with him on the contract was 'a friend,' but not someone he was sure he ought to rely on in the current situation. The guy was Grieve's neighbor, evidently, and had done his contracts for years. Had a law degree. But he didn't practice full time. Worked for the city department of records. Something like that. Practiced a little law on the side."

"Graduate of Southern Law School?" Preacher asked quietly about the law school of the black university in Baton Rouge with its lamentable record of turning out graduates unprepared for the bar examination.

"Yes," I said.

"Shit," Preacher said.

"Yeah. Shit," I said. "And it didn't take Joan long to figure out just how much shit this guy had allowed Grieve to step in. Grieve outlined the broad parameters of the situation to her, and she agreed to review a copy of the contract he had negotiated with Retif for the acquisition of the Thomas Jefferson Magnet School Corporation. There were significant problems with the contract, but Joan still felt that Grieve had a case. A damned solid one, in fact, despite the bad legal advice he'd had. So she called Grieve and agreed to contact Retif on his behalf. Retif, of course, wouldn't talk to Joan himself, and she dealt instead with Tammy Dieter-White, an attorney with the firm of Wallace and Jones. Ms. Dieter-White informed Joan it was the position of her client that the Retif Realty Company had been granted the Certificate 34 to build Thomas Jefferson Magnet High School and that said certificate remained and had always remained in the possession of Retif Realty. The only relationship Retif Realty had ever entered into with Grieve General Contractors was its role as agent in the sale of a tract of land on Morrison Road in which Grieve was purchaser. And that was that. Neither Ms. Dieter-White nor her client would budge from that position."

"And given that response," Wilson said, "Joan had Grieve file suit. For what? Possession of this Builder's Prerogative Certificate?"

"Exactly," I said. "Joan and Tom briefly discussed a strategy of having Grieve General Contracting go forward with plans to build the school and then try to force payment from the school board. Such an approach was extremely risky, though. If it failed, Tom Grieve would almost surely be completely ruined. Even if it worked it wasn't likely to gain him the friends and positive attention that were his real goals. And besides, despite the problems in the contract, Joan was confident she could win a quick and easy verdict in Grieve's favor. She even expected at the outset that Retif would back down soon after the suit was filed in federal court. To her mind, the case was that cut and dried."

"Why was the case tried in federal instead of state court?" Preacher asked.

"Joan was able to bring the suit in federal court because Grieve General Contracting showed an official corporate address out of state in Gulfport, Mississippi."

Wilson responded, "I thought you said Tom Grieve was a life-long New Orleanian."

"He was. But this is another of the case's little messy parts. For the first ten years Tom Grieve was in business for himself, he did pretty well. By the early seventies, he was doing very well indeed. Louisiana was riding high on oil, and Grieve had moved from doing home repairs to doing subcontracting construction work and finally into the relative big time of building his own spec homes. The standard suburban stuff, brick ranch style, four bedrooms, two and half baths, wall-to-wall carpets. But then came Nixon's national housing bust, and Tom was caught with a huge amount of borrowed money tied up in houses he couldn't sell. His first company went belly up. He lost everything."

"So he moved to the Gulf Coast?" Wilson asked.

"Well, no, he didn't," I said. "But there were accusations leveled at Grieve by some of the firms who had subcontracted for him. Nothing was ever proven. Nothing even went to court. But there were allegations of fraudulent mismanagement. And Grieve was embarrassed enough that he just switched his base of operations out of state for a while. He wasn't going to go back to driving nails for the Sheldon Retifs of this world, so he got a new bill of incorporation in Mississippi with headquarters in Gulfport. It was a pain making the one-hundred-thirty-mile round-trip drive for a few years. But it allowed him to get back into business and reestablish both his confidence in himself and a reputation for quality work."

"Who all knew this?" Wilson asked. "And did it become a factor in his losing the original bid for Jefferson Magnet?"

Preacher laughed. "Woman, you act like you think people in this city behave in systematic and principled ways."

"*If* it was ever some kind of factor," I said, "nobody made mention of it on the front end. Retif got the Builder's Prerogative and that was that. Joan always suspected, of course, that nobody at the school board even examined the other bids."

"Because the fix was in for Retif," Wilson interjected.

"Because the fix was in for Retif," I affirmed. "Joan couldn't prove that, of course. But she sure as hell believed it. On the back end, of course, things changed. One of the points that Tammy Dieter-White tried to make at trial was that Grieve was ineligible for the Certificate 34 all along because he was a Mississippi builder."

"And was this true?" Wilson asked.

"Let's put it this way," I said. "No state law, local ordinance or administrative procedure prohibits awarding bids to out-of-state companies. Maybe there ought to be something like that. But there isn't."

"What about in practice?" Wilson asked. "Is there an established *practice* of only awarding contracts of this sort to in-state firms?"

Preacher laughed again and said, "Mike's already told you. The business of government in Louisiana is the business of people I'm in business with. And people in Louisiana are in business with whomever it's good for them to be in business with."

"Out-of-state firms land government contracts in this state all the time," I said.

"So then Retif's attorney's argument about this was bullshit," Wilson said.

"Basically, yes," I said. "Though that's not to say it might not have carried some weight with the judge. As did, perhaps, the allegations of fraud that were leveled against Tom Grieve some years earlier."

"The judge allowed testimony about that?" Preacher asked.

"No," I said. "He sustained Joan's objections to all such testimony in that area."

"But the jury heard it?" Wilson asked.

"There was no jury," I said. "The case was heard by Judge Leon Delacroix. And he made the decision."

"Why didn't Joan opt for a jury?" Wilson asked. "I mean, Tom Grieve is a black man and most juries in this parish end up being overwhelmingly black. No offense, Carl. But I was a cop, and I saw black juries acquit black defendants time after time."

"Only juries full of T.N.O.N." Carl said in a tone so flat we couldn't tell if he was being sarcastic or not. *T.N.O.N.* was a popular local acronym for the expression *trashy New Orleans nigger.*

We waited for him to elaborate but when he didn't I said, "Joan could have demanded a jury trial. And she certainly considered it.

She even considered the race factor, both Tom's and the prospective jurors'. But she knew that Retif's attorneys would put people like Hastings Moon on the stand to testify that Retif could walk on water. And that, presumably, would pretty well have neutralized whatever advantage Tom's skin color might have given him at the outset."

"Judge Delacroix is black?" Wilson asked.

"No," I said. "Why do you ask?"

"I don't know," Wilson said. "I've never seen him, but somehow I thought he was black."

I looked at Carl who stared back at me blankly. Slowly he turned to Wilson and said in his flat tone, "You probably thought he was black because he was Southern and liberal."

"Maybe that's it," Wilson said sharply. "You know how we cops and ex-cops are, bigoted and all."

"What bigotry, girl?" Preacher said. "All liberal judges are either niggers or faggots. Everybody knows it. Most of 'em, as I understand it are actually both."

Wilson's face reddened and she laughed, perhaps embarrassed at having snapped at Carl, uncertain now if there was any venom in Preacher's sarcasm. "I'm probably confusing Delacroix with somebody else," she said. "Actually, I don't know much of anything about the federal judges in this town. On my beat I'd probably only get involved with a federal judge if there were suspicions one was on the take."

"Leon Delacroix isn't on the take," Carl said irritably.

"How do you know?" Wilson demanded, aggressiveness back in her tone.

"Yeah, how do you know?" I repeated.

"I know," Carl said. "It's my business to know who's on the take and who isn't. Right? And if Delacroix was dirty, I'd know it."

Wilson started to say something, but I cut her off. "If I can get back to my point," I said. "It's true that Delacroix is an almost completely unblemished liberal. And that was another reason Joan was content to let him hear the case without a jury. She respected him immensely. And she trusted him not to be swayed by the bullshit Tammy Dieter-White was sure to pull in trying to make Retif look like a saint. I can remember the surge of confidence Joan had the day Delacroix ruled on the first pre-trial motion. Dieter-White tried to get the whole case dismissed for plaintiff's failure to state a cause of action. Or something like that. I think the exact terminology may be a little different in federal court. But anyway, Delacroix just dismissed that approach right out of hand. After listening to Dieter-White hold forth for a while, he said something like, 'Thank you very much for your efforts to help the court in this matter, Counselor, but I'd have to disagree. Whatever the ultimate outcome of this case, Mr. Grieve has most certainly stated a cause of action.' And Joan thought that he was sending Retif a message not even to bother fighting on."

"But in the end Delacroix ruled against her." Wilson said.

I blew out a noisy breath of air. "In the end Delacroix ruled against her, all right. And there's a sense in which she never got over it. You should have seen her the day she got Delacroix's judgment vacated by the Supreme Court. And then . . . and then it didn't even matter."

"Why did Delacroix rule for Retif?" Wilson asked.

"That question bugged Joan till the day she died," I said. "Her argument for *Grieve* was simple. But it never occurred to her that she wouldn't win. Basically, she argued that Tom Grieve bought the Certificate 34 from Retif when he purchased the Morrison Road property and the Thomas Jefferson Magnet School Corporation."

"But the purchase contract between Retif and Grieve didn't state that fact specifically, did it?" Carl asked.

"No," I said. "There was no mention of the Certificate 34 anywhere in the contract."

"And that was obviously a problem," Wilson said.

"Sure," I said. "But Joan pointed out a whole series of things that supported the notion that Tom Grieve must have presumed he was purchasing the 'Builder's Prerogative.' Retif had already made a public announcement that he'd chosen the Morrison Road site for the school. Tom Grieve purchased that exact property. Furthermore, he purchased a corporate entity called the Thomas Jefferson Magnet School Corporation. Why else would he have paid more than the land's appraised value? That was the point Joan kept hammering on. And it's a hell of a point. And why else would Grieve have agreed to pay a real estate commission of $100,000 had he not presumed he was buying the right to build a school for which the city would pay him six million dollars upon completion?"

My friends were all sitting over empty glasses. I swallowed down the last of my tea and waved at a waiter that we wanted another round. Preacher lit up an unfiltered Lucky Strike and offered his pack around to the rest of us. I declined with a shake of my head, as did Carl. "It's bad enough I smoke these," he said, taking out his pack of Camel Lights and lighting up. A streetcar rattled down the avenue across from us.

When the waiter had brought us fresh drinks, Wilson said, "Joan's argument sounds almost unassailable to me, Mike."

"But not to Judge Delacroix," Preacher said.

"So how did Retif's attorney respond?" Wilson asked.

"Basically," I answered, "Dieter-White relied on the language of the contract itself. She harped on the absence of any language dealing with a sale of the Certificate 34. She stressed that the contract stated money changed hands only for the purchase of the land. The transference of the Thomas Jefferson Magnet School Corporation was invalid because it wasn't executed as an exchange for value. But, even if valid, the Certificate 34 wasn't transferred along with the Thomas Jefferson Magnet School Corporation because Thomas Jefferson Magnet School Corporation never possessed the Certificate 34. The Certificate 34 was granted to Retif Realty and always remained in the possession of Retif Realty. As to the commission that Grieve paid Retif Realty on the land transaction, Dieter-White argued that Retif Realty was due such a commission as the listing agent of record for the Morrison Road property and though it was certainly true that commissions were usually paid by the seller, it was hardly unprecedented for a contract to obligate the purchaser to pay the commission."

"In other words," Preacher said, "Retif's argument boiled down to the proposition that the white man took the black man to the cleaners because the black man was too stupid to get good legal advice."

"It's just such bullshit," Wilson said. "I don't care who's black and who's white in this case, and I don't care about all the legal technicalities. It's clear that Grieve got ripped off. And I can't believe the judge didn't see it the same way."

"But he didn't," I said, reaching inside my jacket pocket for the copy of the judge's opinion I'd gotten at federal court earlier in the afternoon. "In fact, Judge Delacroix mainly saw it almost exactly like Tammy Dieter-White. I remember Joan complaining at the time that Delacroix's opinion seemed to have been lifted whole cloth from Dieter-White's brief."

"Meaning he upheld Retif's position right down the line," Wilson said.

"Right down the line," I said, opening the pages of the opinion and glancing it over. "At the outset, Delacroix states that elements of the contract at issue may be considered 'unorthodox, misleading and at points, arguably, even deceptive.' But then he goes on to reflect on the highly public nature of matters surrounding Thomas Jefferson Magnet School. He calls Sheldon Retif a 'reputable businessman' with 'an outstanding record of public service.' He refers to Tom Grieve as 'a seasoned businessman of wide experience.' Then he basically parrots back Dieter-White's argument, adding the point of his own that the contract transferred the Morrison Road property from Retif to Grieve. The property had value at the time of the transaction and continued to have value. So Grieve was not damaged, he maintained, in that connection."

"Slightly diminished value," Preacher said, "now that it wouldn't be housing a school, of course."

"Yeah, well he's got some stuff in here about that, too," I said. "Says that in the absence of specific language in the contract, he cannot accept plaintiff's arguments concerning a sale price in excess of appraised value as designed to compensate Retif for the Certificate 34. Market value, he says, and appraised value are seldom in precise synch."

Preacher snorted, "Old Judge Delacroix really did a number on Mr. Tom Grieve, didn't he."

"Yeah," I said. "But, now listen to this, the way he ends this thing."

I read directly from Delacroix's opinion. "'In a contemporary court of law, one hesitates to invoke the old principle of buyer beware,' the judge argues. 'But contract law rests on the presumption that all the terms of what may be agreed to shall be written and bound within the pages of the contracting document. A careful examination of that document can lead but to a single conclusion, namely that plaintiff is without legal remedy for circumstances he himself willingly committed to. And on those grounds, I hold for the defendant.'"

"Jesus Christ," Wilson said. "What passes for justice in this country."

"It's a simple enough formula," Preacher said. "He who has power and influence and money may also get justice. He who has neither power nor influence nor money will usually get fucked."

Wilson turned to Carl. "You're the investigative reporter," she said. "Why haven't you ever looked into this business?"

"He did," I said. "A couple of years ago."

Carl ran his fingers through his graying knit of hair, took a drag off his cigarette and breathed out a dragon's breath of smoke through his nostrils. "Right after Tom Grieve died . . ." he began.

"Grieve is dead?" Wilson said. "How?"

"Heart attack," I said.

Wilson shook her head.

"Afterwards," Carl said, "Joan asked me to check into this for her. I told her sure. But I didn't find anything."

"So what do you think about the missing folders?" she asked.

Carl shrugged.

"Do you think Mike ought to poke around in this shit?" she inquired.

"I think that Mike is a film critic and he ought to critique movies."

"Meaning you'll do the digging for him?" she wondered.

"I didn't say that," Carl responded. "I already checked into this mess once and I didn't find anything, okay?"

Carl drummed his fingers on the table and then added, "Look, I think Mike's right about aspects of this business. Sheldon Retif is a political user. Nobody's ever caught him with his hand in the cookie jar, but that doesn't mean he hasn't got sugar under his fingernails. And there are lots of other unsavory characters involved. Hastings Moon is the kind of black politician that makes you ashamed to be black. And Leon Delacroix's political affiliations stretch into the thicket of old time New Orleans gambling operations. He's married to Charles Mason's daughter, for Christ's sake. All of that certainly argues there's something rotten here. But the one thing that says maybe there's not is the judge himself. He's been in public life for four decades, and there's not a stain on him. I'd know if there was, and there isn't."

Carl pulled the straw out of his drink glass and took a swallow of gin. "More important," he continued, "and I know Mike doesn't want to hear this, I'm just not sure the whole thing is such an important story. Not if you look at the big picture. This town and state are riddled with corruption, and whatever went on here looks like relative small potatoes to me." Carl turned to me with somber eyes. "I'm sorry, Mike, but compared to other stuff, like city government managed sales tax fraud . . ." He shrugged and looked back to Wilson. "Mostly, I think Mike ought to try to forget about this business. He thinks it's important because it had to do with Joan. But it's not going to do him any good to go stirring around in this shit."

Wilson shook her head, took a sip of her beer, looked back at me and said with a sigh, "Anyway, the story doesn't really end with Delacroix's decision, right?"

"Oh no," I said. "That's really just the beginning. The case dragged on for years."

"But meanwhile," Carl said, "even while it was dragging on, Retif built Jefferson High School on the campus at the university."

"That he did," I said.

"So how did it all turn out?" Wilson asked.

"You're not listening girl," Preacher said. "He who has neither power nor influence nor money will usually get fucked."

"But I thought Joan won at the Supreme Court," Wilson said.

"Oh she did," I said. "But not on the merits of the case. She couldn't even get the Supreme Court to hear the case on its merits. And she lost the appeal on a split decision by a federal appeals panel. The majority held quite simply that Judge Delacroix had made no procedural errors. What was remarkable, in a way, was that the dissenting judge was so vehement in his argument in Grieve's favor. I think he smelled the same stink she did."

"Well what *did* Joan win at the Supreme Court?" Wilson asked.

"The issue before the Supreme Court was one of judicial recusal," Carl interjected. "A kind of technicality Joan came up with."

"Technicality?" Wilson said.

"Well, I think *procedural irregularity* is the proper term," I said. "But basically, yeah. Irony of ironies. Delacroix ruled against Grieve on the technical grounds that he had an incompetent lawyer who approved a contract that didn't even spell out what he was trying to buy—though that point was pretty damned obvious to everybody in the world *except* Judge Delacroix. And then Joan got Delacroix's verdict set aside on—on another technicality, if you will."

"Which was what?" Wilson asked.

"She discovered that Delacroix was on the board of trustees for the University of New Orleans."

"So what?" Wilson asked.

"So he had a conflict of interest," I responded.

"How?" Wilson wondered. "All U.N.O. did was donate the plot of land for building the school."

"True," I admitted. "But U.N.O. had an awful lot to gain prestige-wise by becoming host to Thomas Jefferson Magnet. Everybody knows the kind of struggle that institution has had through the years trying to capture the attention of a town dominated by Tulane people. The front-end public relations coup for the university was enormous. And in the aftermath of the school's getting built, people would clamor to get their kids into Jefferson High, which meant sending them to school on the U.N.O. campus. It was a way for the university to assert itself into the center of the lives of professional New Orleanians and to continue to do so for generations."

"Okay," Wilson said. She tapped the fingernails of her index and middle fingers against her teeth. "I concede U.N.O. had powerful reasons for wanting Retif to build the school on its land. But I still don't quite see the connection for the judge. How'd he get on the U.N.O. board, anyway?"

"Appointed by the governor," Carl said. "Standard political appointment."

Wilson looked at me and cocked her head. "I guess I'm confused, Mike. I can see that, however intangibly, U.N.O stood to gain, even gain significantly. Therefore, I'll concede that Delacroix had a conflict of interest. Technically, that is. But surely he wouldn't have made an unfair ruling against Tom Grieve just to benefit U.N.O. I mean, board or no board, what does he care about U.N.O.? Right? He was probably already a judge by the time the place first opened its doors, so he's certainly not a graduate. He's probably a Tulane man."

"He is," I confirmed.

"You see what I'm driving at?" she asked.

"Of course, I see what you're driving at," I said. "It's exactly what Retif's lawyers drove at. But you have to remember that Joan was a damned good lawyer. She argued simply that Delacroix's judgment against Grieve carried with it an appearance of impropriety. She didn't bother to argue that Delacroix had done anything wrong. Only that this appearance of impropriety existed and that the judiciary was such a sacred American institution that it should avoid even the appearance of bias."

"And the Supreme Court bought that?" Wilson asked.

I laughed. "By a five-to-four majority, yes."

"To paraphrase another notorious windbag," Preacher said, "the wheels of justice grind perversely, but they grind with exceeding irrelevance."

"What the fuck does that mean?" Wilson asked.

Preacher replied, "No matter what the Supreme Court ruled or why, the school still got built at the university."

"The Supreme Court didn't hear the case until April of 1986," I said, "and didn't make its ruling until June of that year. Thomas Jefferson Magnet began its classes on the U.N.O. campus in the fall of 1983, just as the Builder's Prerogative required."

"Couldn't Joan have gotten a restraining order," Wilson asked, "to have kept Retif from going ahead with the building?"

"She tried," I said. "But it was denied. By Judge Leon Delacroix."

Wilson shook her head. "If the school was already built," she asked, "what exactly did Joan win from the Supreme Court?"

"The right to a new trial before a different judge," I said. "But by then Thomas Jefferson Magnet High School had been completed for so long it had already had a graduation class."

"So the case was moot," Wilson said.

"Well, not technically. Grieve could have started over with a suit for the Certificate 34. But that obviously wasn't in anybody's interest. There couldn't be *two* Thomas Jefferson Magnet High Schools. And besides, Grieve's plan all along was to have used his building of Jefferson as a launching pad for his business. By this time, everybody pretty much saw him as the bad guy, trying to disrupt the city's gleaming new secondary institution on the Lakefront. That pretty much eroded his will to fight. So he settled."

"What did he get?" Preacher asked.

I laughed a single bitter ha. "Joan asked Retif for the $200,000 premium Grieve had paid for the Morrison Road site. Plus interest. Dieter-White countered with an offer of $20,000. And much against Joan's advice, as you can imagine, Grieve took it. But the whole affair ruined him. He defaulted on his loans for the Morrison Road property and was forced back into bankruptcy."

"What happened to him?" Wilson asked.

"Well, he didn't live long after that," I said. "And that was a blessing, I guess. He had to find work as a carpenter again. He was the most earnest guy. Gave Joan the whole $20,000 of his settlement. That was only a fraction of what he owed her, of course, but she was never in this case for the money. She tried to resist, but he insisted she take the twenty grand. Then once he was working again, he'd stop by every Friday evening. Evidently, he'd stop off at a bank and cash his check; anyway he'd bring Joan a $50 bill. It seemed to mean everything to him that he was making progress, slight as it was, to paying her off. When we first knew him, he was driving a late model Cadillac Seville and always wore a suit when he went to Joan's office. At the end, all he had was a second-hand pick-up. I used to watch him climb out of the truck and dust himself off before he'd come up to the house. Once I came out of the house and found him washing his hands under the faucet off to the side of our front porch. Wanted to be as presentable as possible, I guess, before he rang the doorbell."

I looked at Carl who had an elbow propped on the table and most of his face covered by his large dark hand.

"And then he died," Wilson said.

"And then he died," I said. "Mercifully, I guess. He was still a young man. But this thing cracked his spirit."

"And that was it," Wilson said. "That was the end of the case."

I pinched the bridge of my nose between thumb and forefinger. "Except in Joan's mind," I said, "that was the end of the case."

Wilson said, "This story is just too sad for fucking words."

"As far as Joan was concerned," I said, "it was the saddest story of her life. I so hoped she'd let it go after Tom died. But she couldn't. In her mind, the injustice of it all had come to transcend the specifics of what happened to Tom Grieve. It meant that the system didn't work. And Joan really believed in the system. I'm not saying she believed the system was perfect. She wasn't naive. But she believed *in* the system. She believed that it could be made to work. For if the system didn't work, all the Tom Grieves of the world were vulnerable. So she kept digging on the case, even when she no longer had a client to dig for, even when she had a husband she had to hide her digging from."

"What was Joan looking for?" Wilson asked me.

"A motive, I guess," I said. "A motive for Retif to have bribed or blackmailed Delacroix. Some other personal motive for Delacroix to have ruled against Tom Grieve."

"And she never found it?" Wilson asked.

"Not to my knowledge," I replied. "Though that's what's been bothering me since my house was robbed. While we were jogging on the day of Joan's accident, she said she had something new to tell me about the case. And I figure it must have been fairly significant for her even to bring it up to me, given how I always bugged her to just let it go. Now I think maybe what she was going to tell me was in the folder that isn't in my study any longer but isn't in the file at Herbst, Gilman either."

"Like what?" Carl asked.

"Like the motive she was looking for—Retif's or Delacroix's or both."

Carl shook his head. "I don't think there was any motive for her to have discovered. I certainly wasn't able to find one."

"But I think you must have missed something," I said to Carl. "There's that one ingredient you were never able to explain."

"I never said Delacroix's decision wasn't rotten," Carl responded. "I just said that I couldn't see that Retif had any motive for bribing or blackmailing the judge. The stakes were too small for him. And in the absence of that, I certainly couldn't see Delacroix's motive."

"But you never accounted for why Delacroix lied," I said to Carl.

He shrugged and shook his head.

"What are you talking about Delacroix lied?" Wilson asked me.

"Delacroix definitely lied," I said. "And whenever Joan got hung up on the absence of a motive for either Retif or Delacroix, her suspicions were rekindled by the fact that Delacroix lied."

"Lied about what?" Wilson inquired.

"Lied about what he knew and when he knew it," I said. "Sounds like something out of Watergate, doesn't it? Delacroix had already rendered the judgment by the time Joan learned that he was on the U.N.O. Board and thus had a conflict of interest. But the case was still under his control. It was less than a week later. Two days only, I think. The statutory time delay that makes the judgment final and official hadn't yet run. So she went to see him and asked him to vacate. He said he didn't know what she was talking about. Admitted that he was a U.N.O. board member, but denied that fact constituted a conflict of interest. When Joan formally filed a motion to vacate the judgment, Delacroix refused."

"Well you can't blame him about that?" Wilson said. "I mean, I could buy that Delacroix screwed Grieve for some mysterious reason, but surely not to benefit U.N.O."

"The key thing about the U.N.O. connection," I rejoined, "is that Delacroix didn't recuse himself from the get go. That's what he should have done, a fact that he admitted in his deposition to the Supreme Court. Only he claimed he was unaware that U.N.O had a material interest in his verdict."

"And why couldn't that be true?" Wilson asked.

"Because Joan subpoenaed minutes of the U.N.O. board meetings where the land donation was discussed. Over and over U.N.O. Chancellor McConnell stressed the advantages to the university. And this is critical: Delacroix was present at every meeting. When the donation was finally approved, he cast an affirmative vote."

"Jesus," Wilson said. "So Delacroix did lie."

I responded, "And that's the thing that drove Joan nuts till the day she died. *Why* did Delacroix lie?"

I looked up from our table and out to St. Charles Avenue at a brightly lit streetcar clacking by in the dark. Save for the driver shrouded by the black curtain that separated him from his missing passengers, the streetcar was empty. It seemed to be laughing at me as it passed, like a gigantic jack-o'-lantern baring a dozen yellow and taunting teeth.

I had a screening of a new documentary picture by Errol Morris called *The Thin Blue Line* scheduled at the Prytania early in the morning. It was very late, and we were tired. I knew that it was time

I allowed my friends to go. I hadn't been drinking, but I felt almost as if I had been. In my fatigue I craved a drink, and I wondered if this would be the night when I would once again reach for the uncomplicated companionship of Black and White.

*   *   *

At home that night, I fought my life-long battle with insomnia, this time turning over and over in my mind all the details of Joan's *Retif* case and the central mystery of Judge Delacroix's surprising decision. Somewhere around dawn I fell into a brief, fitful sleep unsettled by my persistent baseball dream. This time as I rounded third and tore for home, the catcher made only a half-hearted attempt to block the plate. I saw that I could easily avoid him and score standing up. Instead, I veered deliberately left and ran him down. The collision caught him utterly unawares and seemed to break him in half. I stood over his crumpled body in a swirl of dust. And I looked down at a black face I couldn't identify. I couldn't identify it, but somewhere, somehow, it was a face I knew.

CHAPTER NINE

One of the formative moments of my baby-boomer youth occurred when Perry Mason requested permission in his weekly murder trial to be allowed an unusual procedure. The judge was perplexed and undecided and turned for comment to prosecuting attorney Hamilton Burger. Burger suggested that Mason be allowed to proceed, remarking that the object of a murder trial, after all, was truth, that its goal was not victory but justice. And so I was instructed still again about an element in American democracy that made us distinctive as a people.

In the thirty years since that particular episode of "Perry Mason" blinked off the tube, I have, I hope, waxed more sophisticated in my grasp of the complexities of the American system of justice. But not even my own admittedly increasing level of cynicism prepared me for the withering attack on that system waged by Errol Morris's The Thin Blue Line. The Thin Blue Line *is not an easy motion picture to typify. It is highly stylized and employs performers for the reenactment of certain scenes. In its heart and soul, though, the film is a documentary. It examines a particular murder and ultimately proves beyond the shadow of a doubt that the man convicted of the murder, and still serving a life prison sentence, is innocent. In so doing it impugns the intelligence of the police officers who investigated the crime, the motives of the assistant district attorney who prosecuted the case, and the worthiness to sit on the bench of the man who heard the case as judge. And in the final analysis, the movie calls into question just how often our adversarial system results in such horrifying miscarriages of justice.*

The details of the murder case in The Thin Blue Line *are complex. Shortly after midnight on November 29, 1976, a Dallas policeman named Robert Wood stopped a blue compact automobile for driving without lights. As his partner waited in the police car, Wood approached the violating vehicle. He planned to issue a verbal warning and send the driver on his way. But when he stepped alongside the window, a series of shots rang out. The fatal rounds were fired into Officer Wood's head after he had already fallen to the ground. The small blue car then sped away into the cold autumn night.*

Officer Theresa Turko, Wood's partner, did not manage to get the license plate number. But she did offer the observation that the driver was alone in his car and was wearing a jacket with a large fleecy collar. Beyond that, the Dallas police were able to generate very little to go on. On December 3, 1976, after notices of a $20,000 cash reward appeared in Dallas newspapers, a woman named Emily Miller came forward and filed a written affidavit claiming she'd passed the crime scene moments before the shooting. The driver of the blue compact, she said, was "a light-skinned Negro or a Mexican."

Dallas police spent thousands of man-hours studying automobile tire tracks and examining auto registration records for Chevy Vegas, the make of the car identified by Officer Turko. But by the third week of December, they were still without substantive leads and admit in the film to a feeling of public humiliation. Never before in the department's history had they failed to apprehend a cop killer within forty-eight hours. The break in the case came on December 19, 1976, and came from a most unexpected quarter. Three hundred and fifty miles from Dallas, in the small town of Vidor on the Texas-Louisiana border, local authorities arrested sixteen-year-old David Harris for a crime spree in early December of that year. In the process of their investigation, Vidor police ascertained that Harris had recently stolen a blue Mercury Comet and a .22 caliber pistol and used the latter while committing several burglaries and an armed robbery. Furthermore, friends of Harris told investigators that for nearly a month Harris had bragged of having "offed a pig in Dallas." Led by Harris, Vidor police retrieved the .22 revolver from a nearby swamp, and it proved to be the weapon with which Officer Wood was murdered.

When interrogated by Dallas police, however, Harris maintained that he was innocent. His story of killing Wood was told to "impress his friends." The actual shooting, Harris now asserted, was committed by a twenty-eight-year-old Caucasian laborer named Randall Adams, a hitchhiker Harris had picked up in Dallas on the day of the killing. Harris claimed to have witnessed the murder from the front seat of the stolen Comet, which, he said, Adams was driving. He did not report the crime because the (stolen) murder weapon was his. Randall Adams had no prior record, but on December 21, relying on Harris's testimony, Dallas officials arrested him and charged him with the murder of Officer Wood.

During his interrogation, Adams admitted that he had been given a ride by Harris on the morning of November 28, 1976, and that the two had spent a large portion of the day together driving around Dallas. In the early evening the two of them had purchased beer and attended a drive-in screening of two teenage sex flicks.

The court proceedings began on April 26, 1977. Adams was prosecuted by Douglas Mulder, an assistant district attorney with an undefeated record and an astonishing reputation for convincing juries to return recommendations for the death penalty. The court-appointed defense attorneys were Edith James, who had never before worked a case involving a capital felony, and Dennis White, whose specialty was real estate. At the trial, Harris repeated his accusations against Adams. The defense attempted to impeach Harris's testimony by referring to his Vidor crime spree and his statements to associates that it was he who had killed Wood. Judge Don Metcalfe disallowed such rebuttal, however, ruling that Harris's statements and activities after the murder were not relevant to the issue of Adams's guilt or innocence. Officer Turko testified that Adams's bushy hair probably looked like the fleecy jacket collar she had described earlier.

Still, going into the last day of the trial, defense counsels White and James thought that they were surely going to win, that the state had not proved its case. But when they arrived in court on that fateful Friday, April 29, 1977, Mulder produced three surprise witnesses, all of whom identified Adams as the driver of the blue compact. The most damaging witness was Emily Miller, who dramatically named Adams and further claimed that she had picked him out of a police line-up.

Shaken and confused, White and James made critical errors at this point. Namely they did not confront Miller with her earlier statement that the driver was "either a Negro or a Mexican." Nor did they reserve the right to recall her and the other witnesses at a later date. The trial recessed for the weekend with the defense case in tatters.

And it got worse the next Monday. Defense had now prepared a strategy for impeaching Miller in particular. But she was not in the courtroom. And prosecutor Mulder informed the judge that she had been dismissed and had subsequently disappeared. In her absence, White requested permission to show the jury Miller's statement from December 3, 1976, but Judge Metcalfe refused, stating that since Miller was unavailable to defend herself against the impeachment, such a procedure would be unfair.

In his closing remarks to the jury, Dennis White argued that David Harris was easily the most likely killer, that both the car and the weapon were his, that he had a long record, and that at the time of the shooting he was in the midst of a crime spree. Furthermore, White submitted, the primary case against Adams derived from Harris's evidently self-interested accusations. Speaking last, though, district attorney Mulder stressed the final day's testimony from Miller and the two others. In an eloquent closing, Mulder spoke of Officer Wood, his widow and family, and of all courageous policemen, as a "thin blue line" who protect civilization from the omnipresent threat of anarchy. "But who protects the police officers," he asked. "Who picks up their banner when they fall in battle?" Judge Metcalfe recalls to this day how moved he was by Mulder's summation. And a stirred jury returned both a guilty verdict and a recommendation for the electric chair.

The Thin Blue Line *takes us through the years since that verdict, through Randall Adams's repeated appeals, through his stay of execution by U.S. Supreme Court Justice Lewis Powell three days before he was to die in 1979, and through the 1980 commutation of his sentence to life imprisonment by Texas Governor William Clements, a move that denied Adams retrial on the facts of the case. It also takes us through the subsequent years in the life of David Harris, through his enlistment in the U.S. Army and subsequent arrest by military police in 1978, through his 1979 apprehension and 1980 conviction for a California crime spree that included the attempted murder of a police officer and his efforts at trial to blame the incident on a hitchhiker, through his arrest for attempted rape, through his arrest and conviction for the murder of a man he first wounded in a gun battle and then dispatched with three deliberate shots to the head. And much more.*

Much much more.

Director Morris produces evidence that Miller and the other surprise witnesses lied, that Harris was carefully coached by the prosecution and that district attorney Mulder deliberately withheld and misrepresented evidence.

Why? Because Dallas was crying for vengeance. Because David Harris was only sixteen and could not be tried as an adult and could not be given the death penalty. Because Randall Adams was twenty-eight and could. Because assistant district attorney Mulder had a perfect trial record and couldn't bear to lose. And because, as Mulder told one of his associates, who reported the incident to Morris: "It takes a skilled prosecutor to convict even a guilty defendant. But it takes a great prosecutor to convict one who's innocent."

Errol Morris has produced a daring and gripping piece of cinema, one of those rare films that demands a second viewing. Anyone who has ever contemplated the merits of capital punishment should see this film before adopting a final stance. The Thin Blue Line will intrigue you. But it will leave you sick at heart. How in this great country can such atrocities happen? How can Randall Adams still be in prison, his most recent appeal, in May of 1988, turned down by a justice crony of Doug Mulder?

There is but one answer: the lessons of Perry Mason are a mirage; as a people we are not nearly as good as the principles to which we give lip service.

*   *   *

I would have written the above review, I believe, even had Joan still been alive. *The Thin Blue Line* is an unsettling piece of cinema. It rots your confidence that the American system of justice is anything more than a sham, a ritual we perform that has no more relationship to the truth than did the dunking of suspected witches in seventeenth-century Salem.

In the aftermath of viewing *The Thin Blue Line* I found temporary solace in the fact that as a result of publicity generated by the movie, Randall Adams was finally released from prison. I found fleeting comfort that a work of art could somehow spawn justice in a real-life world. But such solace as I thought I'd momentarily found was abruptly dashed just weeks after Adams's release when he filed suit against Erroll Morris to stop the filmmaker from making further profit off the circumstances of his life. So much for decency and honor. So much for gratitude. So much for the redemptive power of art. So much for the foolishness of taking solace in anything produced by men.

*   *   *

I shared such a sentiment in the bitterest possible terms when I got together with Preacher Martin at Mandina's the next evening to eat turtle soup and fried oysters. Actually, I was so tired from lack of sleep that I'd wanted to cancel, but getting in touch with Preacher had proved typically impossible.

I was alert enough through my screening of *The Thin Blue Line* in the morning. But I began to bog badly in the afternoon. And that led to a most embarrassing development when I went over to the Downtown Joy for a screening of *Without A Clue*, a thoroughly delightful comedy positing that Sherlock Holmes (Michael Caine) is the invention of a fiction-writing physician and amateur sleuth, named Watson (Ben Kingsley). The wonderful conceit of the movie is that as Watson's books found a wide readership, his creation got out of control, and Watson found himself in the infuriating situation of having to play second fiddle to a figment of his own imagination. But I am able to make such comments about the film only after having arranged a second screening of it. For at my first screening I must have fallen asleep during the opening credits. And I didn't awake until some minutes after the end when the manager spotted me still sitting in the theater and approached me to ask what I thought.

I hate that by the way. And I suspect all film critics do. I have to write about a film. And the analysis I bring to what I have seen emerges as I write. It doesn't leap full blown from my head like a child of Zeus. In other words, what I think requires digestion and reflection. I don't *know* what I think the second the end credits blink off and the lights come up. I don't know, in the fullest sense, until I've finished writing about the film. And then my thoughts are too complicated to express to someone as I make my way from a theater. So I gave the theater manager my stock answer when he asked what I thought.

"I think it's the kind of movie I'm going to have to see twice before I make a judgment," I told him.

Only that remark had never before been quite so true.

Despite sleeping through most of a movie, I was still so groggy I ached to just go home and crash. But I couldn't very well stand Preacher up, and all efforts to contact him proved futile. He wasn't at the paper, he didn't answer his phone at home, and he didn't respond to the message I left on his machine. I could never figure out when Preacher wrote his books, since he never seemed to be home during conventional working hours. And he'd be damned if he'd ever tell you where he'd been, either.

"Out makin' a nuisance of myself," was all he'd ever say if you asked him. And, actually, he meant that. He was like Tom Joad in *The Grapes of Wrath*. If there was trouble, he'd be there. He'd showed up in Little Rock in 1957 and in Selma in 1964. He was in Chicago in 1968 and on the campus at Jackson State in 1970. In more recent and quieter days Preacher's activities had been less glamorous. He did a lot of work with the homeless. Undramatic stuff. He made visits underneath the overpasses where people lived. Just talked to them for the most part. Gave them things. He liked to give *things* rather than money.

He had started a little foundation that sponsored this largess. Called it the Prince of Peace Fund. Preacher's success as a novelist and short story writer had resulted in his meeting a lot of people in the entertainment business. He counted among his friends an array of filmmakers, actors and big-time journalists. He seemed to have formed particularly strong bonds with a whole host of performers in the country music business. Anyway, a number of his rich pals made fairly regular donations to the Prince of Peace Fund. Preacher was the sole executor. He'd find somebody needy, and give that person something the person needed.

To illustrate the way Preacher worked, one exceptionally cold night in January of 1984, he came by my house and asked if I'd go for a ride with him. Wouldn't tell me where or why. "You're either goin' or you ain't," he said. "And if where matters to you, I wouldn't want you along anyhow."

As I was getting into the cab of his pick-up, I noticed he had the bed of his truck piled with boxes. I asked what was in them, but he wouldn't tell me that either. "Find out soon enough," was all he'd say.

He drove us down to the French Quarter, stopped the truck, told me to get behind the wheel and drive up and down the Quarter streets slowly. "I'm gonna be standin' up in the back there, so no herkin' and jerkin' around," he ordered. "If I hammer on the roof of the cab here, you ease to a stop."

I did what I was told, and Preacher proceeded to holler at people he saw huddled in doorways. "You gotta place to sleep tonight?" he'd call out. Then he'd bang on the roof, and I'd stop, and he'd talk to folks a minute or two. If they were going to have to sleep on the street, he'd give them one of the boxes from his truck bed. Inside of each box was a sleeping bag. No lengthy interrogation. Just, "You gotta place to sleep?" And, "You gotta a way to keep warm?" And if the answer to both questions was, "No," he'd ask if the person wanted a sleeping bag. To any who said yes, he tossed a box. Then he'd wham on the roof, and we'd drive off down the street to talk to somebody new. We covered the whole Quarter and then worked our way along Claiborne Avenue under the Interstate from Esplanade back uptown until Preacher finally handed out his last box at Poydras.

On the way home, I asked him where he got all the sleeping bags. He told me a friend of his had put $5,000 in the foundation fund, and he figured tonight was a time to do something with it. I asked him if he wasn't worried some of the people he gave sleeping bags to didn't really need them and that others who did need them might sell them to buy alcohol or drugs.

"Son," he said. "If you stop to examine whether everybody you help really deserves it, you ain't ever gonna help anybody. And if you worry that some you help who do need it are gonna trade your help for alcohol or drugs, then you might as well get out of the helpin' business altogether."

Generally speaking, I looked forward to spending time with Preacher Martin. He was riotously funny. I loved to listen to his adventures in the world of New York book and magazine publishing, about the editors at competing magazines who loved the opposite halves of one of Preacher's recent stories or the book editor on Preacher's Vietnam novel who chastised him that they were publishing in the Reagan Era and then went through the manuscript and changed every *shit* to *turd*. Even more, I loved to listen to Preacher's stories about the early days of the Civil Rights Movement when blacks still seemed to believe in the notion of black and white *together*. But on this particular occasion I was so tired and generally depressed I really didn't feel like spending the evening with anybody. Not even Preacher. Still, when I couldn't contact him, I went to meet him. He might have forgiven me if I'd stood him up, but I couldn't have forgiven myself.

I parked in the drive-through bank lot next to the restaurant and found Preacher at the bar, his hand around a glass of Wild Turkey. He was dressed in his usual uniform, faded jeans, a blue cotton work shirt and a Chicago Cubs baseball cap. Mandina's was the kind of place where such attire was acceptable, where it wasn't considered impolite if you left your hat on all through dinner.

As the evening wore on, and we finally got seated and served, I wanted a drink so badly I repeatedly came within seconds of ordering one. I was agitated and out of sorts. And I wanted little so much as enough whisky in my gut to make me stop noticing how bad I felt.

I didn't get drunk that night. I restricted myself to non-alcoholic beer. But I did get maudlin, a condition that Preacher tolerated just about the same way he tolerated everything else.

I asked Preacher where he'd been when I called trying to cancel, but, predictably, he wouldn't tell me.

"You're the biggest horse's ass I ever knew," I told him.

"Just living up to my calling," he said. "Some people are called to be doctors. Others are called to be movie reviewers. I was called to be a horse's ass. And I'm doin' my dead level best at bein' one."

"Goddamnit," I said. "If you won't tell me where you were, tell me something else. You seem to think the world is worth the effort to try saving. Tell me why."

"What crawled up your ass?" Preacher asked.

"The world crawled up my ass," I retorted. I smacked a hand down on the table top so hard water sloshed out of our water glasses. "And I'm so angry I could eat glass."

"Not advisable, son," he said. "Glass gives you an awful pain goin' down. And usually gives you piles comin' out the other side."

I laughed, but not with a great deal of enthusiasm. He stared at me, picked his cap off his head with one hand and smoothed wispy strands of hair back over his bald pate with the other.

"Who all you mad at, son?" he asked.

"I'm mad at the whole fucking world."

"I'd say you are," he agreed

I drank my Sharp's, and he sipped his Wild Turkey.

When I didn't say anything else he prompted, "I'd say you're mad at more than the whole world. Or the whole fucking world, I think, is the way you termed it."

"Meaning what?" I asked, out of sorts.

"Meaning you tell me."

I laughed mirthlessly. "What? You gonna play preacher me on, Preacher? You want me to say I'm pissed off at God? Is that it?"

"Are you pissed off at God?"

"I don't believe in God," I said. "I used to believe in God, but my believing in Him didn't save Joan, did it?"

"Nope. Didn't," he concurred.

He took a sip of Wild Turkey.

"Course not believin' in God," he added, "ain't gonna bring her back either."

"Fuck God," I said venomously.

Preacher nodded at me, reached inside his shirt pocket and brought out a package of Luckies. He put a cigarette to his lips and lit it.

"So what say, Preacher," I said, extremely weary. "Even you've got to be offended by that, huh? Fuck God. The ultimate blasphemy."

"Fuck God in the ass!" Preacher said. "That's what I say. I'm tired of the heavenly fucker's superior routine, just like you. What a goddamn piece of shit the world He made is. Poverty. Disease. Snot. Shit. Death. Son-of-a-bitch seems to have made all of 'em. Fuck the bastard in the ass. Cornhole the motherfucker. Cornhole his wimpy son Jesus, too. Good for nothing quitter."

Preacher took a drag on his cigarette and blew out a cloud of smoke. I swallowed the last of my Sharp's.

"You have to be the craziest person I've ever met," I said.

"No," he corrected. "I'm the biggest horse's ass you ever met. I'm true to my calling. You're the craziest person you ever met."

"Why am I crazy?" I asked

"You're crazy because you think that God's gonna give a shit that you're mad at Him. You think you can get even with God by cursing Him."

"Come on Preacher, it's not . . ."

"Don't interrupt me, goddamnit," Preacher commanded. "You gotta get it straight that I'm the preacher and you're the preached at. You're gonna tell me some silly shit like it's not that simple. It's exactly that goddamn simple. Your wife died and a piece of you died with her. And you wouldn'ta been you if that hadn't happened. And now you've lost your piecea shit bit of faith in God, too. Well who gives a fuck, son? Who gives a fuck. God sure as hell don't give a fuck. That's what preachers like me mean when we talk about grace, goddamnit. God don't give a fuck that you've lost your faith. He does give a fuck that you've lost your wife, however. That I can assure you. But He understands that you don't believe it. He forgave you for not believing it the minute you squeezed out of your old lady's snatch. Do I make it plain enough for you. You're just a goddamn little pipsqueak. You ain't gonna erode the Rock of Gibraltar by spitting on it. And you ain't gonna affect God's grace by not believing in Him, much less by saying stupid ass things like 'Fuck God.'"

During this speech Preacher's cigarette had burned down almost to his knuckles. He fished a new smoke from his back and lit it with the glowing butt.

"Do I make myself plain, son? You don't deserve it any more than I do. But there's no way we can get away from it. God loves us, and we can't fuck up enough to make Him stop."

CHAPTER TEN

Memory. Memory is always painful. Even those memories we cherish the most are purchased only with the currency of acknowledged loss, of accomplishment become irrelevant, of vanished youth. And yet we remember. When memory comes to us, we choose to suffer its pain. When memory comes, we even savor it. For in the end, memory is all we have.

*   *   *

I remember Joan every day that I live. I do not do it willfully, but I always embrace her memory when it comes. Her memory plays in the cinema of my mind with the immediacy of an event in progress. Sometimes the trigger is a song I hear playing on the radio. Other times it's a film Joan loved, a bit of which I stumble across while mindlessly pressing buttons on my TV's remote control. Many times, it seems, it's a smell. When we moved into our house, Joan planted jasmine in our tiny front yard, and it blooms now every summer evening. I can seldom make my way through the thick sweetness of its fragrance without being captured by a memory of her.

I smell the jasmine today, and I remember another day when cherry blossoms were in bloom and Joan and I have traveled from New Orleans to Washington, D.C.

*   *   *

"I'm not wearing any panties," Joan whispers in my ear. She kisses me loudly on the cheek and then whispers again, "Does that give you a jiggle? It better!"

I hug her to me and whisper back, "Slut!" I am used to her games, and I love them, of course. I am always surprised and delighted when she begins to play them. Yet, I am always amazed that this normally no-nonsense lawyer who is my wife, this fierce barrister who can make witnesses cringe under the assault of cross-examination, this decorous professional, can unabashedly reveal herself to be so wantonly sexual.

"There's a time and a place for everything," I say out loud, smiling at her. "And this is neither."

"Sez you," Joan rejoins.

"What does Mike say?" Allan Gilman asks. Gilman, who is a senior partner in Joan's law firm, has just walked up.

Joan turns to him. "He says I done good. What do you say?"

Gilman steps closer to her, bends from the waist somewhat awkwardly and kisses her lightly on the cheek. "I say you done good, too."

The three of us are standing on the wide plaza in front of the United States Supreme Court Building in Washington. It is a balmy afternoon in April and the cherry blossoms are in bloom on the avenue behind us. Inside the building, Joan has just finished her oral arguments in the case of *Grieve versus Retif* on which she's been working for five years.

And she has done good.

As she knows going in, the justices allow her to make little more than an opening statement before they begin barraging her with questions, one after another until her entire thirty minutes is exhausted. As much as anything, as they do with every attorney who stands before them, they use her as a sounding board, arguing with each other through the questions they throw at her. But she acquits herself well, unbelievably well I think, neatly parrying the thrusts of Justices Rehnquist and White, who apparently are leaning against her, and time after time knocking right out of the park the set-up pitches lobbed to her by Justices Stevens, Blackmun and Brennan, who seem to be leaning her way.

From the look of Allan Gilman's expression, as the three of us briefly replay the salient moments in the argument, it is evident that Joan's boss shares my assessment that she has performed extraordinarily well. Shortly, we are joined by the others who have come to watch Joan's argument, Allan's wife Helen, Marshall Lieberman, Marshall's wife Charlotte, and Jason Roux. Jason has worked on *Grieve versus Retif* fairly extensively, and has argued two previous cases before the Supreme Court. He is considered the team's "oral argument expert." The night before, I escort Helen and Charlotte to dinner at Old Ebbitt's Grill while the lawyers order up from room service and make their final preparations.

The seven of us luxuriate for some minutes now in the glow of an exhausting job, finally satisfactorily completed. As the others relive relished moments in the exchange between the Justices and Joan, I drift a step back from this circle of allies who have just concluded their bracing assault on the world of big-time law. I fantasize that I'm the director of a fictionalized movie about Joan's legal career. I'm riding a director's crane, swooping smoothly about a scene staged for the glory of my star.

A pace away, I stare at Joan with the devotion of Alfred Hitchcock watching Grace Kelly. Her blond hair billows onto the shoulders of her gleaming white suit into the curls I've seen her create that morning at The Hay-Adams Hotel where we are staying in a wonderfully spacious room with two bathrooms. She looks, I think, like Carole Lombard in *To Be or Not To Be*.

Then I study her critically, the director looking for some correctable flaw before ordering the cameras to roll. My gaze is hungry, suddenly yearning with physical desire; my eyes roam from her face down the curving expanse of slender body to where her knee-length skirt gives way to shapely legs. But another well-wisher joins the circle, and I am jerked from my fantasy to be introduced as Joan's husband.

The newcomer is Samuel Buck, the attorney who has just argued the opposing side in Joan's case. He is on his way to his car, he says, but wants to stop and compliment Joan on her performance. "One always hopes for an ill-prepared or incapable opponent," he says.

"But alas, you were neither. On the contrary, I'm afraid, I'd have to admit that you were rather, well, smashing."

She blushes.

And I feel a sudden stab of jealousy, a dagger through my heart that takes away my breath. I feel abruptly spastic and fear myself able to speak only in indecipherable grunts. I stare at Samuel Buck talking quietly with Joan. It seems that the two of them have become a circle unto themselves, while the group posture of the other five leaves me in no circle at all.

The wind stirs, rustles through the trees and sweeps a wave of debris across the plaza. The traffic seems to jump to life, as if a blockade on the avenue has been lifted and a jam of impatient cars has burst down the street behind me. A distant, numbing roar, like that of gigantic seashell, swirls through my head, and I find myself unable to hear what anyone is saying. I am no longer the director of this film about Joan's life. Instead, I am the lonely, longing moviegoer, who can almost smell the perfume of the luminous star on the screen, but can no more possess her than catch and hold light in a moist and pathetic hand.

I scrape my feet on the blanched pavement in a clumsy, shuffling move to draw closer to Joan. I turn my head trying to catch her conversation with her trim, immaculately dressed opponent. I have watched Samuel Buck during his half hour before the court. And even though I am confident Joan bests him, Buck impresses me as a man of obvious intelligence and unusual presence.

Now he strikes me, too, as a man handsome enough to be a movie star.

"This was my eleventh," I hear Buck say as I move closer to Joan. Buck smiles in a way that indicates he doesn't want to be misunderstood as bragging. "Some of the senior members of my firm have argued over thirty. What about you? You surely must have been here before."

Joan blushes again. And the knife in my heart twists and makes me shiver.

"Oh, no," she says, laughing. "This was my first." She laughs again. "I shouldn't say it like that. I can't imagine that I'll ever do this again. Among my partners, only Jason Roux," she points out Jason with a fluttering hand," has ever argued a case here. Besides, I was petrified.

When I saw the green light go on and knew I had to croak out 'Mr. Chief Justice and may it please the court,' I was shaking like a shimmy dancer."

I want to interrupt and say, "Like a shimmy dancer sans underpants, *Dear*." But instead I just scrape my shoes on the pavement again in a way I hope will say, *Excuse us, Mr. Buck, but we have to go somewhere now where you aren't and won't ever be able to find us.*

Ignoring my rasping shoe soles, Samuel Buck wrinkles his tanned brow and says to Joan, "This was really your first case before the court? Lord, I wish I had done so well my first time."

I begin to have visions of Joan walking off with this guy and flying directly to some place where adequate grounds for a quickie divorce can be provided with the statement, "I've found someone much cooler than the person I'm currently married to."

I feel desperate to find some way to disrupt their instantaneous society for mutual admiration and am ecstatic to hear Allan Gilman say, "Excuse me, Joan, I think we're going to head on back to the hotel for a victory drink before dinner. You and Mike please come join us when you get back."

Allan offers his hand to Buck again and says, "It's a victory for us Louisiana folks just to appear before this court. I hope you won't think us guilty of counting our chickens before they hatch."

"Not at all," Buck says. "Given the performance of my adversary today, you have every reason to be brimming with confidence."

As the other New Orleanians step to the curb to hail a cab, Buck turns to Joan. "I mustn't keep you from your celebration," he says. "Again, my congratulations."

"Thank you," Joan says. "And mine to you."

"I'd wish you luck," Buck says, smiling like Cary Grant in *Notorious,* "but I'm sure my client would disapprove. So let me wish you all the best in your career—however the verdict on this case comes out."

Buck extends his hand toward me. "Nice to have met you," he says. I shake his hand without comment.

As Buck turns to leave, he cups his hand around Joan's shoulder. "Goodbye," he says warmly.

I feel my right hand ball into a fist and think, *I've got some goodbye for you right here, asshole.* I am light-headed and disoriented as Samuel Buck walks away in his perfectly tailored, thousand-dollar suit.

Joan tugs at my jacket sleeve and says, giggling, "Come *on*. We've got ourselves some serious partying to do."

As we walk toward the street to get a taxi, we see that Jason doesn't try to crowd into a taxi with the other four. I call out to him to catch a ride with us.

"Y'all go on and take the next one," Jason says as we walk up.

"That's stupid," Joan says. "There's plenty of room for three."

"But I'm not going back to the hotel just yet," Jason says. "And besides, y'all probably want to feel each other up or something."

"Such a wickedly delicious idea," Joan says, laughing.

I clear my throat.

Just then a taxi pulls up to the curb, and Joan says, "You go ahead and take this one, Jason." He doesn't argue, and she elicits a smile from him as he slides into the back seat when she adds, "Mike and I always like to get started feeling each other up before we get into taxis."

"Poor Jason," Joan says as the cab pulls away. "I just hate to see him so lonely." I put my arm around her and squeeze. She breathes deeply and sighs. Then she leans her head against my shoulder and changes the subject from Jason to her argument. "Did I really do okay?" she asks.

I laugh and hug her to me again, "Jesus, Joanie," I say. "Did you do okay? You were fucking Clarence Darrow."

"Clara Darrow," she says. "Don't forget my gender."

In the backseat of the cab on the way back to The Hay-Adams, Joan snuggles up against me and whispers, "Did I mention to you that I'm not wearing any panties?"

I laugh and then crackle in a hoarse whisper of my own, "You are the craziest woman who ever lived. And I know goddamn well you are so wearing panties because I watched you put them on this morning."

"Uh uh," Joan says.

"Uh uh what?"

"Uh uh."

"Are you trying to tell me I *didn't* see you put on panties this morning?"

"Uh huh."

"Well, how's this, they're one of your white pairs with leetle biddy red roses on leetle biddy green leafy stalks. Tell me if I'm wrong."

"Oh, those," Joan says.

"Yeah, those. I make it a point to be pretty observant when it comes to your underwear."

"Well . . ." Joan says.

"Well, what?"

"Well . . . I took 'em off."

"When?"

"When you weren't looking."

"That must have been when it was." I roll my eyes.

"Why?" Joan asks.

"Because I didn't see you when I *was* looking."

"See! That settles it, then."

"Not entirely."

"Not entirely, why?"

"Well, it may establish *when* you depantsed yourself. But it doesn't deal with where or why."

"Where is easy. In the bathroom. Downstairs in the Supreme Court Building. You thought I was just powdering my nose, but I was really taking off my panties."

"Uh huh," I say, "and why?"

"Why is easy too," she replies, pursing her lips and nodding her head like Shirley Temple in *Heidi*. "Why to drive you crazy, of course."

"That part is succeeding," I say, laughing. "Am I to understand that you argued a case before the United States Supreme Court in a dazzling white suit tailored to make you look like a movie star's imitation of a lady lawyer, sort of Veronica Lake, Attorney at Law, so to speak, and underneath it you weren't wearing panties?"

"That's the skinny of it," Joan giggles. "So to speak."

We get out of the cab in the driveway at the door to The Hay-Adams. I pay the fare and hand the receipt to Joan, who puts it in her purse.

Joan grabs my arm and stops us in the hallway between the lobby and the bar. We are alone, and she kisses me full on the lips, opening her mouth and darting her tongue against my teeth. Then she steps back and says, "I've got to whisper something else to you."

I make a face but lean my head toward her. She puts her arms around my neck and her lips against my ear. When she speaks, her tongue touches me wetly in caress. "This is the second grandest day of my life," she says.

I pull away from her to arms' length. "What in the world was the grandest?"

She puts her lips against my ear again. "The night you kissed me that first time. Up against the fence of the yard next to my parents'. Remember?"

"Of course I remember. You turned your head away."

She draws back now to face me, her chin tucked against her neck in remonstrance. "We were only fourteen. I didn't know anything about kissing. And I didn't think we should be doing that sort of thing. When we were only fourteen."

"Then why was that the grandest day? I just turned your face back and kissed you anyway."

Her lips against my ear again, whispering, "That's why. I knew you would. And you did."

I squeeze her in a bear hug. "I'm going to have to have you committed, you know."

"I've been committed for years."

I laugh. "Let's go in before everybody wonders where we are."

I grab her hand and drag her into the bar to celebrate with our friends. I order Black and White on the rocks, and she has Glen Livet with a splash of water. We are seated around a low coffee table in wingback chairs and on a camelback sofa. The talk is serious for a time. The lawyers analyze the legal exchanges we have all just witnessed, crediting Joan's skillful parrying of Justice Scalia's repeated hostile thrusts and praising her gentle ability to bring Justice Marshall up to speed on a case whose essentials were evidently eluding him. Just before we go in to eat, Allan Gilman offers a solemn toast: "To Joan, our brilliant colleague and to the forthcoming victory she so richly deserves." We clink our glasses and each concur, "Hear hear!"

Our dinner in the hotel's John Hay Room is equally festive, and Joan resumes being naughty. We have a wonderful meal that starts with a toasted goat cheese appetizer, topped with a light vinaigrette dressing. After that the waiter rolls a cart next to the table and makes Caesar salads for everyone. People choose a variety of entrees. Joan has lamb medallions with a bearnaise sauce. I have poached salmon with a bordelaise sauce. Mine is very good, but hers is better.

The mood at the table is celebratory. Our friends order two bottles of wine, finish them and order two more before the meal is over. Joan and I aren't wine drinkers and so stay with our Scotches. Halfway through the Caesar salad, Joan begins to get a little sloshed and starts playing footsie under the table cloth. Footsie and then handsie. Little darting sorties to squeeze at my crotch.

When I finally respond, though, she grasps my hand firmly just as it steals to her knee and announces to the entire party, "I have something I'm going to have to say to my husband privately right now. I hope nobody thinks I'm rude."

"I certainly don't think you're rude, dear," Helen Gilman says. "Especially not after you've asked permission."

"All you have to do is tell us exactly what you're going to whisper," Jason Roux says, "and then it will be perfectly all right."

Everybody laughs and makes buzzing sounds as Joan whispers in my ear. "You better not put your hand up under my skirt, honey. I'm very hot for you right now. But I'm not wearing any panties, remember? And I wouldn't want you to get your fingers all wet and sticky."

"Okay. Okay, Mike. What did she say?" Marshall Lieberman asks when Joan takes her lips away from me.

"She said, uh, she said, uh . . ."

Joan says, "I know this is going to embarrass Mike, Marshall. But since you asked, I told Mike I thought there was something wet. Or sticky. Or something." She turns to me, eyes shining in merriment. "Right here." She suddenly reaches out and dabs with her napkin at my face. "Right here in his mustache."

She turns back to the others at the table and rolls her shoulders up. "I'm the custodian of our family's facial hair," she says. "What can I say?"

Finally recovering, I manage, "I've always maintained that the loneliest man in the world is someone without a friend to tell him he's got food on his face."

Everybody laughs. And as they do, Joan darts her hand back into my lap. She finds there an erection that doesn't diminish through the rest of the meal.

When dinner is over, after a knockout crème brûlée for dessert, followed by snifters of warmed brandy for everyone at the table, we go upstairs to our room where we fall into a mad embrace the minute we close the door behind us. And this is unusual. Our lovemaking is most often slow and deliberate, filled more with talking and laughing together than with breakneck panting. But now Joan strips out of the jacket to her white suit and flings it toward a chair. She isn't wearing a blouse, only a slip underneath. Almost as if in frenzy, I throw my suit coat toward the same chair and begin to tug at my tie. But we fall back together before I can get it off. She unbuckles my belt, pulls my zipper down and my pants fall to the floor. With both hands she pushes my underpants down around my thighs. I give up trying to undo the zipper on her skirt and gather it into a bulky band around her waist. Then my hands slip back down her waist to the curve of her buttocks.

And I scream, "You rotten lying bitch. You are so wearing panties. The very same panties I saw you put on this morning."

"What of it," she says, taking me in her hand and stroking me slowly in her closed fist. "I intended to drive you crazy, and the evidence, your honor, suggests that I succeeded in that regard exactly as planned."

"Yeah," I gasp. "And what about all that 'wet and sticky' talk at dinner?"

She takes my hand and slides it down into her panties, across the pale white scar at the top of her pubic hair and between her legs, which she spreads so she can ride on my cupped fingers as if they formed a tiny saddle.

"Come on in," she says. "The water's fine."

*   *   *

After we make love, we lie together under the covers in our room's king-sized bed. I am on my back, Joan on her side, her head on my chest, her knee hooked over my thigh. My right arm stretches down her back; my splayed fingers knead gently at the Y-shaped pad of flesh over her tailbone. Repeatedly, absently, I rub my hand down the valley of her spine and up the swell of her buttocks.

We talk about the glory of the day with an antiphonal refrain. "I really did it," Joan says.

"You did it as well as it can be done," I respond.

Finally Joan says, "Do you think I won, Mike? I do think I did my best. But do you think I won? It matters to me. I'm right. And I ought to win."

"Of course, you're right," I say. "And you ought to win. But Rehnquist and White seemed against you from the beginning. O'Connor seemed on the fence. Marshall seemed not yet to understand the issue. So who knows? Being right doesn't have anything to do with winning."

"And he was good too, wasn't he?"

"He who?"

"Samuel Buck," she says. "He made their position, which is so fucked, sound so reasonable. Made it sound as if we were asking for something entirely irregular."

"Bam-you-all Suck? Yep, Bam-you-all Suck was very good. Very good indeed."

"You know, I don't think he understood the real issue of the case either. He didn't seem to grasp the fact that Delacroix screwed us and that his ruling stank to high heaven and that a tainted judgment erodes public confidence in our entire system of justice."

"I'm sure you're right. Old Bam must have misunderstood or else he wouldn't have waxed so eloquent. For I can only presume that Bam-you-all Suck is as principled as he is handsome. Isn't that always true of the Bam-you-all Sucks in this world?"

"Quit calling him that," Joan says, shifting onto her back so that her head rests now on my shoulder.

"What? Bam-you-all Suck? I thought that was his name. Bam-you-all Suck."

Joan sits up in the bed facing me, crosses her legs underneath herself and pulls my face around to look at her. "You don't think I liked that guy, do you?"

"Who? Bam-you-all Suck? Why would I think that? Just because he's as handsome as Robert Redford, as wily as Rhett Butler and as smart as Robert Oppenheimer? Nah."

Joan bends forward and kisses me on the lips, her mouth opening to me with the sweetness and the succulence of a ripe plum. "I don't think you're really jealous," she says, nibbling about my eyes and over the bridge of my nose. "Because I'm sure you realize that you'll never have a single cause to be."

Lying still, I pretend not to respond to Joan's attentions. But my ruse is revealed when she reaches under the sheet and finds me hard again.

"What's this?" she inquires.

"I don't even know what you're talking about," I reply.

"You don't suppose saying that *suck* word over and over has jump started its engines again, do you."

"I don't even know what you're talking about," I say.

"I suppose you're in no way involved with the renascence of *this* thing," Joan says, stroking me.

"I don't even know what you're talking about," I say.

Joan laughs as she scoots down the bed and positions herself. "Well," she says, "let's see if you can make out what I'm *humming* about."

*   *   *

We lie intertwined again, and Joan says softly without looking at me, "The greatest thing of all is getting to have you, for a whole life, as my best friend."

The intensity of the love I feel for her is such that I think I'm going to burst open from its pressure. I remove a strand of hair from her cheek and caress her face with the back of my hand. "I'm gonna do something someday," I say, "that will make you really proud of me. Win a Pulitzer maybe. I don't know, write a screenplay or a novel or something. Something that will make you really proud. Just you wait and see."

Joan strokes my stomach with the flat of her hand. "Oh Mickey Barnett, you typical Southern macho asshole. All these years. Haven't you figured out yet that there's not one single thing you could ever do that would make me proud of you? I'm proud of you all on my own. And it's already done. And there's not one fucking thing you can possibly do about it."

PART THREE

CHAPTER ELEVEN

Summer in New Orleans arrives, usually, in mid-May. And it arrives with a vengeance, a hammer blow of heat and humidity that saps strength and turns our entire citizenry irritable. But our characteristic distemper is accompanied by a distinctive incapacity for sustained fury. We become like old dogs, willing to snap at those who venture near us, but not at all willing to bestir ourselves for a chase, not even to run down and bite an enemy. The murder rate in our city rises during the summer. But the rate is driven up by wife killing husband and neighbor killing friend. Anonymous assaults go down in the summer. It is simply too hot, and our people become too lethargic to go out of their way to harm strangers.

And summer in New Orleans, as any resident can grimly testify, most always invades months that other sections of the country reserve for fall. A walk down one of our streets in October is accompanied by the rumble of air conditioners whirring in the windows of house after house. Sticky November and even December nights may leave us sleepless, tossing and turning in damp sheets.

By the time I discovered my house had been burgled in July of 1988, the city was in the grips of summer's insidious, numbing malaise. And I myself was in the snare of an amber net of self-pity, spawned by grief, nursed with bottles of Black and White.

But I knew something about myself and my year of grieving. There was a voice that whispered to me in the dead of night when my most recent daze of Scotch had worn off, and, without a sense of waking, I found myself full of thought, wide-eyed and staring into the darkness. This thing that whispered to me was created by Joan, I think; certainly it was nurtured by her. It resided inside me, and it took note of my actions. It was my secret, critical Otherself. It watched me as if I were a character in a movie. And it gave me bad reviews when I behaved in ways that weren't true.

I had allowed my life to cease. I had gone to work, seen my films, written my reviews. But I had allowed my life to cease all the same. Now, after a year, I felt cramped from inactivity. A zygote shaping itself into embryo, I needed to stretch, to move. The path lay clearly in front of me. I should pick up where Joan had left off. I should act in her stead.

*   *   *

The remarkable thing to me about Joan's response to the whole long nightmare of the *Retif* case was her buoyance. She was stunned by Judge Delacroix's decision against Grieve in the original trial. But for years she didn't lose faith that the system would work in the end. "That's why they have appeals courts," she used to insist when I would wax pessimistic. She was incredibly excited when the Supreme Court agreed to hear her argument on judicial recusal. She knew that such an issue was a technicality. And, more important, she knew that the court cared very little about the specific facts of *Grieve versus Retif*. The justices were interested only in settling a procedural dispute between two different appeals courts about when and under what kinds of circumstances trial court judges were obligated to disqualify themselves from hearing a case. But much as she understood the technical nature of her opportunity to begin again, she maintained that such technicalities represented a significant way in which our system arrived at justice. And she was elated when the court ruled in her favor.

Sustaining her optimism through the long years between 1981 and the Supreme Court's ordering of a new trial in 1986 was no mean accomplishment. Joan and Tom Grieve were peppered with negative publicity from the very outset of the case. Most all the parents in the city, except those in the immediate Kenilworth area, preferred the U.N.O. site for Thomas Jefferson Magnet over the location on Morrison Road. Even the black parents in New Orleans East warmed pretty quickly to the idea of being able to send their sons and daughters to high school on a university campus. Thus, few in the city cared about the moral or legal issues involved. Sheldon Retif managed to portray himself as the man who had bowed to the will of the people. And he was supported in that self-portrait by his long-time ally School Board President Hastings Moon. The parents of New Orleans had demanded a more central location for their new flagship high school, and the holder of the Certificate 34 strove only to deliver what they wished for their children. That was the view of himself Retif promoted. And it was the view people soon took.

Tom Grieve, on the other hand, was portrayed as a spoiler, a self-interested black climber who was willing, for his own profit, to force the city to build a school where it didn't want to. Joan was depicted as the stereotypical greedy lawyer, almost a gangster's mouthpiece in some quarters. To promote her client's interest, she was willing to defy the best interests of the city, which would have to pay Grieve six million dollars for his school on Morrison Road, whereas Retif had announced he'd deliver the school at U.N.O. for only four million. The negative publicity became particularly detestable in the summer of 1983. The case was still winding its way through the judicial system, still years from any kind of finality, yet Retif was nearing the end of construction work on Jefferson High. Joan's attempts to block groundbreaking had failed shortly after Delacroix's original ruling. When she tried to impede the school board's occupation of the property at the university, she was blasted in every quarter, if not in name, then unmistakably by thinly veiled inference.

The Old Man ordered our editorial page editor, Jeffrey Rouse, to prepare a statement of opinion decrying any effort to further delay the opening of Jefferson Magnet. Jeff called me into his office to tell me about it. He was sorry, he said, but emphasized that he agreed with the Old Man's stance. A day later, he showed me the editorial. He had drafted it, he told me, out of deference to me, without naming Joan, or Tom either for that matter. But the attack was sharp. And, of course, to my mind it illustrated how utterly confused Jeffrey and seemingly everybody else had gotten about this matter. "In this troubled city," the piece ended, "in these troubled times, too many seek to put their own personal gain above the welfare of their neighbor."

But Joan weathered all that.   And she weathered it without complaining indignantly that 1983 was the last year Tom Grieve was able to pay her anything. He was humiliated by this, of course. And to the day he died he pledged that he'd come back as he'd come back before and that he'd make good his debt to the people who had stood by him. I believe he would have, too. But as happened to Joan, time ran out when he was behind.

What was hard for me was witnessing the effect Tom's decision to settle the case had on Joan. She was depressed for months, for a large part of the time she had left to live. Tom's settling under the conditions he did meant that the system failed. And Joan wanted to be able to believe in the system again. She wanted justice, if no longer for Tom Grieve who wasn't there, then for all the other Tom Grieves of the world who were there, lined up like cattle in a slaughter house, helpless as they waited for the hammer of a malfunctioning system to smash them into abjection.

In the last months before her accident, I had taken to discouraging Joan from continuing to concern herself with the issues in *Grieve versus Retif.* I had come to believe that her refusal to let the case go was bad for her emotionally. But my attitude was different now. Looking back, I admired her Sisyphean resolve. Who knew whether such a thing was even possible, but I knew she wanted to be the agent of righting all this wrong. Now I would have to stand in her place. To honor her determination and commitment properly, I had to try to solve the riddle she died too soon to unravel. I had to sober up and straighten up and pay her back for taking me on when I was too stupid to appreciate her, pay her back for nurturing me through an adolescence that might otherwise have lasted a lifetime, pay her back for taking me to movies and showing me what I wanted to do with my life. As Preacher told me, when Joan died, a major part of me died with her. Now with what was left of me, I was going to have to live for both of us.

*   *   *

For the rest of our relentless summer and into the hot, pregnant months of fall, I devoted myself to research about Leon Delacroix. The police were indifferent to the files which were missing from my home and Joan's office. I couldn't be certain, of course, but I was convinced they'd been stolen. If they'd been stolen, then somebody stole them. If somebody stole them, he (or she, I guess) did so for a reason. And that reason must have been that those files might have contained something the thief wanted to keep a secret. If I was to figure out who stole the files and why, then I needed to discover the secret of what they might have contained. So I decided to start with Leon Delacroix. He had ruled against Tom Grieve in a decision that had flabbergasted Joan. I reasoned that part of the secret, at least, must be embodied in why he did so.

For the most part my search was a painstaking, eye-ruining process, hour after hour in the microfilm room at the paper's morgue, spinning reels of celluloid, chasing down the highlights of Delacroix's forty years in public life, looking for a clue I knew I might never find.

What information our own files at the paper didn't provide, I gathered in person. Simple, straightforward, old-fashioned reporting. Ask and you shall be told. I called the judge's friends and professional associates, and they all talked to me gladly, without reservation. I identified myself half-truthfully as a *States-Tribune* reporter; it's always amazing to those of us who work for the paper how eager people are to talk for the record if they don't anticipate getting in trouble for doing so. Few people even inquired why I was seeking information about Judge Delacroix. Presumably, they regarded him as enough of a public figure that the daily paper's interest in him struck them as in no way perplexing. The one or two who inquired about the nature of my interest in the judge I satisfied quite easily by explaining, in a decidedly hushed tone, "Well, this is sort of embarrassing, you see, but we like to keep our obituary files as up-to-date as possible. And, I want to assure you, though we haven't the slightest suspicion that the judge is in ill health or anything, well, you know, he's past seventy now and . . ."

Deviousness flows from my mouth as easily as Scotch flows into it.

*   *   *

Here is what is known about Judge Leon Delacroix: He was a reputable, in many ways extraordinary man. He was widely admired. There had never been even the hint of scandal associated with his long career. He had been a federal court judge since 1962, an appointee of President John Kennedy, the result, presumably, of Delacroix's long-time association with New Orleans Mayor Denoux Leblanc, who had joined President Kennedy's administration in 1961 as Ambassador to France.

Delacroix was born in 1915, the second son of prominent local businessman Francois "Frank" Delacroix. Frank's oldest child, Robert, was ten years Leon's senior. Robert was followed in the family by two daughters—Cecile, who died before her first birthday, and Rachel, who married a Tulane medical student and moved with him to upstate Ruston. Leon was the last of the Delacroix children to survive into adulthood, though his mother, Denise (née Thibault), endured two more pregnancies, both of which ended in miscarriage. Robert, Rachel and Leon grew up in the family's lavish mansion on Esplanade Avenue in an area of the city known as the French Garden District. They attended public schools. And they went to college at Tulane, though Rachel married in her sophomore year and never completed her degree.

In 1935, Frank suffered a heart attack and Robert, at age 30, succeeded his father as head of the family's Delacroix Steamship Company. Leon was still an undergraduate at Tulane. The Delacroix's family fortune had been made in Mississippi River shipping, and by the mid-1930s, they owned a fleet of tugboats which dominated industrial hauling on the lower river. In addition to his tugboats, at his death Frank Delacroix operated two sprawling warehouses on the riverfront and about 70 barges. Under Robert's management the company expanded quickly into oil leases and increased its wealth four fold during the second half of the Great Depression.

As was true of Robert before him, Leon spent a year in Paris after high school before starting college. Unlike Robert, he spent another year in Europe after graduating from Tulane in 1937 with a degree in English literature. From June of 1937 until September of 1938, accompanied by college chum Brett Williams (third son of sugar magnate Hannibal Williams), Leon made the grand tour, sailing from

New York to London aboard the Queen Mary and spending weeks apiece in Paris, Rome, Athens, Madrid, Copenhagen, Stockholm, Vienna and even Berlin. The U.S. was mired in a depression that had defied recovery for nearly a decade, and Europe was busy appeasing madmen in the forlorn hopes of avoiding the most fearsome war in human history. And two young privileged Southern boys were living the lives of modern-day royalty.

Delacroix returned home to take up his legal studies at Tulane Law School in the fall of 1938. Dedicating himself to Robert's expectations that he prepare for a career managing the far-flung legal aspects of the family's expanding business, Leon took courses in Admiralty Law as well as Oil and Gas. And he was a splendid law student. He graduated first in the class of 1941 and teamed with Brett Williams to capture first place in a state-wide moot court competition. Even before he had passed the bar that July, Leon accepted the title of Vice President with the Delacroix Steamship Company and settled into his office on the eleventh floor of the Maison Blanche Building, presumably expecting to work there for a lifetime.

In the days immediately after graduation in May of 1941, Leon and Brett purchased a house on St. Ann Street in the French Quarter and created fabulous bachelor digs for themselves. There was a whole floor of entertaining space on the ground level and an apartment above for each of the young men, Leon's on the second floor, Brett's on the third. They instantly threw themselves into the swirl of elite New Orleans society. A social column about them from October of 1941 details a party they hosted for music patrons at the beginning of the symphony season that fall. A photograph shows the two young friends and their dates, all holding champagne glasses. Leon and Brett are both in tuxedos, the young ladies in white frilly dresses. Brett is tall and slender. He looks slightly intoxicated; a lock of blond hair hangs down messily on his forehead. Leon is comparably slim, but noticeably short, shorter than his high-heeled date. He is wearing gold wire-rimmed glasses, which stand in bright contrast to his dark hair and complexion. He appears perfectly sober, but his expression is somber, unsmiling, and one suspects that something has happened that has dampened his pleasure in the party's gaiety.

Two months after the symphony party, of course, the Japanese attacked Pearl Harbor, and the nation was plunged into war. Leon joined the Navy's Judge Advocate General Corps and spent the whole of World War II overseas, first in England, then in the Pacific. He returned from the service, evidently, a changed and more serious young man. He was thirty years old and only now really able to begin a career. One can only wonder at the reaction by Robert to the course Leon chose for himself. Leon returned to his position as Vice President of Delacroix Steamship but used it primarily as a base for flinging himself into local politics. By 1946 he was thoroughly identified with Denoux Leblanc's insurgent group of young reformers and was an officer in his family's company in name only. Leon served for two years as an assistant to the mayor, after Leblanc wrested that office from incumbent Samuel Anselmo. He then served an abbreviated term on the City Council from 1948 to 1950. In 1951 Delacroix was elected Civil District Court Judge. In 1955 he moved to Louisiana's Fourth Circuit Court of Appeals where he remained until President Kennedy appointed him to the federal circuit in 1962.

As history will, of course, time has tarnished somewhat the reputation of Leon Delacroix's friend, Denoux Leblanc. Leblanc was beloved of the city's progressive elements of his era. But many of his actions now seem strangely and sadly shortsighted. The Union Passenger Terminal that was opened with such fanfare was obsolete almost from the moment of its dedication. Today it's a bus depot fighting against a creeping decay as insidious as cancer. The new City Hall and Municipal Civic Center, modeled after New York's United Nations Building, is an architectural monstrosity, astonishing in its unsightliness. And no one today can conceivably imagine why in God's name Leblanc saw progress in ripping up the streetcar tracks on Canal Street's neutral ground and replacing them with a concrete median to be plied by carbon-monoxide-belching buses.

Whatever the specifics of Denoux Leblanc's failures, he occupies an almost mythic position in the childhood years of our city's baby boomers. In the white community, at least, his persona and years in public office represented a time of growth and optimism that this city had not known since the Civil War and was not able to sustain long beyond Leblanc's death in 1965. He brought to the city the finest public recreation program in the country. He oversaw the construction of the Greater New Orleans Bridge which spanned the Mississippi River at midtown to connect the city with undeveloped land on the West Bank. He initiated a system of expressways to connect the heart of the city with its suburbs.

But Denoux Leblanc's very achievements were carved in hues of black and white, and it's unlikely he could have survived with his political base intact had he not moved on to the national administrative landscape when he did. White adults today will speak with nostalgic wonder about the New Orleans Recreation Department programs of their youth. But they seldom remember that those programs were segregated and extended only spottily to that third of the city's youngsters who were black. The Greater New Orleans Bridge and the expressway system heralded a smooth, brisk ride into a promising future. Instead, they provided a rapid escape route for white families fleeing the integrated schools of the city for the *de facto* segregated schools in Jefferson and St. Tammany Parishes.

Denoux Leblanc was a racial moderate in the 1950s and early 1960s, and in the mouths of members of the White Citizens Council and other, even more extreme organizations, of course, that made him a "nigger lover." He spoke the litany of approbation for segregation that was required of any Southern politician, but he was widely seen as humane and devoid of the overt racism so typical of such men as Jimmy Davis in our state, Ross Barnett in Mississippi and George Wallace in Alabama, who were his contemporaries. He integrated public transit in our city without incident and in 1960 called on his fellow citizens to allow the desegregation of our public schools to move forward without the kind of ugliness that had erupted in other Southern cities from Little Rock, Arkansas, to Norfolk, Virginia.

But, in the end, as with his evident taste in architecture, Leblanc's political legacy has to be characterized as distinctly lacking foresight. He wasn't ready for the school desegregation order when it was handed down for November, 1960. And the plan to integrate a handful of schools, a year at a time, was almost laughable in its tokenism. What it provided more than anything was a damn good head start for half a generation of parents to get the hell out of town before they discovered that the world wouldn't end if their daughter had to sit at a school desk next to a black boy and their son sent a valentine to a black girl.

Historians, too, suggest that neither Leblanc's private nor public ethics would meet today's more strenuous standards. Reminiscent of his White House mentor, Denoux Leblanc survived four terms in City Hall with the reputation for being a ladies' man, and even before his untimely death in 1965, he had scandalized some Crescent City voters through his well-publicized relationship with a Hollywood actress. Most damning, it seems probable that Leblanc accepted campaign support from and turned a blind eye upon the activities of certain shady elements involved in the city's notorious illegal gambling operations.

It is surely remarkable, then, given his long-time personal and political alliance with Denoux Leblanc, that none of these failings, neither those of omission nor those of commission, ever became associated with Leon Delacroix. To be sure, Delacroix benefited from moving out of administrative and into judicial responsibilities. He was not as much on the political spot in the late fifties and early sixties as the South was forced to amputate Jim Crow from its legal body, if not from its soul. But once he ascended to the federal bench he distinguished himself time and again as a proponent of civil rights for all Americans, of whatever racial complexion. He saw the future, it would seem, much more clearly than Denoux Leblanc did. His opinions insisted on justice and would tolerate no exception to the principle that justice delayed was not justice at all. Thus, he was openly hostile to the white political strategy of compromised retreat. And alongside such of his contemporaries as John Minor Wisdom and J. Skelly Wright, he moved to strike down as either unconstitutional or in violation of federal civil rights legislation state statute and local ordinance after state statute and local ordinance which were meant to delay until some uncertain tomorrow the black American's access to the full benefits of citizenship in this great country.

Such decisions hardly rendered Judge Delacroix widely popular with his fellow whites. And there were a half dozen years in the late sixties and early seventies when his name all but disappears from *The States-Tribune* society page. But what stood as remarkable for such a political man in such a politically corrupt state was the seemingly utter sense in which Delacroix managed to avoid even the hint of scandal. He evidently conducted himself with such devotion to principle and in a manner of such consistent high-mindedness that he was regarded as beyond reproach.

The only negative word I got on Judge Delacroix was from one of his old political foes, Brandon Broussard, the man whom Delacroix defeated in his 1948 race for the City Council. Broussard called Delacroix a wimp and accused him of having run a campaign where every other word was *reform* but where real proposals for the future weren't ever forthcoming. The charge of empty reformism, of course, was made repeatedly by those who lost to the Leblanc political machine of the era.

The most controversial years of Leon Delacroix's career were spent in an era when the bedroom shenanigans of John Kennedy were becoming backroom legend in Washington and the national (double) standard for sexual activity winked at most any kind of male infidelity as long as it was heterosexual and accompanied by devout, if hypocritical, pronouncements about the sanctity of home, family and motherhood. Denoux Leblanc, Delacroix's political mentor, was tarred with rumors of indiscretion from early in his career forward. Delacroix's pal Brett Williams was involved in a messy divorce in 1959 that included the outright accusation of adultery, the naming of a co-respondent (a secretary, of course) and whispered talk of his participation in "Roman" orgies. But no such gossip ever included the judge.

In the late forties and early fifties, Delacroix was regarded as one of the city's most eligible bachelors. He was wealthy, cultured and politically and socially well-connected. The social column in his bachelor years pairs him with any number of the city's well-bred young women.

It was not until his fortieth year, however, during his race for the Court of Appeals that he finally married, in August of 1955. His bride was a thirty-six-year-old brown-eyed brunette named Jessica Mason. Jessica's father, Charles Mason, traced his ancestry to the earliest Americans who came into New Orleans in the first decade of the nineteenth century. The Mason family had made its fortune in the cotton exchange. In the twentieth century they had sustained and augmented their wealth through land acquisition. But the closest point that the taint of scandal came to Leon Delacroix arrived in the person of his father-in-law. Jessica's father had lost a great deal of money during the years of the Great Depression, and it was rumored that he had rebuilt his fortune by joining forces with several other well-positioned Uptown New Orleanians to take over the illegal gambling industry during World War II. Charles Mason's operations supposedly included the infamous numbers racquet which largely preyed on poor people, slot machines which were maintained in brazen defiance of the law in various quarters of the city, pinball payoffs that were mostly confined to barrooms and bowling alleys, and even black-tie casinos for high rollers from both inside the city and out. Typical of New Orleans, however, Mason's association with gambling didn't prohibit him from becoming a part of Denoux Leblanc's political inner circle and didn't exclude him from the highest reaches of local society. Socially and politically, therefore, Jessica was an especially good catch for Leon Delacroix, even despite the fact that, as one of my sources put it, "If old Chuck hadn't paired her up with Lenny Delacroix, he was gonna have to hang an oat bag over her face and get her mated at the Fairgrounds." In sum, though she was slender enough of figure, she was notably unattractive, the key factor, no doubt, in her remaining single for so long.

Owing to their separate religious affiliations—Leon was Catholic; Jessica was Episcopalian—they were married in a well-publicized non-denominational ceremony at Gallier Hall. Mayor Denoux Leblanc presided. Priests from both St. Louis Cathedral and Christ Church Cathedral were present to add a proper religious air, and both were called upon to offer prayers for the couple's union.

A reception was held after the ceremony at the Roosevelt Hotel, and all the city's movers and shakers were in attendance. A *States-Tribune* photograph at the reception shows the bride and groom just after they've cut their wedding cake. Leon is still thin, graying at the temples now, clad in what the social columnist describes as an off-white dinner jacket with black tuxedo pants. Just as the photo was snapped, he has turned his head to the right, away from Jessica, toward, presumably, some well-wisher who has called out to him. You can only see the side of his face, but he is smiling. Like his date to the symphony party a decade and a half earlier, Jessica is taller than he is. The story describes her tailored white suit and matching pair of shoes as "wickedly elegant." She has a small, round, straw hat on her head. An ornamental veil reaches down from the hat to about the center point of Jessica's forehead. She, too, is looking to the right in the photo, and her movement has caused her to lift the knife, which is in her left hand, away from the cake. The perspective of the picture makes it appear that she has just stuck the knife through her new husband's coat and into his heart.

The article on the wedding states that the couple would delay their honeymoon until after election results were tabulated in Delacroix's race for the Fourth Circuit Court of Appeals. Leon has joked to the society columnist that if he wins they may go to Europe. But if he loses they'll probably have to settle for the Mississippi Gulf Coast. Jessica has informed the columnist that their passage to London, Paris and Rome is already booked.

The Delacroix's only child, a daughter, Marie Mason Delacroix, was born in 1957. She attended private schools in New Orleans and graduated from Sophie Newcomb College of Tulane in 1979. In 1980 she married an L.S.U. medical school graduate practicing radiology in upstate Alexandria. In 1982 and 1984 Marie presented Leon and Jessica with their only grandchildren, a boy and then a girl.

Shortly after their wedding, Leon and Jessica took up housekeeping in a Greek revival mansion on Third Street, a half block off St. Charles Avenue in the heart of the Garden District. The real estate section of the paper which noted their purchase did not state how much the couple had paid for their new home. Its market value in the late eighties, though, approached a seven figure sum. Leon certainly couldn't have afforded such a place on his judge's salary. He continued, of course, to draw some income from Delacroix Shipping. But I could only presume that the Third Street house was purchased with some combination of funds that included a significant contribution of Jessica's money.

My researches uncovered no indebtedness, no marital disharmony, no reason that the joint resources of Mr. and Mrs. Delacroix weren't more than adequate to meet their needs, however luxurious those needs may have been. But there was evidence that his lifestyle with

Jessica Mason exceeded his individual means. Could money have been the key to Leon Delacroix's decision to rule against Tom Grieve? Is it possible he could have been bought by Retif?

CHAPTER TWELVE

July had given way to August, August to September. The crush
of summer had lifted. And though the city remained hot and
uncomfortable, there was a period of comparable coolness in the
evening that promised a more genuine relief in the days to come. But
I felt myself burning out even as summer eased. I had devoted myself
to more than two months of investigating Leon Delacroix and had
learned only that he was a prosperous and influential man who had
taken the side that I applauded in most every issue that had come
before him.

I got what seemed like my first break in early October when I called
Jason Roux and asked him to meet me again for lunch. Maybe Jason
could remember something I had overlooked. So I wanted to pick his
brain. About Leon Delacroix. About Sheldon Retif. About absolutely
anything he could remember from the *Retif* case. Anything. I was
stuck. And I had to keep pushing to get unstuck.

The alternative, I was afraid, sang to me like a Siren's song. And it
emanated in golden tones from the mouth of my quart bottle of Black
and White.

*　　　*　　　*

Jason and I agreed to meet for lunch at Galatoire's, a luncheon
indulgence I seldom allowed myself. Galatoire's was the restaurant

Joan and I went to on special occasions, occasions which became ever more frequent and ever more frivolous as the years passed and we became ever more prosperous. Old and elegant in its determined simplicity and lack of pretension, it was such a treat that I never thought of it as a place to eat lunch, though, of course, it was a favorite luncheon spot for many in the local legal and business communities.

Galatoire's didn't take reservations, and if it was full, you waited. Joan and I frequently stood in line to eat at Galatoire's in the evening. The waiting was part of the ritual. We got drinks from the bar on the corner of Iberville and Bourbon and made pleasant idle conversation with those waiting behind and ahead of us. One of the privileges of being even a semi-regular at Galatoire's was the treat of being allowed to ask for a specific waiter. Once inside, we always asked for a waiter named Randy. That was part of the ritual too. Without needing to speak to us, Randy would bring our cocktails, Black and White on the rocks for me, a Glen Livet with a splash of water for Joan. And when he brought the drinks and the silverware, he would always kiss Joan's hand and make some nice comment to me about one of my recent columns.

Two weeks before her accident, Joan and I ate the last of our many meals together at Galatoire's. We were celebrating the fact that we'd gotten back the photographs of our trip to Alaska from which we'd returned a couple of weeks earlier. Randy brought our drinks. We ordered Crab Meat Maison to start. Joan had Sweetbreads Bordelaise as her entrée; I had Pompano Meuniére. Afterwards we split an order of Crêpes Maison and finished with Café Brûlot which Randy flamed for us at our tableside. While we drank the Brûlot, we passed the photographs back and forth between us, making sure we agreed on just what we'd photographed before Joan wrote a short caption on the back to jog our future memories.

We paused for several moments over each of the pictures we'd taken on our day-long trip through Denali National Park. Joan was most assuredly not a sentimental person, not nearly as sentimental as I am, for instance. But sometimes when she drank, her emotions seeped out as if around a leaky gasket of her normal reserve. That last night at Galatoire's, stimulated by Scotch and the brandy in the Brûlot, she got misty over pictures we had taken of a mother bear and her two frisky cubs.

"I just can't believe we got these," she said. "They are just too adorable for words." She wiped a finger under each eye, and laughed at herself. She took in a breath, opened her eyes wide and smiled. "Sometimes I act just like a *girl*."

I touched her hand, and we interlaced fingers on the table top.

"My girl," I said.

She wrote her captions on the bear photos and turned to one taken by a fellow traveler of the two of us on the rim of Denali's central valley, Polychrome Mountain rising across the way behind us. We had our arms around each other and smiled brightly for our anonymous photographer.

"Do you remember who took this of us," I asked.

She was still struggling a bit with her emotional reaction to the bears. "No," she said, swallowing and then clearing her throat. "Do you?"

"No," I admitted, laughing. I took a swallow of my drink. "It's as if the picture was taken by God Himself. In fact, when I think about our trip, I don't remember there being another single person anywhere around."

Joan laughed and said, "Me neither."

"I think we must be what Kurt Vonnegut called in *Cat's Cradle* a *duprass*, you know, a two-person group requiring no one else for wholly satisfactory interaction."

Joan dabbed her lips with her white linen napkin. Her eyes shone in merriment. "The only kind of duprass the two of us are," she said, "is just a couple of middle-class, middle-aged duprassholes."

*   *   *

Jason and I agreed to meet at Galatoire's at precisely eleven-thirty so as to be sure to make the first seating. Neither Jason nor I had schedules so flexible that we could wait an hour in line at lunch. Consequently, compulsive as always, I arrived at Galatoire's at eleven-fifteen. Five tables worth of customers were already ahead of me.

Waiting in a shaded line on that bright and refreshingly breezy October morning, I reflected on the oddness of meeting Jason Roux for lunch. For the briefest moment I thought about his sexual proclivities and wondered whether I'd be mistaken for the new man in his life. Not that I gave a damn what people thought. I don't think. But such a worry, I knew, if it was a worry, was needless. New Orleans, its French Quarter in particular (where Jason resided), had long been notorious as a haven for male homosexuals. And the city possessed a partially benevolent attitude toward gays. For we were, after all, The Big Easy. But acceptance of homosexuality had its limits. And the legal world was outside those limits. Joan and I knew that Jason was gay. A limited number of others at Herbst, Gilman did too. In the early '80s, if a dinner party was small and he knew all who would be invited, Jason used to bring his roommate Preston Parkerson. After Preston's death he'd sometimes come to such parties with a current male friend. But he always brought a female date to larger gatherings or any formal firm function. And he otherwise conducted himself in such a fashion that no one would suspect he was gay. Joan always said that she was not sure Jason would have made partner had the nature of his sexual orientation been known to all the firm's senior members.

As I waited, I pondered the extent of my friendship with Jason. We had never really been good friends, not even when Joan was alive. But we'd always been cordial. I liked him, and I was confident he liked me in return. Right now, though, I needed Jason for something momentarily more important to me than friendship. I needed him as a connection. I needed him as an ally. I don't think he realized this, or at least not fully. I suspect that he thought I was lonely, in need of companionship since Joan died. And he was kind enough a person to try to fill a void in my life. I appreciated him for this and felt guilty that my motives were more manipulative and more obsessive.

Jason joined me just as the maitre d' opened the front door and began directing us to tables. As we seated ourselves at a deuce against the mirrors along the left side, I asked for Randy. When Randy came to take our orders, I had to fight the impulse to request a glass of Black and White. Galatoire's waiters pour the most generous glass of whisky anywhere in the world. But, for another moment, I was strong and asked for iced tea. Jason had a vodka martini. We asked Randy to bring us appetizers and told him that we'd order entrées when they arrived. I chose the Shrimp Rémoulade; Jason had Oysters Rockefeller.

As the busboy set a loaf of hot bread between us, I asked Jason to tell me everything he knew about Leon Delacroix, and he complied. Randy showed up with the appetizers. Jason ordered a filet with Bernaise sauce as an entrée, and I selected the stuffed eggplant. As we ate the appetizers it became clear that Jason knew far less about Delacroix than I did. It was a shame to waste such delicious food in an atmosphere of such disappointment.

Randy appeared at the tableside. "Excuse me, Mike," he said. He moved the bread plate closer to the mirrors and set a plate of soufflé potatoes beside it, "I'm afraid the entrées are going to take just a moment longer. I hope this will tide you over."

Typical superlative, generous, thoughtful Galatoire's service.

Jason picked up a puffed potato and began to smear it with butter. He looked at me pointedly. "You really have to let this business go, Mike. It's over. The case is closed."

"It isn't over if justice wasn't done," I said, so passionately I embarrassed myself.

Jason lifted his drink glass and stared at me over its rim as he sipped from it.

"Listen to this," I said.

I reached into the inside jacket pocket of my blue blazer and pulled out my dog-eared copy of Delacroix's ruling in *Retif.*

I knew that Jason was familiar with the language of Judge Delacroix's opinion, but I read him its concluding lines anyway.

He listened patiently. When I finished, I closed the pages of the opinion back along their lengthwise crease and waved them toward Jason. "What do you *make* of that?" I said.

He shrugged and slowly brought his napkin from his lap to his lips.

"What do you want me to tell you, Mike?" he asked. "You know as well as I do how very disappointed we were with Judge Delacroix's ruling."

"I think it stinks," I said. "I can't get over how much it stinks. Joan never got over how much it stank."

"I couldn't agree with you more," Jason said.

Randy arrived with our entrées and set them in front of us. We busied ourselves for a moment with food almost good enough to make me think that the world couldn't be as bad a place as it usually seemed.

When I had eaten several forkfuls of rich, delicious crabmeat (there's very little eggplant in Galatoire's stuffed eggplant), I drank from my tea and said, "Jason, I'm not sure you really do agree with me. Not *really*. You say Delacroix's judgment stinks. But I think you mean that only in an abstract way."

I reached into my jacket pocket again for the opinion. "I want you to listen carefully," I said, "to what the man wrote."

Jason raised a hand palm outward to me. "Please don't read that to me again, Mike. I'm thoroughly familiar with the opinion. Really I am."

"It's a travesty," I said.

Jason nodded and said very slowly, "It doesn't read like something Leon Delacroix would ever write. It's blatant sophistry. It reads more like something a slimy lawyer would try to put over on a typically stupid jury. It seems more like a ruse than a judgment."

I thumped a closed fist down on the white tablecloth.

"Then you do see," I said.

"I see that you're upset by this," Jason said quietly. "And I'm very sorry."

I put my elbows on the table, laced my fingers together and laid my outstretched index fingers against my teeth. I blew out a breath and picked up my fork.

"Jason," I said, "When I say that Delacroix's decision stinks, I mean it. I mean it stinks because something is rotten. Something is wrong. I know a lot about Leon Delacroix, now. I've bothered to find out. And nothing in his twenty-six years on the federal bench suggests that he's the kind of man who would resort to a dictum of 'buyer beware.' It was plain as day that Sheldon Retif was screwing Tom Grieve. And prior to this decision, Delacroix was the kind of man who would have stopped him."

"So you're saying something crooked happened. Bribery. Blackmail. Something of that order."

"That's exactly what I'm saying. Why was Joan's *Retif* file stolen from my home?"

"Well, now you don't know for sure that file was actually stolen."

"I know for sure it isn't where it ought to be. And you and I both know that her last year of records on the case are missing from your office?"

"Well, again, to use your language, I know that those records aren't where they presumably ought to be. But . . ."

"What conclusion *can* we reach," I interjected, "*other* than that they were stolen?

"There are perfectly innocuous explanations," Jason said.

"Such as?"

Jason shrugged. "I don't know, Mike. I'd say . . ."

"You say there are maybe innocuous explanations. I say maybe not. I say maybe somebody wants to make sure this case remains as closed as you think it is."

We finished our meals. Randy brought us coffee, a full-bodied luxury I was always forced to forego on my many evening meals at Galatoire's with Joan for fear of not being able to sleep afterwards. Randy asked if we wanted dessert. I was tempted to order the wonderful cup custard, but when Jason passed, I wisely did too.

While we sat with our coffees, forcing myself to be calm, I asked Jason why he wasn't suspicious that the last year of *Retif* files were missing from Herbst, Gilman.

He looked at me ruefully and said, "Mike, Herbst is a very big law firm. You've seen the size of our back-file storage facility. *Retif* is a finished case, a *settled* case for Christ's sake. And they don't get any more finished than that. The empty file drawer for 1987 you're referring to would have contained records for the year *after* the case was settled. Maybe such records were never generated."

Jason held up his hand when he saw that I was about to interrupt him again.

"Okay, Mike, I know you've said that Joan had some kind of large working file that she carted back and forth between office and home. I'm not disputing that. But maybe that's all that would have been in the 1987 drawer. See? And maybe that file was in her office when she died. And maybe in the aftermath of her accident we never got the file in the place where it belonged. See what I'm getting at. God knows what happened to all the material in Joan's office at the end. The active files were passed on to other attorneys. But something like a *Retif* file, a file on a settled case. It could have gotten put in the wrong place. It could have gotten thrown away. We've got an empty file drawer where there might have been some file materials. But I just can't conclude that means the files were actually once there and have since been stolen. You see what I mean?"

Randy came with the check, and I was too exasperated to resist when Jason insisted on putting the meal on his account. He coded in his account number and signed his name, and we made our way back outside. The brightness of the early afternoon sun hurt my eyes. Both Jason and I put on sunglasses.

Jason had an early afternoon appointment with an antique dealer client and walked with me a block over to Royal and down river a couple of blocks toward the paper.

"Who would have had access to that file room at Herbst," I asked him.

He sighed and said, "Mike, you've got to let it go."

I smiled. "Indulge me," I said. "Okay, buddy?"

He snorted a laugh and shook his head. "Go ahead."

"Who at Herbst, Gilman would have had access to that file room?"

"Everybody at the firm," he said. "Every attorney, every paralegal, every clerk, every secretary. Two hundred different people. Some of whom don't even work for us anymore."

"Who doesn't work for you anymore?" I asked.

He laughed. "Jesus Christ, Mike. Lots of people don't work for us anymore. People come and go all the time."

Near St. Louis Street almost to Brennan's, we stopped at a shop where Jason had his meeting.

"Who doesn't work for you now that was in any way involved with *Retif*?" I inquired.

Jason looked up into a high blue sky that was adorned with only the occasional wisp of cloud. He slipped off his sunglasses and dabbed at each eyebrow with the back of his wrist. Then instead of putting his glasses back on, he placed the end of the plastic-coated right temple into his mouth.

"Johnny Chambers has left us," he said.   Only he didn't say it to me.   He had tilted his head backwards again and spoke upwards, toward the heavens. Across from us, to the side of the Wild Life and Fisheries Building, a muledrawn tourist carriage pulled away from its stand that stretched the block from Royal back to Chartres. "He actually left when Joan was still with us. But . . ."

"Johnny Chambers," I said. "The associate whose office was next to Joan's. Between yours and hers."

Jason looked back at me, nodded and went back to chewing on his glasses.

"Young guy," I said. "Short. Perpetual case of runaway dandruff. Worked with Joan some on *Retif*."

Jason laughed. "That's the guy," he said.

The tourist carriage turned the corner in front of us and headed toward Canal Street. In its wake, a breeze stirred off the river and filled our block of Royal with the biting stench of mule urine.

"Where did he go?" I asked.

Jason made an exaggerated underbite and clicked his teeth together. "He's at Wallace and Jones," he said.

I licked my lower lip. "Johnny Chambers is working for Wallace and Jones," I said slowly.

"Yes, he is," Jason answered.

"Why did he leave Herbst, Gilman?"

"He wasn't going to make partner with us."

"And yet Wallace and Jones made him an offer?"

"When I heard the news, I was pleased for him," Jason said.

He took a deep breath and put his sunglasses on. In the bright sunlight I could see myself mirrored twice in the dark lenses.

"It's always painful," Jason said, when a negative partnership decision affects someone with whom you've worked. Johnny said that they liked his experience, particularly in educational law and in real estate."

"What you're telling me is that Johnny Chambers is now working for Tammy Dieter-White," I said.

Jason breathed in deeply through his nostrils and lifted his eyebrows high enough that they rose like twin accent marks above the dark round ovals of his glasses.

"That's what I'm telling you, Mike. Johnny Chambers is working for Tammy Dieter-White."

* * *

Jason agreed to get in touch with me after he'd had time to reflect on what we'd talked about. He went into the shop for his meeting, and I crossed the street toward the Wild Life and Fisheries Building, turned left and walked on toward *The States-Tribune.* The urine smell was overpowering and I turned my head away from the river in disgust as I crossed St. Louis. But as I was stepping up onto the curb in front of the Royal Orleans Hotel, I was affronted by an even stronger and more offensive odor, a blast of sewer gas that seemed to rush from the bowels of a city in the agony of wasting disease. I almost gagged. I rushed down the street toward the paper, dizzy and sickened and somehow trapped in a ubiquitous cloud of stink.

CHAPTER THIRTEEN

Four days after beginning my efforts to reach Joan's former associate Johnny Chambers at his new offices with the firm of Wallace and Jones, I received a phone call at the paper.

"Mr. Barnett?" a vaguely familiar female voice inquired.

"Yes," I said.

I get a variety of phone calls from my readers. Some callers want to praise what I've written. Others want to argue with an opinion I've expressed. Some are merely seeking information. I assumed the current caller would fall into one of those broad categories. But I was wrong.

"This is Tammy Dieter-White," Tammy Dieter-White said. "I'm an attorney with the firm of Wallace and Jones."

"Yes?" I said, instantly on guard at hearing Tammy Dieter-White's name.

"You are Joan Barnett's husband," Tammy Dieter-White said. "Is that correct?"

"I *was* Joan Barnett's husband," I corrected. "My wife is deceased."

"Yes, of course. I'm sorry," Tammy Dieter-White said without managing to put the sound of anything like sympathy in her voice.

"How may I help you, Ms. Dieter-White?" I asked.

Don't you just hate people with hyphenated last names. It takes so long to address them.

"I understand you've been trying to reach one of my associates here at Wallace and Jones. Mr. Johnny Chambers."

"Yes I have."

"May I inquire what about?"

I pondered that.

"Well," I said, "let me first inquire why you're calling me on Mr. Chambers' behalf."

"As I've stated, Mr. Chambers is my associate here. In fact, he does most of his work for me. I thought then maybe perhaps . . . "

"My business with Mr. Chambers doesn't involve his work with Wallace and Jones," I interrupted. "At least I don't believe it does. And I'm certain it shouldn't."

"I need to ask what that means, Mr. Barnett."

"It means, Ms. Dieter-White, that why I'm trying to reach Johnny Chambers is none of your concern. Being a Southern gentleman, though, I was trying not to state the proposition quite so crudely."

Tammy Dieter-White was extremely cool, unflappable in the way a good trial attorney had to be. I thought she was scum. But I knew she was a good lawyer.

"Mr. Barnett," she said. "Let me repeat. Mr. Chambers is an associate at a firm where I am a partner. He does most of his work for me. I think that makes his business, my business."

I laughed. "What I need to talk to Mr. Chambers about has nothing to do with his work at Wallace and Jones."

"I wish you'd let me be the judge of that," Tammy Dieter-White said.

I covered the mouthpiece of my phone, shot her the bird and said to the ceiling of my office, "I'll let you be a judge of this, bitch."

Into the phone, I said, "As a writer, Ms. Dieter-White, I find redundancy aggravating, but I repeat, why I need to speak to Johnny Chambers is none of your business."

"Mr. Barnett," she responded. "I'm afraid I just won't be able to authorize your speaking to Mr. Chambers unless I know the subject of your conversation."

That cracked it.

"Look, lady," I said. "It may only be because I'm in the newspaper business, but I happen to know we have something in the First Amendment to the Constitution of these United States, something called freedom of speech. And when you couple that right with another First Amendment privilege called freedom of assembly, I think I'm on pretty safe ground telling you I'll goddamn well talk to Johnny Chambers whether you authorize it or not."

Told her, didn't I.

And I'm not the sort of man who makes idle threats. I did goddamn well talk to Johnny Chambers. That night I called him at home and talked right to him.

"Is this Johnny Chambers?" I inquired.

"Yes," Johnny Chambers answered. His voice was nasal and whiny.

"This is Mike Barnett," I said.

After a short silence, Johnny Chambers responded, "Yes."

"Joan Barnett's husband," I explained. "We've met several times. You were over to the house, I think."

"No, I don't think so. When?"

"Several years ago. When the *Retif* case was going before the Supreme Court. Didn't you and Joan do some work on a Sunday afternoon?"

"Oh, of course. Yes, I do remember that."

"Actually, Johnny, it's the *Retif* case that I wanted to talk with you about."

"I don't think I can do that."

"Do you realize that the last year of Joan's files on the *Retif* case are missing?"

Silence.

"Johnny? Are you still there?"

"Look, Mike, I'm under strictest orders from my boss not to talk to you."

"Why in the world would that be?"

Silence.

"Johnny?"

"I hope you don't mind if I just hang up here. I mean, I don't intend to be rude or . . ."

"Of course, I mind if you hang up on me, Johnny. And it would be rude. I'm not asking you anything . . ."

"I really can't talk to you about this."

"Why in hell not? You don't even know what I'm gonna ask?"

"I don't care what you're gonna ask. I'm under orders."

"Do you have any idea what might have happened to that last year of file materials? For instance, you didn't go back to Herbst at some point to collect some old belongings and accidentally . . ."

"Like I said, Mike, I'm gonna hang up now. I liked Joan. She was a good person. But I work at Wallace and Jones now. So . . ."

"So just talk to me about your work at Herbst, Gilman."

Silence.

"Johnny?"

"Really, Mike. I don't mean to piss you off. But I gotta hang up now."

"Just let me ask a question or two about when you were still at Herbst."

"Like I said, Mike. I'm at Wallace now. And, and as you know Wallace represented Sheldon Retif. There's all kinds of legal ethics involved here. I've got my orders, and I've got my job to keep. So really, I gotta hang up."

"Johnny, just let me ask . . ."

Dial tone.

So much for freedom of speech. I'd have gotten more information out of a parrot.

*   *   *

October turned into an unusually chilly November, nighttime temperatures frequently dipping into the forties. My attempt to make sense of *Retif* waxed just as cool. I was stymied. Johnny Chambers wouldn't talk with me. I had no other leads.

A gray Thanksgiving approached without my feeling the slightest bit thankful, no matter what Preacher Martin might argue. The weatherman reported the possibility of freezing temperatures in the days ahead, and I thought of the inevitable annoyance sub-freezing weather meant. Like most residences in our city, mine had exposed water pipes. My water pipes ran underneath my house which stood on brick pillars about four feet off the ground. Abnormally cold weather could freeze and break the pipes in a matter of hours. The only defense was to run my floor furnaces and hold their heat in a closed cavity created by stapling thick sheets of plastic to the sills and weighting them down with a supply of bricks I kept stacked under the house for this express purpose. But this was dirty, exhausting work, made all the more irksome by the debris which inevitably fell into my eyes as I lay on my back and wielded my staple gun. I never did it unless it was absolutely necessary, although that strategy meant flirting with disaster every winter.

Fortunately, though the weatherman warned of an especially cold winter ahead, the Thanksgiving cold snap didn't reach into the twenties, and I was saved this onerous duty for a while at least. But I was too despondent to feel appropriately thankful for this respite. I felt bloated and clumsy. I didn't even feel all that thankful when Wilson Malt invited me to her West Bank home for Thanksgiving dinner. I was generally frustrated enough that I almost didn't go, though finally I relented and accepted her invitation. And ultimately I was glad I did. If I'd stayed at home and eaten a Swanson frozen turkey dinner, I'd have commenced feeling powerfully and pointlessly sorry for myself.

Some members of Wilson's family were also invited, her mom and dad, a brother and a sister, their spouses and three children. Wilson had also invited Preacher Martin and Carl Shaney, she said, but neither could make it. Carl was having a big family Thanksgiving at his parents'; Preacher had gone to Shreveport to be with his daughter's family. But Amy Stuart from the paper came to Wilson's with her husband, Andy. We watched the football games on TV and ate ourselves silly.

The meal was traditional and sumptuous, and we seemed to go on eating for hours. People finally began to drift away about nine p.m., but I stayed to help Wilson clean up. I washed. She dried and put things away. When we finished about midnight, Wilson asked if I'd like to have a nightcap before I drove back across the bridge. I agreed, and we sat in her living room. She had a glass of white wine; I had a cranberry juice.

Wilson asked me how my investigations on *Retif* were going, and I brought her fully up-to-date. When I'd finished my account and confessed my frustration, she remarked that she wasn't sure my snooping was really doing me all that much good.

"What's good?" I asked her.

"Being happy is good," she replied.

"Then I'm not sure anything is going to do me any good," I said.

Wilson told me that I owed myself a happier existence but to get it I was going to have to seize control of my life. "We don't just drift into happiness," she said. "I've come to believe that happiness is something we have to earn through the hard decisions we make about how to live."

"You sound as if you're speaking from experience," I said.

"I am," she replied.

"You talking about your decision to leave N.O.P.D.?"

She shrugged.

I didn't push her with another question. We sipped our drinks, and after a while she volunteered, "My granddaddy was as sweet a man as ever lived. He was a cop in this town, but he had a sunny disposition till the day he died. My daddy isn't nearly as optimistic a person as Granddaddy was, though I think he may have been when he was young. Momma says so anyway."

She reached behind herself and gathered her long hair together and pulled it over her right shoulder. "Don't get me wrong," she said. "I've always admired the hell out of my father. I think he raised me and my brothers and sisters right. We were taught right from wrong and we were loved and Daddy and Momma scrimped and saved and saw that all of us got a chance to go to college." She sipped her wine. "It's just that Daddy has gotten angrier about things as he's gotten older. I saw some of it at home, but once I was on the force I saw it in a way I hadn't before and it frightened me."

"The world has changed," I said, "and some people have trouble adjusting."

"You'd have trouble adjusting, too," Wilson said sharply. "The bad guys have automatic weapons now, and they don't bat an eye before deciding to blow you away. And the bad guys wear a lot of different faces. The average cop is scared shitless every time he takes to the streets. The guy who wastes him may be a thirteen-year-old kid. Hell, he may be a ten-year-old kid. That does something to your motto about serving and protecting, doesn't it? As far as most cops are concerned, the people they're supposed to serve and protect *are* the enemy. That's my daddy's attitude now. And I can damn well understand it."

We finished our drinks, and she walked me to the door where I stopped at the coat rack to slip into my topcoat.

"Turn around here," Wilson said.

"What?" I responded, tugging at my jacket sleeves and at the collar of my overcoat.

She grabbed me by the shoulders and turned me around to face her.

"You're a nice man, Michael Barnett," she said, eyes shining in the yellow hall light of her entrance foyer.

"Well," I said, suddenly clumsy and ill at ease. "You're a nice person, too. I appreciate your inviting me over."

She lifted her hands to my face, pulled my head down to her and kissed me very gently on the lips. Then she stepped back and smiled.

"Good night, Mike," she said.

I cleared my throat.

"Good night, Wilson," I managed to reply.

I turned to leave, opened the door, and felt the damp, cold air on my face.

As I stepped outside onto the concrete front stoop, she spoke again, "The next time I kiss you, Michael Barnett, I'll expect you to kiss me back."

*   *   *

The Friday night after Thanksgiving, something odd, perhaps even ominous happened. Or at least I thought it was ominous upon subsequent reflection. Wilson had called to ask if I would take her to see *Without a Clue*, which was still running at Canal Place. A significant advantage of being a film critic, I guess, is that you know all the theater managers in town, all of whom let you and your guests into their movies for free. Under most circumstances Wilson and I probably would have agreed to meet at the theater. But she said she was working on a story Uptown and would prefer just to stop by my house afterwards. So we made plans to eat Mexican food at Cuco's on Carrollton, and then go down to the nine-thirty screening of the movie.

I got home around six and, as always, stood at my mailbox, transferring junk mail directly to the garbage can which stood just inside the picket fence to the right of the squeaky gate I never seemed to get around to oiling. About the time I finished sorting mail and had started up the steps into my house, a white Cadillac pulled up in front of my house.

From inside the car, a well groomed black man called out to me, "Excuse me, you know how to get to Longue Vue Gardens. I guess I must be lost."

I laughed and walked over to the fence to talk to him. He was rather farther off track than most, but he was hardly the first person to be thwarted in a quest to locate Longue Vue.

"It's on Bamboo right near the New Orleans-Metairie line," I said.

He shook his head and grinned. "Several people told me that," he said. "I live out in New Orleans East, and I never really get in this part of the city. But I've about decided that Bamboo don't really exist."

"Well, it's not easy to get to," I admitted.

And then I started trying to give him the detailed directions which would land him out-bound on Palmetto and ultimately to Bamboo and his destination. But he quickly started shaking his head and said, "I got a map here. Maybe you could show me."

He got out of his car, paused a second behind the opened door, evidently to button his pin-striped suit coat, and stepped to meet me at the gate. As he lifted the map to me, I noticed that he was wearing a diamond pinky ring and a gold Rolex watch. This guy seemed living proof that upward mobility was a genuine possibility for contemporary black people in our city. I wondered what he did for a living.

"Kinda hard to see this in the dark," he said.

I suggested that he come up on the porch and that I'd turn the outside light on. I was just getting my key in the metal burglar door when we heard the gate squeak behind us. The man with me seemed to flinch, as if he'd been poked. I turned to see Larwood Dupre standing at the steps with two plastic grocery bags in his hands.

"Evenin' Mr. Mike," Larwood said. "The Mrs. just sent me over here with some Thanksgivin' leftovers. She said she bet you done ate your Thanksgivin' dinner at Popeyes or somewhere. Got some good stuff for you, little white meat, a leg, some gravy, and a messa dressin.'"

Delinda prepared me little care packages of food about twice a month. When Joan was alive, Delinda often sent stuffed artichokes, but she knew from cleaning out my refrigerator in the last year that I seldom ate them. Most everything else Delinda prepared, I dined on with relish.

"Y'all are too good to me," I said as I got the wooden door open and stepped inside. The man in pin-stripes cleared his throat and shuffled his feet as if impatient. "Bring that stuff on inside and stop to have a beer with me," I said to Larwood who came on up the steps and into the house. "This gentleman here is in need of some directions to Longue Vue Gardens," I told him as he passed.

"He'll need Moses hisself to lead him over there," Larwood said and then went on into the kitchen and started putting the food away. The other man and I stood just inside the front door to my living room and looked again at his map. I took a pencil from my jacket pocket and traced the route he needed to follow. But he didn't seem to be watching. He kept looking out the door toward the street and then to the kitchen where Larwood had retreated. Then, as I handed the map back to him and looked at him for the first time in the light, I realized that I had seen this man before. Only I couldn't remember where. His face, the slight twist of his nose? Was he a lawyer I'd met at some function with Joan?

I started to say something, but before I did, I heard "Yoo hoo," from the sidewalk in front of my house. Wilson was coming through the gate.

"My date," I said to the black man as I stepped around him and out onto the porch. After a moment's hesitation, he hurried out after me.

"A man in need of directions," I said to Wilson by way of introduction. "Longue Vue Gardens."

I opened the gate and he brushed past us without comment. I started to follow him out to the car but Wilson grabbed my arm and held me in the yard behind the fence. She snapped open her purse and thrust her right hand inside.

"It's not impossible to get there from here," I called out laughingly to the man as he slid behind the wheel of his car. "It's only improbable."

*   *   *

"Who was that," Wilson asked me as the man drove away. Slowly, she released whatever she'd grasped in her purse and closed it back up.

I shrugged. "Guy asking directions. I did think he looked sort of familiar though."

"Why'd he have a pistol in his belt?" she asked.

"Come on," I said. "He didn't have a pistol in his belt."

"Think he did," she responded.

"Nah," I countered. "Guy was on his way to some fancy party at Longue Vue. Dressed to the nines. What you probably saw was the glint of a gold watch chain."

"Man was packin," she asserted. "And if he'd reached for it, I'd have blown his black ass to kingdom come."

I shrugged and then shivered. "It's like we're living in the fucking Wild West," I said. "I guess I ought to be more careful."

"Damn straight you ought to be more careful. Your house has already been burgled. You don't want to become a robbery victim, too."

We walked back toward the house to have a beer with Larwood before we went to dinner. I casually put my hand flat against her back as we stepped through the front door. "Tough day on the crime beat," I inquired.

"Grisly," she replied. "Two murders last night. One in the Quarter, one over by Tulane. One was white. The other was black. But the M.O. was the same. Both of the deceased had their heads blown open with a thirty-eight. Both had fresh semen in their mouths."

"Women?"

"Men. Cops are afraid this is the front end of some kind of serial thing. Some lunatic blowing away gay guys. God I hate this city sometimes."

"Not me," I said. "I hate the whole fucking world."

*   *   *

In mid-December I took Carl Shaney with me to a preview screening of Alan Parker's *Mississippi Burning*. The film wasn't set to open locally until January, but Orion Pictures was maneuvering to land the film on top ten lists even in cities where it was yet to play. The company was very high on the picture, thinking Oscars in a number of categories, confident of enthusiastic critical response. The word of mouth on the film was excellent. Parker, it was said, had done the extraordinary and made something "important" as well as something entertaining.

But I found *Mississippi Burning* as thoroughly disturbing a motion picture as I'd seen in some time. When Carl and I stopped by

Napoleon House after the screening to talk about the movie, I was relieved to discover that he shared many of my reactions.

Our discussion of *Mississippi Burning* segued into an exploration of the racial problems in our city. After a time, the conversation didn't go well. We agreed that New Orleans had been severely damaged by the extensive white flight in the sixties and seventies. And we agreed that the runaway population explosion in the black underclass was straining city services beyond the city's capacity to deliver. You couldn't allow people to starve. But as a result of already inadequate efforts to attend to the needs of the poor, the grass in the parks and on the city's neutral grounds wasn't being cut. Policemen, firemen and teachers were relocating to communities offering higher salaries. The city seemed caught in a vicious downward spiral from which it couldn't escape.

My suggestion was simple, however much an instance of political pie in the sky. Centuries old political boundaries had placed the City of New Orleans in a geographical straitjacket. It could not expand beyond the crowded confines of Orleans Parish. Meanwhile, the suburban residents of mostly white Jefferson and St. Tammany Parishes enjoyed the benefits of being New Orleanians without the obligation to pay their share of the cost of keeping the city safe and clean. Our metropolitan area had more than doubled in size since 1950. But the municipal population was smaller than it had been forty years ago. Since 1960, the city itself had lost roughly fifteen percent of its population or nearly 100,000 people.

What my argument to Carl boiled down to was an observation that New Orleans as an organic place was being crippled by arbitrary political distinctions. Those distinctions allowed the residents of suburban Kenner in Jefferson Parish to have better schools and safer neighborhoods than the residents of the Ninth Ward inside the city limits. It allowed the residents of Metairie to escape paying for the policemen who patrolled for Saints games at the Superdome. And it allowed the residents of St. Tammany to enjoy the festivity of a New Orleans Mardi Gras without having to pay for the colossal clean-up costs afterwards.

"Fundamentally," I asserted to Carl, presuming I was preaching to the converted, "the system is anti-democratic. The burden of government is not being shared equally by all who enjoy its benefits."

Carl sat silent over his gin and tonic. I sipped fervently at my Sharp's.

"And in the long run," I added, "though I'm sure you couldn't convince them of this fact, the residents of Kenner and Metairie and Covington will suffer for the advantages they've enjoyed. In fact, I think they're suffering already. Oil went kaput. And the kind of high-tech, low-pollution, light industry we need to locate in this town to turn our economy around won't come because our educational system is too goddamn poor and our crime rate is too fucking high. And that hurts the people in the suburbs, too. They don't belong to the underclass. But a lot of them are out of work and facing relocation because there aren't any jobs on the horizon."

"So what are you proposing?" Carl asked.

His head was over his drink, and his voice was oddly flat in tone.

"I'm proposing metropolitan government, of course. Whoosh." I snapped my fingers. "Kenner and Metairie and Covington are no more. Mandeville and Slidell and Laplace are just neighborhoods of one united metropolis. No different than Carrollton and Gentilly and Lakeview are now. Everybody suddenly the same. One police force, one fire department, one tax structure. We'd still have to get a sensible real estate tax system and assessors who wouldn't peg the price of everything a nickel under the homestead exemption. But we might have a fighting chance then. Fact is, same approach might apply to a lot of urban America: Chicago, Detroit, Atlanta."

"I could never support such an idea," Carl said.

At first I misunderstood him.

"Well I'm not saying that the nitwit legislature in this state would ever enact such an idea," I said.

"I'd lobby against it if it were being considered," Carl said.

"Why, for Christ's sake?" I wanted to know.

"Because, man, if we had metropolitan government, we'd go back to being ruled by white men," Carl said. "I grew up in this town being ruled by white men. I rode on the backs of buses and watched white men take seats from elderly black women. I was bossed around by white cops when the very idea of a black police officer was as laughable as the idea of a Martian police officer. This city is shit now. White people think it's shit now. Well, understand something.

It's always been shit for black people. Only there's a difference now. We've got a black mayor, and we're gonna keep on having a black mayor. We've got a black majority City Council, and we're gonna keep on having that, too. We've got black cops, and as time goes along we're gonna have more and more black cops. See what I mean? We've got black judges now. And we're gonna have more black judges. We're not going back to the days when whitey ran things and put his brother in charge of this and his cousin in charge of that."

I admit being taken aback by the intensity of Carl's response. We had hardly always agreed on things. We certainly did agree, however, on the fact that our city was in serious trouble. Acutely, there was the madman on the loose having oral sex with gay men and then blowing their heads off immediately afterwards. Chronically, the city was diseased with poverty, infested with drugs and crippled by political corruption. So I was shocked that he was so hostile to my theoretical idea for forcing metropolitan area whites to assume their fair burden for putting the city back on its feet.

"Carl," I said, "You've built a career exposing political corruption. You can't seriously mean, then, that racial politics are more important to you than good government."

Carl laughed, drained his drink, waved at the waiter for two more, and looked at me as he shook his head.

"This is all bullshit," he said. "We both know that. But since we're arguing it, what makes you think your metropolitan plan would translate into good government?"

He had me there. In the State of Louisiana the term "corrupt politician" was considered a redundancy. Still, I thought he was missing a significant point.

"Okay," I said. "Good government is too much to expect. But making everyone assume a fair share of the tax burden isn't."

"At the price of disenfranchising the black people of this city, the cost is more than I'm willing to pay," he asserted.

"What disenfranchising black people, Carl? What are you talking about?"

"I'm talking about a black majority city. Which is what we are now. You're talking about a white majority Metropolitan New Orleans, and I'm telling you I wouldn't go for it."

"I read an article in *Newsweek*," I said. "About the new suburban poor. One of the case studies was this suburb of Chicago called Ford Heights. All black town. Population of ten, fifteen thousand. All of them poor. Worse off than poor people in Chicago because of the services Chicago is able to provide for *its* poor. Cheap public transportation. Job counseling. Certain municipal welfare programs. And so forth. Ford Heights is so broke they can't even afford to open the municipal swimming pool."

I took a sip of my drink, toyed with idea of smoking one of Carl's cigarettes but rejected it.

"You see what I'm saying?" I asked. "I'm saying that I want to know what keeps New Orleans from becoming an urban Ford Heights. The city becomes ever more black. Its tax base erodes away as more and more white professionals give up on the city and move to Jefferson and St. Tammany. Or Timbuktu for that matter. And pretty soon the city is incapable of providing even limited services. We don't get the side streets paved in this town now. How long is it before this place becomes like Port-au-Prince or Caracas. Sky scrapers downtown. Dirt ruts for neighborhood streets. When I was growing up, I thought of New Orleans as one of the emerging leaders of the modern world. Now I'm afraid I'm going to die in the Third World. And I haven't moved fifteen blocks."

Carl crushed out his cigarette and proceeded to rub a finger back and forth under his nose.

"You remember a city where the City Park Golf Course was so nice the pros played the New Orleans Open there," Carl said. "You remember a rental house in Audubon Park where you could rent paddle boats and canoes or a bicycle built for two."

"Exactly," I said.

Carl snorted.

"Exactly," he said. "And now that rental house in Audubon Park is boarded up and the boats and bicycles are gone Godknowswhere."

"Yes," I said. But uncertainly. His tone suggested he was setting me a trap.

"And the golf course in City Park gets in such bad condition sometimes you can lose a ball in ankle-deep grass in the middle of the fairway."

"Well," I said. "I don't play golf, actually."

"Well neither do I," Carl said. "I don't play golf because when I was growing up, that nice City Park Golf Course wasn't open to blacks. And I never went boating in City Park lagoon for the same reason. Do you see *my* point now? The New Orleans I grew up in was like this Ford Heights you were talking about. I don't have your memories of any time when this was a city of the modern world. It was always the Third World to me. See, we agree that this town is shit now. But you seem to think there was a time it wasn't shit. And that isn't true to the experience of anybody black who grew up here. But there is something different now. And that's the fact that black folks are running the show. We've got problems. We've got T.N.O.N. who'd rather stick a crack pipe in their face than put food in their baby's mouth. And we've got Oreos at City Hall who'd rather put a Volvo in their own garage than a decent teacher in a Ninth Ward school. And we've got plenty of our own political crooks; boy do we have our share of crooks. And so we may not get it done. But we *know* the white man isn't going to get it done. He ran things for more than a century after the Civil War, and as far as black people are concerned, he didn't even get started. So don't talk to me about some metropolitan government shit where the white man takes over again."

"Come on, brother," I said, "we can . . ."

Carl put his hand on my arm and stopped me.

"Don't call me brother," he said.

He said it quietly, without menace or even rancor, but I was cut to the quick just the same. I shouldn't have called him 'brother.' I had never done so before. I wasn't the kind of person who aped a kind of hipness I didn't have. But the fact is, I had always thought of Carl Shaney as a kind of brother, as a soul mate. I thought of us as belonging to the same fraternity of people who looked at the world in similar, cynical and angry ways. But he was right; we weren't brothers. And we couldn't be. Not yet. For though we were both native New Orleanians. And though we both loved the city of our birth. We couldn't be brothers. Because I had grown up white. And he had grown up black. And that was all the difference in the world.

*　　　*　　　*

Carl and I didn't stay at Napoleon House much longer that December night. But shortly before we left, he asked me if I was still digging around on Joan's old *Retif* case.

"Yeah," I told him. "Sort of."

"What's 'sort of' mean," he asked.

I toyed with his pack of cigarettes. "Well, I've looked at a whole bunch of stuff. Asked myself a lot of questions. But I haven't come up with any answers."

Carl let out a long breath. "Maybe there aren't any answers to come up with," he said.

"Well there sure as shit are the same old questions. Why are the files missing? Why did Delacroix rule as he did? Why did he lie about his conflict of interest? And some new ones now, too. Why won't Johnny Chambers talk to me. What's the bug up Tammy Dieter-White's butt?"

Carl looked at me hard for a long moment before he finally said, "You're our film critic, Mike. And you're a damn good one. You have something to say. That's what you should do. You should leave investigation to someone who's good at *that.*"

"Like you?" I asked.

"No, not like me, dammit," Carl said with surprising heat. "I've already told you a hundred times, this shit doesn't lead anywhere. It's a dead fucking end."

Added to his comment about not calling him 'brother,' Carl's instant irritation about the *Retif* business cast a shroud of suffocating discomfort over us. Suddenly we were unable even to make small talk. I had never before felt so awkward with him.

Barely speaking to each other save in grimaces and grunts, we paid the check and stepped out onto Chartres. As we turned to head in our separate directions, I muttered good night and Carl clapped me on the back without responding.

*   *   *

As I turned the corner off Burthe Street and into the 800 block of Dante, I momentarily glimpsed a white Cadillac turning off Dante onto Maple at the far end of my block. I had the sudden unsettling idea that it was the same car driven by the black man in pin-stripes Wilson was so certain had had a pistol tucked in his belt. But such a notion was crazy, of course, and it served to heighten my depression. I felt on the verge of crippling despair. To fight my sense of hopelessness, I went into the house, took the Zenith out of its backpack and wrote a draft of my commentary on *Mississippi Burning*.

When I finished, I went into the living room and sat in front of the TV. For three hours, from one a.m. until four, I used my remote control to channel-hop from one station to the next, watching five minutes of news on CNN, bits of old sit-coms on Nickelodeon, snatches of three different movies on TBS and WGN. And while I sat, and pressed buttons, and let my mind go almost utterly blank, I drank three-quarters of a fifth of Black and White.

CHAPTER FOURTEEN

Near the beginning of Alan Parker's Mississippi Burning, *Gene Hackman tells a joke I first heard as a fifth grader in 1958. "Do you know what has four 'eyes' but can't see?" he asks Willem Dafoe. The answer to the riddle, "Mississippi," is obviously a simple wordplay about spelling. But in* Mississippi Burning, *the joke has a greater resonance. The movie is based on the 1964 murders of three civil rights workers in rural Mississippi. And so in the context of the film's narrative, the joke implies that the people of Mississippi can't see the vicious injustice of their entrenched racism. More than that, the joke is a comment on the film's two lead characters. Rupert Anderson (Hackman) and Alan Ward (Dafoe) are FBI agents who have been assigned to investigate the murders. Anderson is rumpled, folksy and unorthodox, but in the film's view he instinctively understands what measures must be taken to bring the guilty to justice. Ward's by-the-book approach, in contrast, proceeds practically nowhere. Clean shaven, straight-laced and intellectual, bespectacled Alan Ward is the typical bleeding heart liberal "four eyes" who just can't see what steps are necessary to defeat the forces of unrestrained evil. Regrettably, I find that Hackman's opening joke echoes in still another, unintended way.* Mississippi Burning *is the creative product of two men, director Parker and screenwriter Chris Gerolmo. Together these two have made a motion picture of undeniable power and considerable artistry. But in ways thoroughly dismaying, in their blindness both to salient points of history and the transcendent lessons of the American Civil Rights Movement, Parker's and Gerolmo's are the four eyes that evidently cannot see.*

I am not alone in objecting to Mississippi Burning, *of course, but for the most part the film has been greeted with critical hosannas. And a host of prominent critics have designated the picture the year's best. Given such praise, I find it ironically fitting that I sit revising my commentary about the film on the birthday of Martin Luther King. For Dr. King, I believe, would be saddened by it, would agonize that if Alan Parker's understanding of the lessons of the 1950s and '60s is that of all America in the 1980s, then perhaps those brave soldiers of the Movement marched, suffered and sometimes died in vain.*

Mississippi Burning *fictionalizes one of our nation's darkest passages, the officially sanctioned Ku Klux Klan violence during the "Freedom Summer" of 1964. The story doesn't address the courage and commitment of the young men and women who journeyed to Philadelphia, Mississippi, that year to register black people to vote. Rather,* Mississippi Burning *concerns itself with the FBI's investigation into the murders of three young activists and with that the endeavors of the federal government to break the back of Klan lawlessness in the South. To accomplish their goals, the federal agents must overcome the race prejudice rife among even those who aren't members of the Klan. Parker's story structures itself as a kind of mismatched buddy picture. Both federal cops assigned to the case are determined to bring the guilty to justice. But they are utterly different kinds of men, with widely divergent approaches to their jobs.*

Rupert Anderson is a native Mississippian. He grew up with racist parents in a poor rural community near Memphis and thus possesses an inherent understanding of the people in the town where the civil rights workers were murdered. He's repelled by racial hatred, but he knows the socio-psychic womb from which it's born. Alan Ward, on the other hand, is a Harvard-educated Northerner. He's a Kennedy liberal who, before switching to the FBI, worked in the Justice Department and accompanied James Meredith during the Ole Miss integration crisis in 1962. Ward is appalled but almost stymied by the racial violence in the South. And initially he suspects that Anderson may secretly sympathize with his fellow Southerners.

This suspicion develops in part because Ward is so determined, first to prove a murder has been committed (the bodies haven't been found) and then to identify the murderers, that he's always calling for reinforcements until the town is aswarm with more than a hundred federal agents. Anderson, in contrast, wants to keep the investigation small and low key. He's worried that a greater federal presence will result in increased violence, that the suffering in the black community will be escalated rather than diminished. In short, Ward is an idealist, Anderson a pragmatist; Ward is an optimist, Anderson a cynic. They constantly put a different slant on the same events. Expressing his sympathy for an infuriated black community that riots in its own shantytown, one says, "If I was a Negro, I guess I'd feel the same way." The other rejoins, "If you were a Negro, no one would give a damn how you feel."

Mississippi Burning *is praiseworthy for its effectiveness in reminding us of the horror of racial segregation and the relentless violence blacks had to endure to crack Jim Crow's spine. And that's hardly an insignificant achievement. In a day in which the former Grand Wizard of the Ku Klux Klan, David Duke, has emerged as a political power in our own supposedly New South, we need reminders that the legacy of the Klan dangles from the loop of the lynchman's noose and explodes from the barrel of the assassin's gun.* Mississippi Burning *communicates that legacy with memorable efficacy. From its opening image of a "Colored Only" sign above a public drinking fountain, to its closing shot of a chipped tombstone bearing the words "1964 Not Forgotten,"* Mississippi Burning *is a searing reminder of a bitter past not nearly long enough gone. To this end director Parker exerts his considerable cinematic gifts, most notably in the murder sequence which follows the opening credits. In the shadowy gray of a Southern summer night, violence hides in the swale beyond every hillock, and menace drapes like Spanish moss from every roadside oak and cypress.*

The lingering wound the movie inflicts on our consciousness, however, derives from keen details in Chris Gerolmo's script. Anderson has another little joke he likes to tell. "You know what baseball is?" he inquires. "It's the only situation in which a black man can wave a stick at a white without causing a riot." How telling and effective a line of dialogue; how it causes the dividing walls in our memories to collapse and the information stored in separate compartments to mingle and interact. 1964 was the year the St. Louis Cardinals marched to a

National League pennant and a World Series victory over the New York Yankees behind the pitching of Bob Gibson. By 1964 Jackie Robinson had been retired *from baseball for almost a decade. The great Willie Mays was more than halfway through his storied career, his finest seasons already behind him. And still, none of these men could have found a motel room in rural Mississippi. None could have eaten at a bus station dining counter anywhere in the state. None could have taken a downstairs seat in a Southern movie theater. Not nearly enough of us acknowledged the bitter anomaly of that fact in 1964. And it is valuable for all of us to be reminded of it today.*

However far we are from true racial harmony in America, however far from genuine racial equality—and statistics about the disproportionate suffering of black people from poverty, unemployment, illiteracy and other social ills ascertain that we are far indeed—the world has changed since 1964. Jim Crow is dead. Legions of blacks hold public office all over the South, in small towns as well as big cities. Jobs, housing and public facilities are open to blacks now in a way they most certainly weren't twenty-five years ago. Thus, however much it needs further alteration, the world had changed enough in the quarter century since the setting of this film that its events seem like tales from the Dark Ages. But 1964 is hardly so far in our past. This is what Mississippi Burning *reminds us. 1964 was in* my *lifetime. It was in the lifetime of most of you who read these reflections. And Gerolmo's screenplay has something to say to all of us who were alive in those days. It comes from the lips of Alan Ward. Ward pronounces a kind of benediction for the town's mayor who has hung himself even though he wasn't Klan and wasn't in on the murders. "But he was guilty," Ward says. "Anyone is guilty who watches this happen and pretends it hasn't.*

Elsewhere, in a story Anderson tells about his own father, Gerolmo's script shows a particular sensitivity to the seemingly intractable rootedness of Southern racism. Poor and demeaned in the world at large, Anderson's father derives a toehold of dignity from feeling superior to blacks. "If you ain't better than a nigger," he argues, "who are you better than?" With comparable insight, Gerolmo has Anderson question the judgment of certain (presumably white) civil rights leaders who seem anxious for blood—particularly white blood—to be shed in Mississippi so as finally to focus the outraged attention of the (white) nation on the violent resistance of the South to the end of segregation. In this one deft development, Gerolmo underscores both the bedrock racism of the supposedly tolerant North and the tarbaby nature of American apartheid which seemed to soil the hands of so many who touched it.

The element in Mississippi Burning *which proves most viscerally powerful and emotionally satisfying, however, arrives in two scenes in which we see evil receive its due. In one, Anderson grabs the genitals of the film's most viciously racist character and taunts him with his momentary helplessness. In the second, a black FBI agent threatens to emasculate the town's mayor unless the mayor cooperates with the Bureau's investigation. Prior to these scenes Parker and Gerolmo have accosted us with repeated instances of unspeakable white-on-black brutality. In the most shattering of these, a ten-year-old black boy has knelt to pray in front of his church while around him hooded Klansmen are using baseball bats to beat his parents and the other members of his congregation. A Klansman approaches the boy, curses him, and then, taking vicious aim, kicks him, once in the stomach, a second time in the head. Thus, by the time the FBI has the Klansmen in its clutches, our anger has been built to such a pitch that we lust for righteous retribution. The violence of those who oppose the racists is earned, we are made to feel. And we want swift and brutal justice, vengeance for all those innocents we have been made to watch suffer. When Anderson undertakes the tactics that bring anguish to the Klan, he is our "liberal" Rambo, and we cheer that he has come to Mississippi.*

But powerful and gratifying as such scenes are, they could not be more wrongheaded, more thematically disastrous, more deeply perturbing. And they provide crucial insight into the confused nature of what Mississippi Burning *has to say and how the picture goes about saying it. The film's "satisfying" ending is palpably false. Subtitles under stop-frame photographs of the picture's villains announce the prison sentences they've received. The emotional crescendo that Parker has orchestrated creates the feeling that significant justice has been done. But it hasn't. None of the murderers were sentenced to prison for longer than a decade. Few actually served half that long. Some of the collaborators were acquitted outright. Most, still today, walk the streets of Philadelphia, Mississippi, largely unpunished for their crimes.*

More significantly, Parker fails to develop but a single sympathetic character among the white Mississippians. I'd even argue that there's a whiff of (presumably careless and unintentional) class prejudice in Parker and Gerolmo's depiction of the racist white Mississippi populace. Granted, the filmmakers include the town mayor among its cast of villains, and the head Klansman seems a man of some affluence and standing in the community. But for the most part, the face of evil in Mississippi Burning *is positioned upon a red neck. And I submit that racial subjugation became an institution in the South precisely because it served the interests of those in the upper, reputedly genteel, reaches of Southern society. On the one hand, Parker and Gerolmo don't show us those white characters with whom we can identify and sympathize. On the other they let the ruling Southern classes off the hook without proper indictment. In sum, their facile portrait dresses Mississippi racism always in the white robes of the Klan and seemingly never in the vested suits of the business place and the reversed collar of the white church.*

Comparably, Parker neglects to illustrate the extent to which Klan violence intimidated whites who might not themselves have been brutes. As Nicholas Von Hoffman writes about the era in Mississippi Notebook, *"there was a special molecule in the air: fear. Everyone watched and everyone was watched." Plenty of white people feared that speaking out against the Klan meant risking their lives. It is fully arguable that rural Mississippi in 1964, for both white and black citizens, was in the grips of a paralyzing terror. Depicting nigh all white Mississippians as Klan collaborators diminishes the reach of that terror and underestimates the vast extent to which the tide of racial hatred had extinguished the spark of human liberty for Mississippians and other Southerners of whatever color.*

Defenders of Mississippi Burning, *such as Chicago Tribune columnist Mike Royko, have argued that the movie must be understood as a work of fiction. "You don't go into a movie theater expecting to see and hear facts," Royko posits. "The best you can hope for is a sense of reality. And that's what* Mississippi Burning *provides." I beg to differ. A whole generation has come of age since 1964. Those approaching their mid-twenties have grown up, black and white alike, without having to experience the ugliness of legal segregation. For many of those young people, Alan Parker's movie represents an exercise in popular history. And that is traumatically sad. For this film suggests all manners of things about the Civil Rights Movement and the death of Jim Crow that are patently false. First, it is more than a little unseemly to make FBI agents the heroes of this struggle. As there were certainly sympathetic white Mississippians in the 1960s, there were no doubt honorable members of the FBI. And I'll grant that Parker and Gerolmo labor to establish that Anderson and Ward are disgusted by racial hatred and discrimination. But, to choose a deliberately extreme example, making the FBI into civil rights heroes is as distasteful as making Hitler into a founder of Israel. Throughout his career, Martin Luther King complained about the indifference of the FBI to the Southern black man's struggle for legal equality. And we know without qualification that FBI director J. Edgar Hoover harbored disturbingly racist ideas and possessed an almost pathological hatred for Dr. King, whom he called "the most notorious liar in America." To state the proposition baldly, the FBI's behavior during the civil rights crusade was appalling. Rather than being dedicated to helping black people achieve justice, the Bureau spent most of its energies trying to besmirch the reputation of the Movement's most prominent leader, going so far even as attempting to humiliate and blackmail Dr. King into suicide.*

But even more troubling than the filmmakers' glorification of the FBI is their diminution of black people to solitary roles as victims. Viewed from this vantage point, Mississippi Burning *says something alarmingly wrong: that black people weren't central to the struggle for their own civil rights, that white oppression in the South was ended by the federal government rather than black activism. The film never makes clear that the activist murder victims weren't isolated interlopers interfering in somebody else's business but rather were pacifist soldiers in a battle for true democracy. It never discusses the whole push for voter registration that was "Freedom Summer," a drive led by such black organizations as the Congress of Racial Equality (CORE), the Student Nonviolent Coordinating Committee (SNCC) and Dr. King's Southern Christian Leadership Conference (SCLC). The leaders of these organizations and their legions of followers were rather more than mere helpless victims, who, as in this film, occasionally marched in a protest parade, but always fled in panic before the onslaught of* violence. *On the contrary, those who demanded equal standing before the law of every state in the land did so with a defiant courage all the more remarkable because it was done in the name of brotherhood. That's the realism that's missing from* Mississippi Burning, *Mr. Royko, the realism of black people uncowed, looking evil in its jaundiced eye and declaring for all the world to hear, "We shall overcome someday."*

Still, the greatest failing in Mississippi Burning *resides in its confused and objectionable theme. The filmmakers take one of history's few instances of the triumph of right over might and turn its legacy inside out. It's important to recognize that this movie is less the heir of the Civil Rights Movement than it is the product of the Reagan Era in which it was made. The film has evident sympathy for the suffering of Mississippi blacks. But in concocting a fictional justice to compensate for that suffering, the film embraces an ideology execrable to the Movement that black leaders founded and to which the black populace flocked. In order to stimulate our appetites for such an ideology, Parker and Gerolmo shamelessly manipulate our emotions—with scenes of the praying black boy, defenseless before the Klansman's jackboot, and notoriously, with their devotion to footage of burning black churches. But there is method to their inflammatory madness. We grow as incensed with the Klan as we do with the rapists and killers in Clint Eastwood and Charles Bronson movies. We yearn for an Eastwood or a Bronson to set matters even. And that's just what Anderson does.*

The American Civil rights Movement remains a beacon of courage and inspiration into the current day, proclaiming the world can actually be changed through nonviolent resistance and civil disobedience. How alarming then for Anderson to come to such a diametrically opposite conclusion. "These people," Anderson states, referring, it seems, to all white Mississippians, though perhaps only to Klansmen and Klan sympathizers, "crawled out of the sewers. Maybe the gutter is the place we have to go to fight them." In short, Anderson advocates engaging the Klan on its own violent turf, employing its own means of physical intimidation. The lesson of Anderson's approach, embraced and proclaimed by the film, is that the end of achieving civil rights for one group justifies the violation of the civil rights of another group. And that, of course, is a philosophical position with which the Klan would feel fully comfortable. Martin Luther King, on the other hand, would find it a crushing repudiation of everything that he believed in, a desecration of the banner under which he asked his followers to march.

*   *   *

My column on *Mississippi Burning*, I think, pretty much speaks for itself. And that's a good thing. I surely couldn't speak for it. Not on the morning after I finished drafting it. I could barely speak at all. When I woke up at eight a.m., I was still drunk. Not just hung over. Actually still drunk. Dizzy drunk. Sick drunk. I called Carl and told him I was sick and wouldn't be in. He accepted this news without comment.

I went back to sleep until about one p.m. when Wilson called to check on me. She asked what was wrong. I told her the stomach flu. Yeah, she said, she'd heard some of that was going around. Right, I thought. It was going around your nearby bottle of Black and White. She said she'd stop by that evening with some chicken soup. I thanked her but argued that such a visit was really unnecessary. Unnecessary or not, she said, she'd see me about six or six-thirty.

My head was throbbing, and I felt the glare of disorientation that was unique to a Scotch hangover. I took four aspirins and tried to sleep again. But I found myself turning the questions of the *Retif* case over and over in my head once again. Why had Judge Delacroix ruled as he had? Why did he lie about his conflict of interest? Where were Joan's files? Why was Tammy Dieter-White so determined to keep Johnny Chambers from talking to me? I was tormented. Finally, it seemed more agonizing trying to sleep than it might if I got up and did something.

I straightened up the house and took a shower, all of which took about an hour, none of which made me feel any better. I thought about trying to eat something but quit thinking about it when my stomach flip-flopped at the very idea of food. Finally, desperate to ease my general sense of ill being, I did something I had never done before. I poured myself two fingers of Scotch and knocked it back neat. When it hit my empty stomach, I thought I might throw up. But I fought the impulse. And within minutes I started feeling better.

This was a very scary solution to my problems.

I got out my notebook in which I'd kept the notes of my research on Leon Delacroix, set it by the phone, and dialed the number at Wallace and Jones. When the switchboard operator answered, I asked for the office of Johnny Chambers. I wasn't sure the proposition was altogether logical. But if Tammy Dieter-White didn't want Johnny to talk to me, then she must think Johnny had something to tell me she didn't want anybody to know. The call was transferred to Johnny's secretary, who picked up and asked if she could say who was calling

"Uh, Mickey," I said. "Mickey, uh, Michaels."

I hadn't prepared my lie in advance. So when I delivered it, I didn't manage to do so smoothly. Perhaps the secretary became suspicious.

"May I say what your call is concerning?" she asked.

"Real estate," I said, more crisply this time. "I'd like Mr. Chambers to handle a real estate transaction for me. Commercial property."

"I'll see if Mr. Chambers is in," the secretary said.

Boy, doesn't that piss you off. A secretary gives you the fucking third degree and then says she'll *see* if her boss is *in*. She'll see, of course, if her boss has any interest in speaking to you and will be back on the phone to claim he's out of the office until sometime after the turn of the century if he doesn't. But Chambers must have heard the crinkle of cash folding itself into his wallet because he came on the line.

"What can I do for you, Mr. Michaels," he said brightly.

"Hi, Johnny," I said. "This is Mike Barnett, I wonder if you've . . ."

That's when I got the dial tone.

Three minutes later my phone rang. I answered.

"Mr. Barnett?" a female voice said.

"Yes," I responded.

"This is Tammy Dieter-White," Tammy Dieter-White said.

"Miss Dieter-White," I said. "How nice of you to call. You don't mind if I call you Tammy, do you? Your last name is, well, so hyphenated."

Tammy Dieter-White didn't dignify my question with an answer.

"I understand," she said, "you have persisted in trying to make contact with my associate."

"Freedom of speech *is* a thorny thing, Tammy."

It felt so good being nasty to Tammy Dieter-White that I thought of pouring myself another shot of Black and White. I knew that would be a bad idea, of course, so I resisted. For the time being.

"We believe in other freedoms in this country, too, Mr. Barnett."

"Call me Mike, Tammy."

She ignored me.

"Like the freedom from being harassed," she said.

"I hope you aren't insinuating that I have been harassing Mr. Chambers."

"I'm not insinuating it," she said. "I'm charging you with it."

"My goodness," I responded. "Tell me, Tammy. I'm sure you won't begrudge me a minute's worth of your legal expertise. Is asking a person a question a felony or a misdemeanor?"

"Mr. Barnett," Tammy Dieter-White said, "I will give you one free piece of advice. If you want to avoid legal action, I advise you to stop pestering my client."

"Your client?" I asked.

"My associate, Mr. Chambers. Excuse me."

"I need to get my head around this, Tammy. I hope you'll indulge me. You're threatening legal action if I persist in trying to speak with Johnny Chambers."

"I'm not threatening, Mr. Barnett. I'm promising."

"Ooooh," I said.

"Mr. Barnett, I don't think you're taking me seriously. And I don't think you realize what a mistake that is."

"Tammy, I might ask you just what kind of legal action you're contemplating taking against me. But before I do that, why don't I see if I can't possibly save us both a lot of trouble. Let me ask you the questions I've been trying to ask Johnny."

"I don't think that's . . ."

"No, no, no," I said. "Let me ask the questions before you begin refusing to answer them. Since Johnny Chambers left his position at Herbst, Gilman, a group of files my wife had compiled on the *Grieve-Retif* case has disappeared. Is it possible that Mr. Chambers, who, as I'm sure you know, worked for a time with Joan on *Retif*, is it possible that Mr. Chambers returned to Herbst to collect others of his possessions and took the *Retif* materials as well. Accidentally, of course. I'm certainly not suggesting industrial espionage or whatever the appropriate equivalent in the legal world."

"May I ask what business this is of yours, Mr. Barnett?"

"I asked you first," I said.

"Mr. Barnett, you are making an allegation that an associate member of the firm of Wallace and Jones is in possession of property belonging to Herbst, Gilman, Roquevert and Ivy."

"You're calling it an allegation," I said. "I was only intending to ask a question."

"In what capacity are you asking this question? As a member of the media? As a representative of Herbst, Gilman?"

"Lady, I was just asking the question. As one human being to another."

"Then you admit you have no standing to be delving into this matter."

"What does that mean? Standing? This isn't a court case. I'm looking for a missing file."

"It would seem to me," Tammy Dieter-White argued, "that if a Herbst, Gilman file is missing, then it's the business of Herbst, Gilman. I don't see how it's any business of yours."

I was suddenly inspired with what seemed a very bright idea.

"Well, Tammy," I said, sweetly, "as I'm sure you know, the *Retif* case settled some time ago. So Herbst, Gilman hasn't any use for the file, though they did consent to let me look at it. You see, I'm writing a memoir about my wife. And as you know, the highlight of her legal career came when she argued one of the issues of *Retif* before the U.S. Supreme Court."

And kicked that rod you wear up your butt another two inches toward your narrow little humorless brain, I wanted to add, though, of course, it was actually hired gun Samuel Buck's butt Joan had actually kicked at the Supreme Court.

Tammy Dieter-White's tone changed, at least a tad, when she'd heard my (purported) reason for inquiring about the missing file.

"Well, Mr. Barnett," she said. "We might have been able to avoid a certain level of acrimony had you made your desires clear from the outset."

"Well, ma'am," I responded, "I thought maybe you knew that I wasn't an attorney. And my only conceivable use for the file would be as source material."

"Yes," she said. "Well, as I'm sure *you* know, *Grieve* was a long and difficult case for us. There were some pretty bad feelings on both sides. I think, now, everybody concerned would just like to see the case lie. But anyway, I don't think we'll be able to help you."

She delivered this last line in a way that suggested she was ready to bring our conversation to a close.

"Just a couple of questions before you run, ma'am."

"Yes?"

"You said, that you didn't think, quote, *we'd* be able to help me."

"Uh huh."

"And you see, it never occurred to me that you might have the missing materials. I mean, what would you be doing with it, right?" I hurried on. "What I thought might have happened is that Johnny Chambers might have had occasion to return to Herbst at some point and accidentally removed the file along with some of his own."

"Well, I'll be sure to ask Mr. Chambers to have a look, Mr. Barnett. Will that satisfy you?"

"Well, it would satisfy me if he found it," I said with a little laugh. "But I'd appreciate your asking him for me."

"I'll do it as soon as we ring off."

Her tone suggested that she hoped that would be immediately.

"There was one other thing," I said.

"Yes, Mr. Barnett."

I could almost hear her teeth gritting.

"You said that everybody concerned would just like to see the case lie. By which I presume you mean not resurrected in any way."

"Yes, Mr. Barnett."

"Well who all exactly were you including in this everybody you referred to?"

"That was just a figure of speech, Mr. Barnett."

"Were you referring to Mr. Retif. Is that what you meant? That Mr. Retif would just . . ."

"Mr. Barnett, I have clients waiting."

"Well I wouldn't want to keep you, ma'am. But I was just wondering if . . ."

"Thank you for calling, Mr. Barnett. I'll make sure Johnny checks his files for you. On the off chance something of your wife's got accidentally mixed in."

"I was just wondering . . ."

"Goodbye, Mr. Barnett."

Dial tone.

My blood was up after my conversation with Tammy Dieter-White. I certainly didn't feel good. But I felt stimulated and unusually alive. I thought she was hiding something. And if she was hiding something, that meant there was something to hide. I fought off the urge to down another couple of fingers of Scotch, and dialed Carl instead.

"Got a minute," I asked when he answered.

"What's up?" he responded.

"I just got off the phone with Tammy Dieter-White," I said. "Woman who represented Sheldon Retif."

"Yeah," he said.

"She called me."

"So?"

"So. So let me ask you a question. As an expert in the craft of investigative reporting.

I could hear Carl breathing into the mouthpiece of his phone.

"I've been trying to reach Johnny Chambers at her office. I told you about that. See if he knows anything about Joan's *Retif* file which is missing from Herbst."

"Mike, I thought I . . ."

"Chambers won't talk to me. Says Dieter-White won't let him. Today he hangs up on me. A couple of minutes later she rings me up and starts threatening legal action if I don't leave Chambers alone. Now what . . ."

"Mike, I thought you told me you were sick."

"I am, Carl. I was throwing up this morning."

"But you're not too sick to keep stirring around in this Leon Delacroix business."

"I just made a phone call. And then . . ."

"If you're well enough to make phone calls at home about some shit I keep telling you to forget, you're well enough to get your ass down to your office and start earning your salary."

"What the fuck are you talking about?" I demanded.

"I'm talking about the fact that this paper has treated you like a privileged character for a long goddamn time and you don't even have the sense to realize it. Other people get their butts to the office every day and . . ."

"I told you I was sick, goddamit."

"You also told me you been on the phone with some white bitch lawyer."

"What the fuck is eating you, Carl?"

"You're the fuck is eating me right now."

"I don't get this shit. You know goddamn well I haven't ever missed a deadline. If I'm not at the fucking office, then I'm at a screening or at home writing. And as long as you get my copy . . ."

"You ain't gonna write any copy on this magnet school bullshit."

"Maybe I am."

"No, you're not. You're the goddamn movie critic. And you're gonna write movie reviews."

"What is this shit, Carl? I'd give you this goddamn story if you'd take it. You afraid I'm gonna steal your thunder? What the fuck is going on?"

"What the fuck is going on is I'm gonna kick your ass the next time I see you."

And for the third time in less than an hour, somebody hung up on me, and once again I found myself listening to the insistent, irritating whine of an empty phone line.

*   *   *

By the time Wilson got to the house at six twenty-five, I had conquered my depression with the aid of about seven ounces of Black and White. I wasn't drunk. But if Wilson hadn't shown up, I would have been within another couple of hours.

As soon as she came in, she immediately began to boss me around as if she had just graduated from the National Academy of Motherhood and Nursing. She wanted to know what in the world I was doing up and dressed. Didn't I have the good sense to know that bed rest was the best medicine for any kind of illness. I seated myself at the kitchen table to endure this bawling out while she stirred about making me something to eat. She had brought two plastic containers of homemade chicken soup. Without even asking for directions, she began banging around in the cabinets under the kitchen counter until she found a pot to her liking. Once she'd found it, she emptied the containers of soup into it, and set it on the stove over a low flame. My low level alcoholic daze seemed enhanced by her domestic energy.

"Now, you, Mister," she said, turning from the stove to face me. "I want you up and out of those clothes. Go put on your pajamas. And then we'll decide whether I let you eat this at the table or make you have it in bed."

"I don't own any pajamas," I said.

"What do you sleep in?" she asked.

"Well, I sometimes sleep in a chair. But usually I sleep in the bed."

"Okay, wise guy," she said. "What do you wear when you sleep?"

"I don't usually wear anything," I admitted.

"Uh huh," she said. "Probably a holdover from your hippie days in the sixties."

"Actually," I said, "in the sixties I didn't wear clothes at all, day or night. But only as a political statement."

"Yeah," she said. "My daddy used to say hippies and queers were the same thing."

She laughed. Then she stepped over to me and placed her hand on my forehead.

"Hmph," she said. "You feel clammy."

To confirm this assessment, she bent from the waist and laid her cheek against my forehead. As she did, I looked straight down into her blouse and breathed a scent of perfume and powder which seemed to waft directly from her breasts.

"I don't think you have a fever," she said.

"No," I agreed. "I don't think so either."

"But you're pale. Have you thrown up?"

"Yes," I said, embarrassed admitting this to her.

"Just this morning? Or since then?"

"Just this morning."

"And diarrhea?"

I cleared my throat.

"Uh, no," I said.

"Hmmm," she responded. "Maybe it was just something you ate then."

No, it was something that I drank. And kept on drinking. But I didn't tell her that.

"But it doesn't matter," she added. "Treatment's the same. Mild food. Bed rest. What have you eaten today?"

"I haven't eaten anything."

"No. That's no good. You have to eat something. Just not very much."

She touched my forehead again. As if my temperature might have changed since she'd last touched me a minute or so ago.

"Soup'll be ready in a second," she said. "I want you to get out of those clothes. Put on a robe or something. You do have a bathrobe?"

"Yes," I said.

"Okay. Put on your robe. You'll eat the soup. And then I'm putting you in bed."

And that's just what she did. I ate the soup at the kitchen table in my bathrobe. And afterwards, she insisted on my going to bed.

"Do you really sleep naked?" she asked.

I rolled my eyes and laughed.

"Yes," I said.

"Don't you get cold?"

"No," I said. "If it's cold, I turn on the electric blanket. But my body heat is such that that's seldom necessary."

"I get cold," she asserted. "And I'm big, just like you."

I laughed again.

"No, Wilson, you're not big like me. You're tall. I'm fat."

"You are not fat, Mike. You're just big."

"Yeah. Well, let's put it this way, I'm bigger than I used to be and bigger than I ought to be and bigger than I want to be."

"Right now," she said, "you're gonna be a big boy who does what I tell him. Which is get right in bed. Now go on."

I got up and started toward the bedroom.

"Since you're going to have to make yourself naked," she said, "I'll wait until you're under the covers to come tuck you in."

If I hadn't been one part seriously depressed and another part not exactly sober, I don't think I'd have gone along with all of this.

But somehow I lacked the energy to resist her incredible maternal energy. I got undressed, got into bed, and pulled the covers up to my chest.

"Wilson," I called out. "I'm in bed and all decent."

"Okay," she said. "Can I bring you something?"

"Uh, yeah," I responded. "I've got a headache. You can bring me some aspirin. They're in that basket on the spice table."

She stuck her head through the French doors so she wouldn't have to shout again. She was holding the bottle of aspirin in her hand, and she rattled it at me.

"How many?" she asked.

"Four," I said.

"I will *not* bring you four aspirins. What's the matter with you?"

"I've got a headache," I said. "I always take four aspirins for a headache."

"Yeah, well not when I'm the nurse," she said.

She brought me three aspirins and half a glass of tap water. I took the aspirins and made a face.

"What's wrong?" she asked.

"Warm water," I said. "I always keep a bottle of cold water in the fridge, and I always take pills with cold water."

"I think maybe the main pill in this house," she said, "is a film critic who likes to sleep naked."

"I'm sorry," I said. "I guess that did sound sort of ungrateful."

I handed her the glass back, and she set it on the nightstand.

"You really naked under there?"

She grabbed the top of the covers and jerked her hand as if she was going to snatch them off me.

"Hey!" I said laughing.

"Oh, don't worry, Michael," she said. "Your virtue is safe with me."

She walked over and sat on the yellow cushions of the wicker couch across from the bed.

"Well, what are we gonna do now?" she asked. "We have to have an activity for this to be a proper date."

"I didn't know this was a date," I said.

"Sure it is. Didn't you just hear me call it a date. And that means we need an activity. How about TV?"

"I don't watch much TV," I said. "I never have time, since I'm always out at the movies."

"Maybe we can find a movie to watch," Wilson said.

"I'd rather just talk," I said. "If you don't mind."

"Talking's fine with me," she replied. "What do you want to talk about. Seen any good movies lately?"

I laughed.

"Really," I said. "I'd like to talk with you about the *Retif* case."

Wilson made a face as if she'd just tasted something unpleasant.

"Carl thinks you ought to let all that business go," she said.

"I know he does. And I guess he thinks I'm fucking myself up worrying about it. But really, Wilson, something stinks about this business. I know it does. And I can't figure out why Carl doesn't think so, too."

I reviewed my various suspicions with her, including Tammy Dieter-White's obvious and continuing hostility to my nosing around the case at all. We went over again everything I knew about Leon Delacroix and how confident Joan had been of winning the case in Delacroix's court. Wilson remarked, as she had once before, that her daddy had always complained that Delacroix was the worst of the bleeding heart liberals. And at the end, we concluded that I was pretty much stymied. And Wilson could tell, I'm sure, how much that fact depressed me.

She got up from the couch where she'd sat for the three hours of our conversation and came to stand by the bed. She put her hand on my forehead again and announced that she thought I was doing better.

"I believe you'll live," she said.

Then she bent her face down to mine.

Just before kissing me she said, "Remember what I told you at Thanksgiving."

Dutifully, I kissed her back. It was an extremely odd sensation for me, and I felt thoroughly uncomfortable. Wilson Malt was the first woman other than Joan I had kissed a real kiss since I was in junior high school. And it was a real kiss, distinctly different from the peck on the cheek or dry smack on the lips I'd exchanged with countless female friends over the years. It wasn't a long kiss or a hot kiss. But it was real, and to my surprise, I liked it.

When she had her coat on and her purse over her shoulder, she stepped back to the bedside and laid her hand on my arm. And in a gentle voice she said, "Whatever it is you've got, Michael, drinking whisky isn't the medicine you need to make it better."

She patted my arm and then rubbed it, pursing her lips a little as she looked down at me. I didn't say anything. And then, before she left, almost as a parting gift, Wilson suggested something I hadn't thought of. She suggested I talk with Amy Stuart, who had covered the Thomas Jefferson Magnet School story as part of her education beat.

"Maybe Amy has something in her notes that would help you," Wilson speculated.

That was to prove a very valuable conjecture indeed.

CHAPTER FIFTEEN

This time memory captures me when I'm watching television. Or I should say when I'm staring at television, letting its vacant buzz provide the incantation of my discontent. I sleep awhile after Wilson leaves my house. But then when the Scotch wears off, I wake and sleep will not return. I lie in the dark, thinking of the kiss Wilson gives me just before she leaves. In a way I cannot control, I am embarrassed.

I rise, go to the living room and sit before the television where I push buttons and jump hopelessly from this late night talk show to that sitcom rerun, from the news on CNN to a contest of Australian rules football on ESPN.

And this time memory is unleashed by a commercial. A slinky blonde reclines on a sofa. Call her, she urges. Tell her *anything*, she implores. She *wants* to hear. Across the bottom of the screen a disclaimer warns how much this phone sex is going to cost. But the blonde purrs repeatedly about her phone number. All I have to do is dial HOT-HOTT.

*   *   *

"HAHT," I say in the cinema of my memory.

I walk out of Joan's bathroom and into our bedroom holding a small plastic pillbox. The pillbox is rectangular and pink and perforated across the bottom with five rows of holes so that foil-encased capsules can be squeezed by a thumb out of the box and into your palm.

"HAHT," I say again, sounding like a cawing crow.

"What?" Joan says.

She is wearing her typical morning costume of panties and dress shields. She is standing in front of her closet when I come into the room, selecting items to be packed for our trip. The slip and dress that she will put on later are spread on the bed behind her.

"HAHT," I repeat.

I'm not quite managing it, I realize, but I'm trying to render the sound of discovery made by the intergalactic bounty hunters in John Sayles's *The Brother from Another Planet.*

"What?" Joan says, turning to me.

The connective straps of Joan's dress shields shape themselves like a bra without cups and frame her breasts in triangles of elastic. The waist band of her skimpy panties stretches just below the pale white scar on her lower abdomen. I see her like this almost every morning and seldom fail to make some kind of lewd comment or suggestion. I have other games on my mind now, however. I wave the pillbox like a fan, back and forth in front of my face.

"HAHT!" I croak.

"What are you saying, goofball?" Joan asks.

"Not WHAT. HAHT!"

"Hot?" she asks. "You're always hot. So what else is new? Tell me when you're not hot. That'll be the day worth remarking upon."

"H.," I say, spelling out each letter. "A. H. T. Husbands Against Hairy Tits. I've been checking up on you. You haven't taken your estrogen tablet this morning. And you haven't packed them to take with us on vacation. I know you're doing that just to spite me. I'll be the only husband around whose wife has hairy tits. What an unbelievable humiliation."

I march up to her stiff-legged like a toy soldier. I hand her the pillbox.

"Bad woman," I say. "All power to HAHT."

Joan tosses the pillbox toward her purse, which stands open on the bed next to her dress and slip.

"You are the craziest man God ever made," she says.

"HAHT!" I reply.

I reach out with both hands and grab a breast in each, stroking lightly down until I'm holding a nipple between each thumb and forefinger.

"I think I can already feel the fuzz starting to grow," I say. "I think I have no choice but to initiate more detailed examinations."

"If we miss our plane, you're going to be able to make a more detailed examination of your ass," Joan says, "because I'm gonna have kicked it up around your neck."

"God, I love it when you talk dirty."

I bend and rub my face against each of her breasts. Then I pop the elastic of her dress shields.

"As long as you wear this," I say, holding one of the straps between the fingers of my right hand, "I will always be able to find your tits. I've always said they're as pretty as a picture. And I'm delighted to see that you've taken me seriously enough to start framing them."

"I thought you were doing a hairy-tit test, not a pretty-as-a-picture-tit test."

"Right you are," I say. "And I hate to report that they've got a distinctly fuzzy feeling to both hand and face. If you miss taking your estrogen another single time, I'm afraid you may start growing an Adam's apple and have to find work with the circus."

"As the hairy-titted woman?" Joan says.

"As the hairy-titted woman with an Adam's apple," I correct.

"I didn't forget to take my estrogen, you know," Joan says.

"Liar," I say. "You are a liar who sets my pants on fire. I have inspected your dated pillbox. You have not yet taken today's tablet."

"True," Joan admits. "And I could tell you that I had put the box out to remind me both to take this morning's pill and to pack it."

"But somehow I don't think that's what you're gonna tell me."

"No. I wouldn't want to lie to you. The truth is that I didn't take the pill on purpose."

"Oh well," I say. "I hope you'll have the furry kind of tits. Not the coarse, bristly kind that will give me a rash when I do it to you."

"That's something else I need to talk to you about," Joan says.

"Oh my God, it gets worse."

"You won't be able to do it to me a lot, once I have the hairy tits."

"I'm a flexible kind of guy," I say. "I mean if the tits are furry and all, I'm sure I could get used to them."

"Perhaps," Joan says. "But you see, I'll be out of town so much of the time."

She slips her hand down the front of my pants.

"With the circus, you see."

"Ah," I nod. "Yes. With the circus."

*   *   *

I shouldn't, but I do anyway. Like an addict who knows fully well the painful aftermath of his high but craves the momentary rush of its elysium all the same, I deliberately summon memory. I switch off TV and step to the armoire in the dining room. On a shelf inside is the photo album of the vacation trip Joan and I took to Alaska the month before she died. I take it to the couch in the living room and set it on my knees. On the first page is a photo of the Captain's Lounge aboard the M.S. Noordam, the cruise ship we took through the Inside Passage from Vancouver, British Columbia, to Ketchikan and Juneau.

*   *   *

"I'm your Hostess Veronica," the blond woman says.

She is so perky that in another mood I feel sure I'd want to strangle her.

"I'm your activities director Barb," the taller, thinner brunette announces.

Barb is pretty perky, too, although in Barb I think I can detect just a hint of saving irony.

"And my name's Billy," the male of the trio says. "Every afternoon I run the bingo game right here in the Captain's Lounge. During the game, or before if you really have to, you can call me 'Bingo Billy.'"

"Bingo Billy," one of our fellow passengers calls out. And the whole room buzzes with laughter.

I lean over to Joan and whisper, "I'd like to bingo that guy with a billy club."

"Hush," Joan says, laughing.

Your Hostess Veronica, Your Activities Director Barb and Bingo Billy are providing the passengers with an overview of the various activities available during the cruise. Joan and I are seated at a round cocktail table sipping frozen margaritas through straws.

"Don't you feel unredeemably bourgeois?" Joan whispers.

I look around the room at our fellow passengers. "Mostly I feel unbelievably in the need of a license in geriatrics," I reply. "I thought these cruises were supposed to be big singles affairs. Everybody here looks like they were last single in the nineteenth century."

Joan says, "Everybody here looks like he or she *was* last single in the nineteenth century, Mr. Award-Winning Journalist."

"I'm glad to see that we're in *agreement* on that," I say, deadpan.

"After the bingo game," Bingo Billy says, "I conduct a horse race each afternoon also right here in the Captain's Lounge." He steps to the side and points out six wooden horses all festooned with various colors of ribbon, each mounted on a movable aluminum stand.

"A roll of the die, your horse advances," Billy proclaims. "Winner take all. Pari-mutuel betting isn't just allowed; it's practically required. Doesn't that sound like fun?"

"Neeeeeeeeigh," someone calls out and sets the room laughing again.

"Are we gonna lose I.Q. points during this trip?" Joan whispers to me.

"I am," I whisper back, flashing my eyebrows in imitation of Groucho's most famous leer. "'Cause in lieu of bingo and horse racing, I'm gonna fuck my brains out."

The entertainment trio are winding up their presentation. "If it's sports or exercise you're interested in, you see me," Your Activities Director Barb says.

"See me for bingo and horse racing," Bingo Billy says. Like a hammy actor in an amateur production of *Showboat*, he makes a gesture toward his chest with his right thumb.

"And if it's anything else, you see me," Your Hostess Veronica says. She smiles so broadly you can see her gums. I thinks she is about to do a twirl in imitation of Vanna White just about to flip a letter on *Wheel of Fortune*."

"Tell me," I say to Joan, "do top-of-the-morning blow jobs qualify as 'sports and exercise' or 'anything else'?"

"You're not thinking of this vacation," she responds, "as an occasion for unlimited sex, I hope."

"Not at all," I say. "My limit is three times a day. Four tops."

Joan looks pointedly at her watch.

"It's five-thirty," she says. "Dinner is at nine. If we finish up here pretty quickly, I think we can grab showers and work one in before we eat. After we eat, we'll be full, of course. But I guess we can manage another one by, say, eleven. And that's gonna wipe me out, I'm sure. So I guess you're right. Either Your Hostess Veronica or Your Activities Director Barb is going to have to stand in for the last one. Which one do you prefer?"

"Well," I say, "Your Hostess Veronica is the blonder of the two. And I perceive that she might not require much in the way of small talk. Just a drink before and a cigarette afterwards. Slam bam thank you ma'am in between."

"You're such a conventional man, Mike Barnett," Joan says.

"How's that?" I inquire.

"Choosing the blonder one."

"I'm sorry," I say. "I thought choosing the blonder one would meet with your approval, given your own persistent blondeness."

"You're on vacation. You need to do something different, something new."

"You're suggesting I've got a surfeit of blondeness in my everyday life?"

"Well, yes I am actually. Unless I've been falling down on the job."

"I could do with some more of your falling down on your knees," I say. "If you follow my insinuation."

"Oh Mickey," Joan rejoins. "You make so many fellatious statements. If you can perceive a vowel change here, a different consonant there."

"And you make so many suckful responses," I say, laughing.

"I aim to please."

"So you think I ought to choose Your Activities Director Barb for my third tumble every day?"

"Well," Joan says. "She *is* the taller and more brunette of the two."

"And you can never underestimate the importance of tall non-blondeness."

"Mostly I just know you'll hate every minute of doing it with her," Joan says. "Given her excessive tallness and inadequate blondeness. Think what a fabulous change of pace that'll be."

"How's that?"

"All the rest of your life," Joan responds, "you've been limited to doing it with somebody you absolutely adore."

"And that's become so déclassé, I guess."

"No doubt the very essence of unbridled peasantry."

"Maybe I could skip Your Activities Director Barb and just pretend that I hate you. How does that sound?"

Joan looks at her watch again and slurps up the last of her drink.

"If we hurry," she says, "there may be time for a couple before dinner."

We get up and walk hand-in-hand from the Captain's Lounge toward the staircase that leads down to C Deck and our starboard-side cabin.

"You're a bitch," I say. "You're cruel. You're humorless. You're stupid. Oh, and I shouldn't forget that I find you absolutely repulsive physically. I can't imagine what I'm doing with you."

"Stop it," Joan says. "I'm so wet I'm afraid I'm leaving tracks."

*   *   *

Our cruise aboard the *Noordam* is more than merely a marathon of sex, though it is that indeed. It is a time of splendid isolation. We sail aboard a mammoth floating hotel, surrounded by fifteen hundred other passengers and a crew of equivalent size. And yet we are as alone together as if on a backpacking trip. Our modest affluence is a particular treasure to us because it provides opportunities like this one. And together we are grateful for the stroke of good fortune we know is ours.

We enter a contest trying to guess the mileage the *Noordam* will sail in the first twenty-four hours of the cruise. We miss by over a hundred miles, and consequently surrender plans for new careers in oceanic navigation. We enter the daily written trivia contest and twice come within a single answer of winning a prize. We go to bingo with Bingo Billy every afternoon without ever coming within three numbers of winning. We swim in the ship pool, even though we freeze ourselves silly doing so.

In our determination to avail ourselves of every recreational facility the ship offers, we rent equipment for games of paddle tennis and shuffleboard. Joan even insists on using the batting machine which occupies one net-draped corner of the top deck.

"I never learned to bat when I was a girl," she explains. "Maybe I can make up for it now."

I try to argue that there isn't any thrill in hitting the ball inside the batting cage because you can't tell how well you have hit or how far it might fly. But Joan reminds me of our quest to try out every piece of equipment that the *Noordam* offers. The batting machine has several speeds, including a slowest one called "Pokey." But all the speeds are too fast for Joan's untrained batting coordination. She sometimes manages to get her bat on the ball. But even a foul tip is unusual. Despite my depositing five dollars in quarters into the machine's operating slot, she never succeeds in hitting the ball squarely. But she is altogether typically undaunted by her failure.

"One of these days," she declares, "I'll learn to bat well enough that I can knock the ball out of the Superdome."

"That'll be some feat," I say, "given that the Superdome has a roof over the top of it."

"I never like to set insignificant goals for myself," she retorts.

*   *   *

Joan always turns our vacations into a sexual Olympics. And that is never more true than on our Alaska trip. The demands of our separate careers frequently find us at the office late or out fulfilling the social obligations of our jobs. Over the course of an average working year, we probably average sex about twice a week. Joan likes to use vacations to make up for what she considers this deprivation. Thus she informs me when we leave home that she plans on making love at least twice a day. And she sticks to that pace, adding spice by repeatedly initiating sex in strange and "dangerous" places: in a restroom aboard the Alaskan Railroad on our trip from Anchorage to Denali, in the woods off a mountain trail above the gold rush town of Skagway, on a pier at Glacier Bay Lodge in the afterglow of a magnificent midnight sunset.

The wildest of such escapades, though, Joan orchestrates when we are still aboard the *Noordam*. It is our last night on the cruise.

At about eleven-thirty Joan says she wants to go out on deck one last time. We put on sweaters, gloves, knit caps and our matching Burberry overcoats and take a long stroll the whole way around the promenade deck. It is late and very cold in the wind. There are a few others out on deck, but not many. And none of the others is willing to brave the frigid wind tunnels which form on either side of the bow to stand at the very front of the ship. Alone at the front, Joan makes her move. I stop and lean back against the metal wall of one of the forward meeting rooms, empty now at this late hour. Joan leans back against me, and we stand for a time, relishing the bite of the wind in our faces. Southerners, the idea of being cold like this in July is almost sinfully delicious. Joan tilts her head back and kisses my earlobe.

Then she whispers, "Put your hands up under my skirt. I've got a surprise for you."

"I hope you're not about to start what I'm afraid you're about to start," I say, laughing.

"Just put your hands up under my skirt, Okay?"

"I won't be able to feel a thing. I'm wearing gloves."

"Take your gloves off," Joan directs.

"I still wouldn't be able to feel a thing. My fingers are frozen."

"That sounds so kinky," Joan says. "I want you to fuck me, Mickey."

I laugh. "I got no problem with that. Let's go."

"Uh uh," Joan says. "I want you to fuck me right here."

"Did anybody ever tell you that you have a dirty mouth? You are not doing your part for the international image of the Southern Belle."

She puts her lips to my ear and whispers breathily, "I want you to fuck me in the ass."

I laugh again. "Not only a dirty mouth, but a sodomite to boot. If you're going to propose such kinkiness, you're going to have to do so in a ladylike fashion."

"I want you to bang me in the butt until I babble," Joan says. "I want you to corncob me."

I laugh still harder. "I think the expression is 'cornhole me,' dear."

"I don't want to corncob you," she responds. "I want you to corncob me."

"You are undoubtedly the craziest woman who ever walked the face of this earth."

"I want you to fuck me," Joan says. "I want you to fuck me in the ass on the bow of the *Noordam*, eight hours south of Juneau, Alaska, in June, 1987. I want to do something that will make us remember this moment forever."

"Joanie," I say, "Someone could come walking around the deck any minute."

"No one has walked up here since we've been here."

"But that doesn't mean they won't absolutely any second."

"The wind will blow them back. It's too cold."

"It didn't blow us back," I point out.

"But we came up here to fuck like bunnies on the bow of the *Noordam*, eight hours south of Juneau, Alaska. So that we'd have done something to remember this moment forever."

"You aren't the only kinky person in the world, you know. Maybe some other couple might come up here for the same reason."

"Then they'd understand," Joan says.

*   *   *

Far more even than the climactic act of sexual release, I relish the mutual tenderness it is my blessing to share with Joan, the wordless closeness I have never known and will surely never know with another human being. I can never get my fill of touching her. I treasure the period we spend intertwined in one another's arms after sex as much as the act of sexual union itself. I like to touch her face, softly, with the backs of my fingers. I like to lay my cheek next to hers. I like to hold her against me till she twitches and then stills with sleep. I like to watch her while she sleeps, knowing that she will make me stop if she wakes, for she is always embarrassed that I behold her with such unqualified adoration.

*   *   *

At Glacier Bay, we take a day-long boat tour led by a man we quickly take to calling Your Naturalist Frank. Frank is the kind of guide who has a thousand things to say, not one of which is illuminating. He invokes every wilderness cliché ever invented and repeats it like clockwork, it seems, once an hour. But he is such an earnest and evidently well-meaning young man, so obviously in love with the natural splendors of his adopted state, that we come to feel bad making such cruel fun of him. At the day's end we tip him exorbitantly and Joan praises him profusely in an exchange before we leave the vessel. I love the dual facts about Joan that she can be such a wicked and satiric mimic but will always go out of her way to encourage those she judges in need of it.

The highlight of our Alaskan vacation comes in Denali National Park. We have to rise at four one morning to catch our scheduled bus tour of the park. And we begin the day with some apprehension. We regularly contribute to Greenpeace and to the Sierra Club. But we are not sentimental about animals. We visit the fine Audubon Park Zoo in New Orleans only when we have out-of-town visitors. Neither of us has ever owned a pet. But like every other aspect of our trip, we are delighted with our visit to Denali. We see several moose, several herds of caribou, and a fox.

Then on a hill above a turnout for viewing Polychrome Mountain, we are treated to a mother bear eating blueberries while keeping a wary eye on her two wildly cavorting cubs. The cubs wrestle with one another, pull on the mother's hind leg only to be swatted away, scamper and somersault, try to climb a spruce sapling which they quickly bend to the ground. The show goes on for the better part of an hour. And at the end, when the bus driver announces he has no choice but to move on, Joan has tears in her eyes.

That night, hours later, we sit until closing in the lounge at the McKinley Chalet and drink frozen margaritas until we are both tipsy. Finally, I ask her why she'd cried while watching the mother bear and her cubs.

"I don't know," she says. "They were just so precious."

I don't say anything. So uncommon for her, no doubt stimulated by drink, Joan's eyes fill with tears again.

"It's so stupid," she says.

She smiles. But the tears burst through her eyelashes and run in large drops down both cheeks.

"It's so stupid, I'm embarrassed," she says. "But those cubs reminded me of the children that you and I aren't ever going to get to have."

*   *   *

I close the album and return it to its shelf in the armoire. And I make matters worse. I walk into my bedroom, fumble through a chest on which the bedroom TV stands. I find the videotape I'm looking for and slide it into the VCR. As it plays, I undress and stretch out on the bed. On the screen a blonde woman manipulates her clitoris and probes at her vagina with a vibrator. I touch myself, but I am soft. And I find that I am crying. Sex without Joan makes no more sense than a Moon without an Earth around which to orbit.

*   *   *

When I finally fall asleep again, I dream that Joan is still alive, that I am still in bed and, as always, Joan has risen before me to shower and dress. I dream that I have moved onto her side of the bed and have stretched myself in the sheets that she has warmed. I dream that I pull her pillows against me and in them I can smell the fragrance of her hair. I dream that I can hear her emerging from the shower. I dream that she comes to me all brisk and eager and kisses me on the nose to wake me. In the amber world between the magic of my dream and the bleakness of waking, I do stretch into her side of the bed. But it is unwarmed now, of course, and its cool stretch of patterned cotton forces upon me anew the agony life feels without her. As I wake I feel as if some slow-working acid has been injected behind my eyes, slowly dissolving away all perception save for that of overwhelming sorrow. I rise resentfully, wishing to retreat to the world of dreams where Joan and I can still be together. As I prepare for the day, her absence hangs on me like the weighted shroud of a sailor prepared for burial at sea.

CHAPTER SIXTEEN

Exhausted both physically and spiritually, I nonetheless arrived at the paper before eight the next morning. I was determined to get Carl off my ass by churning out a barrelful of work. And I wanted to talk with Amy Stuart as soon as possible.

I walked into Editorial to discover that the Christmas spirit had manifested itself in a decorated office. A giant string of silver letters stretched from one side of Editorial to the other bearing the cheery greeting "Merry Christmas." Sprays of pine needles were tacked up on the corners of every door. And mistletoe dangled from every archway. I felt a brutal stab of heartache at the realization I was going to have to spend another Christmas without Joan who so cherished the holiday season. And I retreated quickly to my office and the sanctuary of my work.

I had already placed three short pieces in Carl's basket before he arrived at nine. They were just little filler spots, rewrites of news releases about the box office success of this picture and the plans of that star to appear in such-and-such a film that was scheduled to go before the cameras on you-can-bet-they're-guessing projected future date. This was the kind of stuff I usually did as "breathers" between working on my feature pieces and reviews, or frankly, left for an intern to practice on. But I wanted some sort of communication with Carl. And the best I could think of was this: If you really want me to be an office drudge, I guess I can turn out rewrites as speedily and surely as anybody on staff.

But when Carl came in, he picked up the pieces without comment and carried them into his office where he uncharacteristically closed the door. He didn't slam the door. But he shut it forcefully enough that he jingled the little bell someone had hung from the doorframe.

At about ten I went out on the floor and sat in the chair next to Amy Stuart's desk. In keeping with the spirit of the season, she had outlined three sides of her desktop with a strand of tinsel. Amy was one of those people who seemed perfectly suited for her calling in life. In years of covering education for the paper, she had come to look like a school marm. She wore her long brown hair pulled back in a bun and was never to be seen without her reading glasses dangling from a chain around her neck or perched on the end of her nose as she stared at her computer screen or rummaged through her notes. She wasn't an unattractive woman, still slender as she neared fifty. But she seemed to be oblivious to changes in clothes styles, and always dressed in something that looked as if it needed to be ironed.

Asking for her confidentiality, I gave Amy a brief account of my investigations into Judge Delacroix and the Thomas Jefferson Magnet lawsuit. She listened without comment. She didn't probe at me about why the film critic was doing an investigative piece. Probably she thought I was suffering from some sort of bereavement dementia. And in that, no doubt, she wasn't far wrong.

Carl came out of his office while I was talking to Amy and glanced in our direction. But he turned immediately away from us and walked straight to the coffee room. He returned with a cup in his hand a couple of minutes later and didn't lift his head in our direction.

Amy remembered the case very well, of course, and assured me that like all good newspaper people, she had a back file with all her old reporter's notebooks on the story.

"Do you think I could look through your notebooks?" I asked her. "Maybe I'd find a clue of some kind."

"I don't mind if you look at them, Mike. Can you read shorthand?"

"Oh Christ," I said.

Amy laughed. "I'd have been surprised if you could. I'm sure somewhere there is one, but I've never met a man in my life who knew shorthand. Damn dumb of them too."

I sighed in defeat. "Another dead end," I said.

"What are you talking about?"

"Oh, Wilson just thought there might be something in your notes that I hadn't come across elsewhere. Some loose end that I could use to unravel the knot I'm tied up in."

Amy smiled and patted my hand maternally. "Let me pull out the notebooks and see if I come across anything interesting."

"I'd be in your debt," I said quietly.

"I'll let you pay off in whiskey sours at Napoleon House."

*   *   *

In the continuing silence that raged between me and Carl, I worked unusually hard all week, filling his basket with rewritten short items most of which we both knew wouldn't find space in the paper. More productively, I finished my annual selections of the year's best and worst films for publication in our year-end entertainment tabloid and filed reviews of all the Christmas releases, the last of which made their debuts that Friday noon. I was used to making a hard push the week before Christmas. For traditionally, Joan and I had taken vacation time the following week, between Christmas and New Year's. I was in a position to do so this year, too. I almost literally had nothing else to do for the next week, but until I got rip-roaring drunk at the office Christmas party Friday afternoon, taking a vacation hadn't even occurred to me.

The party started at three. By four I had achieved a measure of the Christmas spirit. By five I was imparting Christmas cheer to everyone at the party, all of whom seemed like the best damn colleagues a man could want, the finest, most talented and committed writers anywhere in the South, hell in the whole goddamn country. At five-thirty I was standing with my arm around Carl Shaney who had managed a few cups of red vodka punch himself. We didn't speak of the tenseness between us the last couple of days. Our conversation concerned the burning topic of the Saints' having failed to make the NFL play-offs.

"Gonna kick those bastards' butts," Carl announced, referring to the fact that a team of Saints and ex-Saints played in our spring softball league. We had never beaten them. And it wasn't likely that our team of writers was about to beat them anytime soon. But every year when they missed out on the playoffs, Carl declared he'd get even for their letting him down by humiliating them at softball the following summer.

"Gonna beat 'em like a goddamn drum," I concurred.

And in the dream of our forthcoming athletic triumph, he and I were united against the world once again.

I had this notion that in other parts of the country, such flamboyant and public drunkenness was frowned upon a great deal more than it was in New Orleans. I had this notion that an employee would be pretty careful about getting shit-faced in plain view of those who signed his checks every week. But maybe I was wrong, of course. I hadn't held a job in any city other than this one. So I didn't really know. Maybe occasional wild behavior was tolerated everywhere, so long as it didn't interfere with work performance. Maybe all of American society qualified as The Big Easy. But even if that was so, New Orleans still had to be The Big Easiest. Every year at the paper's Christmas party people got almost as drunk as I did. And a lot of other shenanigans went on as well. Rumors of couples humping in the toilet stalls circulated after every Christmas party. And not couples who were themselves couples either. But couples who were normally paired with other people. I never saw anyone humping—in toilet stalls or anywhere else. But I believed that it went on.

And I disapproved. I disapproved because I wasn't into humping. I was into drinking.

By six o'clock Carl had shown the good sense to go home, but I eagerly consented to join a group of younger staff members who were headed over to Pat O'Brien's to drink hurricanes and get really crazy. It was my good fortune that Wilson Malt was among the hardy partiers. I hardly needed another swallow of alcohol to be more than thoroughly blitzed for the rest of the evening, but that fact had never stopped me before. And it didn't stop me now.

There were eight of us altogether. We marched out into the courtyard bar and pulled together two of the meshed metal tables to accommodate us. As was true every cool winter evening, the giant heaters buzzed and popped and turned this walled outdoor space cozy under its canopy of oaks. We were all full enough of Christmas cheer, though, red punch coursing like anti-freeze through our veins, that we'd probably have been perfectly comfortable without the heaters.

A waiter appeared, ecstatic to have eight of us to wait on, and we gave him our orders, hurricanes around.

"I need a hurricane the way this country needed Ronald Reagan as our president," I declared forcefully. "But I'll goddamn have one anyway."

Some of our members had the good sense to pass when a new waiter appeared to take orders for a second round. But not I.

"I need a hurricane the way this country needed Ronald Reagan as our president," I declared once again.

"You've already used that excuse," somebody pointed out.

"Damn straight," I said. "And just like the country, I'm gonna have to give the hurricane a second chance to get it right."

By the end of my second hurricane, I found I was no longer into talking. Wilson wasn't exactly sober, but at least she could still speak. And she could walk well enough for the both of us. She held me up all the way to her car and got me upright and seatbelted into the front passenger's seat. That's the last I remember of Friday, December 23. I passed out on the way home. It's obvious I was too big for Wilson to have carried into the house, but I have no recollection of having walked there myself.

That night I dreamed of Joan and our Alaska vacation. And I dreamed of a very specific act of lovemaking. But the next morning when I awoke with a headache I thought might blow my brains out the top of my skull, it wasn't Joan in bed next to me, of course. It was Wilson Malt. We were both naked. But I didn't know whether I had made love with her or not. And that's not exactly the sort of thing you want to admit to the naked person sleeping next to you.

I crept out of bed, put on a bathrobe and went into the kitchen. The clock on the dining room mantle read eight o'clock, but I didn't know if that meant we'd slept a long time or hardly slept at all. I hadn't the slightest idea what time we left Pat O'Brien's, much less what time we got home and went to bed.

I found the aspirin bottle, shook out four tablets and swallowed them down with a gulp of ice water poured into my mouth directly from the bottle. I felt extremely uncomfortable. I hadn't made even

secret plans for getting involved with Wilson Malt. I liked her. I didn't
like her political attitudes. But I liked her personally, difficult as it
sometimes was for me to make such a distinction. Yes, I admitted to
myself, I was attracted to her. In purely sexual terms, I was attracted
to her. She was pretty, and she was warm, and she was pleasant to be
with. Perhaps I was just feeling my year and a half of celibacy, but I
found something very sexy in the way she wore her clothes and the
way she smelled and the way she moved.

I poured myself a large glass of water, stepped back into the
bedroom and looked around for clues to exactly what had taken
place after we got home. She had presumably undressed me, though
maybe I had been "walking blind." My clothes were piled in a clump
at the foot of the bed approximately where I threw them on a daily
basis. Wilson had folded her skirt and blouse and placed them neatly
on the wicker sofa. Her bra and panties were placed on top.

I looked over at her lying in my bed. Lying on Joan's side of the bed,
I couldn't stop myself from thinking. She obviously hadn't figured
out how to adjust the electric blanket, because she had flung it
off. She was lying on her stomach, her long brown hair flowing
down her shoulders and back, spilling over onto her face which
was turned away from me. Her left arm was raised up toward her
head and her left leg was raised toward her waist, separating her
buttocks. I felt a rush of indecency, staring at her the way I might
some picture in a girlie magazine. But I stepped farther into the
room, almost directly behind her now so that I could look between
her legs. Beneath the oriental rug that had been a gift from Joan's
father, a floorboard creaked. Wilson stirred. She didn't wake, but she
turned on her back, showing me for an instant her breasts with their
milk-chocolate circles of flesh around her nipples. She had grown
cold, evidently, because the nipples were hard. Still without waking,
she pulled the sheet across herself and brushed the long strands of
hair from her face.

I didn't know what I should do. I didn't have the energy or desire
to stay up. My head was throbbing. And I knew the only treatment
for that, in addition to aspirins and water, was going back to sleep. I
considered opening the sofa bed in my study and going back to bed
there, but given that Wilson and I had already slept together—even

if we hadn't done anything *but* sleep—it seemed pretty pointless to arrange separate beds now. More, it could very well be that she'd interpret such an action as rude. What the hell, I finally concluded, too fuzzy headed to figure out what I *ought* to do. I took off my robe and dropped it on the pile of my other clothes and slipped underneath the sheets beside her. She seemed to wake a little as I did. She mumbled something. Or at least she moaned, a low hum from the base of her throat that worked its way up into her mouth without ever quite forming itself into words. She turned on her side toward me and opened her eyes for the briefest moment. She licked her lips and smiled and closed her eyes and threw her right knee up on my thigh.

When I awoke again, at quarter of noon, Wilson had her head on my chest. My arm lay around her, my hand flat in the small of her back. I felt a wetness and a tickle under her face, and as I gained consciousness, I realized what had awakened me. She was licking my right nipple. This was an instance of intimacy that I had never before experienced. I had never thought of my nipples as particularly erogenous and had never asked Joan to stimulate them. But now less from the physical sensation than from the psychological, I found what Wilson was doing wildly erotic. I stroked my hand up the length of her back and then down the long tresses of her hair.

We didn't speak. We didn't kiss. We didn't look into one another's eyes. But our hands never stopped the slow and sweeping caresses. She eased on top of me and slid her hips down. Her breasts pressed against my chest, her face flat against my shoulder, she lifted herself only from the knees. Gently, unhurriedly she rose and fell against me.

This was different. Sex with Joan had always been riotous and funny, experimental and deliberately wild. We made noise when we made love, and we took keen delight in giving each other pleasure. We treated sex as a private amusement park; pleasing each other was the thrill of a roller coaster ride. In contrast, this act of lovemaking with Wilson evoked the subtler experience of rocking back and forth in a front porch swing on a breezy spring day.

*   *   *

Saturday afternoon Wilson and I left town for the Mississippi Gulf
Coast and in so doing, with a mixture of misgiving and relief, I left
Retif behind for a while. We had booked reservations at the Comfort
Inn in Gulfport just east of the Edgewater Shopping Center. I was
still a little shaky from the previous evening's debauch, but I drove
the eighty miles out through the swamps of New Orleans East, across
the Interstate twinspan over Lake Pontchartrain and amidst the piney
woods of the Pearl River Basin. The trip was so spur-of-the-moment
that Wilson didn't think to call her parents to cancel plans for lunch
the next day until we were already in Mississippi. It was Christmas
Eve, and Wilson and I had no presents to exchange save for the gift of
one another's companionship. We ate Eggplant Josephine at the White
Pillars Restaurant. I had a couple of glasses of Scotch before dinner
and a brandy afterwards. But otherwise I was good. I didn't even open
the quart bottle of Black and White I had brought from home.

We watched the annual telecast of Frank Capra's *It's a Wonderful
Life* on television and turned out the lights before midnight. And we
made love again in the same quiet way we had that morning.

On Christmas morning, Wilson wanted to go to church, and I
agreed, though I didn't like having to attend without wearing a
tie, which I had neglected to include in my hasty packing the day
before. Sometimes I am capable of the most ridiculous obsessions.
Joan would no doubt have termed this one something like
religiosanscravatphobia, the fear of going to church without a tie. I
made such a point of complaining about going to church tieless that
Wilson joked she'd know exactly what to get me for Christmas every
year for the rest of my life. I needn't have expended the breath, of
course. There were plenty of fellow tieless Christmas churchgoers
that bright Mississippi morning. Thank God Wilson had the instincts
needed to puncture the expanding balloon of my embarrassment by
starting to tease me as soon as we got to church and refusing to let
up for the rest of the day. As we settled into our pew, she whispered
her hope that we would shortly be singing "Bless Be the Tie That
Binds." When we didn't, she declared herself "just fit to be tied." And
later that evening as we watched a football game on TV, long after
I thought the episode was ancient idiosyncratic history, she seized
every opportunity to confess her fear the game would end in a tie.

We attended Christmas services at a Baptist church for reasons impossible to reconstruct. I wished afterwards we had gone to a Catholic church. Wilson still practiced the faith of her rearing, whereas I darkened the door of the Baptist church where Joan and I had belonged as children exactly as often as Christmas rolled around. But without thinking, I drove us to the big Baptist church on the Gulf Coast Highway and began to get the creeps I associate with organized religion almost as soon as I stepped inside. Few others, I think, Pat Robertson and Jimmy Swaggart among them, of course, can attain the same heights of oleaginous, self-righteous piety that a Baptist preacher achieves with the merest effort of opening his mouth. Baptist preachers have long made me chagrined at having been born, raised and lived my life as a Southerner. I am sure that many of these men are sincere in their beliefs and public pronouncements. But when I hear a Baptist preacher sermonizing, my hypocrite alarm buzzes almost as loudly as when I hear a Louisiana politician speechifying. I was thankful, at least, that Wilson seemed oblivious both to my embarrassment and to the Biloxi preacher's unctitude. And though we didn't sing "Bless Be the Tie That Binds," the service did include a large number of Christmas carols which, I'm sure, everybody present enjoyed singing.

After church we were able to find a cafeteria open on Pass Road and treated ourselves to a Christmas turkey dinner with all the trimmings. The afternoon was bright and mild. It was too cool for swimming, and we hadn't brought bathing suits anyway. But it was perfect for walking along the beach and letting the anemic waves of the Mississippi Sound trickle up over our bare feet. Late in the day, we fetched the duffle bag of balls, bats and gloves I always carried in my trunk and hit flies to each other. Wilson was well-coordinated and strong. She could throw a baseball with a straight overhand motion that hadn't even a hint of girlishness. She knew how to position herself under a fly ball and how to squeeze the glove down on a catch. She sometimes whiffed when she tried to hit flies to me, and she wasn't good at gauging how hard to hit the ball, but when she connected she could knock it high and long.

Sunday night we decided to stay the week. Wilson had already arranged a vacation week for herself, something the paper liked during this notoriously slow news period. No new movies would be released until mid-January, and so I hadn't any reason to go in either. I called Carl to tell him to charge me with five days of vacation time as well. He wasn't at home, but I left the message for him on his answering machine.

As I presume is true of any couple in their first days of romantic involvement, my holiday week on the Gulf Coast with Wilson Malt was mostly about sex. We had sex every day that we were there, in the morning before we got out of bed, at night before we went to sleep, sometimes in the afternoon, too. Such passion, as we all know, sadly burns like kindling wood, powerfully hot, but extremely fast.

Throughout the week I could not help comparing Wilson to Joan. I had, after all, prior to Wilson, slept with only one woman my entire life. Comparisons forced themselves into my consciousness even when I didn't want to make them. Almost from the beginning of our relationship Joan had exhibited an utter obliviousness about being naked in front of me. She just lacked that quality about her body that is often termed *modesty*. Wilson wasn't like that. By the end of the week, she no longer kept a sheet pulled up to her neck when we weren't actually making love and no longer scrambled into a caftan the minute she got out of bed. But she remained conscious of being naked in front of me. In certain ways, I found her "modesty" unexpectedly sexy. She had a habit of cupping one breast in her hand and partially concealing the other with her arm. When she would stand in front of me naked, she had a way of turning slightly, shifting her weight onto her right hip, and lifting her left heel off the floor so as to point her knee across her right leg and thereby somewhat cover herself with her thigh.

Physically they were so very different, one slender, the other full-bodied. And they not only looked different, they actually felt entirely different. Thus, every instance of making love with Wilson produced a series of tactile shocks, somehow like those you get when you drive a different automobile and aren't yet used to a tighter brake pedal and a clutch that engages at a different point. Joan was so slight, she always felt frail in my arms, and though Joan was not an unusually small-breasted woman, Wilson seemed unusually large-breasted. More important than the difference in size, though, Joan's breasts were soft. Wilson's were so firm I thought of them as almost hard.

Between their legs, they were different too, Joan so sparse-haired and small, Wilson so lush and so large. I had to fight the impulse to withdraw my hand every time I touched Wilson there, not because the sensation wasn't pleasing, but because years of touching one woman made touching another seem alien, momentarily, foolishly of course, even wrong.

I also had to adjust to a difference in Wilson's sexual habits and desires. From the time we were teenagers Joan and I had talked to each other frankly about what might please us and what probably wouldn't. This was the result of her doing, I'm sure, and not mine. She never hesitated to tell me what she wanted to do, how she wanted to act out a fantasy, what her fertile imagination had most recently devised, where she wanted me to touch her and how. I asked Wilson directly what she liked, and she responded, cooing, that she liked everything I did. I asked her to tell me how to please her, and she whispered that sex wasn't for talking about, but was for doing. Joan was so partial to oral sex, that save for our efforts at procreation, we seldom had it any other way. I found it astonishing, then, that I spent what amounted to nine days in bed with Wilson without having oral sex even once. The one unbidden time I tried to introduce an act of oral lovemaking, she pulled me away from her with the gentle remonstrance, "Come here, honey, you don't want to do that."

The difference between them was profound but in the end perhaps inconsequential. Making love with Joan was like downhill skiing, flat-out, breathless, exhilarating. Making love with Wilson was like curling up on a rug in the ski lodge, warm and cozy before the fire.

On New Year's Eve we paid for a champagne buffet at Mary Mahoney's. The food was good and plentiful, and the waiters kept our stemmed glasses full of sparkling wine. Shortly before midnight we walked down to the beach to watch a fireworks display put on by soldiers from nearby Keesler Air Force Base. It was a little cold, and we put our arms around each other to warm ourselves against the chilling breeze blowing off the water. As the first rockets burst against the black sky, and I passed from my fortieth into my forty-first year, Wilson turned and raised her face to me. She tasted pleasantly of the champagne, and she opened her mouth to me. Kissing her, I thought, was like falling through dreamscapes into pillows of satin.

*   *   *

When I arrived back home New Year's night, I was greeted with an ominous sign about the year and the life which lay in front of me and in front of the city which was my home. I noticed as I went to the breadloaf-shaped mailbox which sat on my brick front steps that a hole had been punched in its top. At first I thought this an act of petty vandalism perpetrated by one of the neighborhood teens. But when I started to pull the week's accumulation of mail from the box, I realized that the hole penetrated the letters and magazines and bills that lay inside. And at the bottom of the mailbox, in a dent of metal that had finally stopped its flight, I found a .38 caliber lead slug.

The likeliest explanation for this lay in a menacing, stupid, absolutely reprehensible habit of my fellow New Orleanians. In particular, though by no means exclusively, black New Orleanians like to stride onto their porches on New Year's Eve, or on July Fourth, or at Mardi Gras, and fire their pistols in the air in celebration. This activity, a kind of poor man's fireworks, has been deplored repeatedly by city leaders and the media. But it goes on. Every holiday season there are reports of bullets falling through roofs and car tops, doing untold damage. One day, of course, a celebratory bullet was going to fall into somebody's skull, just as I now assumed it had fallen into my mailbox. And then maybe we'd learn our lesson. But probably not even then. For the joy of the cracking shot always outweighs any responsibility for the bullet's flight.

Of course, I couldn't be certain that my mailbox had been damaged by a partying New Year's Eve gunman. So I thought again of the pin-striped black man who had stopped to ask directions and who, Wilson thought, had been carrying a pistol in his belt. And I remembered the subsequent time I thought I'd seen his white Cadillac turning off my block just as I arrived home. Was it possible that this man had come into my yard and fired a bullet into my mailbox. For what reason? To leave me what kind of message?

CHAPTER SEVENTEEN

In the first weeks of the new year, Wilson Malt became the one stabilizing factor in my life. I had sought for months to find a solution to the puzzle of the burglary at my home the previous summer. But all I found were more puzzles: missing files, the strange behavior of Tammy Dieter-White and Johnny Chambers. Perhaps Amy Stuart would eventually find a lead for me in her notebooks, but through the holidays she hadn't had the time to go through them. And so I was stymied. This search had been my companion, but the search had gone nowhere. Now I had Wilson. She arrived with her winter clothes at my house late on New Year's night. Within a week she brought a recipe book and her favorite pots and pans.

Living with Wilson required a series of adjustments—on both our parts, of course. But since the house we were living in was mine, I myopically tended to see myself as having to do most of the adjusting. Wilson needed closet space, naturally. And that simple enough need produced our first tiny squabble. My little house wasn't long on closet space to start with. But Wilson didn't give up her own apartment on the Westbank, so I could probably have made space in my own closet for the things she wanted to keep at my house. My closet was certainly full of pants I could no longer squeeze into and shirts I no longer wore. Lots of my clothes could have been donated to Goodwill without affecting my functioning wardrobe. But I didn't think to create space in my own closet. And worse, I couldn't think of anything else either.

For a couple of days Wilson's winter skirts and blouses, still on hangers, lay across the dining room table where I'd draped them when she first arrived on New Year's night. Finally, she asked where I'd like her to put them. I was absolutely dumbfounded. I *knew* the obvious answer. But I was resolute in refusing to discover it. For Joan's closet was even more tightly packed than mine. Her job had required a greater degree of dressiness, and she had always tried to keep reasonably current with ever changing women's fashions.

"Is there room in here?" Wilson inquired. She was standing in front of Joan's closet. I was lying on the bed reading. When I didn't respond, Wilson opened the closet door and studied its cramped contents, occasionally running her hand along the fabric of a jacket or suit. Holding one of Joan's cocktail dresses to examine at arm's length, she finally put the point bluntly, "Why don't we give Joan's clothes to Catholic Charities or the Salvation Army or something. It's a shame to let such nice things go to waste."

There was nothing aggressive or baldly insensitive about Wilson's proposition. But I was horrified. "That's absolutely out of the question," I said.

She turned to me with the squint of question marks in her eyes. "Why?" she asked.

"Because . . ." I said. "Because . . . because, I don't know."

She sat on the bed next to me, pushed the paper I had been reading down on my lap and took both of my hands in hers. "Honey," Wilson said, "God knows I understand how much you loved Joan, but she's been gone over a year now and you . . .

"Just throw her fucking clothes in the garbage," I shouted. I shoved Wilson's hands away from me and abruptly got up. "I wasn't married to her goddamned clothes." As I strode from the bedroom to my study, I added cruelly, "Anyway, Joan and I had our best times when she wasn't wearing any clothes."

Wilson didn't respond to that needlessly mean remark. I think she just sat for a while on the bed where I'd left her. As I sat at my desk and stirred through the new month's stack of bills, I heard the bed springs squeak a time or two, presumably as she shifted her weight. After a time she came into the study and stood to the side of my desk so that I had to spin around in my chair to face her.

In a soft voice, she said, "I just need a . . ."

"You're absolutely right about this, Wilson," I said in a matter-of-fact tone. "You're absolutely right. Do what you want with Joan's things. I really don't care."

I did care, of course. And though I recognized that the reaction was irrational, I felt as if each box of clothes we loaded into Wilson's car to be donated to Goodwill was another piece of my own flesh sawed away without anesthetic.

*　　　*　　　*

In ways rather astonishing to me, though, Wilson was a most capable and industrious housemate. For one thing, she liked to cook, and thus for the first time in nearly twenty years I began to eat at home regularly. I never learned to do much more than heat soup and grill a steak. After ten and eleven hour days at the office, Joan hated the bother of cooking. So for most of my adult life, I had taken the vast majority of my meals in restaurants. My love affair with New Orleans's great dining establishments hardly ended, but I found I liked the routine and convenience of eating most meals at home. Wilson's skills in the kitchen didn't make that change very difficult.

Wilson was also incredibly self-reliant around the house. Joan and I had long had Delinda Dupre, of course, to do the major cleaning chores. And Joan was both relentlessly neat in her own right and pretty effective at goading me out of an innate slothfulness. But it never occurred to either of us to attempt serious handymanning. If the water pipes burst after an infrequent freeze, we called a plumber. If an appliance went on the fritz, we called a repairman. Delinda continued her once-a-week cleaning chores now. But if we had problems other than basic dirt, Wilson's instinct, in contrast to Joan's and mine, was first to try to solve such problems on her own.

At the end of our first week together, I came home from a screening she hadn't attended with me to find her laboring over the toilet in the back bathroom. Her white T-shirt, stretched tight over her bosom, showed dark circles of sweat under each arm. Her pleated dungarees were rolled up to the bottoms of her calves. The bathroom floor was wet all around the toilet, and Wilson was cranking a plumber's snake into the bowl.

"What in the hell are you doing?" I asked.

She mopped at her damp forehead with the back of her wrist. "This goddamned toilet is stopped up," she said, "and I'm gonna unplug it if I have to get a snake that will stretch from here to Sewerage and Water Board." She explained that when she'd discovered the problem she'd first tried a plunger and when that didn't work she had called her dad and borrowed his plumber's snake.

"Your father owns a plumber's snake?" I remarked.

"There isn't a tool smaller than a crane my father doesn't own," she replied.

I laughed and inquired, "Why didn't you just call a plumber? Lot less trouble."

"And a lot more money," she responded.

I shrugged. "So what?"

"Plumber didn't plug this toilet," she said. "I did."

"What's that mean?" I asked. "Although I'm not sure I want to know."

"I flushed a goddamn Tampax," she said.

"Is that a problem?" I asked.

"Is this toilet stopped up?" She continued cranking the snake.

"I think Joan always flushed her tampons," I said. "I mean, I don't think we had a conversation about them, but . . . she must have flushed them."

"Yeah, well," Wilson grunted with her work. "Did you have problems with stopped up toilets?"

"No," I said.

Wilson twisted her head in a gesture of resignation to life's inevitable injustices, then a smile started to play across her lips. "Know what elephants use for tampons?" she asked.

I had to laugh at the mere fact she was telling a joke in the middle of her obvious aggravation. "No," I said. "What do elephants use for tampons?"

"Sheep," she replied.

I laughed more loudly.

"See, that's just another difference between me and Joan. She was small and could get away with flushing her petite size tampons. I'm a fucking elephant woman who has to moonlight as a plumber because I was stupid enough to flush one of my goddamned sheep."

The next day, when we went to do our grocery shopping at the Superstore, she steered our basket down the aisle containing feminine hygiene products with the remark, "Better do some sheep herding here while I've got the chance." After that day, Wilson took to noting on our grocery list her need for a fresh box of tampons with the single word *sheep* and began referring to her menstrual period as "straddling sheep," "Bo Peep time," or "pogoing fleece."

In some respects, she *was* a woman after Joan's own bawdy heart.

*   *   *

Wilson was there for me now every night as I faced the hours at home that had proved so agonizing after Joan's death. She cooked, and we ate together, and she talked with me while I washed the dishes. She provided me a sounding board for engaging my problems and through her companionship helped distract me from them.

Wilson got me back into a routine of regular exercise. She wasn't the runner that Joan was, but she liked to take long brisk walks and quickly started insisting that I walk with her. Wilson's favorite walking course stretched along the Mississippi River levee which rose on the other side of Leake Avenue just a block and half from my house. Afternoons after work and weekends she would hound me into a sweatsuit and jogging shoes and lead the way across the railroad tracks and up the grassy slope to the shell path on the levee's summit. Light permitting, we tried to walk for an hour, far enough upriver to take us past Ochsner Hospital before we turned back.

We liked the upriver route because it took us by the horse stables where Leake turns into River Road. Those stables, we discovered to our amazement when we first started walking, also boarded a full-grown camel. The second time we saw the camel, the day was overcast and New Orleans cold, the temperature in the low forties. The camel was out in a corral behind the paddocks, milling about with his equine stablemates. The horses kept their heads down, but the camel looked up at us as we passed and seemed to follow our progress with curiosity. Every time he exhaled, his breath condensed into a gray cloud of mist. So we took to calling him Smokey. And despite the scores of different people who walked and ran the same course along the levee every day, Wilson and I liked to pretend that Smokey was a secret known only to the two of us.

Occasionally, Smokey's bearded, overall-clad owner ("Who else but a hippie would own a camel?" was the way Wilson jokingly put it) would take Smokey for walks on the levee path. And we were always struck by the creature's patience and his gentleness. We had both heard stories that camels were ill-tempered beasts given to biting those they could reach and spitting at those they couldn't. But "our" Smokey wasn't that way at all. He always drew small crowds when his owner walked him outside the corral. Dogs sniffed at him and nipped at his heels. Children scurried about between his legs. And all the while he stood impervious to the stir he inevitably caused, twisting his head as if in wonder as each new person arrived to gawk at and pet him.

Smokey was more animated when he was alone in the corral with the horses. He galumped around in that awkward stride characteristic to his species and was forever bumping or nuzzling his stablemates. One day in a pose that would have made a wonderful photograph, Wilson and I saw Smokey muzzle to muzzle with a horse pal, engaging in an activity that could only be called kissing.

At home afterwards I remarked, "Poor dumb Smokey. He's evidently too ignorant to realize he isn't a horse." And after a moment's reflection I added, "Or maybe it's the horses who are too dumb to realize that Smokey's a camel."

Wilson said, "Maybe Smokey's pretty lucky actually. If there were a bunch of camels at the stable, the horses probably wouldn't be nearly so friendly."

Such idylls as our levee walks were illustrative of the ways in which Wilson and I sought to form a bond with one another. And at times, despite the differences in our ages and aspects of our sensibilities, I thought we might have a chance to forge a lasting relationship. But it was not easy for me to relate to a woman other than Joan. Joan and I were together so long that all the rough edges between us had long since been worn smooth. Though this was entirely inflexibly petty of me, I realize, it seemed to me now that many of Wilson's habits were "wrong." Wrong meaning different from Joan's, of course.

First came a struggle over bathroom identity. I wanted there to be a *my* bathroom and a *her* bathroom. Mine was mine and hers was Joan's. But this was a concept she didn't quite grasp at first, child as she was of a family with eight children. Then when Wilson had been living at my house a week or two, I came home from a screening one evening and found her hanging her lingerie all over the shower curtain rod and from every other place in her bathroom that could serve as a hook. Pairs of panties, bras and slips dangled from light fixtures and toilet handles and lay draped across bathtub and sink.

"This place looks like the lady's tent at a Turkish bazaar," I said.

"Yeah," she replied, fatigue in her voice. "I'm just a Middle-Eastern washer woman at heart."

"Why don't you just put all this stuff in the dryer?" I asked.

"Oh, I never put my underwear in the dryer," she explained. "I wash it out by hand and then hang it up to drip dry."

"You don't even wash it in the washer?"

"Nope."

"Why not? Joan just threw her underwear in the washer and then in the dryer. Right along with everything else."

A flash of anger flamed momentarily into Wilson's eyes, but then she breathed deeply, sighed and said, "I've found that the elastic in my underwear dries out and cracks when I put it in the dryer. And I've found that it's scratchy when I machine wash and then drip dry it. So now I do it by hand. It's sort of a pain, but it's no big deal."

"Sure makes the bathroom into a mess," I said.

"Well, then I bet you're glad we got all the business about the his and hers bathrooms straightened out."

I shrugged and then said under my breath as I turned to leave her to her work, "Joan's underwear never seemed to crack or scratch."

Her sharp tone stopped me at the bathroom door, "Hey, Mike, it's gonna take some time evidently. But eventually you're gonna have to figure out that Joan and I aren't alike about everything. She had a tiny little butt, and I got a big sloppy ass. She had pert little breasts, and I got big saggy tits."

"Hey that's not true. You're at least as fit as she was. And anyway it's not what I . . ."

"She was modern and she was efficient and she didn't sweat and she didn't stain her underwear and she probably only washed it . . ."

"Stop it," I said.

"No, you stop it. Stop comparing us all the time. Joan was my friend. She was a good person. Don't make me end up hating her because you think the two of us ought to be just alike."

Sometimes I feel like one of those out of control drivers who keeps swerving from one side of the road to the other, always over-reacting to the dangers of first one side and the other. Only days later we had another little flare-up that I ignited in a very different way. Wilson had fixed what I thought was a particularly delicious meal. It was simple enough, I guess, just a roasted chicken breast, deboned and served in cream sauce over angel hair pasta. But I loved it, and despite Wilson's protestations, I kept raving about it all through the meal, bite after scrumptious bite.

"So all right, already," Wilson said finally. "I'm glad you liked it, but it was nothing. Really."

"I guess I'm just not used to home cooking," I said. "Joan and I never cooked at home."

"I know. You've told me. But Joan was an extraordinarily busy woman."

"She was also a terrible cook."

"Oh, I don't believe that," Wilson said.

"Really, she was," I said. "She couldn't even boil water. When we first got married, she used to try to make toast for us every morning for breakfast. Burned it every time. She was amazing. Never could understand that a stove burner had more than two positions—on and off. Used to cook lima beans. How hard is that, right? Scorched. Every time."

"Stop it, Mike," Wilson said.

"Stop what?"

"Stop making this show of putting Joan down."

"I'm not putting her down. She was a terrible cook, and I'm just illustrating the ways in which she was terrible. When we were out at U.C.L.A., she made this Chinese dish for some friends who were coming over. Chicken ptomaine or something. Sauce was okay. But she fucked up the rice totally. She must of have run it under hot water instead of boiling it. It was so crunchy it was like eating pretzels. Only not that tasty."

"Are you gonna stop it?" Wilson said.

"Don't you think it's a funny story?"

"It's a funny story. But I don't think you're telling it because it's a funny story."

"Why am I telling it then?"

"You're telling it to show me you think I do some things better than Joan."

"And what's wrong with that?"

We had finished eating, and Wilson began to scrape and stack together the dishes on the table.

"What's wrong with that?" I repeated.

Wilson carefully folded her napkin into a perfect rectangle and laid it in front of her. "What's wrong is that Mike Barnett loved his wife with all his heart. And I don't want to be the woman he remembers as making him, even for a fleeting second, sully that wife's memory."

I pondered that for a moment and got up from the table to begin moving the dishes to the sink. After a time, I said, "You're a smart woman, Wilson Malt. I hope you know that."

She came and stood behind me at the sink, put her arms around my waist and laid her face against the back of my neck and said softly into my hair, "Somebody really smart once said that new love is like riding a bucking bronco; it's a thrill, but you got to do your damnedest to hold on."

I turned around to her and kissed her on her forehead. "Who said that?" I asked.

"Wasn't it you?"

"No," I laughed.

"Oh," she said. "Then I guess maybe it was me."

*   *   *

The placid nature of my three-week idyll with Wilson ended on the evening of January 15. It was Martin Luther King's birthday, and I had just finished the final revisions on my *Mississippi Burning* review which would run that Friday concurrent with the picture's New Orleans opening. The phone rang and it was Amy Stuart.

"I finally got a chance to look through my notes on the Jefferson Magnet story," she said. "I'm sorry it took so long. First it was the holidays and then . . ."

"That's okay, Amy. I hardly expected you to put your life on hold for this."

"I had to comb through a whole bunch of stuff," she said, "given that the story played itself out like it did over such a long period of time."

"I hope you didn't go to too much trouble," I said.

"Oh, no, it was kind of pain, but it was sort of fun too, if you know what I mean. I just didn't want you to think I'd blown the whole thing off or something."

I felt as if a tiny foot were kicking at my insides as I asked the next question, my casualness all a pretense. "So, what did you find? Anything interesting?"

"I don't know," Amy said. "The whole thing's been a long time, and my memory isn't what it used to be. But I found my interview notes with a man named Cheney Hickman."

"Just a second," I said. "Let me get something to write with."

When I had written down Cheney Hickman's name, I told her to go ahead and she said, "I can barely recall the guy. He was older. Used to be in the fishing business. Owned some land that once figured in the Jefferson Magnet business."

"So why do you think he might be helpful," I inquired.

"Because my notes contain the observation, 'Manner implies he knows more than he's telling. Particularly in second conversation.'"

Amy's connection to Cheney Hickman proved a very crucial lead indeed.

PART FOUR

CHAPTER EIGHTEEN

Cheney Hickman owned the wide expanse of empty land that stretched from West End Boulevard across to Pontchartrain Boulevard and was bordered on the north and south by Robert E. Lee and Harrison Avenue. For a time in the early eighties, a portion of Hickman's property had been under consideration as the site for Thomas Jefferson Magnet School.

The phone number Amy Stuart gave me for Hickman connected me with a company in the marina that claimed never to have heard of the man. But I found a residential listing for a Cheney Hickman on Chickasaw Avenue in Bucktown, Jefferson Parish. Hickman answered when I called. I identified myself as a reporter for *The States-Tribune* and ascertained that I had indeed reached the Mr. Cheney Hickman who owned the West End tract. I asked if I might stop by to see him at his home that night. He agreed, but he told me to get there early because he didn't much stay up after nine anymore.

Bucktown is one of the oldest neighborhoods in Jefferson Parish. Located just across the Seventeenth Street Canal from the marina area of the city proper, and curving along the south shore of Lake Pontchartrain, Bucktown was originally a community of working class people, many involved in some aspect of the seafood industry. Certain aspects of that original character abided to this day, though the long tentacles of more middle-class Metairie had deposited four-bedroom, two-and-half-bath, ranchstyle brick houses onto many of the blocks where frame houses and even fishing camps once stood.

Cheney Hickman's house, which occupied the entire north half of its block, looked as if it belonged in a stand of Mississippi woods, rather than in an urban area of one and a half million people. The unpainted wood house was shaded by live oaks, whose wide canopy of leaves was so thick that only patches of grass grew anywhere in the unfenced front yard. The house's tin roof swept down from a high pitch and over the supporting posts of porches both in front and behind. A weeping willow stood directly in front of the house and provided a center point for a semi-circular, shell driveway that arched off Chickasaw up to the front steps of the house and back to the street. Just beyond the top of the arch, parked so that its back bumper didn't impede access to the wooden steps which rose from the shell to the wood-slatted porch, was a black 1988 Cadillac El Dorado.

I arrived just after seven p.m. and pulled my car to a stop behind the Cadillac. But before I could get out, someone called out to me, "I wouldn't leave a nice shiny car sittin' just where that one is if I were you. Not even seein' as it's Japanese."

"Excuse me?" I said in response.

In the dimness of a faint yellow porch light, I spotted a man on the porch sitting in a tattered cloth rocker to the right of the steps. A white fringe of close-cropped hair showed out from underneath a red baseball cap that was pulled down snug on his head.

"I'm advisin' you to back your car up there," the man said.

I was mystified by this, but I put the Camry in reverse and backed it up twenty-five feet or so.

"I'm Mike Barnett. From *The States-Tribune*," I said as I stepped up on the porch.

The man didn't respond.

"I called you earlier today," I explained. "You said I could stop on by early this evening."

The night was chilly now that the sun was down, all the more so under the porch roof where rays of sunlight never fell. The man was dressed warmly enough, I guessed, in overalls and a wool shirt with the cuffs folded back to reveal the white sleeves of cotton long johns.

Still, I was surprised that he would want to sit outside at this time of the evening. I stepped up to him and extended my hand.

"Mike Barnett," I repeated, hoping for some assent of recognition.

"You said that once," he responded. "And whatever else I am, I ain't deaf."

"Are you Mr. Cheney Hickman?" I asked.

"I guess I can admit to that much," he responded and accepted my hand.

The hand I shook was large and strong. Thick calluses scraped against my softer palm. Cheney Hickman was a man, I estimated, in his early seventies, lean and sinewy in the fashion of a man who had done hard physical labor for a lifetime. He didn't look like a man who would own what surely had to be one of the most valuable undeveloped pieces of real estate in New Orleans. He hadn't shaved in a day or two. A white stubble covered his angular face, including his bulging left cheek. He was chewing tobacco. And when he now launched a missile of spit over the side of the porch and onto the shell driveway, I realized why he'd suggested I move my car out of harm's way.

Hickman hadn't asked me to sit, but he pointed with a thumb now at a chair to his right and I sat in it, next to him, the two of us staring out at the dark yard.

"Cold?" Hickman asked.

"A little, yes," I admitted.

I rubbed my hands up and down the sleeves of my blue blazer. Hickman spit again.

"We'll go inside in a minute," he said. "Got a fire goin' there in the front room. I'm only sittin' out here myself because Mother don't like me chewin' in the house. Can't say as I blame her actually. Nasty stuff chewin' tobacco. Gotta spit in a jar if I'm inside. And I don't think that's any more polite than she does."

He spit again.

"Picked up chewin' tobacco when I first went out on the shrimp boats," he said. "Fifty-six years ago. Right out of high school and not wantin' to go to work with my daddy down on the river front. Chewin's not such nasty business out on the water. Just spit over the side. Mother never liked the fact I chewed, and I reckon that's why I kept goin' out with the boats a long time after I had to. Chew all day. Didn't even want to at night. Not like that anymore. Fleet's sold. I just work in that garden behind the house. Mother won't let me chew back there. Says she wouldn't eat what I spent months spittin' on."

Hickman laughed at his account of his wife's concerns for vegetable hygiene. And then he spit again and stood up.

"Well, let's go in," he said, "and hear what you've come around for."

He showed me into his living room and pointed me to a seat in a wooden rocking chair in front of the fire. To the left of my chair was a stack of old newspapers that the Hickmans presumably saved to help in getting their fire started every morning.

"I'm gonna just go spit this plug in the commode," he said. "Mother don't like for me to spit in the fire. Says it stinks. Probably right, too. Used to just spit it out in the yard till a neighbor's dog ate a plug and like to died."

He laughed, evidently at the memory of his neighbor's sick dog.

"Served the dumb mutt right, don't you think? Never liked dogs. Specially never liked a neighbor's dog in my yard. But then the bastard was gonna sue me for makin' his dog sick, and it's easier just to flush a plug down the commode. I'll be right back."

Somewhere in the back of the house I heard a toilet flush, and shortly Hickman joined me and sat in a wing-back chair across from me.

"Okay," he said. "Let's hear it."

"You are the Cheney Hickman who owns the West End neutral ground?" I asked.

"Told you that on the phone earlier today," he said, his tone registering less irritation than his words.

"I just didn't want to be bothering you unnecessarily," I said.

"You ain't bothering me, yet," he remarked. "And the land ain't a neutral ground. Though people always refer to it that way."

"A colleague of mine at the paper," I explained, "Amy Stuart, talked to you some years ago about the prospects of locating Thomas Jefferson Magnet School on your property."

"I remember well," Hickman said. "Talked to me twice about two weeks apart. Sometime after Thanksgiving in 1980. I remember the year because I was negotiatin' to sell my fleet then."

"Your fleet?"

"Shrimp boats. Started with just one. Had eleven when I sold 'em off. Closed the deal in February, 1981. That's when I retired, I guess you could say."

"How long have you had the West End tract?"

"Bought it in 1952. Coast Guard owned it before me. Part of their Lake Pontchartrain Installation. Korean War was on. Guess the government needed cash more than some parcels of empty land. I kinda thought myself patriotic buyin' the property at the time. Had all the shrimp boats I could manage. Lake was a big bowl full of shrimp in those days. Puttin' my nets down in it was like scoopin' up potfuls of money. I had more money than I knew what to do with. Decided to put it into land. Somebody told me that's what smart folks did when they had money burnin' a hole in their pockets. Coast Guard put the place up on sealed bids. I went and made me one and damned if I didn't win. Got the whole plot for two hundred thousand dollars. But I was just a dumb fisherman. Bid twenty thousand more than anybody else."

"Why've you held onto it all these years?"

"Well," he said. "I didn't need to sell it is the main reason. I always made more money than I could spend off my shrimp boats. Least I did until the lake got fished out. Then it started gettin' tougher and tougher. Had to move my operations base over to Pass Christian. And that was a pain in my backside about every time the sun come up. In the late seventies the Vietnamese came in and that made things tougher still. Though I gotta say I admire those little slanty-eyed bastards. They know what a full day's work is, just like I did when I started out. But tell the truth, I hung on to my West End land in most part because I always felt a little stupid for payin' so much for it in the first place. Got a lot of offers for the plot through the years, but I was suspicious of every one. Didn't want to get taken on the back end, like I sort of did on the front."

"Ms. Stuart says you led her to believe you were close to a deal with Sheldon Retif that would have located Thomas Jefferson High on the West End plot."

Hickman smiled at me, and his eyes gleamed in the firelight.

"Oh, we were damned close all right. I was in the process of gettin' out of the shrimp business. Kinda shuttin' things down for my so-called

golden years. Figured I might as well liquidate everything. Keep my
kids from havin' to do it when me 'n' Mother finally kicked off."

"What happened?" I asked. "What caused the deal to fall through?"

Hickman got up from his chair, shifted another log onto the fire,
and moved it around with a poker until he got it situated where it
would catch and burn. He turned toward me and warmed his back
against the fire.

"Pretty simple matter," he said. "Mr. Retif wouldn't meet my price."

"Amy remembers getting the feeling that you were awfully close to
a deal with Retif the first time she talked to you."

"It's what she put in the paper, isn't it?"

"But the second time she talked to you, after the deal fell through,
she felt like you knew more than you were telling."

"Said that, did she?" Hickman said.

"Well, something like that, yes, sir."

Hickman laughed and returned to his chair, rubbing his hands
together.

"Well, I didn't *know* more than I told Ms. Stuart. But I figured. And
I still figure I figured right."

I cleared my throat.

"Could I get you to tell me what you figured?" I asked.

"You might could," Hickman said, "if you tell me why you want to
know."

Explaining my reasons could have taken all night, of course. I didn't
know what I should tell him, and what I best not.

"My wife handled a law suit against Sheldon Retif," I said. "She died
about a year ago, well more like a year and a half ago now. And . . ."

"Your wife was Joan Barnett," Hickman said, "poor Tom Grieve's
lawyer."

"Yes, sir, that's correct."

"And she's dead now? Tom Grieve's dead now, too."

"Yes, sir, she is. They both are."

"And you want to know about my negotiations because of your wife."

"Yes, sir. In a nutshell, that's correct."

"I see," Hickman said.

There was a short pause in which the only sound in the room was
the crackling of the fire. I squirmed in my chair, sore-backed and

achy. I felt swollen, and I felt that the fate of seven months of digging hung on what Hickman said next.

"Well," he said, "I'd judge you have fair enough reason for wanting to know what I figured, so I'll tell you. For what it's worth."

"I'd appreciate very much your telling me," I said.

"Retif came to me with a proposition to purchase a piece of the West End tract along in the spring of 1980 and . . ."

"The school board didn't grant Retif Realty its Certificate 34 for building Thomas Jefferson Magnet until August," I interrupted.

"Well mind you now, Retif didn't mention anything to me about building a school. Not at the time. Said he wanted to 'develop' the property, whatever the hell that means. Build a shopping center on it or something is what I figured at the time."

"It's much too big for a shopping center," I said.

"Oh, he didn't offer to buy the whole tract," Hickman said. "Just the southernmost piece of it from Harrison to about where Bragg Street could be cut through."

"I see," I said. "That's just about the right amount of land for the school."

"Maybe," Hickman said. "But I don't think Retif was ever really interested in buying just that one section."

"Why did he enter negotiations for it then?"

"Two reasons, I figured. First, he wanted to see if I was willing to sell at all. Second, he wanted to see about how much he was gonna have to pay."

"How do you, uh, figure this?" I asked.

"Well we talked for a while about the southernmost section, see. Then I didn't hear anything from the man for a couple or three months. I'd about forgot about the whole thing when he gets back in touch with me again."

"When was this?"

"Sometime in July."

"Jesus Christ," I said.

I looked at Mr. Hickman, fearful that he wasn't the kind of man who took the Lord's name in vain.

"Excuse me," I said. "It's just that July is still a month before the school board awarded Retif the builder's prerogative."

Mr. Hickman laughed. "You forget," he said, "I was a man who earned his living at sea. I'm sure you've heard the expression curse like a sailor. Not that I'm all that bad myself. Mother wouldn't have had it. But there's little I haven't heard a man say in my life. And I've learned you don't take the measure of a man by what he says, but by what he does."

"Anyway," I said. "Sorry to have interrupted you. What did Retif want in July?"

"Wanted to buy the whole kit 'n' kaboodle."

I was perplexed by this revelation.

"Why would he want to do that?" I asked.

"It's what he wanted all along," Mr. Hickman said. "Way I figure it, the discussion we had earlier he was just feelin' me out at that point. Like I say, I was suspicious enough when it come to that land in the first place. When Retif came back sayin' he wanted to buy all the land instead of just a piece of it, I was mighty suspicious then."

"Did Retif say what he planned to do with the property?"

"Said same as before. Wanted to 'develop' it."

"Didn't mention anything about building a school, though?"

"Never mentioned anything about building any school. Not then. Not later in the fall."

"Not even after August when he had clear title to the Certificate 34?"

"Nope. Building a school was never a part of any of our discussions. Course, no need to have been. Remember that. I might ask him what he was gonna do with the land, but he wasn't under any obligation to tell me."

"Did you ask him?"

"Course I did," Mr. Hickman said with a chortle. "Wouldn't you? I'm as curious as the next person."

"But Retif wouldn't say anything other than he was going to 'develop' it?" I asked.

"Absolutely all he'd say. Maybe mentioned the shopping center this time."

"But at some point you tied the whole thing to the new magnet high school."

"Damn straight I did. I figure Retif had me pegged for some dumb redneck who'd baked his brains to mush haulin' shrimp nets his whole life. See, when he come back to me with an offer for the whole plot, he wanted to pay less an acre than we'd talked about for just the one section down by Harrison. Been a time I'da taken his offer and been glad to gotten it. Then he made some nonsense noise about 'bein' willin' to take the whole thing off my hands,' if, he said, I'd be willin' to let the whole thing go 'wholesale rather than retail.'"

I started to ask Mr. Hickman to elaborate on this last point, but he glanced at his watch, abruptly stood up and rubbed his hands together.

"Eight o'clock," he said. "I always have myself a toddy at eight o'clock. Drink it any earlier, I don't stay awake till nine. Mother says a man who drinks before eight in the evening is a man a woman can't count on. Don't know that she's right. But don't know that she's wrong either."

Mr. Hickman walked from the room, and I could hear cabinets being opened and closed in the kitchen. He returned momentarily with two glasses, each holding three ice cubes, and a bottle of Jack Daniels Black. He handed me one of the glasses.

"You a drinkin' man, Mr. Barnett?" he asked.

The question struck me like a body blow.

"Yes, sir," I said. "Sometimes even before eight in the evening."

"Well, now," he remarked, "I don't know that I can approve of that. If Mother were here, I might have her speak to you about it. Spoke to me when I was a young man like yourself. And I been okay ever since."

"Where is your wife?" I asked.

He poured enough whiskey in my glass to cover the ice cubes.

"I hope Jack Daniels is okay," he said. "Don't keep anything else in the house."

"It's fine," I said, though, of course, I almost never drank bourbon.

Mr. Hickman poured a like amount of whiskey in his own glass and sat back in his chair.

"I lost Mother three years ago this past June," he said. "Cancer of the liver. She went in three months after they found it. Couldn't do a thing for her. I've got a bad habit of speakin' as if she was still with me. I know that. But we lived together a long time. And you get used to sayin' things a certain way. And they don't sound right if you say them some other way. If you know what I mean."

"Yes," I said. "I do."

We each sipped at our whiskeys for a moment. I listened to the fire crackle. I presume Mr. Hickman did the same.

After a moment, he said, "So, where were we, Mr. Barnett?"

I glanced at my notebook.

"You were telling me how Retif was trying to get you to sell the whole West End tract at a price less per acre than you had discussed for the southernmost section."

"Right," he said, "Said he wanted to buy wholesale rather than retail."

Mr. Hickman laughed at the memory.

"And I gather you were having none of that," I said.

"Damn straight I wasn't. I figured he was up to something, see. And I wanted to know what. So I stalled him for a while. Hired me a snoop to find out what he was up to."

"A snoop?"

"A private detective. Man named Crowell. George Crowell. Used to be a cop."

"And what did Mr. Crowell find out for you?" I asked.

"Found out all about the magnet-school business."

"This was still before the school board awarded Retif the Certificate 34?"

"About two weeks."

"So what did you do when you realized what Retif wanted the land for?"

"I raised the price. Twenty-five percent. And that's over what we were talkin' about originally. Not this bull wholesale business he'd been talkin' about."

"And Retif didn't say no."

"Damn straight he didn't say no. Poor mouthed around a little bit about how I was driving such a hard bargain. But I could see he was gonna take it."

"But he didn't?"

"No. I didn't."

I looked up at him, puzzled.

"Wait a minute," I said. "*You* backed out on the deal? Why?"

"It's like I told you. I had this spot in me that felt embarrassed about that land all along. Once I saw Retif would buy the land at the price I was askin', I started wonderin' just how high he'd go. Then I got to askin' myself a very important question. Retif could build that school on the section of land down off Harrison. What'd he need with all the rest of it?"

"I've been wondering the same thing myself."

"Well the answer is plenty simple enough. Retif wasn't ever all that interested in building the school. There was money in building the school. But there wasn't significant money. The big money really was in development. Retif knew it. That's how he came to be a rich man."

Mr. Hickman drained his drink and poured himself a second drink, smaller than the first, just enough to cover the shrunken ice cubes.

"Always make your second smaller than your first," he said. "And always make your second your last. Two rules to live by, Mother says."

He raised the bottle to me in silent inquiry if I wanted to join him in a second round.

"No thanks," I said.

I sucked on an ice cube.

"Mr. Hickman," I said, "Pardon me for being dense. Which I'm sure I am about this stuff. But you backed out of the deal because you figured out that Retif wanted to develop your property. But that's what he said he wanted to do all along."

Mr. Hickman smiled at me and then sipped slowly at his whiskey.

"I just put two and two together," he said. "And it added up to millions."

"You're going to have to elaborate, sir. I'm sorry."

"Rather than my just spillin' it out to you, Mr. Barnett, why don't I let you figure it yourself."

He pointed at the stack of newspapers to my left.

"Pick up a fistful of that paper," he instructed.

Mystified, I did so.

"Now thumb through there till you find a real estate section. Don't matter what date. Any date'll do just as fine as the next."

I shuffled aside newspaper sections until I came to one titled "Real Estate."

"Here's one," I told him.

"Fine. Now look in it until you find the listings section that contains houses for sale in the Lakefront area of the city."

"Okay," I said, when I'd located the correct page.

"Now scan down until you find the specific listings for Lake Magnolias." Lake Magnolias was the fancy new subdivision directly across Leon C. Simon from the University of New Orleans.

I ran my finger quickly down several columns looking for the right heading.

"Got it," I said when I found it.

"Start reading the ads," he commanded.

I did. The first one read:

> ENCHANTING LAKE MAGNOLIAS
> Splendid 4 bdrm, 2 and 1/2 bath home.
> Jacuzzi. 2 car garage. Near Jefferson
> Magnet. 5814 Wainwright. $290,000. Betty
> Daniels. 555-8177.

The second one read:

> NEW IN LAKE MAGNOLIAS
> Spacious floor plan. 4 bdrm, 3 bath. Master
> suite has f/p, huge walk-in closet, jacuzzi
> tub. Pool w/ sweep. Intercom and alarm
> system. Jefferson High area. 5911 Wildair.
> $319,000. Jessica Dunn. 555-1700.

The third one read:

> LAKE MAGNOLIAS' FINEST
> French Provincial two-story. 4 bdrm, 2 and
> 1/2 bath. Formal lv-rm w/ f/p. Den w/
> beamed ceiling. Huge kitchen. Bkfst rm and
> dnrm. Garage. Pool. Short walk to Thomas
> Jefferson High. $345,000. 5700 Warrington.
> Jessica Dunn. 555-1700.

I didn't have to proceed beyond the fourth one, which read:

CLOSE TO JEFFERSON MAGNET
Desirable Lake Magnolias brick ranch. 4
bdrm, 2 and 1/2 bath. Paneled den w/ built-
in book shelves. Jacuzzi. Gazebo.
$295,000. 5717 Waldo. Betty Daniels.
555-8177.

"They all advertise their proximity to Thomas Jefferson High School," I said to Mr. Hickman.

"That they do, my friend," he responded. "That they do. And what does that tell you?"

I bit my lip, then sucked at an ice cube a second.

"It tells me," I said, "that Retif wanted all your land to build homes for a new generation of rich people."

"Exactly," Hickman said. "For Sheldon Retif, Jefferson High was going to be a magnet school in more than one sense. And the main sense that he cared about was that it was going to draw people willing to pay premium prices to get their kids close to a new topflight school."

"Mr. Hickman," I said. "Do you think I might be able to have that second drink now?"

"I'll even get you some fresh ice cubes," he said, "seein' as how you've eaten all those I gave you the first time."

While Mr. Hickman was in the kitchen with my glass, I tried to contemplate the various implications of what he'd helped me see. First, it was clear that the fix was in for Retif to get the Certificate 34. That much wasn't in question, though knowing it was obviously easier than proving it. And the motive for the fix was also clear: money. Lots of money. Plenty for Retif. Plenty for whomever he had to pay off to make sure he got the Builder's Prerogative. But then came a list of big problems. Why did Retif suddenly in January of 1981 announce that he was going to build Jefferson Magnet in the Kenilworth area? And why thereafter, at Mardi Gras of 1981, did he sell the Kenilworth property and the Thomas Jefferson Magnet School Corporation to Tom Grieve? And why, finally, did he allow his big scheme to collapse and agree to build Jefferson High at U.N.O.?

I posed the first of these questions to Cheney Hickman when he returned to the living room with a fresh glass of ice for me.

"I don't have any doubt," Mr. Hickman responded, "that Retif announced his intention to build Jefferson High in New Orleans East in order to get me to close the deal."

"I'm afraid you've lost me, again," I admitted.

Hickman handed me my glass of ice and poured in a healthy belt of whiskey on top of it. As he sat back in his chair, I noticed he'd replenished his own glass with ice as well.

As he poured himself another glass of Jack Daniels, he said to me, "Always make the second drink your last, unless you're drinkin' with company."

I laughed. "That another of your wife's rules?" I asked.

"Nope," he said. "One of my own rules. Mother can't be right about every last thing on earth. Which is another one of my own rules."

I laughed again, and we each sipped our drinks.

Then Mr. Hickman looked up at me solemnly and said, "Retif didn't stop negotiatin' with me for the West End tract after he announced he was going to build the high school on Morrison Road."

"He didn't?" I said, as confused as ever.

"Hell no."

"But why?" I asked. "I thought you'd just led me to believe that . . ."

"I led you to believe correct, Mr. Barnett."

"But I'm . . ."

"I am without a doubt Retif made that announcement to convince me I was wrong in my suspicions about his intentions and I'd better sell before he changed his mind. Furthermore, I'm without a doubt that he was still planning on building that school on my land."

"You mean you think he was willing to endure all the controversy parents raised about building the school in New Orleans East just to get you to lower your price?"

"First of all, Retif wasn't worried about a bunch of yakkin' parents. Hell, if you think about it, he could have orchestrated the whole thing, couldn't he? Dissatisfied parents helped him screw Grieve in the end, didn't they? Second, my askin' price wasn't the important thing. Getting me to sell at whatever price was the thing he was after."

"What made you think that?"

"Crowell," Mr. Hickman said.

"George Crowell," I said. "Your private investigator."

"Yep," Mr. Hickman said.

"Crowell told you that Retif wasn't really planning on building Jefferson High in New Orleans East?"

Mr. Hickman laughed and slapped his knee. "On the contrary, Mr. Barnett. He told me Retif *was* going to build in Kenilworth."

"Jesus you've got me confused," I said.

"Think about it," Mr. Hickman advised. "Crowell is working for me, and he tells me what Retif is up to. And what he tells me turns out to be pretty damned on target. Course in gettin' that information Crowell is goin' to have to be stickin' his nose around, askin' a lot of questions. And that draws attention to himself. Can't help it. He tells me what he finds out. I'm informed and grateful. I pay him what I owe. Then he ain't workin' for me anymore. Right?"

"Okay," I said

"I got what I need. I've paid Crowell off. And he's out doin' whatever he does to keep a roof over his head and meat on the table. And I keep raisin' the price on my property and draggin' my ass like maybe I'm not gonna sell at all. You follow what I'm sayin'?"

"Yes," I said, uncertainly. "Keep going."

"Then in January Retif makes his announcement about building the school off Morrison Road. And I'm supposed to be shook up. I've screwed the pooch. Blown a bankful of money."

"Right," I said.

"And you know what? I *was* shook up. But then Crowell shows up here one day. All apologetic. Says he musta gotten the whole thing wrong. That was curious enough. But what clinched it for me was when he offered to give me back the money I'd paid him. Then I knew he was lyin'. Simple enough. He was a workin' man. He'd worked for me. That's when I figured he must be workin' for Retif now."

"So you decided to continue holding out for your price," I said.

"No sir," Mr. Hickman said. "I decided at that point I wouldn't sell my land to the son-of-a-bitch for all the profit he was planning on makin' off it."

"And so negotiations fell apart," I said.

Wrong as usual.

"Nope," Mr. Hickman said. "Negotiations continued. Just because I wasn't gonna sell him the land didn't mean it wasn't fun to let him think I might. Course I couldn't stall him off forever. If he was gonna build that school himself, he was gonna have to get started at some point to avoid the penalty clause of the Certificate 34."

"And that's why he made his deal with Tom Grieve," I speculated.

"Way I figure it," Mr. Hickman explained, "Retif and his cronies at the school board had Grieve on the line all along. They just reeled him in at this point. If I'da cooperated, they may have cut Grieve loose, somethin' I've felt damn bad about, but then it might not be true either. See I figure Grieve was a kind of trump card Retif was holdin'. He played it as a last chance to convince me to let go of my land. Convince me I'd figured the whole thing wrong from the get-go. That's one thing. Course if I didn't sell West End, then Retif'd just as soon Grieve build that school in New Orleans East, if that was where it was gonna have to go. Wasn't no land around the Kenilworth site for him to cash in on big time. So the whole deal was small potatoes, and it was easier to take the premium Grieve was willing to pay and just walk away to some other scam. Let Grieve put up with the complaints from all the white parents who didn't want the school way out there. Course if lettin' it appear the school was gettin' built on Morrison Road shook the West End tract outta me, why they had the contract with Grieve written up in such a way that they could screw him if they wanted to."

"And in the end, they did want to," I said.

"But not on account of me, thank God," Cheney Hickman said. "Once Grieve was in possession of the Morrison Road property, they'd only have had incentive to screw him if I'd caved in and sold. Or that's what I thought, anyway."

"Why do you think you were wrong about that?"

"I hadn't foreseen Retif gettin' ahold of the Baseview Apartments in order to build Lake Magnolias."

"Whoa," I said. "I'm lost again."

"You remember the Baseview Apartments?" he asked.

I shrugged. "Bunch of ratty old buildings across from U.N.O. Where Lakes Magnolias is now. On all those cross streets that start with a W, Wildair, Wadsworth, Wainwright, whatever."

"Right," he said. "And you remember what those buildings were originally?"

"They were officers and officers' family quarters on the old naval base, weren't they?" Founded in 1958, the University of New Orleans had been built on the site of a Naval Air Base which had been abandoned in the 1950s. In its early days the university had converted barracks into classrooms and runways into parking lots.

"That they were," Hickman affirmed. "Stretched clear from Leon C. Simon to Robert E. Lee and from Elysian Fields back to the London Avenue Canal."

"I first remember driving past them when I was a little kid and my parents used to take me to the amusement park at Pontchartrain Beach."

"Probably everybody in this town over a certain age remembers them the same way," Mr Hickman said. "Everybody white least ways. What lotsa folks don't remember is that when the Navy donated its land to the state for building a new university, it also donated all those apartment buildings between Leon C. Simon and Robert E. Lee."

"I guess I'm among those who didn't realize that," I admitted.

"For a couple of decades, the university did pretty well with the apartments as a revenue source. But by the late '70s they'd become a big nuisance. They weren't built worth a damn to start with. And as they started to age, they also started to eat up in repairs most everything the university could collect in rent. So the university started looking for a buyer. Woulda been a time when they'd had bidders a plenty. Knock down those rattle traps and put up just the kind of houses they got there now. But like everybody in this town knows, by the late seventies the housing market inside the city limits was all cattywhompus. Public schools had gone black. All the white people with any money were buying their houses out in the parish or across the lake."

"And what you're saying," I interjected, "is that Jefferson Magnet changed that dynamic."

"That's exactly what I'm saying. It's what Retif was counting on to sell all the houses he was gonna build on my land. And as you can see from those newspaper ads, it's precisely what sold all those houses across from U.N.O. Houses that made the developer of Lake Magnolias a bankful of money."

"And you're saying that developer was Sheldon Retif." I was scribbling furiously in my notebook. "That's easy enough to ascertain," I said. "If Retif bought the land from the university, it'll be a part of the public record and we can find it."

"He's a little slipperier than that," Mr. Hickman said.

"Meaning?"

"Meaning I checked on that land sale a lotta years ago. The buyer was a man named John Broom."

I stopped writing and looked up at him. "What are you telling me," I asked.

"I'm telling you what I know," he replied. "Now I'll tell you what I believe. You dig hard enough, Mr. Barnett, and you'll find out that John Broom and Sheldon Retif are somehow one and the same person."

*   *   *

The implications of Cheney Hickman's information and speculations were enormous. If indeed John Broom and Sheldon Retif were connected, then Retif managed to convert his School Board fix for the Certificate 34 into millions. The Certificate 34 gave him the right to build the school. Possession of the Baseview Apartment tract gave him the land to build luxury homes for people who wanted to locate their kids in the neighborhood near the school.

Critically, the millions Retif stood to make were plenty of incentive for Retif to have bribed or blackmailed Leon Delacroix. And keeping secret the fact of the bribe or the circumstances of the blackmail was reason aplenty for Delacroix to have lied about the conflict of interest arising from his membership on the U.N.O. Board of Trustees. The various pieces of the puzzle did indeed all fit together. And because they did, Retif or Delacroix either one had reason to burglarize my home and somehow raid the storage room at Herbst, Gilman in order to see how many of those pieces Joan had managed to assemble.

*   *   *

Before I left Cheney Hickman's Bucktown home that evening, he and I drank another "toddy" together. I asked him what he was going to do with the West End tract now. He told me that he had worried over that a good deal once his negotiations with Sheldon Retif had fallen through. He was glad, of course, that they had, he said, since he wouldn't want anything he had ever owned to be so soiled.

"My kids would like me to find another buyer," he confided. "More cash for them when I go on to join Mother. But I already gave them more than I got to start life with. I gave them college diplomas and professional degrees. And a hell of a lot of money to boot. So I been thinkin' of some other kind of thing to do with the land."

"What's that?" I asked.

"Well a park, actually," he said. "Not a park with golf courses and tennis courts. We're doin' okay on that front, I reckon. And not some damned amusement park with rides. But a park that would be dedicated to the memory of Lake Pontchartrain the way it was when it was a live lake you could swim and fish in and earn a livin' off of. The way we're goin' in this godforsaken state, somebody'll suggest we pave the lake over someday and we'll goddamn do it before somebody with good sense suggests it's a bad idea. Course, the way our coastal wetlands are disappearin' and we're fishin' out the gulf the way we already done the lake, probably won't be anybody left in this city to visit my park if I could get the damn thing built. But I think I'll try to build it anyway. Just to spite the bastards."

I also asked him why he hadn't come forward when Grieve's law suit was so much in the news. He said he had.

"Did you talk to my wife?" I asked, astonished. "Did you talk to Joan Barnett?"

"Yes, I did." he said.

Something unspeakably outrageous was suddenly occurring to me. But I pushed the idea away. Fighting for calm, I swallowed hard and said, "Tell me about your conversation with her."

"Well," he said, "when I first saw in the papers what they were doin', I gave Tom Grieve a call. And he asked me to talk to your wife. Didn't get a chance to, though. Not at the time. Called the office where she worked and ended up talkin' to some young fella at your wife's firm. Said he was workin' with her on the case. He 'uh huhed' me a while on the phone, then rang off sayin' he get back to me. But he never did."

I interrupted him. "You remember the attorney you spoke with?" I asked.

"No, can't say that I do."

"Could it have been a young man named Johnny Chambers?"

"Coulda been," Mr. Hickman said. He removed his cap and scratched at his crewcut white hair. "Can't say that it was. But coulda been."

I breathed deeply. "Sorry," I said. "Please go on. What happened after you spoke with the associate who was working with Joan on the case?"

"Well, that's the last I heard of the thing for a long damn time. Directly, anyway. After the case went to trial and all, and Tom lost, I got in touch with him again. Asked him if he thought he got good legal advice. He was kinda distant, I thought. Kinda in a hurry to get off the phone. Said he appreciated my interest, but said his lawyer had . . ."

"Excuse me, Mr. Hickman," I interrupted him again. "I thought you said you talked to Joan herself."

"I did. I'm comin' to that."

"But when did you talk to her?"

"About a year and a half ago."

The idea was insistent now, demanding to be consciously acknowledged. I felt as if someone huge was sitting on my chest. I could breathe only with the greatest effort.

"I'm sorry, Mr. Hickman. Could you by any chance determine the exact date you talked to my wife?"

"Why I know the date exactly, Mr. Barnett. No doubt about it at all. Your wife sat right there where you've been sitting tonight and ate birthday cake my son's wife had brought over for me the day before. It was the day after my birthday. And that'd make it July twenty-fourth. It was a Friday, she was here. My daughter's family took me round to R & O's to eat catfish later that evening. Your wife left here late afternoon. I remember thinkin' she must be a hard worker, 'cause she said she had to go back to the office. Said she had somebody she had to talk to."

"You had told her what you told me?" I croaked.

"Yes sir, I told her much of the same thing."

"About Retif somehow being connected to this John Broom and through him to the Baseview Apartments acquisition and the development of Lake Magnolias?"

"Yes sir, I think I probably told her all that. I tried to tell that young fella who worked with her all the same things, some years before. When the trial was all in the news. Not that he really listened to me."

"And what did Joan say to you, Mr. Hickman?"

"She thanked me. She said I had been a big help. She said she'd probably need to get in touch with me again later on. But she never did."

She never did, of course, Mr. Hickman, because she barely lived another week.

*   *   *

On the way home from Cheney Hickman's I was in such a state of agitation that I missed my freeway exit and ended up driving clear downtown before I could get off and turn around. Why hadn't Joan told me? For a week she had breakthrough information on the most important case of her life, and she hadn't told me about it. Why? Had I pushed her that hard to let go of the case? Had she somehow risked herself needlessly because she felt she couldn't confide in me? I couldn't get around the logic that stemmed from what Hickman had told me: My wife had been murdered. I couldn't stand the thought. I couldn't stand the fucking thought! The bastards had killed her. Joan was on to them. She was going to bring them down. They knew it. And they squashed her like she was some fucking insect.

The more I thought about the implications of what Cheney Hickman told me, the more I was possessed by a cold blind fury. I hadn't been there when she needed me. Now, I'd be damned if I was going to let Retif and Delacroix get away with this. I pounded the goddamned steering wheel of my goddamned car. I screamed aloud into the indifferent night: "I'm going to get you fuckers if I have to kill you with my own hands."

CHAPTER NINETEEN

I am capable, of course, of astonishingly self-destructive behavior. Given my mood after returning from Cheney Hickman's, the last thing I needed was to chase the several glasses of Jack Daniels I'd had at his house with shots of Scotch. But that's exactly what I did. Wilson wasn't home for me to talk to. A message on the answering machine said she was staying late at the office to finish a piece on the serial murders of presumed homosexuals. Only one of the victims, it had emerged, was avowedly gay. I called Wilson's desk at the paper but got no answer. And so, crazy with anger, I got out my bottle of Black and White and a cup of ice and drank until I lost even a semblance of good sense.

After a time I began to pace the house from front to back, stopping only to pour more Scotch into my glass. The corruption associated with Thomas Jefferson Magnet obviously went much deeper than I had ever imagined. The fix was in for Retif to get the Certificate 34 many months before the case even came before the school board. The certificate was worth millions in a way I'd never quite understood. And it now seemed possible that Joan's case was sabotaged all along from the inside by Johnny Chambers. If that was true, then Tammy Dieter-White was no doubt also somehow involved. The money provided all the motive needed for either bribing or blackmailing Judge Delacroix. And to keep the whole stinking mess from coming out, somebody had hired a black hit-man to run over my wife.

Finally though late, needing to take some kind of action, I called Pat Finley, our real estate editor, and asked him what he knew about John Broom. He knew nothing about John Broom, he reported, save for the fact that he'd developed Lake Magnolias. I asked if Pat knew of any relationship John Broom might have to Sheldon Retif. He knew of none whatsoever. He did know, however, that Retif had a son-in-law named Lloyd Broom.

I thought the top of my head was going to come off. I poured two inches of Scotch into my cup and knocked it back in a single draught. Sheldon Retif was Satan Incarnate.

Had I been sober, I hope I would have been far less rash. But my fury was fueled by the high octane alcohol I'd been pouring into my bloodstream at an increasing rate over the last four hours. My best move was surely cold calculation. But I lusted for the more immediate gratification of instant confrontation.

It was nearly eleven p.m., and I called Sheldon Retif's house anyway. A houseman said he was entertaining guests and couldn't come to the phone. I insisted, but was firmly told to call back tomorrow. So I loaded myself a go-cup of Scotch and ice, put my blue blazer back on and headed for Retif's mansion on Lakeshore Drive.

Two couples—the women in cocktail dresses, the men in coats and ties—were walking down the driveway to Retif's imitation Taj Mahal as I drove up. So it was true he'd been entertaining. All the better, I thought, my ability to reason warped by whisky's distortion.

"Hey," I said to the two couples as I got out of my car. "Y'all guests of Mr. Retif's tonight?"

All four people no doubt thought they'd been confronted by a madman. They weren't far wrong.

At first no one responded.

"Y'all been to a party here?" I asked again, waving toward Retif's house with my Mardi Gras cup of Scotch.

Finally one of the women said, "Yes, we've all just been to Sheldon's party. I think it's about over, though."

"No matter," I said. "I don't think I was invited anyway."

The couples began to edge away from me in opposite directions. But I stopped them when I said, "What's it like to go to a party at the house of a murderer?"

One of the women said to her husband but plenty loud enough for me to hear, "Somebody ought to call the police."

"Boy ain't that the truth," I said back to her. "I think I'll just mosey on inside and do that right now."

I left Retif's guests at the street and started up the walk to the house. Taking a swallow of my drink while I waited for someone to answer the door, I noticed the two men had come halfway toward me. I'm sure they wanted to see what I was going to do next, but they didn't want to get close enough to get hurt if I was carrying a weapon. They had no way of knowing that I was armed only with outrage.

A tuxedo-clad butler, presumably the same man I had spoken with on the phone, answered the door. I brushed past him immediately and strode down the entrance hall to the marble-floored living room, softened everywhere with Oriental rugs. The houseman was on my heels blustering that I couldn't come barging in as I had. He made enough noise behind me that the party, Sheldon Retif, his wife and their ten or so remaining guests, fell silent as I entered the room.

"May we help you, sir," a woman, presumably Mrs. Retif asked in a refined Southern drawl.

"No, ma'am," I replied. "If you're Mrs. Sheldon Retif, I think your husband has helped me just about all I can stand for this lifetime."

"Who is this man?" Retif demanded of his servant. Retif was now a man in his mid-sixties, but he strode aggressively toward me, unbuttoning his navy blue suit coat as he did so. His large round face under his fringe of white hair was reddened with indignation. He set his drink glass on a marble-topped lamp table against the wall on his way to meet me. I was busied trying to brush off the butler who was pulling rather lamely at my shoulders. When Retif reached me, he spoke through gritted teeth. "Just who the hell are you, and what do you think you're doing?" Before I could answer he spoke to the butler and ordered him to call the police.

All dressed in their fine suits and stylish dresses, the guests shrank away from me, leaving just Retif and myself in the center of a wide circle. It was as if he and I were bride and groom, just about to begin our wedding dance.

I handed him my drink cup. "How about a refill, Shelley. I'm feeling ever so dry."

Retif looked in amazement at the cup I'd given him and then spoke under his breath again, "I don't know who you are, but I want you out of my house this instant!"

Around me I could hear the hubbub of chatter as Retif's guests shared their consternation at my unbidden arrival. I backed away from the host, spun on my heel and lifted my arms to the others.

"Ladies and gentlemen," I proclaimed, "wealthy residents of our great and historic city, those of you prosperous enough to be business associates and unfortunate enough to be friends of Sheldon Retif, I greet you heartily. I am here to give you a little needed background on your host. Many of you may know this already. But repetition of these matters in a public forum never hurts. Your host is a grafter. But now that's not so bad in the great state of Louisiana now is it? Some of you may even admire him for this trait. How many of you admire the fact that he's also a FUCKING MURDERER?"

"This man is obviously a lunatic," Retif said to his guests.

I could hear the squad-car sirens then, and squealing tires racing up the drive. "None of you knows this now," I hurried. "Most of you will choose not to believe it. But your friend Sheldon Retif murdered my wife."

The police burst into the house about then and began to push me around. But as they were escorting me out, I told the whole ashen-faced assemblage. "Sheldon Retif murdered my wife, and I'm gonna see him fry. One way or another, I'm gonna see him fry."

*   *   *

I awoke the next morning in the drunk tank at City Lockup. My head pounded like a bass drum in mid-parade. There were five other men in my cell, some flung on thin-mattressed bunks, two standing at the bars. All appeared to be street people. Their hair was matted and filthy; they reeked from lack of washing. When I went to urinate in the cell's seatless toilet, I nearly gagged from the smell of vomit. This is what I'd allowed my life to come to.

Sometime in the late morning—the cops had taken my watch so I couldn't be sure of the exact time—a seventh man was placed in our cell. He seemed to come out of the fog of my hangover. He wasn't there. And then he was. And he was different from the others. His hair was cut, badly and too short on the sides, but recently. He was medium height and build, five feet nine perhaps, and about 160 pounds. In a tacky way, he was nattily dressed—dark green pants, two-toned brown-and-white wingtips and a plaid, open-necked sport shirt with the collar pulled out over a beige blazer. Several minutes after I noticed him, he wandered over to where I was standing against the wall in the front corner, my left arm curled through the bars.

"Gotta smoke?" he inquired.

I shook my head, and he took a position to my right, leaning against the wall.

After a time, he patted himself and pulled out a pack of Marlboros. "Hey whataya know. I got some myself." He shook out a cigarette for himself and offered the pack in my direction.

"No thanks," I said.

He lit up, blew out a cloud of gray smoke which seemed to shroud him entirely and said, "So what you in for?"

"Drunk and disorderly," I said, not looking at him, wondering how long it would be before Wilson would get me released.

"Yeah? Me too."

I didn't comment.

He smoked for a second and then he moved a half step closer to me. "Say," he said quietly, "You ain't the guy who made all the ruckus out on Lakeshore Drive are you?"

I turned and faced him.

"Yeah," he said. "You're the guy all right." He pointed at me with the cigarette pinched between his index and middle fingers, the smoke rising in circles as he gestured. "Say, I got a message for you."

"What the fuck are you talking about?"

"It's like the little lady says in the song. You been a messin' where you oughtn't been a messin'." He took a deep drag on his cigarette and then crushed it out on the floor.

"You trying to threaten me, you son-of-a-bitch?"

He blew the smoke in my face. "And one of these days some boots are gonna walk all over you."

I reached out and grabbed him by his shirt front, lifting him up on his toes toward me. "You tell Sheldon Retif I'll fuckin' piss on his grave."

The little man didn't blink, and neither did he try to squirm out of my grasp. He just looked at me steadily, as if faintly amused, patiently waiting for me to let him go. When I did, he calmly tucked his shirt back in his pants and adjusted his jacket around his shoulders. Then he took out his pack of Marlboros and lit up another cigarette.

"You tell Sheldon Retif I'm a long ways beyond being scared off by the likes of him."

The man exhaled a cloud of smoke, this time aimed away from me. He looked at me quizzically? "Who's this Shalton Rateev you keep goin' on about?"

"Fuck you," I said.

"No thanks," the man said. He shrugged, moved away from me to sit on one of the bunks, and continued to smoke one cigarette after another. When the guard came to get me, he began humming "These Boots Are Made for Walkin.'"

"You shut the fuck up," I screamed at him.

He looked up at me as if shocked.

Pointing at the man, I said to the guard, "This man has been threatening me."

The man jabbed at his chest with a thumb and then lifted his hands palms up toward the guard.

"What about it?" the guard asked him. "You been making some kind of threats?"

The guard asked the others in the cell, "Somebody been making threats in here?"

The others cast their eyes away and said nothing.

My tormentor pointed at me and said to the guard, "That man's got a bad case of the D.T.s."

"Come on," the guard said to me and dragged me from the cell.

*   *   *

I was warned not to approach Sheldon Retif again and released on my own reconnaissance with just the drunk and disorderly charge pending against me. Wilson's daddy had protected me from an assault charge. Wilson had given Carl some abbreviated version of what happened to me and thus explained (if not excused) my absence from work. But my life had never been in greater disarray.

I was disgusted with myself. My wife had been murdered by one or a group of New Orleans's wealthy and privileged. And rather than taking the proper steps to bring them to justice, I'd gotten drunk and perhaps made bringing them down more difficult now. I'd tipped my hand, and they were on to me now. I promised myself I wouldn't take so much as a sip of alcohol until those responsible for Joan's death were dealt with.

A pledge of sobriety was something I'd made many times before, of course. But this time I kept it—almost long enough.

*   *   *

The next day I was summoned to a meeting with the Old Man. Carl Shaney was in his office when I arrived. Neither was pleased.

The Old Man sat behind his desk, half-lensed reading glasses resting from a chain around his neck against the chest of his starched white monogrammed shirt. His high forehead, which gave way to a gray-fringed bald pate, shined in the morning sun cascading into the room through Venetian blinds. He bade me sit in a chair across from him. Carl was seated off to the side, but he uttered not a syllable during the entire meeting.

The Old Man never raised his voice. His admonishment was simple and to the point. *The States-Tribune* could not afford to have its employees crashing into people's houses making wild accusations. He realized that any statements I had made concerning Sheldon Retif were made on behalf of my own person and not on behalf of the paper. Still, he'd received a phone call from Ms. Tammy Dieter-White with the law firm of Wallace and Jones threatening to sue the paper because I was its employee. He was not intimidated by Ms. Dieter-White's threats, he assured me. He'd been sued a dozen times in his years as editor of *The States-Tribune*—for stories that had actually appeared in the paper. And he hadn't lost yet. On the other hand, neither he nor the paper ever needed the hassle of defending a lawsuit.

It had occurred to him, of course, just to dismiss me. But he hadn't really considered that response very seriously or very long. Carl had informed him that I had been slow to recover from my wife's death, and that was certainly a circumstance he was ready to take into consideration. Furthermore, I had been with the paper for a number of years, and he had always been more than pleased with my work. I must realize, however, that there could never be a repetition of this incident.

"Mike," he said to me in conclusion, fiddling with his glasses as he spoke, "You're our film critic. And you're a damned good one. I gather you think that Sheldon Retif was somehow involved in your wife's accident . . ."

For the first time I started to speak, but he held up his hand to silence me, "I don't want to hear the allegations, Mike, not now, not in this context. If you have evidence implicating Retif, let's pursue it. Let *us* pursue it. Us, meaning the news and investigative staff. You give what you've got to your friend Carl Shaney, who is worried sick about you, by the way. And then you go to the movies and write your reviews."

The Old Man sat back in his chair for a second and rubbed at either side of his nose with his index fingers. Then he rocked forward toward me and said, "I presume that I can count on your resignation if those terms aren't acceptable to you."

*   *   *

Well, those terms weren't acceptable to me. But I didn't resign either. I supposed I could have lived off my savings. I had $300,000 in the bank, 100 grand of my own and the 200 Joan had left me, including the $100,000 I only learned about when she died. I owned my house and my car. I didn't have expensive tastes. Sure, I could have lived on my savings. But a person has got to work. And I didn't know how to do anything other than write for a newspaper. So I sat mute, letting my silence lie about my acceptance.

After I left the Old Man's office, I waited in the hall for Carl to emerge so that I could speak to him. But he stayed with the Old Man for another half hour after I was dismissed. So after a time, I went back to my own office to work fitfully on a review of Bruce Beresford's awesomely foolish *Her Alibi*. I couldn't imagine what a director of Beresford's talent was doing at the helm of such drivel. But the contempt I expressed for the picture was no doubt heightened by my impatience to get in with Carl and relate to him what I'd learned from Cheney Hickman and the horror Hickman's story seemed to imply.

But when Carl finally returned to his office, he wouldn't talk to me. His eyes were sad when he raised them to me as I rapped my arrival on his door, but his voice seemed stripped bare of emotion. "Let's not talk today, Mike," he said. "And maybe not tomorrow. You need to get your head together. You need to take some time to think about the very deep shit you're in."

*   *   *

The one stabilizing factor in my life now was provided by Wilson Malt. She was the only one really willing to stand by me in the whole Retif business. It was clear to me that if I was going to get to the bottom of Joan's murder, I was going to have to do it without Carl's help. I couldn't afford even to let him know that I didn't intend to abide by the Old Man's direction that I leave the case alone. With Carl almost hostile, it was critical for my mental and psychological well-being that Wilson thought I was right about the import of what Cheney Hickman had told me. She believed that I had been threatened while in jail, and without hesitation agreed to help me see what we could do to nail Retif and everybody else in this cesspool.

My mind turned once more to the file that was missing from both Joan's Herbst, Gilman offices and from our filing cabinet at home. I was sure the connection between Delacroix and Retif lay in that file. Sometime in her last days Joan had made that connection, but she had died too soon to bring it to light. And now that file was gone, stolen from home or office by some one presumably in the employ of Sheldon Retif or Leon Delacroix or both.

*   *   *

The several days following my conversation with Cheney Hickman were a blur of frenetic activity. I had to keep up appearances at work even though proper concentration was almost impossible. Meanwhile,

Wilson faced an unusually heavy work responsibility. There had been another murder in what the paper was now calling the "Gay Stalker" case. And Wilson was the chief reporter on the story. Still, we each gave whatever time we could to trying to generate additional leads on the graft surrounding the building of Jefferson High and Joan's subsequent death.

I first sought to establish Cheney Hickman's promised connection between John Broom and Sheldon Retif. There was no local phone listing for a John Broom, so I tried tracing him through his companies. Dead end. I contacted the Secretary of State's office in Baton Rouge where all companies incorporated in the state must register. But I learned nothing helpful. The Lake Magnolias Development Corporation was no longer in operation.

Momentarily stalled, I decided to call Retif Realty. If a Lloyd Broom was Retif's son-in-law, maybe I could get a lead on John Broom from inside the enemy's own camp.

Sometimes it's better to be lucky than good.

When a company receptionist answered the phone at Retif Realty, I simply asked to speak to Mr. John Broom.

"Mr. *John* Broom?" she replied quizzically.

"Yes, that's it, John Broom."

"We have a Mr. Lloyd Broom?" she said. "He's our vice president. Would you like to speak to him?"

"Gee, no," I said, stalling. "I . . ."

She cut me off. "Oh, you know, I bet you do want to speak with Mr. Lloyd Broom. His middle name is John. Lloyd J. Broom. Lloyd John Broom. I'll connect you. Who may I say is calling?"

"Mitchell Leland."

"I'll put you through to Mr. Broom's office, Mr. Leland."

"Thank you," I said. But I had hung up by the time Lloyd John Broom came on the line.

The relationship between Sheldon Retif and John Broom that Cheney Hickman had predicted was closer than even he'd perhaps imagined.

*   *   *

Wilson took on the task of seeing what she could find out about Jackson Smith, the driver of the car that killed Joan on the St. Charles Avenue neutral ground. It took Wilson a while to cajole her father into helping us get information out of the files at N.O.P.D. But finally he agreed to read over the file on Joan's death and tell us what was in it. What he found in the "accident" file led him to another, an investigation file on Smith himself.

At the time of the "accident" in which Joan was killed, Jackson Smith stated that he had been on his way home to dinner. The responding policeman had found that statement troubling enough he'd noted Smith seemed to be going in the wrong direction, since his stated address was on Garfield Street, which would have required a turn off St. Charles Avenue toward the river instead of across the neutral ground. But Smith responded by amending his statement to say he'd been turning around on St. Charles to go to get food for dinner at the Winn-Dixie on Carrollton between Maple and Hampson. The reporting officer noted Smith was very nervous, but deemed that "understandable under the tragic circumstances." The officer also took a statement from me which he described as "distraught and incoherent." The report concluded that Joan had run in front of the car and that Smith had not been unduly negligent. The case was transmitted to the district attorney's office where an assistant D.A. had rendered a formal conclusion of accidental death.

Jackson Smith's other file revealed that when his car ran over Joan on Saturday morning, July 25, 1987, he was an unemployed black laborer. He'd worked for the city sanitation department but had lost that job when the city turned its sanitation business over to a private contractor. For a time thereafter he'd worked as a janitor at Cohen High School on Dryades Street. The police had kept an eye on Smith for years. He had long been a runner in the city's numbers racket. After he'd moved on to the high school, he'd evidently been promoted to bag man for the backroom gambling operations run out of the city's bars. Smith was such a small fry, though, he had never been formally charged. But the cops had him marked for a sponge they'd squeeze when the time was right. Later, Smith was suspected of distributing to the students at Cohen a concoction called "clickums," an hallucinogen produced by soaking marijuana cigarettes in PCP. He was never arrested for that either, however, and he was dismissed at the end of the 1987 school year for excessive absences.

There was one last item in Jackson Smith's file. In November of last year, his bloated and disfigured body had been found floating face down in the Industrial Canal. The coroner estimated he'd been dead at least a week when he was discovered. The cause of death was listed as drowning, though an autopsy showed a blow to the back of his head and extraordinarily high level of alcohol in the blood. The coroner's report speculated that Smith had been drinking somewhere along the banks of the canal, had slipped and hit his head, and had rolled into the water and drowned.

More and more the winding path of the Jefferson Magnet School case seemed to lead to the morgue.

When Wilson summarized for me her father's findings, I asked her if she could get the files themselves for us to examine.

"Why," she inquired.

"I'd feel better having looked at them myself," I answered.

"You think Daddy wasn't thorough?"

"Of course not. It's just that he may not know what to look for. Something in the files might appear meaningless to him, but might be a connection we need."

"I can't believe Daddy would have missed anything," Wilson said.

"Well goddamnit, he's not Albert Einstein for Chrissake. He's just a cop."

"What's that supposed to mean? He's stupid?"

"Jesus," I said.

"He's not stupid," Wilson said.

I assured Wilson that I didn't think her father was stupid, or incompetent, or anything other than a swell guy. But she continued to resist my request that she ask him to provide us the files themselves.

"I can't ask him to risk his badge," she explained.

"If this isn't worth risking his badge for," I countered, "then I don't know why the hell he's bothering to wear one."

"I just can't do it, Mike. Don't you understand that? I just can't."

I didn't understand, of course. And finally, in exasperation I said, "Goddamnit, Wilson, you're just like everybody else in this fucking town. When push comes to shove you don't give a shit. Or, at least, you don't give a big enough shit to make any difference."

"Is that what you really think, Mike?"

"That's what I really think," I rejoined.

"And you know what I think," she countered. "I think when push comes to shove you don't give a shit about anything except yourself and your precious grief."

*   *   *

For the better part of a week we were stymied. But then a critical break arrived as if a blessing from a caring God.

Wilson and I shared our meal after a late afternoon screening. She cooked up some pasta which she covered with another sensational cream sauce, this one spiced with garlic, tasso and black pepper. After dinner, exhausted, I asked if she wanted to watch one of the movies in my video library. She was no more a TV viewer than I was, so she accepted the invitation, bus driver's holiday that such an idea was.

For no particular reason other than divine guidance—before Joan died I had begun an article on the picture for *Film Quarterly* and needed a fresh viewing if I was ever going to finish it—I chose Claude Lelouch's wonderful romantic comedy *And Now My Love.* As we settled down on the living room sofa to watch, I made the mistake of mentioning that the picture was Joan's favorite. And for a few moments thereafter Wilson argued that she'd prefer to watch something else. But I insisted. And within the movie's first five minutes, she was hooked.

The picture's premise is that true lovers do not so much choose each other as do they find each other, that, in other words, they are made for each other. Stars Andre Dussolier and Marthe Keller do not even meet until the film's very last frames. They never have sex, never even kiss. When the film ends, they have barely spoken. But we know they will love each other forever.

By the time the movie was giddily rushing toward its end where the lovers finally meet for the first time, Wilson was almost literally bouncing up and down with pleasure. When Keller and Dussolier

slid into airplane seats next to one another and Lelouch impishly cut
to their suitcases riding together up the conveyor belt toward the
baggage compartment, just as his bag tumbled over on top of hers,
Wilson turned and said to me smiling broadly, "Jesus, Mike, what a
great movie."

I wished I shared Wilson's joy at that moment. But I didn't. I
couldn't. I'd tried to hide my feelings from Wilson, but throughout
the entire film I kept thinking what a mistake I'd made. I was glad
Wilson liked the movie, but I shouldn't have watched it with her. For
this picture belonged to Joan. And throughout the film I could think
only of Joan.

Ironically, on this occasion at least, that's what I needed to do, what,
if indeed there's a cosmic order to things, I was supposed to do.

That night I dreamed of Joan, dreamed of her working on our
bed, all her legal materials spread out around her on the dust cover,
dreamed of our watching *And Now My Love* one last time together,
giggling together as we always did when Andre Dussolier's suitcase
fell over on top of Marthe Keller's. And I dreamed of our going
for our last run together, Joan striding along easily as always, me
laboring a pace or two behind. And I dreamed as happened in fact
that moments before she would be snatched away from me forever,
she was talking about *Retif*, her settled but unsettling law suit, the
legal case on which she could not stop working. And the words
formed on her lips. And a streetcar rattled by. And I was too far
away to hear. But in my dream I heard. The words were a single
word, a mixture, a compound, a precaution, a clue. Not "suit" and
"case" separately. But joined, one: "suitcase."

I sat bolt upright in the middle of the night. Perhaps I hadn't been
dreaming at all. Perhaps in some process of self-hypnosis, practiced
in the shadowy hall of mirrors that stands as the passage between
sleep and consciousness, perhaps I had been placing memory under
a microscope. Suitcase. The idea appealed to Joan's love of language.
And Now My Love, her favorite. My work, her work. Two into one.
Suitcase.

I eased from bed so as not to wake Wilson and went to the large
dining room closet where Joan and I stored the larger pieces of
luggage we used on our summer vacations. I took her square,

herringbone suitcase down from the overhead shelf and placed it on the dining room table. It would be the last place a hurried burglar would think to look. I spun the combination tumblers and flicked the latch buttons. And inside Joan's suitcase lay a brown accordion file folder labeled on both front and back with the words *Grieve versus Retif.*

CHAPTER TWENTY

So Johnny Chambers hadn't snared Joan's working *Retif* file for Wallace and Jones after all. Still, the existence of the accordion folder, deliberately hidden in Joan's suitcase, didn't account for the entire empty Herbst, Gilman file drawer for 1987. Nor did it account for Chambers' uncooperative behavior and Tammy Dieter-White's pugnacious attitude. They had to still be involved in this somehow.

Sitting at the kitchen table in the middle of the night, trying to work quietly so as not to wake Wilson, I began trying to make my way through Joan's file immediately. It was a slow and confusing process. I wasn't a lawyer and didn't understand much of what the file contained. There were copies of correspondence and reams of Joan's handwritten notes, some on sheets of yellow legal paper, others on the firm's half-size sheets of memo paper, all typically written around her ubiquitous doodles. One memo sheet, for instance, had a heading that read "Dieter-White—Phone—9/25/86" but the note page consisted entirely of the word "asshole" written over and over again.

I finally slept a couple of hours before going into work, but I returned to reading the file as soon as possible when I got home. I found the clue that I had been seeking for months in the very back.

On one of her firm memo sheets was the single word, "Herman," and a phone number. The note was paper-clipped to the top page of a legal tablet which bore the handwritten title, "Delacroix Genealogy." Under that heading there was a short list that read:

Office of Public Health
Records and Statistics
—325 Loyola Avenue
Vital Records
Birth and Death Certificates
—555-5171

The middle of the page was filled with variations of Joan's signature. Sometimes she signed her name Joan Barnett, sometimes Joan Anne Barnett, sometimes Joan Norris, once even Mrs. Michael Barnett. After the signatures came the following diagram:

Leon Delacroix (1915)--w
Francois Delacroix (1883)--w & Denise Thibault (1887)--w

A fresh page showed:

Francois Delacroix
Michel Delacroix (1858)--w & Clarisse Fournier (1860)--w
Jean Delacroix (1834)--w   Jacques Fournier (1830)--w

&   &

Catherine Soniat (1836)--w   Genevieve Lissard (1842)--w

And below that:

Denise Thibault
Jean Thibault (1866)--w & Christine Thibodeaux
(1866)--w
Jean Thibault (1839)--w   Marc Thibodeaux (1846)--w

&   &

Bernice Jarreau (1847)--w   Annette Jeansonne (1848)--?

*   *   *

It took me a second to understand what Joan had been working on. And then, all at once, I grasped it. She was working on the possibility that Leon Delacroix was a person of racially mixed blood. She was trying to establish a circumstance by which Delacroix could have been vulnerable to blackmail. The world at large probably didn't any longer care if a public official was part lizard. But when Delacroix entered public life, it would have cared if Delacroix had been part black, cared enough that any Southerner aspiring to public office would have gone to extraordinary pains to keep the fact secret. Even in the 1980s Delacroix and his family might well have fought to keep such a fact from emerging into the realm of public knowledge.

From what her notes indicated, Joan had managed to learn the race of seven of Delacroix's eight great-grandparents. But she hadn't been able to determine the race of the eighth, Annette Jeansonne. Yet evidently there was a birth record for Annette Jeansonne, for Joan had learned the year of Jeansonne's birth.

Why had her birth certificate not indicated her race?

Instead of going into the office the next morning, I stayed home and called the State Office of Vital Records and asked just that question. But I was told that such information was not available to the public. A concerted amount of insistence on my part didn't get me anywhere.

So I telephoned Jason Roux, and he explained that state genealogical records were open only to family members and attorneys involved in researching cases in which such records were relevant. He was surprised that Joan had gotten such information as she had. He suspected, he said, that she could have gotten it only under at least slightly false pretenses.

"Joan was smart enough, of course," Jason said, "to make up a reason that would have satisfied whatever bureaucrat she had to deal with."

"And you're smart enough, too, I presume," I said.

Jason laughed. "I presume I am," he said.

I asked him if he'd call Vital Records and try to learn exactly how the birth certificate for Annette Jeansonne read. He said he was reluctant, but he agreed, promising to get back to me as soon as he had anything to report.

I then called the number for "Herman" on Joan's memo sheet. The man who answered was Herman Krancke, the popular local political columnist who had written for our city's afternoon newspaper, *The Post-Chronicle*, for fifty years until it ceased publication in 1980, at which point Krancke joined the paper in retirement. "Oyman da Joyman" is the way Herman Kranke was known to thousands of his New Orleans readers. Late in his career he even wrote a column of reminiscences under that title in the Weekend Edition of *The Post-Chronicle*. Now about eighty years old, he was still known about town as a man of galloping curiosity, prodigious memory and unflagging good humor.

As fellow newspaper people, Mr. Krancke and I had met on several occasions around town, though I had no confidence that he knew who I was. When I identified myself, though, he complimented me on my work and claimed to look to my recommendations on every occasion before he ventured out to a movie. Given how old he was, I thought, that was probably not even once a year. But, still, I was flattered.

I asked Mr. Krancke if he remembered a phone call from my wife sometime in the summer of 1987. He said he did not, and it occurred to me that maybe calling Herman Krancke was a piece of Joan's investigation she didn't live long enough to complete.

Krancke apologized for not remembering and explained that people in town called him all the time to ask about some aspect of state or local politics from his years on the political beat. "Can't say that I mind, though," he laughed. "People treat me like I'm some kind of living library. And, well, I kind of like it. Anyway, maybe she rang me up and I'm just too senile to recall."

"She would probably have called you with questions about Leon Delacroix," I said.

"Judge Leon Delacroix?" Mr. Krancke asked.

"Yes," I said.

"You know, I think she did call. A young woman. About a year and a half ago. I didn't make the connection that she was your wife I'm sorry to say."

"Can you remember what you told her about Judge Delacroix?"

Mr. Krancke laughed and said, "Knowing what a windbag I am, I'm sure I told her everything I knew."

And from memory Krancke began to recite the highlights of Delacroix's career, from his early days as a role player in the Leblanc administration, through his brief service on the City Council, to his years as first a state court and then a federal judge.

"In the mid-sixties," Mr. Krancke said, "Judge Delacroix was one of the giants."

"Then you knew him well," I said. "Still know him perhaps."

Mr. Krancke laughed again. "Well, I knew him professionally," he said. "I wrote about him. I admired him. But I didn't know him personally. You're a newspaperman, Mr. Barnett. And you know there are a couple of rungs on the social ladder between a newspaperman and the station of society occupied by Mr. and Mrs. Leon Delacroix."

"I guess that's true," I admitted to Mr. Krancke.

To be honest, I hadn't ever fretted about my social station in life. I had always had Joan, and that was all the society I ever needed or desired. Too, I suspected that class divisions in our city were not as rigid as they had been when Mr. Krancke had come of age. But even today he was right that there were certain influential organizations that a man like me could never enter, no matter what I might accomplish. I could win a Pulitzer for my criticism and still never be considered even remotely worthy for membership in Rex or Comus, two of the oldest and most prestigious Mardi Gras Krewes. Such elite clubs weren't a matter of merit. They were a matter of blood.

"Did you ever know anything about Judge Delacroix to his discredit?" I asked.

"Not at all," Mr. Krancke replied. "He's got a harridan for a wife and had a big-time crook for a father-in-law. A big-time racist crook for a father-in-law, as a matter of fact." And then Krancke related an incident involving Mason's membership in the White Citizen's Council and his role even in the early sixties of keeping Denoux Leblanc from moving more expeditiously to loosen the municipal restraints of Jim Crow.

"But," Krancke continued, "I've always thought the judge himself was as fine a man as ever emerged into public life in this city."

I cleared my throat. "Mr. Krancke," I said, "I need to know if you ever heard rumors that Judge Delacroix was part black."

Mr. Krancke paused a moment before responding, and I suddenly felt extremely uncomfortable.

"I don't want you to think I'm in league with the new Grand Imperial state representative from Metairie," I added.

It was amazing what growing up a white Southerner did to your head. You wanted to assure everybody you met that you weren't a racist. Even other white Southerners. The South had gone through a recent period in which people at least gave lip service to a belief in racial equality. George Wallace, for Christ's sake, had won his last term as governor of Alabama running as a liberal with heavy black support. But with David Duke commanding international headlines from our closest suburb, I found my old paranoia resurfacing and wanted to reassure Mr. Krancke that whatever my motives in asking such a question they were not racist.

"I really do read your work, Mr. Barnett," Mr. Krancke said, much to my relief. "So I'd hardly have reason to think such a thing as that. And I definitely did talk to your wife. I remember that she asked me the same exact question. I am curious, though, as to what this is all about."

"It's a very long story," I told him. "But if I can count on your confidentiality, it boils down to the fact that my wife was suspicious someone may have been blackmailing the judge. She died while she was still investigating that possibility. I'm just trying to learn if you told her anything that might have led her to believe allegations of racially mixed blood could have made Delacroix vulnerable."

"Well, as I told your wife," Mr. Krancke said, "there *were* rumors that Delacroix was an octaroon. I first heard them in his race for City Council back in 1948. Of course, nobody sensible put much stock in such smears. The old Anselmo crowd still thought it could muscle back into power in those days, still thought the Leblanc bunch was made up of short-term, do-gooder lightweights. And you have to remember, Mr. Barnett, accusing a rival of having black blood was a very old tactic. Very vicious. And very old. For a century down here it was leveled at most anyone in public life who wasn't blessed with blond hair and blue eyes."

"Delacroix isn't really dark-skinned, though," I said. "I know lots of Italians, Greeks, Armenians, who are darker than he is."

"What octaroon is dark-skinned, though? I'd say if you put Judge Delacroix in a line with Mayors Beaumont and Fredericks and told somebody new in town that two of the three of them were black, they'd pick Delacroix as often as either of the other two. And up until Delacroix himself ruled such legislation unconstitutional, Louisiana law, remember, defined you as 'colored' if you had as little as one-sixteenth black blood."

"Anyway," I said, "when his opponents alleged he had a black ancestor, I presume Delacroix denied it."

"Well now you have to remember such accusations weren't made publicly. That could have led to serious lawsuits. Or among the well-born, duels for all I know. You smeared a man with a whisper campaign."

"So how did Delacroix fight back?"

"His bunch started a rumor that a *Post-Chronicle* reporter had gotten into the Office of Vital Records and had checked his ancestry all the way back to Adam."

"And that wasn't true?" I said.

"No. The beauty of it from Delacroix's side was that it was true."

"How do you know?"

Mr. Krancke chortled. "I know because I was the reporter," he said.

The breath went out of me. Was this yet another dead end?

"You checked the race designations in Delacroix's family tree all the way back through eight great-grandparents?" I asked, exasperated.

"Couldn't do that," Mr. Krancke said. "But didn't have to."

"What do you mean, couldn't do that?"

"Let me tell you how all this came about," Mr. Krancke said. "I was still a fairly young reporter in those days. About your age, I guess."

It was odd to hear myself referred to as young. Even "fairly" young.

"I'd been covering the Leblanc bunch from their first whirlwind bid for power right after the war. I was sort of one of their promoters in the press, I guess you could say. So when all this stuff about Leon Delacroix having colored blood came about, I guess people around him just naturally figured I might be willing to help out."

"And you were," I interjected.

"Yeah, I don't mind saying that I was. One of his people contacted me and told me they wanted to use me to put an end to the rumors about his ancestry. I told them that was OK by me but that I wouldn't be a party to anything fraudulent. They assured me that they would never think of such a thing. So I agreed to meet one of Delacroix's men at the Vital Records office one night at two a.m."

"How'd that work?" I asked. "The Office of Vital Records doesn't exactly keep round-the-clock hours."

Mr. Krancke laughed again. "I didn't insist that everything we did be legal, Mr. Barnett. I only insisted that I wouldn't lie for Delacroix."

"And Delacroix's man had a key to a public building, of course."

"No one ever said it didn't pay to have friends in city hall," Mr. Krancke said.

"So what did you find?" I asked.

"I found out that Leon Delacroix was a white man. Never wrote a story on it. Wouldn't have. Didn't have to. I saw the evidence. And Delacroix's people put out the word that someone had. And that turned the trick. Story about him being part black resurfaced again in the sixties when he was a judge. But everybody knew that was just pure spite because of the kind of decisions he was handing down, striking down one Jim Crow law after another."

"But," I pointed out, "you said you didn't see the birth records of all eight of Delacroix's great-grandparents."

"Saw seven of them," he said. "White as the cliffs of Dover. The other one was missing."

"The one for Annette Jeansonne?" I asked.

"Don't remember the woman's name," Mr. Krancke said. "Was a great-grandmother, though. Do recall that."

"So how do you know that woman wasn't black? If she was, then Delacroix *was* an octaroon."

"Didn't have to see her birth certificate, Mr. Barnett. Saw her baby's."

"I don't follow you," I said.

"Place on the birth certificate said 'race of mother.' And right in that little square was the word 'white.' Simple as that."

"She could have been passing for white," I speculated. "There's been plenty of that in this storied land of ours."

"Could have been," Mr. Krancke admitted. "But if so, she was doing an awfully good job at it. Husband was white. Baby was white. And she must have had light enough skin that when she told the recording clerk she was white it didn't occur to him to write down anything different."

I thanked Mr. Krancke for sharing his recollections with me so freely, and rang off with a renewed sense of frustration. If he was right, racial mixture disappeared as a possible key to Judge Delacroix's behavior. But it was the best lead I had had in my months of searching. I was desperate not to have to give it up.

Then Jason Roux called me back, and I concluded I didn't have to.

Jason said that he'd made up some bullshit, contacted Vital Records and inquired about the birth record of Annette Jeansonne. Clerk gave him everything he wanted to know. Annette Jeansonne was born in the country out from Baton Rouge in 1848. Her father was a white man named Alain Jeansonne. But there was only a blank space in the area of the birth certificate where the race of Annette's mother should have been shown. The mother's maiden name was given as Marie Toussaint, her age as seventeen and her birthplace as Port-au-Prince, Haiti. There was, obviously, no way of determining whether Marie Toussaint was white or black. But the most interesting thing that Jason had to report concerned what appeared in the blank where the baby's race was identified. Something had once been written there. But it was no longer legible. It had been obliterated with a black smudge.

After getting off the phone with Jason, I decided that I had almost all the case I needed. In the late 1940's, if not for sometime thereafter (including up to the very moment for all I knew), Leon Delacroix had possessed unauthorized access to the Office of Vital Records. He had been accused of having black blood in his race for City Council in 1948. And he had deflated those rumors by showing Herman Krancke the birth records of his ancestors. Only Krancke hadn't seen the birth certificate for Annette Jeansonne, which Krancke had been told was missing. Where was it in 1948? And why was it back in the records office in 1989?

My speculations were simple and straightforward. Krancke hadn't been shown Annette Jeansonne's birth certificate because it had originally shown that she was born black. Some ancient recording clerk had merely neglected to note that Marie Toussaint was a black woman. Delacroix had managed to get the baby's race designation obliterated, perhaps in preparation for Krancke's visit to the records office. But then he'd grown fearful that Krancke would be suspicious of the smudge, and he'd be worse off than before. Presumably, Annette Jeansonne was light-skinned enough that by the time she gave birth to Christine Thibodeaux in 1866 she'd had no trouble listing her race as white on Christine's birth certificate. Or, it suddenly occurred to me, since 1866 was Reconstruction and like every other Southern state, Louisiana was being run by an occupation army and a horde of carpetbaggers, maybe Annette Jeansonne didn't even have to be all that light-skinned to list her race as white. Whatever, there was obviously some problem with Annette Jeansonne's birth certificate that made Delacroix's people want to peg her racial identification from the birth certificate of her daughter rather than from her own. So they told Krancke that Annette Jeansonne's birth certificate wasn't in the records office. It wasn't all that hard to believe a record from so long ago might be missing. And they let Krancke come to the conclusion that he did: if Annette Jeansonne was white when Christine Thibodeaux was born in 1866, she was probably just as white at her own birth in 1848.

All of this was extremely unpleasant business, of course. And I felt soiled just in thinking about the fact that a drop of black blood, however many generations back, could threaten a man's prospects in public life—if my suspicions were correct—right into the 1980s.

What a sick fucking world.

Nonetheless, I judged that what I was abruptly sitting on now was explosive. I knew Retif's motivations for blackmailing Delacroix. Greed. Build Thomas Jefferson Magnet on the U.N.O. site and cash in for years afterwards selling houses on the old Baseview Apartments property at premium prices to parents eager to locate their kids in the neighborhood of the city's best school, a school where a sizable white student body was guaranteed. Retif just hid his involvement with the Lake Magnolias subdivision behind the identity of his son-in-law. So far so good. Probably a little scratch for Hastings Moon and perhaps a little more for some other members of the school board. And then it was just go to the bank with truckloads of money.

Only Tom Grieve tried to get in the way with his lawsuit. Maybe there was a time when they thought they could have just bought Tom Grieve. But Grieve wasn't hoping to build Jefferson High for the money. Or at least not *just* for the money. He saw landing the contract for building the school as his ticket to the world of big-time contracting. He was after the visibility at least as much as the money. So Tom Grieve couldn't be bought.

And the case was a loser for Retif. That's what Joan thought. No doubt Tammy Dieter-White thought so too. That meant Retif had to have the judge. Only Judge Leon Delacroix couldn't be bought either. He was probably too proud for one thing. And he didn't need the money. But he did have a skeleton in his closet, or as that despicable old Southern saying went, a "nigger in his woodpile." And so he was willing to do for the sake of racial purity what he wasn't willing to do for money. Only nobody had counted on the conflict of interest charge Joan brought about Delacroix's service on the U.N.O. board. The judge lied to sidestep that land mine. And even though it finally got him reversed at the Supreme Court, by that time it was too late for Tom Grieve. The school was already built. The residents of Lake Magnolias were already having barbecues around their backyard pools. And Sheldon Retif was drawing interest on his millions.

That's the way I had it figured. And I figured that when Joan had most of the pieces of this infamous puzzle put together, Retif or maybe Delacroix or maybe the two of them together had her killed. But I was still alive, and now I had the pieces put together too. And I was going to fry the bastards.

I called Carl Shaney to tell him so.

"This is Mike," I said when Carl answered.

"Where the fuck are you?" Carl said.

"Home," I said, ignoring his expletive. "I've got something . . ."

"I've got something for you, too," Carl interrupted. "You just got a call from a guy with Universal Studios. You weren't here, as usual, so it got bumped over to me. You know how I dig acting as your answering service."

"I'm sorry, man, but I've really got . . ."

"Guy said they've got a print of the new Spike Lee movie, *Doing the Right Things*, or something . . ."

"*Do the Right Thing*," I said.

"All right, *Do the Right Thing*. Anyway they've got a print they're sending down here. A work print or something the guy called it. They . . ."

"A work print's actually a pretty finished print except for . . ."

"Hey, I really don't give a shit," Carl said. "You're mistaking me for somebody who wants to have a conversation. I want to just pass this information along like the good secretary you think I am and be the fuck done with it. You get my drift."

"What the fuck's eating you, man?"

"You're the fuck's eating me. Your cop woman stops in here this morning and tells me you won't be in because you got a lead on this Jefferson High Magnet shit I told you to stop messing with over eight months ago. I tell the Old Man this, and you're drawing unemployment. I don't like you putting me in that kind of position."

"But I do have a lead on it, Carl. I've got the thing goddamned solved, and I called to get you to lend me a hand with it."

"The only thing I'm lending you, Mike, is this piece of advice: You are the goddamn movie critic at this paper. And I expect you to be working on stories about movies and movie stars and movie directors, not stories about high schools."

And he smashed the phone down in my ear.

*   *   *

I gathered Joan's file together with my notes from my meeting with Cheney Hickman and my telephone conversations with Herman Krancke, Jason Roux and the secretary at Retif Realty and set off for work. At the paper I went immediately into Carl's office, closed the door and sat down in the chair beside his desk.

"We have to talk," I said.

He just stared at me a long moment. Then he picked up the pack of Camel Lights on his desk, shook one out, slipped it between his lips and lit up. He took a drag, blew out the smoke and said, "I hope it's about this *Do the Right Thing* flick? Guy at Universal says they're entering it at Cannes, and it's gonna win first prize."

I took a deep breath. I'd been reading about Spike Lee's movie, and I certainly planned to see it. But I didn't want to talk about it right then.

"When are they gonna have it here?" I asked.

"Tomorrow."

"Where?"

"Canal Place. Two p.m."

"I'll cover it, Carl. You know that. And I'm sorry you got stuck with taking the message."

He took another big drag on his cigarette, ground out the stub and blew a cloud of gray smoke toward the light fixture in the center of the false ceiling.

"I need to talk to you," I said, "about the Jefferson Magnet decision and what I've learned."

"You just won't lay off this, will you?"

"One of these days I'm gonna get you to explain to me why you're so dead set against my working on this story. But for right now I want you just to listen to what I've got."

He didn't respond, other than to light up another cigarette. And so I laid it out for him. He listened without comment through my account of Retif's interest in Lake Magnolias via the personage of his son-in-law, Lloyd *John* Broom.

When I paused at the end of this particular part of my investigations, Carl rubbed at his temples with the thumb and middle finger of his left hand and suddenly said, "Okay, Mike, I'm convinced. You're right. What you've got *is* a story."

I was elated.

"If you can prove it," he added.

"I can prove everything I've told you," I said, "This'll put that bastard Sheldon Retif in jail."

Carl leaned toward me across his desk. "Get serious, Mike. This'll embarrass the man. It'll stain his reputation if he bothers to give a shit. He'll probably make a big deal about demanding a retraction, and he'll file a nuisance lawsuit, which he'll quietly drop after we print a piece saying we stand behind our story. And then that'll be the end of it. If he's broken any laws, from what you've told me so far, it's not the kind of thing that somebody goes to jail for."

"You can go to jail for blackmail, though, can't you?" I said, with more than a trace of smugness.

And then I told Carl the second half of my story, the half concerning Leon Delacroix's parentage. I had this fleeting vision that when I finished Carl was going to rise from his chair and holler "stop the presses" and insist I get right to work for a page one story with a six-column banner headline.

Instead, when I completed my account, Carl looked at me and said, "And you think that's a story, too?"

"Yes," I said.

"Man, that ain't even shit," Carl said.

I was shocked. And not for the first time in my dealings with Carl Shaney about Leon Delacroix, I was surprised and troubled by his reactions.

"Look," I said. "I know we're on awfully sensitive ground here. This business about racially mixed blood and all. But you and I damn well know that lots of white people in this town, most white people in this town probably, fuck, probably most white people in this country, would do anything to keep other people from thinking they had a black ancestor. Even though most of them do, I suspect. If Lucy the Ape Eve, or whatever, is the mother of us all, and she was from Africa, I guess all of us have black blood. And that's fine by me. But it's goddamn well not fine with lots of folks. And that means Delacroix was vulnerable to blackmail. Retif had Delacroix in his pocket for Christ's sake.

Carl lit his third cigarette, puffed on it and carefully rolled the ash against the sides of his ashtray.

"You don't have proof, Mike," Carl said. "That's what you don't have. You don't even have proof that Delacroix's great-grandmother was black."

"I don't need proof that she *was*, Carl. I don't know why you can't see that. I've got proof that rumors about Delacroix's ancestry have been in circulation for over forty years. I've got proof that forty years ago he went to rather extraordinary lengths to disprove those rumors. I've got evidence that somebody has tampered with Annette Jeansonne's birth certificate, and proof that Delacroix had both access to it and reason to want to alter it."

"But you've got nothing to link Retif and his people to Delacroix, no witness to blackmail, nothing of the kind."

"So I don't write it claiming I do," I-said. "I'm not an investigative reporter. But I've been around long enough to know how to pull off a finesse. I write up what I've got on Retif, Lloyd John Broom,

Jefferson Magnet and the Lake Magnolias subdivision. I write up what I've got on Tom Grieve's lawsuit. I note that Leon Delacroix was the judge who rendered a controversial decision . . ."

"You and Joan were the only people in town who thought it was controversial," Carl interjected.

"And Tom Grieve," I said tersely.

Carl took a deep drag on his cigarette. "And Tom Grieve," he admitted, exhaling.

"And if somebody tries to protest my use of the term 'controversial' to describe the Delacroix decision, we do another whole piece on the specifics of the trial. That works to our benefit, not Delacroix's."

"Go on," Carl said.

"We point out that Delacroix was the presiding judge," I repeated. "And then we go into all the embarrassing stuff about the rumors of his mixed blood ancestry, quote Herman Krancke on his experience with being ushered into the Office of Vital Records in the middle of the night. And leave it at that."

"And leave it at that?" Carl said.

"Let the reader draw his own conclusion. We make no accusations. Just juxtapose the facts."

Carl stubbed out his cigarette, leaned back in his chair, and folded his arms across his broad chest.

"I wouldn't run it," he said.

I looked at him, incredulous. "You wouldn't run it?" I said.

"It's not my decision, of course," Carl said, "but with a piece like the one you're describing, the Old Man would ask my opinion, and I'd tell him not to run it."

"Why the fuck would you do that? Why the *fuck* would you do that?"

I was pissed, and I made not the slightest effort to hide that fact. Carl was evidently pissed, too.

"Because it's accusation by innuendo," he said heatedly. "You don't have one scrap of evidence that Retif blackmailed Delacroix. But you're willing to drag Delacroix's name through the mud because you don't like a decision he rendered in a case your wife tried. I don't believe in using the pages of this newspaper for carrying out personal vendettas."

"It's pretty odd coming from you that reporting on the possibility of a black ancestor constitutes dragging a man's name through the mud."

Carl spoke to me as if he were spitting. "It always comes back to race doesn't it, white boy?" he said.

I leaped to my feet. I was absolutely furious.

"You son of a bitch," I said.

"Fuck you, Mike," Carl replied. "You want to call names, why don't we really call names."

"I just called you a son of a bitch. I impugned your goddamn mother. What else do you want me to call you?"

"I want you to call me what you want to call me. What you really want to call me."

I turned around and put my right fist through the fiber board that made up the artificial walls of Carl's office. Carl was on his feet now, too, as mad as I was. Neither of us was any longer in good shape. We hadn't been in years, and we hadn't even played racquetball since Christmas. But we were both big men, natively agile and strong enough to hurt each other if we had done something as pointlessly stupid as starting to fight. Fortunately for both of us, Amy Stuart opened the door and stuck her head into Carl's office at that exact moment.

"Everything okay in here?" she asked.

I rubbed the knuckles on my right hand. Carl abruptly sat down and picked up his pack of cigarettes.

"Mike and I were just discussing his review of Mamet's *Things Change*," Carl said to Amy. "I liked it more than he did."

"I liked it," I said. "I just had certain reservations."

Carl lit his cigarette and looked at Amy. "See," he said. "We can't even agree on that."

Amy looked pointedly at me rubbing my hand and then at the hole in the wall behind me. "You two guys just remember that you're friends," she said.

Carl waved her out of his office with an upward flick of his wrist.

"This is a newspaper," he said to her. "Go write a story."

She backed out of the office and closed the door behind her. I sat back down and leaned over Carl's desk and picked up his pack of cigarettes.

"Mind?" I asked.

"Since when did you ever ask me if you could bum one of my cigarettes?"

"Since you accused me of wanting to pursue a personal vendetta rather than a matter of principle."

"Just take the fucking cigarette," he said.

I lit the cigarette, my first in months. It tasted so awful I could barely manage a second puff. But I did. And we smoked a moment or two in silence.

"Will you listen if I try to make the case, circumstantial as it might be, that Delacroix must have been in Retif's pocket?"

Carl sighed, rubbed at his nose and then his eyes with the fingers of both hands.

"Go ahead," he said.

"Leon Delacroix is a superb jurist," I said. "His record is as fine as anybody who ever sat on the federal bench in this district. And yet he ruled as he did against Tom Grieve."

"But nobody thinks that was wrong except you," Carl said quietly.

"Nobody in this town gave a shit about what was happening to Tom Grieve. Nobody except those directly involved looked closely at the issues of the case. Everybody in town thought the U.N.O. site was better for the new magnet school, and, in fact, it probably was, so everybody wanted it to be built there. Everybody wanted Tom Grieve to lose. But that doesn't mean he *should* have lost. Under the law."

"Okay," Carl said, "but that doesn't mean . . ."

"Let me finish, okay?"

"Okay," Carl said.

"I could get a lawyer in here to convince you of the rightness of Tom Grieve's position, but . . ."

"You don't have to do that, Mike. I concede that Grieve got screwed. I just think the law doesn't always provide justice."

"Well in this case, the law would have, if Delacroix had ruled by the law. But he didn't. And he didn't on purpose."

"That's exactly what you haven't proved."

"Answer me this," I said. "And if you answer it, I'll drop this whole business. But if you can't, you agree to help me."

"Just ask your question," Carl said.

"You remember how Joan got the case reversed by the Supreme Court?"

"On a technicality."

"On the technicality that Delacroix lied," I said.

Carl didn't respond, and after a moment of our staring at each other, I went over the whole thing for him, step by step. "Leon Delacroix knew he shouldn't be hearing the *Retif* case and sitting on the U.N.O. Board at the same time," I said. "He even admitted that if he'd realized it he would have recused himself."

"But he says he didn't realize it."

"That's the lie, and besides it was pointed out to him, Carl. It was pointed out to him while the case was still in his control. He had announced his decision, but the ruling wasn't final. The case was still within the ten-day period for post-trial motions when Joan confronted him with the conflict of interest. He could still have stepped aside. And he should have. But he didn't. And more than that he lied to cover up for himself. Admitted he was on the board, but said that he knew of nothing about his board membership that could be construed as a conflict. Joan didn't know he'd been present and voting on the land transfer until she subpoenaed the U.N.O board minutes. But by that time Grieve was already screwed. Hell, Delacroix was on the board when U.N.O. sold the Baseview Apartments to Retif under the guise of John Broom. He no doubt voted for that too. For all we know his hands are as dirty as they can get in this business. But we know for sure Delacroix lied. And now we've got a connection as to why it was awfully useful to Retif for Delacroix to have lied. Furthermore, we know something about Delacroix that Retif could have used to compel his cooperation if money wasn't sufficient, which it probably wasn't. That's my argument. It may be circumstantial, but I still think it's goddamn powerful. I don't relish going after a man like Leon Delacroix, Carl. But I think he caved in to blackmail and screwed Tom Grieve, and I think he ought to be called into account for it."

Carl sat with his eyes on his desk, watching it seemed, only his hands as they held the round ash tray on his desk.

"And they killed Joan to keep it from coming out," I said.

Carl looked up at me and said softly, "You don't really believe that, Mike."

"I do believe it," I said. "I can't prove it. Yet. But I absolutely do believe it."

Carl just stared at me.

"Look," I said. I'm not suggesting we print such a charge immediately. But you just consider this: Joan talked to Cheney Hickman and got from him what I got. She talked to Herman Krancke. And within a week she was dead."

Carl closed his eyes and shook his head.

"That's really what this is about, Carl. We either put the bastards in jail, or I'm gonna kill them."

Carl got up from his desk and moved to stand by the window of his office which looked down from the second floor onto Royal Street. The stores across the way were decorated with the purple, gold and green banners of another Mardi Gras.

"We have a rule," he said, finally, speaking with his back to me. "If you have charges that you're going to print about somebody, you call that person, reveal the gist of what you plan to write, and give him the opportunity to comment. You can't afford to talk to Retif, so I'll do it. You make arrangements to see Judge Delacroix."

He turned to me only as I was about to step through the door. "And after you've seen him," he said, "you start watching your back."

＊　　　＊　　　＊

As soon as I left Carl's office, I called Leon Delacroix's office in the Camp Street Courthouse and asked for an appointment to see him. His secretary put me on hold for a minute and then reported that I could see him that afternoon.

I was ushered into Delacroix's office at five-fifteen. I was extremely nervous, and I had made an outline of my argument in my notebook to refer to as I talked. The judge stood as I entered his office and came around from behind his desk to shake my hand. To greet him I shifted to my left hand the briefcase in which I had brought my notes, some writing tablets and a tape recorder.

The judge was courtly and gracious. Somehow, mindlessly so, I'd thought he would be arrogant and combative. I felt principled in what I was about to do, but at the same time I felt like an assassin camouflaged in a sniper's lair.

Standing so close to the judge as I was now, I was impressed anew with how short and seemingly frail he was. I suspected that he weighed barely half what I did. I could grab him in an arm lock, I thought, and snap his spine like a dry twig. But I'd take greater pleasure in seeing the justice meted out to him be slow and entirely public.

The judge was wearing a dark gray suit and a red bow tie. I took his hand, which was bony and loose-skinned inside of mine. His grip was firm, however. As we greeted each other, I could smell the strong scent of his cologne.

He asked me to be seated in a high-backed leather chair adorned with shiny brass upholstery tacks. As he moved back behind his desk, I looked at his lustrous office, its walnut bookshelves lining every wall from floor to ceiling, and I reflected that it was in this room, presumably, Leon Delacroix had reached the landmark decisions which had cut off Jim Crow's arms and legs if, sadly, not his head.

"And what may I do for you, Mr. Barnett?" Judge Delacroix asked. "It has been some years since a member of the fourth estate has sought to interview me."

He leaned across his desk at me and smiled. The judge's desk looked as if it had been prepared for a photography session. It was almost obsessively neat, and its polished mahogany gleamed like a mirror. Equipped with a blotter, a brass lamp and several paperweights, there was practically nothing else on it, no papers or folders or books. A clean yellow legal pad lay in the center of the leather-cornered blotter, and alongside it lay a black Mont Blanc fountain pen, uncapped, the light of the green-shaded lamp glinting off the pen's golden nib. Every detail in this room, I thought, represented a world of exquisite finery of the sort that I had almost never encountered.

"I hope you're not preparing an article on the aging judiciary," the judge said jovially. "I was in favor of a mandatory retirement age when I was a young man. But now that I'm an old man, I'm against it."

He laughed and brushed a wayward strand of white hair back off his forehead.

"Judge Delacroix," I said, my voice cracking, "I am preparing an article for the *States-Tribune* about the building of Thomas Jefferson Magnet High School, about the lawsuit which resulted from the circumstances of the Orleans Parish School Board's awarding of its Certificate 34 for the building of that school, about your role in presiding over that case while also serving on the Board of Trustees for the University of New Orleans, and about certain facts and allegations concerning your racial ancestry, which have come to light during the course of our investigation."

I had spoken all this while staring straight down into the notebook on my lap. When I looked up at the judge now, his eyes had gone glassy behind his gold-rimmed bifocals, and splotches of color seemed to break out in U-shaped arcs across his cheekbones.

"We would like to have your comments about the article we are preparing, and to insure accuracy I have brought along a tape recorder, which, with your permission, I'd like to play as we talk."

The judge answered me only with a wave of his hand, and I prepared the recorder and then set it on his desk between us, gently, so as not to mar the desk's shining surface.

"Do you have any comments so far?" I asked.

Recovering a little, it seemed, the judge laughed.

"Not yet, young man," he said.

He slipped off his glasses and rubbed at either side of the bridge of his nose with a thumb and forefinger. He smiled again when I didn't respond or begin.

"I haven't heard what you have to say," he pointed out.

And so I told him, slowly, leaving out nothing, the entire argument from A to Y, if not to the Z of Joan's murder, just as I had laid it out for Carl, just as I planned to write it. Through it all, the judge sat silent. In the early going, he scratched down notes or thoughts on his legal pad. But after a while he stopped, capped his pen, leaned back in his chair and closed his eyes. I paused regularly to give him the opportunity to respond, but he never did. On several occasions I asked directly if he'd like to comment; each time he answered only by lifting his right arm from the elbow, a curled palm outward toward me.

"Is that all?" Judge Delacroix inquired when I finally finished, over an hour later.

He put his glasses back on and sat up more erect in his chair.

"That is all we are planning to print at the present time," I said.

"You have more that you're planning for later?" the judge asked.

"Other details may come to light once we break this story," I said.

"Other details about what?" he inquired.

"One never knows," I said.

I recognized the menace in my voice as I delivered that last line, and I recognized as well the unsavory fact about myself that I took a thoroughly sadistic pleasure in scaring this tiny man. I comforted myself that he deserved far more than what he was getting from me.

"So as it boils down now," the judge said, "I gather that you're alleging I was blackmailed by Sheldon Retif. Is that correct?"

My tape recorder was running, and I chose to be very careful now. I wasn't at all sure of what I could or couldn't, should or shouldn't say. And I knew that I was dealing with a man whose legal keenness was infinitely greater than mine.

"Were you blackmailed by Sheldon Retif?" I asked.

Presumably I couldn't get myself in trouble if I asked questions rather than made statements.

"Would it matter to you if I said I was not?" the judge asked.

"I would report that you had denied being blackmailed," I said.

"But you would run your story anyway."

"I don't make that decision," I said, side-stepping. "I am employed to write stories. Our editors determine what stories actually appear in the paper."

"But you're going to write a story implying that Sheldon Retif blackmailed me to rule against Thomas Grieve?"

"I am going to write only such facts as I have at my command," I asserted, priding myself that I hadn't said yes, but hadn't let him force me to say no.

"And you are going to print this story about my having a black ancestor?"

"I am going to write a story including such facts about your racial ancestry as I have at my command," I said.

The judge laughed and stared at me with eyes full of mysterious meaning.

"Your paper didn't run a story to that effect, my young man," he said, "forty years ago when it would have mattered."

"You hadn't made your ruling in *Retif* forty years ago," I retorted.

The judge rose abruptly to his feet, reached across the desk and snapped off my tape recorder. He started around his desk as if he were going to show me immediately out of his office, but he stopped on the side to my left, as if he'd suddenly remembered something he'd almost forgotten. It occurred to me that he had spent the better part of a lifetime having people defer to him. He wasn't used to the thinly veiled contempt I was exhibiting. I was defiantly ecstatic at possessing the right to speak to him with such evident, righteous rudeness. But such was my Southern rearing, that all in one gamy stew of emotion I felt wildly wrong to treat a man of his position and earned authority with such disrespect.

"You cannot prove a word of what you have said here today," the judge hissed.

"On the contrary, Your Honor," I said. "I can prove every word I have uttered here today. And I intend to."

Judge Delacroix slapped his hand down on his desk top, and the sound exploded into the room like a gunshot.

"You cannot prove that I was blackmailed to render a false decision," the judge insisted. "You cannot do it."

I stood up and began to place the tape recorder and my notebooks back into my briefcase. "A technical distinction perhaps," I said, not looking at him. "You are probably thinking of the kind of proof that is necessary in a court of law. But we're going to try this case in a much more important place for a man like you. We're going to try it in the court of public opinion. And in that court we'll see what I can prove and what I can't."

The judge moved back behind his desk now. He picked up his fountain pen and absently began to click the top off and then on again, over and over.

"Why do you care so much about this, Mr. Barnett? Why would you go to so much trouble to ruin a man you don't know?"

He looked up at me, and I stared at his eyes, filmy behind his glasses.

"My wife was Joan Barnett," I said.

At first he showed no sign of recognition.

"Tom Grieve's attorney," I added. "You ruled against her."

"A lovely woman," he said. "Pretty. And a very good attorney."

I snorted. "My wife is dead, Leon. As if you didn't know. Dead you bastard."

His eyes seemed to focus on me for the first time in minutes.

"Dead?" he said. "But surely you don't think . . ."

He didn't finish his sentence, but instead turned and pulled his chair toward himself and sat down.

When he was seated, he looked at me again and said, "How did your wife die, Mr. Barnett? Surely you can't possibly believe I had anything to do with it."

"You tell me, Judge. She believed you screwed Tom Grieve. And she was out to prove it. And she was getting close. Only about the time she got a handle on your genealogy, she got run over while jogging on the St. Charles Avenue neutral ground."

"I know nothing about this," the judge said.

"Yeah," I said. "And you probably know nothing either about the fact that the man who ran her down, an unemployed black man with ties to the organized crime operations your father-in-law once managed, ended up a shriveled corpse floating face down in the Industrial Canal. You tell me what you know and what you don't know. I'll get every quote absolutely perfect."

"I know nothing about your wife's death, Mr. Barnett. I swear that to you."

"Yeah," I said. "Well, let's just say you're not a man I've come to put a lot of confidence in. You want to change your mind on any of this, give me a call."

I picked up my briefcase and headed for the door. He called out to me, though, just as I opened it.

"Mr. Barnett," he said, somehow as if he weren't speaking to me at all, but to himself, all alone in an empty room, "I doubt that it matters to you, but there's no truth to the rumors that I have black ancestors."

"I'll quote you to that effect exactly," I said, as I closed the door behind me.

*   *   *

With Wilson proofreading pages as I printed them, I began writing the story that night. I got to the office early the next morning, worked straight through lunch, and finished a rough draft about one-thirty. On my way over to Canal Place to see the new Spike Lee movie, I stopped in Carl's office to give him a hard copy of the draft. He greeted me with pained eyes. I asked him to look the story over for me.

"I've never written a piece like this before," I said. "I could use your help."

He placed the sheets of the story in his in-basket, and we didn't speak for an awkward second.

Finally I said, "I've got to go catch that movie. Want to come?"

He did occasionally attend an afternoon screening with me if his schedule permitted it.

"It's the kind of movie we both like," I added. "Lots of bad feelings between the races."

Ignoring my attempt at lightness, he said, "You really going to go through with this piece on Jefferson Magnet and Judge Delacroix?"

"I've written it the best I can," I replied. "You tell me whether it's something you'd recommend to the Old Man. You tell me what it needs to make it right. You help me; I'll fix it."

"I'll look at it," Carl said.

His hands started toying with his pack of cigarettes, though he didn't take one out.

"I'm serious about your going over with me to see the Spike Lee movie," I said. "I'm on my way now."

"Nah, I got work to do," he said.

I kept turning the knob on his door one way and then the other. He began to lightly rap his knuckles on his desk.

"I'm sorry about yesterday," Carl said.

I took a deep breath and smiled. "Yeah, me too," I replied.

I looked around his office. "Sorry about the hole in your wall," I said.

"Yeah," he said. "No big deal."

"Carl?" I asked. "Yesterday, when it got tense, did you think I was about to call you a nigger?"

Carl pursed his lips and then licked them. "Yes," he said slowly. "Yes, I did."

All time seemed to stop. All objects in the room seemed to distort, to sag and melt like the objects in an old photograph which has been discarded into a fireplace.

"Yeah. Well . . ." I said. "That makes two of us."

*   *   *

That night Wilson brought home copies of the files on Jackson Smith. My relentless pressure had paid off. The materials were copied on an ancient and overtaxed Xerox machine. They were grainy and hard to read in places. But Wilson was right that her father had been thorough in summarizing the files' contents. Save for one detail, they provided no further illumination.

The one detail was the second generation Xerox of Jackson Smith's school board employment file photograph. And when I first looked at it, my chest constricted till I thought I might suffocate. For staring straight ahead in that photograph was a face I recognized. The file said Jackson Smith was the man who ran over Joan. But in the chaos of that black day I had paid only the scantest attention to his appearance. My memory registered only a bearded black man, wearing a hat, scruffily attired in the clothes of a day-laborer. Now I recognized him as someone I'd seen recently, and that meant he wasn't a bloated corpse lying in an indigent's grave somewhere in the city. On the contrary, he was the well-dressed, clean-shaven man in a Cadillac who had stopped at my house to ask directions to Longue Vue Gardens.

CHAPTER TWENTY-ONE

At the end of a long, hot summer day, an oversized black youngster walks into a Brooklyn pizzeria owned and operated by a middle-aged white man. He's accompanied by a smaller black man whom the owner had to evict from his establishment earlier in the day. The two young blacks begin to harangue the older white with a barrage of demands. It's after closing hours, and the owner instantly regrets that he'd agreed to stay open to serve four other late arrivals. The large young black man is carrying a boom box with the volume turned up to ear-damage level. He's been in the restaurant previously, and the owner has told him repeatedly that he won't be served unless he turns his radio off. He refuses to do so now. The owner is hot and tired, out of sorts; he loses control of himself. He begins screaming and cursing; he resorts to racial epithets. He grabs a baseball bat that he keeps for protection and smashes the youngster's radio. A fight, of course, ensues. And the result is tragedy.

This is the climactic passage of Spike Lee's controversial Do the Right Thing. *After the violence which closes the film's narrative, Lee ends his picture with two quotes, one from Martin Luther King, the second from Malcolm X. King's message is an eloquent summary of his career-long rejection of violence as a means for achieving civil rights. Malcolm X's statement is more qualified. If violence is committed in self-defense, he says, it isn't violence at all; it is intelligence. No doubt because of the second of these two quotes, Lee has fallen under attack in certain critical quarters.* Do the Right Thing *has been labeled as endorsing racial violence. It has been suggested that the movie may even incite racial disturbance. Summarizing his remarks in* Newsweek, *Jack Kroll has accused Lee of having done the wrong thing.*

Nothing could be further from the truth. Do the Right Thing *is a searing indictment of the current state of racial affairs in this country. It posits that we are sitting on a powder keg in the underclass black community the likes of which we haven't seen since Watts and Harlem in the mid-1960s. It's an angry, at times almost despairing film. But it's also a brutally honest, determinedly fair film. And whatever the implications of the Malcolm X passage (and in the context of the story that precedes it, I'll admit they're murky), and whatever Spike Lee's public comments to the contrary (and I'll admit that Lee's remarks about his own film have been both puzzling and irritating), in the final analysis the picture's stance on violence is unflinching: when violence comes to the black community, those who suffer most and suffer longest are the black residents of that community.*

The narrative in Do the Right Thing *occupies a single day on a single block in the impoverished Bedford-Stuyvesant section of Brooklyn. It's the hottest day of the year with the temperature soaring above the 100-degree mark. The action centers around Sal's Famous Pizzeria, a favored hangout for people in the neighborhood. The pizzeria is run by Sal himself (Danny Aiello) along with his two sons, Pino (John Turturro) and Vito (Richard Edson). Sal is so proud of his Italian-American heritage that he's established a Wall of Fame along one whole side of his restaurant with photographs of such of his heroes as Frank Sinatra, John Travolta, Joe Dimaggio and Robert De Niro. But unlike his older son Pino, Sal isn't at all uncomfortable about plying his trade in a black neighborhood. He's been operating Sal's Famous for 25 years, and he's seen the children of the neighborhood grow into adulthood and bear children of their own. He's proud that many have nourished themselves time and again with food he has made with his own hands.*

Much of Do the Right Thing *is designed to establish the richness of human habitation on the block. We meet a wide array of characters whom Lee sketches quickly but vividly. There's Mookie (writer/producer/director Lee), who works for Sal making deliveries. There's Da Mayor (Ossie Davis), an aging drunk who shares his benign philosophies* with whatever passersby will pause to listen. There is Mother Sister (Ruby Dee), who nurses some secret sorrow and keeps vigilant watch over the block from her second story window perch. And there are the corner men, M.L. (Paul Benjamin), Coconut Sid (Frankie Faison) and Sweet Dick Willie (Robin Harris), who perform like a Greek Chorus, providing obscene commentary on all the events of the day and all the folks who pass their way. Critically, there are two others, Radio Raheem (Bill Nunn), who lives an isolated existence inside the hurricane of sound created by his boom box, and Buggin' Out (Giancarlo Esposito), whose anger at his station in life has turned him foolishly and almost pathetically belligerent.

A host of factors combine like the separate elements in a bomb to produce the explosion of the film's climax. The brutal heat has put everybody on edge. Then Buggin' Out begins to insist that Sal add some blacks to his Wall of Fame. Sal refuses. Buggin' Out tries to get his neighbors to boycott Sal's Famous, but no one will cooperate until late at night when he meets up with Radio Raheem. Radio Raheem agrees to accompany Buggin' Out to confront Sal, though Radio Raheem is little concerned with pictures on the Wall of Fame. He's mad at Sal because Sal makes him turn off his boom box whenever he enters the pizzeria. No one intends it. But no one puts a stop to the escalation of bad feeling. And pretty soon one man is dead, and Sal's Famous has gone up in flames.

Lee elicits memorable performances from his talented ensemble, with Aiello and Davis particular standouts. And he's given them terrific material to work with. The roundedness he achieves with a cast of characters this large is remarkable. If there is a villain, it's the overtly racist Pino, who is hot tempered and capable of needless cruelty to boot. But Lee suggests a ray of hope, however dim, even for a man like Pino. For Pino's heroes are inevitably black; his favorite rock singer is Prince, his favorite basketball player, Magic Johnson, and his favorite movie star, Eddie Murphy. Pino is so confused and stupid that he can praise these men in one sentence and deride in the next all black people as "niggers." When the illogic of his pronouncements is pointed out to him, he can only babble that Prince and Eddie and Magic are "different." But whatever Pino's potential for salvation, and it can be rated slim at the very best, it's important to note that he's essentially a bystander to the violence that caps the film.

The person most blameworthy for the violence that wastes a human life and destroys a business is finally Sal himself. And therein resides the film's tragic quality. For Sal, though guilty of a certain element of latent racism, is a basically decent man. He genuinely likes the people in his pizzeria's neighborhood. He doesn't care for Radio Raheem and Buggin' Out, but then neither does much anybody else. He's kind to Da Mayor. He's solicitous about the welfare of Mookie's hardworking sister, Jade (Joie Lee). And he's sentimental about his relationship with Mookie. He pays Mookie a surprising $250 a week and promises him a job "as long as there is a Sal's Famous." With evident sincerity, he even claims to think of Mookie as a third son. But Sal fails to reach beyond his stubborn certainty that he bears ill will to no one. He makes a living, a good one it seems, off the people of Bedford-Stuyvesant but he neglects to place himself in their shoes. It would be simple enough to grant Buggin' Out's wish, for instance. It would be even simpler to pay Mookie the honor of trusting him in a way we see that Sal won't quite.

But it is essential to understand that Lee's understanding is far too sophisticated to lay sole blame for what happens at Sal's Famous at any one person's feet. Sal loses control of himself at a time that he shouldn't. The cops show up to make things monumentally worse. But the black residents of the block are blameworthy too. Buggin' Out has not been named by accident. He's a troublemaker. Radio Raheem has camouflaged his loneliness in a most anti-social way. Only Da Mayor steps forward to speak a word of caution and restraint. And the movie has long since established that nobody in the neighborhood listens to Da Mayor about much of anything. Even Mother Sister seems to lose her judgment and takes up the chant to "burn it down."

Crucially, it is Mookie who takes the first step that leads to the end of Sal's Famous. And it is therefore fascinating that Lee has cast himself in the role, a way of refusing to place himself above the fray, a way of saying, "And I, Spike Lee too, a part of the human race, must accept blame also." Mookie is the flip side of Sal. Like Sal, he bears no one ill will. But also like Sal, he doesn't rise above himself. He takes advantage of his sister. He's an unwed father who is less than adequately responsible to his son and his son's mother. And in the end he leads a stalled mob to destroy the place of his own employment. His rage is understandable, but so comparably is Sal's earlier. The two of them have sense enough to control themselves. Neither one does. And both are losers for it. Sal loses his business. Mookie loses his livelihood. The neighborhood takes another long step toward hopelessness. And it needn't have happened. If only somebody had been willing to do the right thing.

*   *   *

So said my review.

Do the right thing. Easy to say. Easy to believe. But not always so easy to determine. What is the right thing? That's the question, isn't it? Should we have a metropolitan form of government and expand our tax base? Or should we recognize the need of a minority to have some place they can function as a majority?

Should we solve the abiding problem of de facto racial segregation in our state's universities, for instance, by abolishing the historic black schools which were established during segregation days and merging them into their white neighbors? We already have open admissions at the white schools. Blacks *could* go. But only a few do. A larger number choose to go to the black universities instead. Open admission at the black schools allows any white to attend. But whites don't even apply. So if racial integration is a goal, why not just merge neighboring white and black institutions, faculties and student bodies alike? Presumably we'd achieve racial integration in a way we certainly haven't yet.

Why not? Because aside from bleeding heart types like me, it isn't clear much of anybody is in favor of such an idea. Blacks oppose it at least as readily as whites. Black leaders state a determination to preserve the identities of the historic black institutions. They imply, in fact, racist motives to anyone who proposes the mergers. Is racial integration, then, not what we seek?

I understand the need for the black power movement as advocated by men like Malcolm X and Stokely Carmichael in the 1960s. I understand the rightness of black parents infusing in their children a sense of racial pride. But in the end, I am still an integrationist. In the end, I think our only hope, white and black alike, is to come together. We were separated by white law for three and a half centuries. In defiance of the spirit of the great civil rights legislation of the sixties, we have been separated by white flight and white economic might, by white fear and white selfishness for the last two decades. But more recently we have also been separated by black pride. And I am frightened by the fall I fear that black pride may be leading us toward. In order for there to be a black political power base, do we have to stand by and watch our cities crumble, our urban schools dissolve into chaos? In order for us to retain the identity and the sanctuary of historic black institutions, won't we necessarily perpetuate a system which is inherently separate and unequal?

I am frightened by the inequality because it makes people hostile and makes them desperate. And I am frightened by the separateness because it precludes people from being able to know and thus understand one another. I am frightened by what this separation does to our heads and our hearts and our souls. I belong to that tiny but hardy breed known as the Southern liberal. And I am frightened by what separateness may be doing to me.

I am frightened by the anger I feel at ignorance and at insolence, which, in this city of my rearing, so often sits upon the brow of the black underclass. I am frightened that young black men make me uncomfortable, that I will drive around the block rather than exit my car at night when I see one on my street. I am frightened that when I hear about a rape or a murder, I presume the perpetrator is black. I am frightened that when my house is burgled, I presume the burglars are black. I am frightened to recognize the prejudice unpurged from my heart. More than anything, I am frightened that when I disagree with my black friend, when hostility mysteriously flames open between us, that race becomes an issue. In short, I think that racial integration is our only hope. And I fear that I may think so only because I am white and such an idea is in my own interest.

So what *is* the fucking right thing? I'm not like Sal. I'm not like Mookie. If I could only be sure what it is, I would do the right thing. Wouldn't I?

*   *   *

Was it right, for example, for me to own a gun? Or better to possess a gun, to take one that Wilson owned and, as she suggested, to keep it where I could get at it quickly. Wilson was not as sure as I was that the man looking for Longue Vue Gardens was the same Jackson Smith who had run down Joan. But she believed that I had been threatened with bodily harm while in jail, and she understood that I was frightened, and she was frightened for me. It made the simplest kind of sense to Wilson that I take one of her .38 caliber service revolvers and learn how to use it to protect myself.

And yet, I was reluctant. I'd always believed that we'd be a safer citizenry if the ownership of handguns in this country were practically impossible. But now I had reason to believe that a hired killer was stalking me. Was it the right thing now to make an exception to a life-long principle? My violent fantasies of vengeance against Sheldon Retif and Leon Delacroix never involved shooting them, but rather beating them to death with my fists or a blunt object. And most of all I'd rather beat them to death with public exposure in the *States-Tribune*. But I knew that if Jackson Smith were really still alive, he'd most likely come after me with a gun. Would a gun of my own protect me from him?

I didn't know. That seemed the story of my life. I didn't know.

But I relented, of course. Like most of us save for the likes of Jesus and Gandhi and Martin Luther King, when principle clashed with perceived self-interest, I was quick to set principle aside.

Wilson gave me one of her pistols, and she insisted on showing me how to use it.

"But I don't want to know how to use it," I objected.

"You want to be able to hit what you're aiming at," she said.

"No, I don't," I replied. "I don't want to be aiming at anybody, and I sure don't want to hit them if I do." I tried to explain to her how compromised I felt just agreeing to take the gun in the house.

"Sometimes you act like a sap, Mike," she responded. "Do you know that? Guns aren't toys. I'm giving you this pistol so you can protect yourself. And you can only protect yourself with it if you're willing to use it. And that means you need to know *how* to use it. You don't want to shoot at Jackson Smith at some point and hit a neighbor across the street do you?"

So Wilson took me down to the firing range on Magazine Street and put me through a crash course in the fundamentals. She taught me how to grip the gun with two hands and how to spread my legs and flex my knees into a half crouch for better balance. She taught me how to sight and how to squeeze the trigger with just my finger so as not to pull my aim off line. I didn't exactly turn into Deadeye Dick after one lesson, but my hand-eye coordination had always been good, and Wilson promised I could be an adequate marksman if I wanted.

But I didn't want, of course. I was frightened enough by the prospect of a killer after me that I went through this exercise. But all the while I felt as if I was soiling myself. I was scared enough to take the gun and the shooting lesson, but at the same time I remained incredulous that my life had really come to this ridiculous pass, that I could really be in mortal danger.

For an hour we shot at paper targets of the human form. Wilson hadn't lost her police woman's skills at all. Using her 9 millimeter Beretta she could put a half dozen shots in a row through the heart and then another half dozen between the eyes. On my first round I managed to hit an arm and a leg and a lot of air. Wilson recognized immediately what I was trying to do and chided me sharply.

"Don't be some half-baked liberal asshole, Mike," she said. "It's only in the movies that you can shoot the gun out of the bad guy's hand or wound him without killing him. In the real world, you don't get any second chances." She stepped close to me and turned my shoulders to face her. Then she placed her left hand on the pistol in my right. "If you're in a situation where you have to fire this thing, don't you fuck around for a second. You aim here," she placed her right palm against my chest, "and you keep shooting until he's not moving anymore."

*   *   *

And that was only one of the things I had to contemplate as the merriment of Carnival began to reign all around me. Carl had recommended to the Old Man that we not run my story on Retif-Jefferson Magnet and Judge Delacroix's racial parentage until after Mardi Gras. I didn't want to wait, but Carl insisted the Carnival season was no time to break an investigative story of any kind. I argued with him that Jackson Smith was alive and very possibly stalking me. But even Wilson was reluctant to support that notion, and as a result I suspect Carl thought I was paranoid. I reminded him of the threats I'd received while in Central Lockup, but he responded that I'd been so drunk when I went to Sheldon Retif's house for all he knew I'd been incarcerated in a cell all by myself and had been threatened only by the demons in my own brain.

To make matters in my life worse, I had to endure a sudden, precipitous deterioration in my relationship with Wilson. She had stood by me with tenacious loyalty. But I had pushed her horribly hard to get me access to Jackson Smith's files. And we were both raw because of it, particularly when I felt that Smith's photograph was of the man who actually managed to get inside my house while requesting directions. She was worried about keeping her father out of trouble with his superiors while somebody was perhaps trying to kill me. Then, on the Friday afternoon and evening of the weekend before Mardi Gras, the poisonous things in our relationship festered into a boil.

Though the weather was brisk and a cold front was moving in our direction, Wilson and I decided to turn our Friday lunch hour into an impromptu picnic. We bought oyster po-boys at Acme Seafood House on Iberville and took them to the riverfront to eat. We had barely gotten settled onto one of the benches which face the river, and I was popping open our cans of Barq's Root Beer when a young black couple walked up beside us. The man appeared to be in his middle twenties, the girl with him somewhat younger, perhaps in her late teens. He was wearing black denim pants and a shiny silver shirt he hadn't tucked into his pants. His hair was cut in the flat-top style introduced by movie star Grace Jones and popularized by Olympic sprinter Carl Lewis. The girl was wearing blue jeans rolled up at the ankle, a fuzzy pink sweater and a matching pink ribbon tied underneath her straightened hair into a bow on top of her head.

Because of the coolness of the day, the park was practically empty, but the newcomers nonetheless situated themselves on the bench immediately next to our own where they began to eat a lunch from bags of Popeye's Fried Chicken. Between them they passed a quart bottle of beer sheathed in a brown paper bag. For entertainment, they had provided a boom box which blasted out rap music, the insistent beat of which Wilson and I could feel as well as hear.

The young man and woman were obviously having themselves a grand time, talking and laughing with each other animatedly. We presumed they were thoroughly oblivious to the unspoken irritation we felt that they had not selected a location for themselves on a more distant bench. The serenity of our picnic shattered, Wilson and I ate our po-boys and drank our root beers in silence. We did not remark on our mutual feeling of invasion and did not even comment as the black couple blithely tossed their gnawed chicken bones onto the crushed-rock retaining wall which stretched down to the river.

Finally the black couple departed, taking only their boom box with them. The balled bags of their lunch and the emptied beer bottle they left on the bench as they made their giggling and guffawing way along the promenade toward Canal Street. As we watched them saunter away, Wilson said with unbridled contempt, "Just like a couple of T.N.O.N."

"Don't be racist," I said, softly. "That doesn't help matters."

"I wasn't being racist," she snapped. "I was being descriptive."

"Calling someone a nigger isn't being descriptive," I said. "It's being racist."

"I didn't say the word," she responded. " And besides, *nigger* isn't the key word in that expression. The key word is *trashy*."

"Whatever the *key* word is, how do you think Carl would react to your using a term like *T.N.O.N.*?"

"If he'd been here, he'd have used it before I did," Wilson said sharply. She was still irked and obviously in no mood to be corrected. "You know goddamn well Carl uses the expression T.N.O.N. more than just about anybody we know."

"Yeah, well, I suspect he wouldn't exactly approve of a white person using it."

"Then shame on him for being a hypocrite."

We had finished eating, and I didn't want to argue. But I suddenly felt profoundly unclean. I began to gather up the remains of our picnic, turned away from Wilson and muttered under my breath, "What in the fuck am I doing living with a woman who calls people T.N.O.N.?"

"What?" Wilson said.

I shrugged.

"Let me walk you back to the office," I said, loud enough for her to hear. "Then I need to go see a movie this afternoon."

When we had finished gathering things together, I walked along the riverfront to a garbage container to get rid of our soft drink cans and other trash. I thought that Wilson was walking right behind me. But when I turned around, I saw that she had collected the Popeye's bags and the beer bottle and was down on the retaining wall picking up chicken bones.

*   *   *

My relationship with Wilson reached a crisis point, though, over an issue utterly unrelated to our differing sensibilities on matters of race. When I got home from my screening on that Friday evening before Mardi Gras, I found Wilson sitting at my desk, reading in the entertainment tabloid of that day's paper my review of Peter Masterson's *Full Moon in Blue Water*, a small, quiet, independent film about a Southern bar owner and recent widower (Gene Hackman) who ignores possibilities for a new relationship (with Teri Garr) because he is tormented by loving memories of his dead wife. Spread out on the desk as well was a rough draft of the article I'd been tinkering with for *Film Quarterly* on Claude Lelouch's *And Now My Love*.

Wilson looked up at me as I came into the study. Her eyes were red, and I could tell she'd been crying. Several balls of crumpled Kleenex lay on the desk as well.

"What's wrong?" I asked immediately.

She shook the paper, folded it twice and laid it on the desk. "You're a good writer, Michael Barnett. Have I ever told you that?"

I shrugged my shoulders.

"You put yourself into your work," she said. "That's why you're so good, I guess."

I sat on the sofa in my study. "What are you trying to tell me," I asked.

"I think we're in trouble," she replied.

"And why?" I said softly.

She picked up the manuscript copy of my reflections on *And Now My Love* and began to read aloud. "'The Baptist Sunday Schools I attended as a child surely taught as much hokum as they did wisdom. But I will never forget the lesson that was repeated to us over and over again about the sacred nature of the marital union. The proposition was reduced to a slogan: marriages are made in heaven. And through this slogan my Sunday School teachers tried to communicate that in some mysterious way God's hand is present in the love a man and a woman may be so fortunate as to feel for each other. I have not been a conventionally religious person in my adult years. And I am no longer comfortable ascribing to the will of God events that occur in the lives of men. But in some diffuse way, I find myself increasingly enamored of the magic present in the human spirit. I infrequently now enter a house of worship, but at times I find myself at worship in the human house of cinema. I find, for instance, an allegiance between my Sunday School teachers and the attitude of awe expressed in Claude Lelouch's *And Now My Love*. It is that wonderful picture's premise that true lovers do not so much choose each other as do they find each other. Through God's hand, or better through some magic of the spirit that we have given the name God, two people find each other, once in a lifetime, two people blessed, find each other because they have been made, especially, one for the other.'"

Wilson stacked the manuscript against her knees and laid it back on the desk. "You weren't thinking about me when you wrote that, Mike."

I looked up at the ceiling and blew out a long breath. I started to speak but then shrugged. A denial would have been pointlessly insulting.

Wilson turned to the desk again and picked up my review of *Full Moon in Blue Water*. "'It's not that Hackman is unaware of Garr's interest in and affection for him,'" she read, "'nor even is he indifferent to that interest and affection. He knows and he cares. But in a critical area of his heart he cannot respond. He has spent a lifetime loving a single woman. Death has taken her from him, but death has not taken with it his devotion to her. Hackman is attracted to Garr. And his physical being is capable of reacting to Garr's attentions. But his spiritual being remains, if not cold exactly, then closed. For Hackman understands that sexual union is as much a spiritual connection as it is a physical act. And for the grieving Gene Hackman of this film, sex without his wife makes no more sense that a Moon without an Earth around which to orbit.'"

Wilson looked up at me, and I put my head in my hands. I didn't know how to react. I had certainly not written those passages with any intention of hurting Wilson. But I could see and I could understand the hurt that she was feeling. Joan was dead, and it was Wilson who now slept in my bed. And it was hard to read my words without understanding them to mean that Wilson would always be a stranger in Joan's house.

*   *   *

For several hours that night, after double checking that my doors and windows were locked against the advent of an intruder, I sat in the living room with only three fingers of Scotch for company. I didn't read, I didn't write, I didn't watch television, and I let the Scotch sit undrunk until it was diluted with melted ice and I poured it out. I just sat and stared and tried to figure out how my life had gotten so out of control, contemplated to what unfathomable sense a human being's existence is ruled not by his own will but rather by blind accident. Shortly before midnight, I returned to the study where I found that Wilson had fallen asleep on the sofa while reading. For a second I thought of carrying her to bed. I had carried Joan frequently enough, particularly when we were younger. But I suspected I had let myself get too out of shape to lift very easily a woman of Wilson's size. Another of life's hilarious jokes, I told myself, the wasting effects of age that render a man no longer capable of carrying a sleeping woman to bed. Still, I bent to lift her, but as I slid my arms beneath her body she woke. A lock of her hair had glued itself to her left cheek in the sticky salt residue of her dried tears. Her right cheek was red and creased where she had lain against the sofa's throw pillow. Wordlessly she rose and made her way into the bathroom.

I clicked off the lamp and went into the bedroom where I took off my clothes and climbed between the sheets. As I closed my eyes, I could hear Wilson running water. A moment later she slipped into the bed beside me.

She lay still for a while, but then she began to move in a way that I had hoped she wouldn't. When she did, I realized that she had waited, hoping in vain that I might reach out to her. The contact she initiated was almost furtive, at first just the grazing of my thigh with her hand.

When I didn't move, she rolled against me, laid her head on my chest, drew her right knee up on my leg and splayed her hand out on my stomach. I put my arm around her but held it motionless along her back. She moved her knee back and forth over my thigh and pressed herself against my hip. She licked first my right nipple and then the left. She grasped me with her hand. And when I did not respond, she lowered her head and took me in her mouth.

Afterwards, she lay curled against me again, her head back on my chest.

"Do you like it when we make love, Mike?" she asked.

"Of course, I do," I said.

I stroked my hand down her back.

"Tonight," she said. "Tonight you . . ."

"I've just got a lot on my mind, Wilson. It's late and . . ."

"Do you like it as much as you liked making love with Joan?" she whispered.

I licked my lips but didn't answer other than to move my hand in a small circle against the small of her back.

"Do you?" she said, her voice almost inaudible.

"Don't ask me that, Wilson."

"She did things that I don't do, didn't she?"

"I'm not a man of much experience, Wilson, but I suspect that everybody has certain things they like to do and like to have done to them. Everybody is different. Not better or worse. Just different."

"I could learn to do things."

"You should do what pleases you. What feels comfortable."

"Mike," Wilson said.

"Yes."

"Do you think you could ever love me the way you loved Joan?"

"Wilson."

"I need you to be able to tell me that you could."

She rolled away from me and curled herself into a ball. I threw an arm across my aching eyes.

"I've been living here for two months," she said. "It's not a long time . . . but then it's long enough. So I guess what I'm saying is that I need you to tell me that someday . . . if not today or tomorrow . . . that someday, you could feel about me . . ."

"Stop it, Wilson. You can't ask me that. It's not fair."

I sat up in bed behind her and laid my hand on her freckled shoulder.

"Joan and I . . . Joan and I . . . Look, you're what, twelve years younger than I am."

"So what?"

I shrugged my shoulders.

"So nothing. Look . . . You know that you and I see the world in very different ways. Doesn't that bother you?"

Wilson began to pick at the cuticle on her left thumb.

"I don't think we see the world so differently," she said. "I didn't know that you did."

I sucked my lower lip between my teeth.

"I don't even know what I'm saying, Wilson. Jesus I don't. It's just that Joan and I . . . we grew up together. We had a whole life together. We had the same history."

"And I need to know whether you and I can have a future."

"We have a present, Wilson. I can tell you that we have a present."

"But will we ever have a present as special to you as what you and Joan had in the past?"

I didn't respond and after a time she asked in a composed voice, "When we make love, do you think about her?"

"Never," I said, which was the truth.

"But you believe that sex without Joan is like a Moon without an Earth around which to orbit."

"I said Gene Hackman's character felt that way."

"You can't bring her back, you know."

"Of course, I know that, Wilson."

"I liked her," Wilson said. "I thought of her as my friend."

Wilson's voice was very small and came to me as if from far away.

"I know that you loved her with all your heart," she said. "But you can't bring her back. You have to let her go."

"I know," I said. "I know."

*   *   *

But I didn't know, of course.

I couldn't let her go. And that was the fact that ripped a wound in my relationship with Wilson Malt. For understandably, Wilson could not abide my inability to say I loved her, my incapacity to say that she could ever occupy a place in my heart equal to that reserved for Joan. And the next morning, three days before Carnival, while I had gone to purchase the sheets of plastic it looked as if I would finally need for insulation against the predicted cold snap, she collected her clothes and her pots and pans and slipped from my house on Dante Street without a trace.

CHAPTER TWENTY-TWO

It is the Saturday night before Mardi Gras. Across town majestic Endymion has wound its way from Marconi to Orleans to Carrollton to Canal. The bands have marched; the crowds have swayed. Lovers have stood with their arms around one another and raised unified voices to cheer. Care is forgotten. Festivity is the order of the season. But I sit alone in an empty house.

I sit alone, marking the hours until Mardi Gras passes and Carl authorizes the publication of our story on Sheldon Retif and Leon Delacroix. There is nothing I can do but wait, trying to keep a stopper in my bottle of Black and White. Every gust of wind that rattles a door or scrapes a sycamore branch across a window makes me think that a killer is trying to force his way into my house. And so I sit with the lone companionship of Wilson's pistol by my side.

I sit alone on a cold sofa in a darkened living room. Channel hopping again. The colored light from the television dances through the room but fails to fall upon my consciousness. Until suddenly I push the buttons for Bravo and arrive in the middle of *And Now My Love*. In a ritual not unlike that of returning to Galatoire's again and again to order the same cherished dishes, Joan and I watched our video copy of *And Now My Love* over and over again, always relishing anew its unabashed romanticism and its old fashioned premise that in some magical way true love is destined and true lovers are made for one another. But I have watched it only a single, uncomfortable time since she died.

I have come upon the film by purest, unwelcome accident, and in a movement like a flinch, I reach to press a button for another channel. But its images are quicker than my hand. And they seize me. And they spin me into sad reverie from which I cannot escape. I have tuned in just as André Dussolier, speeding through the French countryside, crashes his car into a horrible accident. He staggers from behind the wheel and collapses on the pavement, his face a mask of blood. I think of Joan, of course, another victim of a speeding auto, and of a husband who had then to live without her. I think of Joan, the love who was my treasured destiny. I think of Joan, the love who was made for me.

*   *   *

I am brushing my teeth and studying my face in the bathroom mirror. I cannot see her, but I know exactly what she's doing. Joan is lying on her back in the center of our king-sized bed. A thermometer protrudes from between her lips. Her long flannel nightgown is rolled up into her armpits and lies across just the tops of her breasts. She has removed her panties and placed two pillows under her hips.

She takes the thermometer from her mouth, turns it to the light and reads it.

"This is it, Mr. Mickey," she calls out. "Let's shake it up. I've got to go to work, and so do you."

"Coming, *dear*," I reply from the bathroom.

Joan shakes the thermometer down, places it back in its plastic case, snaps on the lid, and lays it in the drawer of the nightstand.

"Hey," Joan calls out, "I'm waiting."

I come into the bedroom in my bathrobe. I twirl around once and then spread the robe like a flasher. I open my mouth in an exaggerated grin and lick my tongue over my front teeth.

"Ta da," I sing. "How do I look? Are you turned on? I brushed my teeth and used lots of mouthwash. I wouldn't want to offend. I know you feel precisely the same way."

Joan rolls her eyes.

"Let's go, Mr. Clean," she says. "You got duty to do. Now hop to it."

"I think you mean hump to it, don't you?" I say. "But what's a vowel here and a consonant there. Between husband and wife, I mean."

Joan winces, evidently uncomfortable. She scrunches around with her shoulders and finally pulls her nightgown to the top of her thighs.

"Get in the bed, goddamnit," she says.

"You're so romantic," I respond.

"This isn't about romance," Joan says.

"Well I can't say I disagree with that," I reply. "And I think that may be a teensy weensy problem."

"Lord not again," Joan laughs. "Please don't tell me your weensy is teensy at the very moment all conditions are go. Open your robe again, Mr. Mickey."

I do as I am ordered.

"Well now," Joan says, licking her lips in a parody of lasciviousness, "that's not all so bad now is it? I'd say we've progressed from a state of utter flaccidity to something we might record as noticeably firm. Now if we can just accomplish passable stiffness I'm sure we can shortly achieve genuine tumescence."

I close my robe again and sit down on the bed. I push her nightgown back up over her breasts and pull a nipple between my fingers.

"Speaking of flaccidity," I say. "Judging from a sample areola testing, I deduce you're about as aroused as Sleeping Beauty."

"This isn't about arousal," Joan says. "It isn't about arousal, and it isn't about romance. It's about procreation. Think about that future Little Leaguer you can coach to ram that jumper home from outside the three-point circle."

"I hate it when you mix your sports metaphors, *dear*," I say.

"Or that twirling little ballerina you can bounce on your knee," Joan says, ignoring my interruption. "Think of junior or juniette and the cherished years you can spend preparing to go broke when he or she gets accepted to Yale."

"You make it sound so sexy."

"It isn't about sex, either."

"You can say that again."

"Come on, Mike," Joan says, just a note of irritation in her voice. "We've got to go to work."

I cup her between her legs, rub a finger gently inside her. She moves in response but I pull away.

"We've got a major aridity problem to go along with our previously mentioned flaccidity trouble."

Joan sits up and stirs in the drawer where she put the thermometer. She brings out a tube of K-Y Jelly and hands it to me.

"Here," she says, "use this."

She rearranges her hips on the pillows, and flings her legs widely apart.

"I suppose this will take care of your problem," I say, sighing. "But what are we going to do about mine?"

Joan turns her head toward me.

"You want a blow job?" she asks. "I don't mind giving you a blow job."

"Jesus," I say. "You make it sound as clinical as a rectal exam."

Joan laughs, though I haven't really intended to be funny.

"I'll give you a rectal exam if that'll help," she says. "Whatever turns you on."

"Well, you've now given the term 'truly disgusting' an entirely new meaning," I say.

Joan rolls onto her side and puts her hand on my thigh.

"I'm sorry all the fun's gone out of this," she says. "I really am."

"Sometimes all the joking around doesn't help," I say softly.

"I know," she replies. "In our lives it seems like 'sex' and 'spontaneity' have become antonyms. And I'm sure I get as uncomfortable about this whole process as you do. That's why I joke around. I'm just nervous. Knowing things are weirded out. But what are we going to do? We tried it the normal way, and it didn't work."

"Charlie Ferguson," I say, referring to a college roommate, "always said, 'good fucks make good babies.'"

Joan rubs her hand in a slow circle on my leg, gradually pushing my robe out of the way until her fingers and palm rested on bare flesh.

"I try to be a good fuck," she says, inching her fingers toward my crotch. "You always said I was a good fuck."

I grab her hand and places it on my knee. Then I lay my own hand on the back of her head and stroke her blond hair.

"That's not what he meant, babe. And you know it."

"And you know this is the best chance we're gonna get for a month, Mickey. We gotta go for it. Time's running out."

I nod as if agreeing to something unpleasant. Joan picks up the tube of lubricant, rolls on her back and resumes her spread-eagled position. She squeezes some of the jelly onto her fingers and moves them between her legs to wet herself.

"Okay, soldier," she says. "Your orders are the following. Go directly to the TV. Place your favorite video of *Holly Does Santa While Mary Does Holly* into the VCR. Turn VCR and television on. Lie next to me watching it until, shall we say, the proper moment arises. As soon as it arises, assume the position."

I lay my hand against her cheek.

"Aye, aye, sir," I say.

"That's ma'am sir to you, soldier. And say ma'am when you say sir. And ma'am sir, too for that matter."

After we make love, while I shower, Joan remains in bed for an additional half hour, on her back, her hips raised. This, our doctor has told us, will increase the chance of successful conception.

But it doesn't work.

Over a period of five years we have been to a series of doctors who have provided us with a series of strategies. And none has worked. Both of us are fertile; both are in good health. We are in our middle thirties, and conception is frequently more difficult for would-be parents in that age group. But if we are patient, if we are persistent, there is no reason we shouldn't be able to have a child. That's what we are told by every doctor we see.

A decade earlier, when I am still in graduate school, Joan becomes pregnant accidentally. But we aren't ready for a child then. Joan has not even started law school. It is too soon. And though we discuss with some seriousness the possibility of having the child, in the end we opt for an abortion. We never second-guess that decision. We are right, we believe, to delay our parenting to a time when we can embrace such an awesome responsibility on a sounder financial footing and with greater control over the demands on our time. One doctor does speculate that perhaps the dilation and curettage Joan undergoes somehow scars her uterus in a way that makes it difficult for her to conceive. But another doctor examines her and judges that such a diagnosis lacks any evidence to support it.

On our own we try a regimen of making love every day of the month, even during her menstrual period, just to be on the safe side. Under various doctors' guidance we limit our lovemaking to the days surrounding her presumed ovulation. This Joan measures through something called the "vaginal viscosity test" and through a monthly record of her morning temperature fluctuations. We try sperm pooling, where a fertility lab collects a half dozen of my ejaculatory specimens, all of which are inserted at once into Joan's cervix via hypodermic.

"Robofucking," Joan calls this experience and walks around our house after leaving the clinic, legs apart as if she's saddle sore.

But nothing works.

And by the end of the process, our sex life becomes so artificial that for a time we actually lose our life-long zest for one another's bodies. But we keep at it, whipping ourselves through every monthly disappointment, forcing ourselves into sexual congress when neither is interested in the slightest. At the end we are like amateur runners slogging out the last miles of a marathon. Inertia and stubbornness of will keep us going. But the joy of exercise has been jettisoned far behind us.

What finally brings our procreative quest to an end is biology's last cruel joke. At six o'clock in the evening on the day after I work myself into the needed state of arousal by watching a Christmas-themed pornographic video, Joan calls at the newspaper and tells me to drive past Place St. Charles and pick her up. She is having abdominal pains and doesn't think she can drive home.

I am instantly worried by this unusual request. I am aware that certain women have reputations for melodramatic hypochondria. But not Joan. She is never sick. She never misses work. She never leaves her office before seven-thirty p.m. And I have never known her to declare herself too ill to drive. One of the things that she insists upon from our earliest days together is a car of her own. She regards a car in her own name as the emblem of her independence, from me and everybody else on the planet. Never before has she commanded me to pick her up when her own car is at her disposal.

I pull my light blue Toyota Camry to a stop on the streetcar tracks on the St. Charles Avenue side of Joan's office building. I am so concerned about Joan I ignore the fact that my car will be towed if it's spotted by the police. I've only gotten half way between the street and the building's door, however, when Joan comes out, walking toward me slowly and in obvious pain. She has the canvas satchel she uses as a briefcase over her shoulder, and she clutches a stack of bulging manila file folders in her arms the way you'd hold a child who is growing too large to be carried. I rush to her and take the folders and bag from her. I help her into the front passenger's seat of the car, quickly stow her gear in the trunk, and hurry back behind the wheel to drive her home. As we pull across Poydras Street, she sits bent over in the car seat, both hands pressed against her abdomen, her head almost resting against the dashboard.

"Do you want me to take you to the emergency room?" I ask.

"No," she answers, breathlessly, between gritted teeth.

"Whatever in the world is wrong with you?" I demand.

I accelerate to make the light at Lee Circle and whip the car into a right turn on Howard Avenue. When she doesn't answer immediately, I look over at her. Her face seems utterly bloodless.

"Babe?" I say.

"I don't know what's wrong," Joan says. "It feels like I've got an ice pick stuck in my navel."

Though nothing anywhere nearly as intense as now, Joan has been suffering some occasional abdominal discomfort over the last year. Her gynecologist diagnoses the distress as gas pain aggravated by ovulation and gives Joan pills to alleviate the condition. When Joan takes the pills, the pain always seems to ease, but I am never convinced that the passage of time and Joan's unusually high pain threshold aren't more responsible for her improvement than the doctor's medication. Because of our difficulties in conceiving a child, and because of an increased level of bleeding during her menstrual periods, Joan has even speculated that she is going through an early menopause. But the gynecologist tells her such a notion is nonsense and suggests she take a daily vitamin pill supplemented with iron.

As I steer the Toyota past the Union Passenger Terminal, I ask Joan, "Is what you're feeling now anything like the pain you saw the doctor about earlier?"

She shakes her head, and I take my right hand off the steering wheel and cup it gently around the back of her neck, caressing her in hopes of providing her comfort.

"Before," she says. "I think the pain was lower."

She speaks in short bursts, as if the pressure of air in her lungs helps hold the pain in check.

"Now," she says, "It's sharper. And all over. Instead of just low down."

"Jesus, Joan, are you sure you don't want to go to the emergency room?"

"It'll go away," she says. "I'm sure."

But it doesn't go away. It stays with her through the night, unrelieved by the pills for gas pain. I am concerned she has acute appendicitis, but the pain is centered behind her belly button, and the lower right side of her abdomen isn't tender to the touch. Finally, the next morning, when the pain doesn't subside, I insist on taking her to the hospital. The fact that she relents convinces me that there is something very seriously wrong with her.

As we are driving down River Road toward the hospital, Joan says to me plaintively, "You don't think anything's really bad wrong with me, do you, Mickey?"

"I don't know babe," I respond. "No, of course not. I'm sure you're gonna be fine."

"Maybe I'm pregnant," Joan says. "Maybe when you're an old broad like me, when you get pregnant, it hurts from the very beginning."

But Joan isn't pregnant, of course. An ultrasound test at the hospital shows that some unidentified mass has surrounded Joan's left ovary. The emergency room doctor's diagnosis is that she needs surgery. And she needs it very soon. He advises she schedule an exploratory operation within a week to ten days. Joan informs him quietly that she will need, of course, to get a second opinion. And the doctor concurs that in a situation like hers, such a course is precisely what he recommends.

And that only makes things exponentially scarier.

In all, Joan sees five doctors in addition to the attending emergency room physician at Ochsner Hospital. Six if you count her own gynecologist, to whom she does not return once she realizes that something has been growing inside her and causing her pain for an entire year, and her gynecologist has been prescribing medication for gas. The experience is exhausting and unbelievably frustrating because no two doctors tell her the same thing—except that they all agree she needs surgery to find what is going on inside her. Most disturbing, none of the doctors will rule out the possibility of malignancy.

The problem with Joan is that she is sometimes too smart for her own good. The library at her law firm is full of medical reference books. And within forty-eight hours she has convinced herself she has ovarian cancer.

And ovarian cancer, her researches reveal, has a five year survival rate of only twenty-five percent.

Joan Anne Norris Barnett is the toughest individual I have ever known. When life knocks her down, she doesn't cry and make excuses. She doesn't complain that society is prejudiced against women and that the defeats she suffers are inflicted because of her gender. She regards herself a feminist, but she doesn't derive her identity from any movement. She has always possessed a terrific sense of who she is and what she wants out of life. She is strong, and she is independent, and she is resilient.

And on the morning they wheel her to surgery from her second floor room at Tulane Medical Center, she is crying. And I am crying, too. For I have never known her to be intimidated by a single thing. And I know that if she is intimidated now, the world is a scarier place than I have ever allowed myself to acknowledge. At most any other time in our long relationship, had Joan seen me upset and worried about her, she would have cracked ironically wise and forced both of us to face the general absurdity of life. But she doesn't do that now, as I walk along the corridor with her squeaking gurney while the orderlies roll her toward the elevator. The tears stream down her face, and she squeezes my hand.

At the door to the operating room, I think my heart might break when she tells me in a tiny, slurred voice, the shot they've given her already taking affect, "I'm sorry for upsetting you, Mickey. This all just happened so fast. But I'll be okay, I promise. I'll be tough again tomorrow."

*   *   *

The surgery lasts five and a half hours, far longer than the doctors predict. She is under anesthesia for so long that her body temperature falls to a dangerous level, and she is kept in recovery for an additional three hours as the nurses struggle to get her warm again. She is still wrapped in blankets when they finally bring her back to the room from recovery. Even her head is twined in a white linen wrap that reminds me, incongruously, of a hat Joan Crawford wears in *Sudden Fear*.

I hear the gurney squeaking down the corridor and come to stand just outside the door to meet her in the hall. Joan wants a private room, so that I can stay with her after the operation. The only one available is located, ironically, at the end of the maternity wing. As Joan is rolled past me, I hear a baby cry from a room two doors away. Joan is still sleeping. I try to make contact with the orderlies, to register in some conscious human eye the depth of my concern and relief that Joan has been returned to me. But they ignore me, speaking only to each other as they maneuver the gurney into her corner room. As if they are parking a car into an especially tight space, they cut the wheels and back up three times before they can guide Joan through the door.

A nurse comes down the hall from her station and asks me to wait outside while she and the orderlies transfer Joan from the stretcher to her bed. But before I leave I look for a long moment down at Joan's face. What I see there is a vision of personal apocalypse. Her face has turned the color of slate, and all the flesh sags in a way that suggests the bones of her cranium have turned to clay. Looking at her unconscious form, so helpless and seemingly inert, is like standing on the rumbling ground at the first tremor of a devastating earthquake. She is my foundation, the rock upon which I have built the edifice of a surprising life. And now, with a single glance at her sunken countenance, I feel the earth threaten to give way underneath me.

*   *   *

Joan doesn't have cancer, thank God. The softball-sized mass which envelops her ovary is an endometrioma, the product of a disease called endometriosis in which uterine tissue begins to reproduce itself, like algae, on other organs. In Joan's case it destroys one ovary and is growing on everything else in her abdominal cavity. To stop it, the surgeon performs what the public calls a *complete* hysterectomy and medical science terms a bilateral salpingo-oophorectomy, which designates the removal of both ovaries and both Fallopian tubes plus a hysterectomy, which designates only the removal of the uterus. All of Joan's reproductive organs are damaged by her malfunctioning uterus, which has been too busy reproducing itself, evidently, to hostess the conception Joan and I wanted so dearly.

At about midnight on the day of her operation, Joan finally awakens from her anesthesia. Her eyes open like those of a tiny baby who has just discovered her sense of vision. I am lying on a cot next to her bed. I have positioned myself so that I can watch her at all times. I see her open her eyes, and I smile.

"Hi," she says.

"Hello, my love."

She smiles back at me, and I must fight with myself to keep from crying.

"I'm thirsty," she says, slowly.

I get up from my cot and prepare her a cup of ice chips with which she can wet her mouth. I hold the cup for her and warn her to take only a few slivers into her mouth at a time. As she works the ice about in her mouth, I touch her face, just the back of my fingers against her cheek. She licks her lips again, still obviously dopey from the anesthesia.

"Do I have cancer?" she asks.

"No, my love," I say. "You don't have cancer."

And I make a mental genuflection of gratitude for being able to speak those words.

*   *   *

Joan stays in the hospital for a week after her operation. I shower in her room every morning before leaving for the newspaper. And whenever possible, I set up the Zenith on a coffee table and do my writing in her room. I stop home each day only briefly to check the mail and pick up a change of clothes before returning to her. Sometime around three a.m. every night I am awakened by a crying infant, the newborn next door presumably announcing it is hungry. Awake in the dead of the night, I turn on my side to stare at Joan, ready to comfort her should she need it. But she never stirs.

Joan is under her doctor's orders to stay home for a month after leaving the hospital, but I suspect from the outset she won't do what she's told. Her toughness is important to her, and she pushes herself now to show just how tough she is. She switches from prescription pain medicine to extra-strength aspirin even before leaving the hospital. At home she is quickly off pain medication of any kind. I occasionally catch her wincing when she moves in a way she shouldn't yet, but she denies she feels any discomfort at all. Immediately upon arriving home she demands that I arrange to bring her some files from the office, but this I adamantly refuse to do.

Joan does stay home for two weeks, but she is quickly bored, and soon she's up and busying herself around the house, cleaning and arranging, putting her new post-operative life in her required, systematic order. She makes an elaborate production of sorting through her bathroom cabinet and culling out various items that have to do with birth control and menstrual periods. She makes a "care" package for her secretary that includes a box of sanitary napkins, two boxes of tampons and a pink plastic case for carrying tampons in a purse. She throws away several old packages of birth control pills she doesn't take while we have made our big push to conceive a child. She finds and discards a box of spermatocidal sponges, a tube of spermatocidal jelly and the blue plastic container with the diaphragm we have abandoned years ago when she got pregnant despite using it carefully and faithfully.

Joan has moved all these items to a table in the kitchen and is stacking them into separate paper sacks, one for the garbage and the other for her secretary. I notice, though, that she has set aside two boxes of Assure panty liners. I ask her why.

"Because, I'll still have a use for those," she replies.

"What kind of use?"

I think of the joke in Mike Nichols's *The Fortune* when Jack Nicholson tells Warren Beatty that sanitary napkins are "mouse beds."

"The same use as always, Mr. Nosy," Joan says.

"Uh, I think they forgot to tell you something," I say.

Joan looks at me with mock impatience.

"Maybe they forgot to tell *you* something," Joan says.

"What's that?" I ask, deliberately acting the dolt.

"Women don't wear panty liners for their periods."

"I thought they were a kind of back-up protection," I say. "You know. In case a Tampax doesn't work or something."

Joan walks into the living room with the sack for her secretary and sets it on a table next to the door so that she'll remember to take it with her when she goes back to work. When she returns to the kitchen she resumes stacking items into the bag for the trash.

I wait for her to respond, and when she doesn't, I say, "So I thought panty liners were used as a kind of back-up protection."

Joan doesn't say anything.

"You know, in case a Tampax didn't work or something."

"Are you going to keep saying that until I have to kill you?" Joan asks.

"Well," I say. "I just thought that panty liners were used as a kind of back-up protection."

"Stop it," Joan says, laughing.

"You know, in case a Tampax didn't work or something."

"You asked for it," Joan says.

"I just thought that panty liners were used . . ."

"The vagina is a self-cleaning organ," Joan interrupts.

"Nuff said," I submit, realizing her strategy.

"It cleans itself through the production of . . ."

"I understand perfectly," I say, laughing.

". . . a mucousy substance which seeps from . . ."

"Uncle. I quit. You win."

". . . between the vaginal lips."

"Uncle. Uncle. Uncle. Say no more!"

"And while there is nothing offensive in this substance . . ."

I am laughing almost too hard to speak.

"I'm truly sorry I asked," I croak.

"... it can stain the crotch of a woman's underwear."

"Oh lord, I wish I'd never brought this matter up."

"Now in case you are operating under the misimpression that a hysterectomy renders a woman's vagina non-functional, this is not remotely true."

I suddenly become afraid that my nonsense might have actually hurt Joan's feelings.

"Hey babe, I ..."

"The vagina is an independent organ and functions quite normally after a hysterectomy. Lubrication during sexual stimulation, for instance, is unchanged. Some women note that it seems even greater, perhaps because the fear of pregnancy is removed."

"Joan, I hope that you don't think I ..."

"All of that established with as much clinical exactitude as possible, my dear husband, I think that I can now state that I'm saving my box of panty liners because you can only live life a single time, and I plan to live mine with perennially wet pants. So to speak. Spontaneously, of course."

I laugh and shake my head, marveling at her.

"Am I correct in stating the proposition," I say, "that you regard your business as having been converted from a baby carriage to a play pen?"

"Well put," Joan says. "Not original. But well put all the same."

Two weeks after coming home from the hospital, Joan insists on returning to work. She promises she'll just work half days, but she breaks that promise by the end of the first week. She is preparing the judicial recusal issue of *Retif* which she will eventually argue before the U.S. Supreme Court, and she is not of a temperament, she says, to loll around in bed when there's work to be done. Besides, she says, she's already cleaned out her bathroom medicine cabinet and what the hell else is there to do at home.

On the Sunday evening before she goes back to her office the first time, she takes me into the kitchen for instructions about my new responsibilities. Standing at the spice table where we keep a basket with various jars of capsules, vitamin tablets, aspirin, over-the-counter cold medicine and the like, Joan shows me her packet of blue estrogen tablets.

"Now, as you know," she states in her best schoolmarm voice, "I have to take one of these Estrace pills every morning for the rest of my life."

"I understand," I say.

"Your job is to make sure I don't forget."

"My job is to make sure you don't forget."

"There will be dire consequences if you let me forget."

"There will be dire consequences if I let you forget."

"Do you know what those consequences are?" Joan asks.

"Yes. I would become the laughing stock of all male humanity."

"And why exactly is that," Joan asks.

"Because I would be married to an *it* instead of a woman."

"So sensitively put," Joan says.

"And even worse," I say.

"My God, it gets worse than that?"

"Oh yes."

"How, pray tell?"

"You'd start growing things," I say.

"Growing things?"

"An Adam's apple."

"An Adam's apple, of course."

"Yes. And hairy tits."

"Not hairy tits!"

"Yes. I'm afraid so. If you fail to take an Estrace tablet every morning for the rest of your life, you will."

"Grow hairy tits?"

"Yes hairy tits. Can you imagine?"

"Well," Joan says, contemplating. "I'm worried about the Adam's apple. To hide it I'd have to wear a scarf every day for the rest of my life. And that'd be more trouble than simply taking my Estrace tablet."

"I should think," I say.

"But I'm not really worried about the hairy tits."

"Why not?"

"Well, I figure you're the only one who'd ever get to see my hairy tits."

"And that wouldn't bother you," I say. "My seeing them, I mean."

"Oh no," Joan responds. "You're my dearly beloved. I know that you'd love me, hairy tits and all."

"I promise never to let you forget to take your Estrace tablets every morning for the rest of your life."

"You're so thoughtful," Joan says. "But you know. Hairy tits could be sort of nice I bet. Kind of warm during the winter. What do you think?"

*   *   *

Like images in a kaleidoscope, memories blend together, blur, fuse; one grows organically out of another. Painful happy memory about the departed times of bliss segues into nightmare about suffering unrelieved. Joan in one hospital room, gradually, then fiercely, miraculously recovering. And Joan in another hospital room, fighting, valiantly fighting, even in a coma, I will always believe, fighting.

*   *   *

I sit with Joan in ICU after her emergency neurosurgery. She lies, of course, unconscious, and I sit next to her bed holding her hand.

She looks so very bad, and the doctors give little cause for optimism. And all I can do is sit and watch. Sit and watch and pray without hope. Sit and watch and find distant comfort by touching her. I take her cool hand, hold it in both of mine and watch her face for signs of waking. I try to conjure her into consciousness with the force of my own will.

The outline of the anesthetic mask is still pressed into the skin of her cheeks and chin. A white paste of dried saliva coats the inside of her lips just at the line where pink gives way to polished rose. Her mouth hangs open in an expression I have never seen settle on her face in seventeen years of lying by her side. Her eyes are closed, but so desperately round. I suddenly think in sad horror that she looks like the terrified character in Edvard Munch's "The Scream."

But it is me, actually, who feels like shrieking. I feel like screaming at the unfeeling deity that has included suffering and disease and senseless accident as such central elements in mankind's fate. My wife sleeps in the neverland of her anesthesia, in the mysterious blank landscape of her coma. And I am left alone and awake in an indifferent world that is reeling out of control. I speak aloud to a wife who will never hear the sound of my voice again, "Joanie! Joanie! Goddamnit, Joanie!" Over and over again, I chant this profane mantra as an incantation against my fear. Then, it seems, Joan stirs for a second inside her chrysalis of blankets and sheets. I am momentarily certain she is about to wake. When she doesn't, I feel the earth tremble. And I cling to her hand as a talisman for warding off that ultimate evil whose pernicious name I dare not speak.

PART FIVE

CHAPTER TWENTY-THREE

A brutal late season freeze was being predicted for the height of Carnival. And so approaching Sunday noon, with my house suddenly cavernous and creepy in Wilson's absence, I set about the onerous task of stapling up plastic sheets to further insulate and cut down the freezing draft under my floorboards. I continued to be fearful about exposing myself too openly, but I comforted myself with the slim likelihood that a killer, if one were really stalking me, would try to strike in broad daylight.

In the past I'd always had Joan to help me with the chore of protecting the house against sub-freezing weather. The first year after she died, it didn't freeze all winter. Now I was forced to try doing it alone, a seeming impossibility because the wind was forever whipping the long sheets out of my hands. I had been working two frustrating hours and hadn't even reached my side porch when my neighbor Larwood Dupre showed up and offered to help me. He had been walking home from the grocery store and heard my curses.

"You havin' yourself a pile a trouble. I can sure see that, Mr. Mike. I musta told Ms. Joan a thousand times she oughta let me brick y'all's house up like I done got mine. Then you wouldn't have to fools with this Visqueen ever winter. Maybe now I can convince Ms. Wilson of that fact sometime."

I didn't tell Larwood that Wilson had moved out. Nor did I engage him in the old argument about bricking in the crawl space under my house. For Larwood the right thing was the practical thing. For Joan and therefore me, of course, the right thing was the esthetically pleasing thing. Raised houses were meant to stand open above the ground on their brick pillars. They were less attractive if their crawl spaces were closed off. When the weather dictated, plastic could be stapled up and weighted down with bricks. When the weather eased, the plastic could be removed and the house returned to its original appearance. With Joan gone, though, Larwood's plan seemed a lot more sensible.

But for now the two of us worked with the obstreperous plastic sheets. Larwood did the cutting, fed the lengths of plastic to me and stabilized them in the wind. I did the dirty work, lying on my back wielding the staple gun over my head, using my elbows like a crab to scoot from one uncomfortable position to the next. When we were finally finished, Larwood insisted that we nudge the bricks closer to the house from the position in the middle of the sidewalk where we'd originally placed them. "Ifn we don't," he pointed out, "you gonna come round here some night and stump your toe somethin' awful."

I asked Larwood if he'd like to have a beer and, as he was walking inside, he inspected my front door and told me I needed some weatherstripping. "I'll brings you some by sometime ifn I can remember," he promised. When he left I gave him twenty dollars for his labor with me that afternoon. He took it without protest and said, "You always been good to me and Delinda, Mr. Mike. And we appreciate it; I hope you knows that we do."

I appreciated them too. And I was glad for them that they had each other. For now, once again, I had no one. And relief from the certainty of my loneliness seemed to lie only in the two-faced friendship in my bottle of Black and White.

*   *   *

Late Sunday afternoon I received a phone call from Judge Delacroix who asked if I'd meet with him at his home early that evening. I agreed only with reluctance and trepidation. He wouldn't say what he wanted. Said what he had to tell me he must relate in person. I suspected he wanted to talk me out of the story I had already written. Would he try to buy me?

Or would he try to scare me? I thought again of Jackson Smith in my living room, and a chill swept down my spine and lodged itself in my testicles. I didn't really think Delacroix would try to do me harm at his own house, but nonetheless I warned the judge I was notifying the paper of a meeting at his home. Before leaving my house, I called Carl to so inform him. He wasn't home, but I left notification about the meeting on his answer machine. Furthermore, as an added precaution, I put Wilson's police revolver inside the waist band of my pants.

I arrived at the judge's mansion on Third Street in the Garden District at seven p.m., five days after I'd seen him in his office. Bathed in the shadow of live oaks that hovered over it like giant sentinels on either side and behind, protected in front by a stately magnolia, Leon Delacroix's home represented in its architectural splendor the complexity of emotions I felt about the city of my birth. The house was a glimmering white with fourteen-foot green shutters so dark they appeared black. Paired square columns, tripled at the corners, supported a second-floor gallery which swept around the house on both sides. Underneath the gallery, a tile porch was bordered by azalea bushes. This was a house that King Cotton had built before the Civil War, when our city was the richest in the world. It was magnificent. And I loved it as I loved all of those that King Cotton had built for blocks all around. Judge Delacroix's house and those of his neighbors were monuments to an astonishing period in our city's history, a time when New Orleans was a city of power and influence, a force to be reckoned with in the economy of a rapidly changing world. Then. Not now.

And so at the same time I hated the homes of the Garden District because they stood as taunting reminders of what New Orleans once was and oh so most certainly was no longer. And I thought of the ways in which racial mistrust and hatred were interlaced with the problems which had rendered our city a deteriorating backwater hamlet destined sooner for inclusion in a list of Third World cities than in a list of cities progressing forward toward the twenty-first century. Modern industry avoided our city because our schools were so bad. And they were so bad because they were broke. And they were broke because of the scorched earth policy of white flight. And so I too often thought we were caught in a net of racial enmity from which none of us would escape. And I looked at the mansions of the Garden District, at Judge Delacroix's home which stood before me, and I hated it bitterly. I hated it because I knew its builder had sown in the early nineteenth century the seeds which we reaped on a daily basis late in the twentieth. I was dazzled by the house's grace and immutable beauty. And I was disgusted by the knowledge that it was built with money stolen from the labor of people in chains.

I was greeted at the door by a black houseman in a tuxedo. He told me that I was expected. The judge, the houseman said, would entertain me in the garden. I was shown down the long center hall, the walls of which were hung with Oriental tapestries. Double parlors opened off the hall to either side. The rearmost on the right was a library. At the far end of the hall was a pantry outfitted as a bar, where, behind a half door, a black woman in a maid's uniform was placing glasses onto a silver tray. The houseman turned left into the dining room. There was a woman seated at the close end of the vast dining table, holding a dark-haired child on her lap, a little girl perhaps five years old. Broad-shouldered, square-built, dressed in black with a pearl choker around her neck, the woman pulled the child against her and swiveled slightly in her chair as we came into the room. I recognized the woman under a sprayed helmet of died black hair as Mrs. Jessica Delacroix.

"How do you do, ma'am?" I said. "And young lady."

The smile on Jessica Delacroix's face peeled away like a discarded mask, and she acknowledged my greeting only with a long, murderous stare.

"Through this way," the houseman said.

Mrs. Delacroix turned back to the dining table and the houseman led me behind her, past a hallway to the kitchen, and out a pair of French doors adorned with lace curtains.

The judge was sitting on the brick patio in a modern metal lawn chair, white and luxuriously padded. On a low wire table to his right stood a brandy snifter still holding a swallow of amber liquid. The houseman showed me to an identical chair which faced the judge's. I set my briefcase beside the chair, and as I seated myself, I glanced about at the exquisitely manicured garden setting. If the benefits included the daily opportunity to enjoy a courtyard as beautiful as this one, I suspected that one could get used to being rich very quickly.

"Would you join me in a cocktail?" the judge asked by way of greeting. "A cognac? Or perhaps some bourbon?"

I didn't answer for a pointedly long moment. Finally, I said, "I hadn't seen this as a social occasion."

"Indulge me this one request, Mr. Barnett. I hate to drink alone."

"Scotch," I said to the houseman.

The judge smiled, and tugged the collar of his shirt to a more comfortable position inside his bulky gray cardigan sweater.

"Bring Mr. Barnett a glass of Macallan, Horace," he instructed.

"Would you like water with that, sir?" Horace asked.

"Ice will be fine," I said.

"And I'll have another . . ." the judge said. He held up his glass, and Horace went back into the house to get the drinks.

"I hope it's not too cool out here for you, Mr. Barnett," the judge said. "I should have told you to wear a sweater when I called."

"I'll be fine," I said.

Into the uncomfortable silence that settled over us as we waited for Horace to return with our drinks, I said, "Beautiful place you've got here, Leon. Privilege obviously has its privileges."

The judge fielded my remark as if it were just a pleasantry. "One of my greatest pleasures," he said, indicating with a sweep of his hand that he meant his garden. "I bought this house because of this garden. I've always thought of it as my refuge."

I craned my neck around to examine the garden in more detail. The patio gave way to narrow brick walkways which circled off in both directions around a fountain. In front of the fountain was a stand of rose bushes, oddly ill-kempt in such an otherwise well-tended space. Behind the fountain was an expanse of manicured green lawn enclosed by nine-foot brick walls on three sides. A magnolia grew in a one corner at the back, a silver maple in the other. Beds of pansies bordered all the trees, including the oaks which joined to form a canopy over the patio.

"In about an hour," the judge said, "we'll be able to hear the parade passing on St. Charles Avenue."

He was referring to the Bacchus Parade, which was about to start farther Uptown some twenty blocks from us. Bacchus was always one of the season's longest, loudest, most elaborate and most popular parades. It would take perhaps the hour the judge had predicted to reach us. And it would continue to roll past for well over an hour after it got to us.

"Our daughter Maria has come in from Alexandria with her children for Mardi Gras. I never think of Mardi Gras as a family occasion, but it's a joy to have the grandchildren in the house whatever the season."

I didn't comment. The judged sighed deeply, and a short silence settled over us.

"There weren't nearly so many parades when I was a boy," the judge said. "But I suspect you knew that. There weren't so many when you were a youngster either. Mrs. Delacroix has retained her enthusiasm for Mardi Gras rather more than I, I'm afraid. When we first married I accompanied her to the evening parades. But I haven't done so in some time. I'm glad she'll have family with her again when she joins our neighbors on the corner shortly to watch Bacchus from their porch. I've begged off as usual. The last few years I've confined my carnival participation to Mardi Gras Day. You mentioned privilege. Mrs. Delacroix loves the privilege that my position affords us, such as seats in the mayor's box at Gallier Hall on Mardi Gras Day. She treasures the experience, so I'd hate to deny it to her. Even in my dotage as I've become more than just a bit of a Carnival Scrooge."

Horace reappeared with drinks. The judge hadn't finished all the brandy in his snifter, but Horace took it away and replaced it with the fresh one. He placed my Scotch on the wire table next to my chair. Wilson's gun under my belt pinched my waist as I leaned over to pick up my glass. I smelled the rich aroma of the whisky, steeled myself and set the glass back down without sipping from it.

"You're probably wondering why I've asked to meet with you again," Judge Delacroix said when Horace had returned to the house and the judge had taken a swallow of his brandy.

"Yes," I said. "I presume you have a comment or a clarification you want included in my forthcoming story on Jefferson High."

I pulled my briefcase up on my lap, opened it and took out my tape recorder. The judge raised his hand and flicked it in a way that indicated his desire that I put the tape recorder away.

"That won't be necessary," he said.

I continued to prepare the recorder for use.

"Just for the record," I said.

"I didn't exactly plan to speak for the record," he said.

I slipped the audio cassette into place and clicked down the cover.

"If you didn't plan to speak for the record, Judge Delacroix, then I don't know why you invited me here. We're not exactly drinking buddies."

The judge smiled at me, picked up his brandy snifter and lifted it toward me as if in a toast.

"I've learned a bit about you in the last several days, Mr. Barnett. I'm sorry that I wasn't familiar with your work previously. Mrs. Delacroix and I seldom go to the movies. And thus I seldom read about them. But I understand that you are quite well respected for what you do, and by reputation you are a high-minded, principled man."

I set the tape machine next to my drink glass and pressed the record button.

"Blowing smoke up my shorts," I said, "isn't going to stop me from publishing my story."

The judge chortled at my image and then licked his lips.

"My, what a colorful expression," he said. "But you're wrong to think that I was trying to somehow seduce you with flattery, Mr. Barnett."

"Then I'm still unclear as to what this meeting is about."

I lifted the glass of Scotch toward the judge and swirled the ice.

"I appreciate good whisky as much as the next man," I said. "But I can afford to drink it at home. Even on the salary of a newspaperman."

"In my day, Mr. Barnett, newspapermen weren't held in the esteem they have attained in the eyes of your generation. In my day a man like yourself would have gone into public service, much as I have."

"Forgive me, judge, for objecting to being put into a category along with you."

The judge laughed. He brought the snifter to his lips, tipped back his head and drained it.

"You are right," he said. "I confuse things, don't I? In my day a man like you wouldn't have been accepted into public service by a man like me. You are not a child of privilege, but come from modest roots. No, in my day, a capable, ambitious, well-educated man of modest means such as yourself would have been excluded from any possibility of public influence in this city. That's why men like me, like my father, so detested men such as the Longs, not for what they stood for, but for who they were. Impudent upstarts. No, in my day, Mr. Barnett, a man like you would have been forced to go into business or law. And in either, a man like you would have become very rich. And men like me would have looked down our noses at you nonetheless. The well-born, as I'm sure you well know, have long since been contemptuous of mere merit."

I set the drink glass still untouched back on the table to my left.

"The lesson in sociology is fascinating," I said. "But I've already got my degree. So before I go, let me just ask you a single question. How can the same man who ruled as you did in *Grieve versus Retif* have been such a lion on civil rights during the sixties?"

"I think the key is eyesight," the judge said.

He smiled and lifted his arm into the air, silently squeezing his fingers up and down on his palm.

"I looked at men like Napoleon Beaumont and Charles Fredericks and said to myself, why they're not any darker than I am. And both are a good deal smarter. So why should the law deny them privileges that white people take for granted?"

Horace appeared with a fresh drink for each of us. He placed a second glass of Macallan next to my first.

"Since my tape recorder is running," I said. "You wouldn't by any chance be admitting the allegations I raised about your great-grandmother Annette Jeansonne Thibodeaux, would you?"

The judge sat silent a moment as Horace made his way back to the house.

"Mr. Barnett," the judge said. "As you might expect, I am not used to men speaking to me in the manner you have adopted."

"Sorry, Judge," I said. "I was brought up to believe that respect was something you earned."

"Fair enough, Mr. Barnett. Fair enough."

"You still haven't revealed your motives in asking me here," I pointed out.

The judge tugged at his shirt collar again. Clearly he had gotten his shirt twisted inside his sweater when he'd put the sweater on. He licked his lips and started to speak. But then he stopped and took a sip of brandy from his snifter.

"Mr. Barnett," he said, finally, "I want to request that you not print the story you informed me about two days ago."

I checked to see that the tape recorder was working, and he told me with his eyes he noticed I had done so.

"Why would you ask me a thing like that, Judge?"

He breathed deeply and shifted his weight so that he sat more erect in his lawn chair.

"The allegations about my racial ancestry are not true," Judge Delacroix said.

"I've already told you I'd quote you to that effect," I replied.

"In an effort to smear me at the outset of my career, my great-grandmother's birth certificate was altered by my opponents during my 1948 race for City Council. I cannot prove that fact to you. But it is the truth. And I think you will find it consistent with all else that you've discovered about this matter. You asked me a moment or so ago why I became the kind of judge I became in the sixties. There are many reasons. One is that I wanted to destroy a system of laws that could discriminate against a man for something that happened before he was born. I hope that I had less personal reasons as well. But I know that my first-hand experience with a racist conspiracy was a certain factor in making me the kind of man I became."

Judge Delacroix's statement had the unsettling ring of truth, and I was shaken. I felt abruptly like a stranded sailor, lost at sea, without a compass and without landmarks on 360 degrees of horizon. Without thinking, I took a swallow of Scotch and tried to ponder the implications of what he was telling me.

"Even if what you say is true," I said, "that doesn't mean Retif didn't try to blackmail you. You don't want me to run this story. And maybe you were willing to screw Tom Grieve to stop Retif from putting the story out."

The judge worked his mouth into a sad smile.

"You should have been an attorney, Mr. Barnett," he said. "You argue very well."

"Are you denying now that Retif tried to blackmail you?" I asked.

Judge Delacroix had already rocked me once. He did so now again.

"On the contrary," he said. "I am confirming that Sheldon Retif tried to blackmail me."

I had been holding the glass of Scotch, but my hand began shaking so much I feared I was about to spill it on myself. I set it back on the table and examined my tape recorder again. The spool heads were turning slowly.

"I've got this on tape, Judge Delacroix," I said. "I feel I should warn you about that fact."

"I told Sheldon Retif to go to hell," the judge continued. "I told him this was the 1980s, that my enemies had tried to besmirch my ancestry more than thirty years ago. It hadn't worked then. And I couldn't imagine that anyone any longer cared what color my great-grandmother was."

"Members of your family might care," I quickly pointed out. "Your wife, your siblings, your daughter, her children."

"My ancestry hardly reflects on that of my wife, Mr. Barnett. And my reputed dark seed has been diluted enough so that not even our ancient racist laws would have considered my grandchildren stained. As for my siblings, they haven't had anything to do with me since I embarrassed them with my rulings in the sixties. If I were a vindictive man, I might even take pleasure in such discomfort as they might feel at the revelation that some distant ancestor of theirs was a West Indian Negro."

"I don't get this," I said. "You're telling me that Sheldon Retif tried to blackmail you but that his ploy didn't work."

"You told me something last Tuesday, Mr. Barnett, the most chilling thing I've heard in my entire life—that your wife died under mysterious circumstances perhaps related to this affair. It never occurred to me that the evil in all this might extend to murder."

My throat constricted.

"Are you confirming that Joan was murdered?" I rasped.

The judge looked me straight in the eyes.

"I don't know," he said. "But I intend to find out."

The strains of the first parade band wafted over the garden wall. The band was playing "Dixie."

"I think you're going to have to tell me your story slowly and from the beginning," I said.

"And I need to know whether I can count on your cooperation," he replied.

"My cooperation how?" I inquired.

"In not printing what I tell you."

"You must be crazy," I sputtered. "Of course I'm going to print what you tell me. That's what I do. I'm a reporter."

"I thought you were a film critic."

"I work for a newspaper. I'm writing this story about you and Sheldon Retif and Thomas Jefferson Magnet. I'll use anything you tell me that's relevant to that story."

The judge rose from his chair and walked behind it to a place near the wall. He tilted his head to raise his right ear upwards.

"The only thing I enjoy about the parades any more is the music," he said. "I like to watch the bands, particularly those from our local schools. We're doing such a bad job with our schools. But the youngsters still strut to the music, still rise to it, still give it as a gift to all of those who pause to listen."

I didn't share with the judge my frustrated opinion that New Orleans was a town that would sooner teach kids to play music for a Mardi Gras parade than teach them how to read and write. After a moment he moved back to his chair and reseated himself.

"At first I tried to rationalize my capitulation to Sheldon Retif," the judge said. "And sometimes, if I closed off certain corners of my mind, I could make that rationalization work. U.N.O. *is* a more appropriate site for the magnet high school. It's much better than the Morrison Road location. And the agreement Retif negotiated with Grieve really *didn't* specify the reassignment of the Builder's Prerogative. But I couldn't force myself to embrace such sophistry, to contort my beliefs in order to endorse such a rank miscarriage of justice. So I took another tack."

"So you did allow Retif to blackmail you," I said.

The judge no longer seemed to respond to my questions, no longer, in fact, seemed to take notice of my presence. It was as if he were alone in his garden, speaking his confession directly to heaven.

"I demanded money," he said. "If I was going to soil myself, I wanted to wallow in it. To smear myself with the excrement of degradation, I demanded one hundred thousand dollars. And I got it. I never thought Retif would go so high, but he agreed immediately. He had it delivered to my office in cash in a small valise. I never even counted it. I had one of my clerks deliver it unopened to the Little Sisters of Mercy. Your paper ran an article on the mysterious gift the next day."

"I remember," I said. "People speculated it must be drug money from a stoned dealer hoping to buy expiation."

"I'm not so stupid a Catholic as to believe that expiation can be purchased with cash," the judge said. "From the moment I caved in to Retif I have expected to get caught. And in the beginning I dreaded the presumption of bribery more than the revelation of the truth. Taking the money was my hair shirt. It would allow me to suffer with a pain of my own making once my sin was made public. Retif would have been happy not to have had to pay me, I'm sure. But I insisted. And my insistence allowed Retif to think that I was a man like him—he said almost those exact words to me—and it allowed me to maintain my superiority over Mr. Retif. For it allowed me to know what he didn't. That I wasn't really like him at all."

The judge stopped to take a sip of his brandy. He took too large a swallow and shuddered as it went down.

"I sent the money to the Little Sisters almost by instinct," the judge said. "I have routinely given them money through the years. It occurred to me shortly afterwards that I should have given the money to Tom Grieve. That would have helped make up for what I was about to do to him. But, of course, I realized that such an idea was just another attempt to rationalize my guilt. Tom Grieve wasn't after the money associated with Jefferson High any more than I was. I still should have given it to Grieve, I'm sure. But it wouldn't have expiated my sin any more than giving the money to the Little Sisters of Mercy."

There was a roar from the crowd of parade watchers beyond the wall. A float was going by. And we could hear the insane pleas for trinkets: "Throw me something, mister; throw me something."

"Judge Delacroix," I said, speaking for the record of my tape recorder. "I want to be absolutely clear that you are admitting to me that you rendered a verdict for Sheldon Retif in the case of *Thomas Grieve versus Retif Realty* as the result of Retif's blackmailing you, threatening if you did not rule in his favor that he would reveal the questionable racial ancestry of your great-grandmother."

The judge took another, smaller sip of his brandy and smiled at me.

"I've already explained that he tried such a tactic, and it did not work."

"I am still confused, then," I said.

The judge laughed.

"You've recorded yourself to that effect, Mr. Barnett," he said, and laughed once more.

Judge Delacroix got up from his chair again and stepped over to the rose bushes before the fountain.

"These bushes were my special pride," the judge said. "I planted them myself the year Mrs. Delacroix and I moved into this house. And for nearly thirty years thereafter I had the joy of pruning them and fertilizing them and rejoicing each spring when they brought forth their inimitable bloom. The rose, to me, is nature's most exquisite manifestation of Beauty. Beauty, Mr. Barnett, with a capital *B*. You will notice now that I do not allow the bed to be weeded. The bushes themselves still bloom, but in this confined space and without the fertilizer I have denied them since I ruled in *Grieve*, the blossoms are fewer each year. I have never let the gardener who maintains this lovely space tend my roses. But since I ruled in *Grieve*, I have felt unworthy to tend them myself."

The judge returned again to his chair, seated himself, and rested his palms flat against his knees, holding himself in an unnaturally rigid posture.

"I am a homosexual, Mr. Barnett. That is the secret Sheldon Retif managed to learn about me and used as his cudgel to make me disgrace every notion I had ever maintained about myself."

His secret revealed, the judge allowed himself to lean back in his chair. He picked up his brandy snifter and drained it, his third at least, then signaled to the house for still another.

Leon Delacroix was gay and Sheldon Retif got him to ruin Tom Grieve by threatening to make that fact public. To whom all? His wife? Could she not know? His family? I took a sip of Scotch, set the glass back on the table, but without ever taking my hand from the glass brought it back to my lips and took a large swallow.

"Why are you telling me this, Judge Delacroix?" I asked.

"I am telling you because I feel confident you would have learned for yourself soon enough, as others before you have. You are very close to knowing it all anyway. So I am merely shortening the process. In order to ask a favor."

"I haven't even sorted out all the implications of what you're telling me yet," I said, "but I wouldn't count on my granting you any favors."

He smiled then, as if he knew some secret about me that I did not know about myself. Horace set another snifter of brandy beside the judge and fetched away his empty glass and my first Scotch glass as well.

"People are far, far more open-minded about homosexuality today than when I was a young man," the judge said. "I grew up thinking that there was something desperately wrong with me. I had no interest in women. And I lusted after every handsome young man I knew. I remained a virgin right through college. And then I fell in love. And for what seems now the briefest time I surrendered totally to what I still thought was my unspeakable sin. And though I was certain that I was damned, I was blissfully happy for a period of about four years. But then the war came, and Brett and I were separated. And when the war ended and we returned, it was not to one another, for the war had changed us and ruined us, at least for each other."

"Brett Williams was your lover?" I asked.

"Brett Williams was my love," the judge said. "My first love and one of only two that I have known."

"But both of you married," I said.

"It was inevitable," he replied. "Brett was so scarred by the homosexual witchhunts he'd evaded during the war that he wanted to have nothing further to do with me. He married quickly and lived out the rest of his sadly short life hiring boys to join him in the back rooms of bars on Bourbon and Decatur."

"And you ?"

"I could never have done what Brett did. I don't judge him. But I think I was the happier of the two of us. I was more gifted at celibacy."

The judge took a sip of brandy and held the glass with both hands at his waist.

"And your wife," I inquired, "Mrs. Delacroix?"

"A marriage of . . . convenience," the judge sighed. "I was trying to follow a political career, and there were suspicions to dispel. Jessica needed a husband. And so we conferred upon each other a desperately required respectability. We appeared the perfect couple."

"But you have a daughter," I said.

Judge Delacroix smiled benignly.

"I was not incapable of the heterosexual act, Mr. Barnett, just uninterested. Jessica's desire for a child was both expected and understandable, and for the act of procreation I was able to do my duty. Such a feat is not uncommon among men like me, you know. I desired a child as well. And I found parenting a joy. But Jessica never misunderstood the nature of my true proclivities."

"Then your wife wasn't your other, second love."

"No," the judge said. "My wife and I, at times anyway, have been fond companions of a kind. We certainly shared the treasure of our daughter. But my only love aside from Brett came to me as Horace's predecessor."

"A servant," I said.

"A friend," he replied.

"A black man?"

"A man whose skin is black."

"And where is he now?" I asked.

"He lives here. Not here in the house, but here in New Orleans. In the Quarter."

"And the two of you are still . . . together?"

"Oh yes."

"Why didn't you keep him with you here at the house?"

Judge Delacroix snorted and took another swallow of brandy.

"Mrs. Delacroix was rather adamantly opposed to such an arrangement," he said. "She is obviously not a person altogether orthodox in her expectations about marriage. But she has quite a rigorous sense of decorum."

"What is this man's name?" I asked.

"Ah, that I'll not tell you," the judge replied, slurring his words a little.

"Why are you telling me any of this, then?"

"Because I want you to understand the nature of what I was up against. I was wrong to have surrendered to Retif. That I know. But I did want to protect those who were innocent. Among them, Mrs. Delacroix. Our bargain allowed her a public identity as the wife of a judge, and she relished that. Retif threatened to reduce her status to that of a, of a . . . how does this expression go? . . . of a fag hag—if I may speak crudely."

"Who else were you trying to protect?"

"Brett Williams' family, though I'm not sure that Brett's former wife wasn't the source of Retif's information. And mostly I wanted to protect Arthur—I don't suppose you can make anything of his first name. Arthur was a young man when he came to work for me in 1958. Maria was an infant, and thus I had fulfilled my obligations to Jessica proudly. Arthur had just graduated from Southern University. Imagine that so late in our history a college-educated black man would have to seek employment as a houseman. I helped him through a master's program at S.U.N.O., and he's now a school teacher. Naturally, I do not wish his sexual orientation bandied about in all the newspapers. You may not know this, but the black community is even less tolerant of homosexuality than the white."

I didn't know whether such an assertion was true or not. Nor, at the moment, did I care. Brandy had loosened the judge's tongue more than he no doubt knew. And my thoughts were on a black school teacher named Arthur, a 1958 Southern graduate with a subsequent master's degree from S.U.N.O., presumably in education. It might take awhile, I thought, but I could find this man.

"Now that I have confessed everything to you, Mr. Barnett," the judge said, "I will ask my favor."

"Go ahead," I said, reeling a bit in the backwash of all he was telling me. "But I warn you not to expect anything approaching cooperation from me."

"I plan to ask far less of you than I asked of your colleague, Mr. Shaney."

"Mr. Shaney?" I said.

"Yes," the judge replied. "I asked Mr. Shaney not to publish the story at all."

I had to restrain myself from leaping straight up out of my chair.

"Carl knows this story?" I demanded, heat in my voice.

"Yes," the judge replied.

"For how long?"

"For some time. Since shortly after Tom Grieve's death."

"How did you get him not to report it?"

"I asked him not to."

"And what else?"

"Nothing else, Mr. Barnett. I merely asked him not to. I told him that innocent people would be hurt."

"Yeah. Well you were wrong. Maybe innocent people were hurt because Carl *didn't* report this stinking fucking story. Maybe Joan would be alive if he *had* reported it."

The judge bowed his head.

"I recognize that now, Mr. Barnett, though I assure you I did not at the time. Had Mr. Shaney printed what I told him, your wife might be alive. Though, of course, it was not Mr. Shaney's knowledge that placed her in jeopardy, but rather, I presume, her own."

"What the fuck does that mean?"

"Only that your wife had the same information."

"How do you know what Joan knew and what she didn't."

The judge said, "I know she knew what you do now . . ."

I was on my feet before the judge had finished his sentence.

" . . . because I told her myself."

"You're a liar," I said.

"Really, I'm not, Mr. . . ."

I snatched Leon Delacroix out of his chair with two handfuls of his sweater and screamed in his face, "YOU ARE A GODDAMNED LIAR."

I rammed Delacroix back into his chair, my fists still twined in his clothes. My rage was such I suspect he thought I was going to kill him. And he had cause for such fear. I thought I might kill him myself until Horace rushed from the house screaming that he had called the police. I turned toward Horace, and as I did so my blazer blew open. He no doubt saw the pistol in my belt, for though I never touched it, he suddenly raised both hands over his head and shrank back toward the house.

In a quavering voice, the judge said, "I didn't mean to upset you so, Mr. Barnett. It is my intention to help you identify your wife's murderer, if indeed she was murdered. That's why I request that you not run your story. Not yet, that is."

"You must be stark raving out of your mind," I snapped. "Why would Joan have protected you?"

"I don't know why your wife acted as she did. Frankly, I was surprised that she did. I doubt that her motivation was to protect me, though."

"I don't believe a single thing you're telling me."

"Two days, Mr. Barnett. That's all I ask. Two days. You don't want to run your story during Mardi Gras, anyway, I shouldn't think."

"I'm not listening to you," I said. "For all I know you had Joan murdered to protect yourself and your precious reputation."

"I can hardly blame you for such suspicions, I guess," the judge said. "But I implore you to believe that vile a man as you have every right to think me, I had nothing to do with your wife's death. I am many things. But I am not a murderer. What I'm offering you, Mr. Barnett, in exchange for the favor I ask, is my cooperation. And I believe I'm in the best position to help bring the guilty to justice."

"It's thoroughly obvious who's guilty. You and Retif. And one or both of you had Joan killed. If you didn't do it, then it was Retif."

"You may well be right. But there are things you still don't know, things only I can provide for you. If you can wait two days. Today is Sunday. If you can wait until the end of Mardi Gras Day, you can file your story with all the facts, without any of the pieces missing. Two days, Mr. Barnett, is all I ask."

"I've got everything you've said on my tape machine," I pointed out.

"And you may use it as you will. I realize that. I merely ask that you wait two days before you use it."

"I don't promise to wait two minutes," I said.

"You must go now before the police arrive, Mr. Barnett. I will explain that Horace misinterpreted what was merely a misunderstanding. But please consider what I'm offering you—the certain identity of your wife's killer."

"When do you claim you told Joan all about your precious homosexuality," I asked, "and all this other stuff you've told me tonight?"

Like most everything he told me that evening, Delacroix's answer had the nauseating ring of truth.

"I wouldn't recall the date, of course. But I do remember she told me she had spoken recently with your old colleague Herman Krancke and before that had visited in Bucktown with a man named Cheney Hickman who had helped her piece together information that led back to me."

*   *   *

I fled from Leon Delacroix's house into a swirling, sickening night, the pounding of parade drums reverberating inside my haywire brain. Carl Shaney had known Delacroix's story for years. Worse, Delacroix claimed that Joan had known it too, if only during the last week of her life. A cancerous disorientation crowded into my consciousness. I had been concerned for some time as to why Joan had never confided to me the fact of her meeting with Cheney Hickman. I had long presumed that she was going to do just that on the very day she died. Surely she was going to tell me about her meeting with Delacroix as well. But a malignant memory corroded my confidence in that presumption. Retif had paid Delacroix $100,000 in hush money. And when Joan died, she had $100,000 in savings she had never told me about.

CHAPTER TWENTY-FOUR

Leaving Leon Delacroix's house at the height of the Bacchus parade meant that it took me nearly an hour to make my way back to my house in the River Bend, a drive that one can normally make in just over ten minutes.

Sitting in my car on Dante Street, I felt stymied by confusion. How could Carl Shaney have gotten to the bottom of Judge Delacroix's decision in *Retif* and chosen not to print the story? Joan might be alive if he had. And how could Joan have known that Sheldon Retif had blackmailed Delacroix and not told me? How could she have died with $100,000 in the bank she'd never mentioned? If Retif had hired a black man to run Joan down, why would he have given her the money? Had the money bought her silence for a few days while killing her kept her quiet for ever? I absolutely could not bear it. Joan would never have taken a bribe. There had to be some other explanation. There had to be. But what? I was almost utterly irrational. And in my irrational state, I blamed Carl. If Carl had printed the story on Retif and Delacroix, Joan would be alive, and my memory of her would have been free of taint.

Without even getting out at my house, I decided to confront Carl and fought the traffic all the way back to his apartment on Melpomene. He wasn't home. After I'd waited fifteen minutes or so outside his place, I found a pay phone and called his office. But I got no answer there either. Almost in a frenzy I called Preacher Martin.

*　　　*　　　*

"What could Carl have been thinking about?" I asked Preacher after I'd arrived at his Cape Cod cottage on South Solomon in Mid-City.

Omitting any reference to what Joan knew and when, I'd otherwise explained the essentials of my conversation with Leon Delacroix. Preacher and I were sitting in his kitchen, on either side of the formica table which dominated the center of the room. A glare of white light was provided by a naked bulb which hung by a long cord from the ceiling over the table. Preacher had poured us each a glass of whiskey, and a bottle of Jack Daniels and a bottle of Black and White sat on the table between us.

"Beats me, son," Preacher said.

"Delacroix says he just asked Carl not to print the goddamn story, and Carl didn't do it. What kind of bullshit is that? Carl's an investigative reporter, for Christ's sake."

I took a big swallow of Scotch.

"They must have bought the fucker," I said.

"Coulda bought him," Preacher said. "Most anybody can be bought if the price is right."

"Fuck that," I said instantly.

Preacher did not respond.

"Fuck that," I said again. "Nobody could buy you."

"Nobody ever offered me very much," he replied.

"Quit playing your goddamn games," I told him. "I'm not in the mood."

Preacher stood up and splashed a little more whiskey into each of our glasses.

"Carl has fought me on this thing from the beginning," I said. "Tried to harass my ass off the story for nine months."

Preacher didn't say anything.

"Well what do you make of that?" I demanded.

"I don't know what to make of it, Mike. Maybe he knew something you didn't, had an angle on it you don't see."

"Or maybe he was bought," I said.

"Maybe," Preacher said. "But it was Carl told you to go see Delacroix. And Delacroix didn't try to buy you."

"He knew better."

"Maybe. But it stands to reason that Delacroix didn't try to buy Carl Shaney either. Especially not after the way you say Delacroix came across to you."

"I don't give a shit," I said. "Carl had the goddamn story, and he didn't run it. And I'm gonna fry the son-of-a-bitch for that. I'm gonna put *that* in *my* story. And the Old Man'll have Carl Shaney for breakfast."

Preacher got up and picked up his bottle. "I'm takin' mine in the living room," he said. "Get out of this light. You can join me if you want. Or you can stay in here and get drunk by yourself."

"I'm not getting drunk," I retorted. "I'm gonna pour this goddamn whisky down the drain."

"Ain't your whisky," Preacher said. "But if you want to pour it down the drain, go ahead. Remember this, though. It ain't the whisky's fault. And your wastin' the whisky ain't gonna make your problems any easier."

"Yeah, well, if I pour it out, I won't drink it. And that'll solve at least one of my problems."

"If you pour it out you won't drink the whisky you pour out, and it won't solve shit. There's another bottle just like it in the pantry, and even if there weren't, there's one on the shelf at the Time Saver. There's always more whisky. If drinkin' it is a problem, then you gotta solve that problem by not drinkin' it. Pouring it down the drain is just being plain wasteful."

"Why the fuck are we talking about whisky," I said.

"You know me," Preacher said. "I'll talk about any goddamn thing and whisky a lot sooner than others."

He turned and walked into his living room where he sat in a vinyl recliner he had covered with an old bedspread. I picked up the bottle of Black and White and followed him, seating myself across from him in a rocker. We sat and drank for a while in silence.

Finally, I said, "Why'd Carl sit on that story, Preacher?"

"I figure that's something you better ask him," Preacher replied.

*   *   *

For reasons that are sometimes mysterious to me, God usually smiles on Mardi Gras. The holiday sometimes falls as early as the first Tuesday in February, but the weather is almost always mild and clear. 1989 was different. Weather forecasters aren't regarded as terribly accurate in our city, but they correctly predicted the cold front which moved through Sunday night, bringing with it the year's first sub-freezing weather. I awoke Monday morning before dawn, and when I stepped out of my house to head to work at six-thirty, I was greeted by the uncommon sight of frost on my lawn. I went back into the house for a sweater to wear under my blue blazer.

At first almost alone in the building, I managed an agitated two hours of work before my colleagues arrived. Shortly before nine I'd finished the film listings for Friday's entertainment tabloid. I normally did this work on Tuesday, but only a skeleton news crew worked at the paper on Mardi Gras, a group that never included me.

Carl came in about nine-fifteen, and I confronted him immediately. It was unpleasant business. And he knew I was serious when I laid my tape recorder on his desk and pointedly pressed the button to record.

"I know you've had the Delacroix blackmail story for over two years," I said. I sat down in the chair next to Carl's desk.

"I figured he'd tell you," Carl said. He looked me straight in the face. His eyes were solemn. He turned away from me and shook himself out a cigarette. He offered the pack to me, but I declined.

"I want to know why you sat on it," I said. "I want to know why the *fuck* you sat on the *goddamn* story."

Carl's eyes were downcast. "I wish I hadn't," he said.

I stood up and leaned over the desk toward Carl. "As far as I'm concerned, you killed my wife, you son-of-a-bitch." I slapped my hand down on desk for emphasis and Carl blinked. He didn't say anything. "Why did you do it, Carl?" I felt myself about to cry. "Why in God's name did you do it?"

"I did what I do, man. I worked on a story. I got to what I thought was the end of it. I looked at what I had. And I made a judgment. I . . ."

"You made the judgment to back off, to bury it," I said heatedly.

"Yes, I made the decision to back off. I . . ."

"He buy you, man? *Some*body buy you? Retif buy you?"

"Look, Mike. I know you're upset about this and . . ."

"You're goddamn right I'm upset."

"Well, if you'd let me, I'd try to explain what . . ."

"Fuck you, man. Just fuck you."

I sat back down. Carl sighed, crushed out his cigarette and immediately lit another one.

"Just let me try to explain, Mike. Okay?"

"Fuck you."

"By the time I had the story that Retif had blackmailed Delacroix because of his gay lover, Tom Grieve was dead."

"Joan wasn't dead."

Carl closed his eyes, and when he spoke again, it was in a hoarse whisper. "No, Joan wasn't. What can I tell you, Mike? I made the biggest mistake of my life. I didn't know Joan was still digging around. And until you started putting some of the timing together, I never thought her death had anything to do with this business. If I had . . ."

"Delacroix was still alive," I pointed out. "And so was Sheldon Retif. Both still are. But you let them off. A goddamn federal judge let himself be blackmailed. And you could have nailed him. But you let him off."

Carl took a deep breath and looked at the ceiling.

"Yeah, I let him off. I had to make a call. And that's the one I made. I think now it was the wrong call. But I didn't think so at the time. Leon Delacroix has meant an awful lot to the black people of this city and region. He's revered by people in the black community, at least by those who know the legal history of the sixties."

"So you're admitting for the record that you protected Delacroix," I charged.

Carl looked first at the tape machine and then at me. His eyes were sad. "I made a call, Mike. But if you want to put it that way, yeah, I protected him, I guess. Tom Grieve was dead; he was the victim. The school was built. And it was built in the best location as far as the public was concerned. And me too for that matter. I wouldn't have minded frying Sheldon Retif. He was slime from way back. But he wasn't big-time slime in my view. You see? So it looked to me at that juncture like the primary result of my story was going to be the public humiliation of Leon Delacroix and the conceivable ruin of his lover. And the way I looked at it, Delacroix was a victim in all this, too. He stood up to Retif on the attempted black blood smear. And I think he finally caved in only to protect his lover."

"I know all about Master Arthur," I lied.

"You've talked to Adams?" Carl asked.

And now I knew Arthur's last name, too. Carl was on the defensive and not nearly as sharp as he would normally be. I took a mean delight in having tricked the information out of him. If I continued to string him along, I calculated, I might get even more.

"Not yet," I said.

"Arthur Adams is a very sweet, vulnerable man," Carl said.

"How did you find him?" I asked.

"The same way you did, I presume," Carl replied.

"Through his educational records," I said.

Carl snorted a sad laugh. "You've got an instinct for this dirty business, Mike. I'll give you that."

"What did Adams say when you talked with him?"

"He cried," Carl said. "He cried, and he begged me not to print the story. I talked some bullshit about how this was the 1980s and no one gave a shit if somebody was gay anymore. And he said he'd lose his job, that parents weren't going to let their sons or even their daughters go off on band trips with a queer music teacher."

"So you're telling me that you killed the story to protect Arthur Adams," I said.

"Adams was a complete innocent," Carl said. "His only mistake was in having a thirty-year relationship with Leon Delacroix. But that's not the only reason. I've already admitted that I had come to see Delacroix as a victim, too. I think he's a good man who got his arm twisted and did something bad."

"So you just decided to play judge and jury all by yourself."

Carl looked at me fiercely.

"I decided not to play executioner all by myself," he said.

I didn't comment, and Carl tapped out a fresh cigarette, lit it and took a deep drag.

"I don't apologize for wanting to protect Arthur Adams," he said. "Or Delacroix either, for that matter. Not in the final analysis. But part of my decision was purely professional. Only it was wrong, I'm afraid. And I can't tell you how sorry I am about that."

"What fucking part of your decision was professional?" I asked. "I thought you worked at this paper as an investigative reporter."

"You haven't ever done investigative journalism, Mike, and you . . ."

"I'm going to break this story, fucker," I said, "no thanks to you."

Carl sighed. "What I mean is," he said, "you aren't on an investigative beat. I get leads on stories all the time. There's so much corruption in this city; if I had the manpower, I feel like I could uncover a major scandal every week. But I've learned something about the people of this city. They've got the attention span of flies, and their tolerance for bad news is a lot lower than their tolerance for bad government. You gotta pick and choose. You try to expose an instance of corruption every week and people get to where they shrug their shoulders. You do what I do, you gotta be like Muhammad Ali in his fight against George Foreman. You gotta lie on the ropes and take a lot of punches. And you gotta make sure when you come off the ropes to throw a punch that you knock somebody out. I didn't have any doubt that this story would knock somebody out. Three somebodies actually. But it didn't seem to me that I'd win any championships for knocking out Sheldon Retif. And knocking out Leon Delacroix and a music teacher at W.E.B. Dubois High sure wasn't going to do one damn thing to make this city a better place to live. I could probably have put Retif and Delacroix in jail. But only by fixing it so that Arthur Adams would have had to resign his teaching position. And meanwhile, all the ratfuckers in this town would have hid in the shadow of a scandal that didn't have a thing to do with them."

The tip of Carl's cigarette had smoldered into a long gray ash. He flicked it off, took a drag and crushed out the butt. His fingers toyed with his pack for a second, but he set it back down without taking out a fresh smoke. I picked the pack up and helped myself to a cigarette, lighting it with Carl's disposable lighter.

"When you first told us," Carl said, "me and Wilson and Preacher, that you had started poking around in this business, Preacher said something that was on my mind when I let the story die. You probably don't remember. Wilson asked if Delacroix was black. And you said no. And Preacher said then maybe he was gay. Or something like that. Said all liberal federal judges were either niggers or fags. Well there's lots of people, lots of white people in this town who think like that. Exactly like that. And the way it looked to me when I backed off the story was that all I was going to prove if I went forward was the bigots were right. All liberal federal judges were either niggers or fags. And they'd choose to believe that Delacroix was both. No matter what I wrote, that's the way the story would stick in the public mind. People wouldn't be scared or outraged. They'd be delighted. Businesses in this town were stealing millions of dollars, fucking millions of dollars in city sales taxes, and I'd be helping entertain the masses with a story that boiled down to the fact that Leon Delacroix was sucking a nigger's cock while he wrote the opinions that struck down the state's segregation laws. I just couldn't do it, Mike. Don't you see that. I just couldn't do it. Putting Sheldon Retif in jail just wasn't worth it."

I had lost my taste for cigarettes, it seemed. I tried another puff and found I couldn't abide the taste. I crushed it out practically unsmoked. I had the information from Carl I needed. And I didn't want to listen to his excuses anymore. I stood up, clicked off the tape recorder, picked it up and started out of Carl's office

At the door I paused and said, "And what do you do with the fact that Joan is dead, Carl? What do you do with the knowledge that publishing your story would have saved her life?"

"I pray for forgiveness," he said.

*   *   *

On the way through editorial back to my own office, I heard two of our interns discussing the city's most recent murder. I gathered from their remarks that the Gay Stalker had struck again. I hadn't seen Wilson all day, and that was obviously why. She was out on the story. A body had been found, one of the interns said, but not yet identified.

After my meeting with Carl, I tried to work. I needed to finish off copy for Friday's tabloid before leaving for a one-thirty screening of the new Kevin Costner movie, *Field of Dreams,* at The Prytania, the city's Uptown art cinema. But my concentration was crippled by a complicated mix of emotions. I felt as if a tornado had blown through my soul.

At about twelve forty-five I was standing at my desk, shifting papers into various piles and filling my briefcase with materials to take home, when Carl came into my office.

"I need to tell you something," he said.

I didn't look up at him, didn't even acknowledge his presence.

"I've been working on the story again," he said. "You should know that."

I looked up at Carl now and smiled nastily.

"Now that it's a story, you want in. Is that what you're telling me? You don't want to be a *part* of the story anymore, huh? Don't want to read my account of the big-deal investigative reporter who cut his line instead of pulling his catch into the boat? You want to be in on the *writing* of the story now. That's peachy, Carl. Hey, no problem. So, do we share a by-line? Or does this become a *by* Carl Shaney, *with* Mike Barnett story?"

Carl stared at me a second, then turned around and started out of the office. He stopped and turned back, however, when he got to the door.

"Fuck you, Barnett," he said. "This isn't about a goddamn by-line, and you goddamn well know it. I want to get to the bottom of this almost as bad you do. I fucked up. I made a bad decision. People got hurt. Somebody I cared about is dead. The least I can do is help you finger the bastards. I'll give you anything I get. It's your fucking story. And if you want to make me a part of it, that's your decision. I won't do anything to stop you."

I didn't say anything and busied myself stacking papers and rearranging things on my desk. I wanted to hold Carl accountable because I needed to believe that *somebody* was accountable, that Joan's death wasn't just a random happenstance.

Carl stepped back toward my desk. And when he spoke, despite the icy hardness of my heart, I could hear the anguish in his voice.

"The question, Mike, is who had Joan killed. I don't think Delacroix did. So if Retif did it, how do we nail him?"

I sat down in my chair and put my head in my hands.

"I don't think Delacroix did it either," I said. "But he told me yesterday he's going to give me the killer. He told me he'd let me know right after Mardi Gras."

Carl pondered that for a moment. Then he said, "I'm working on a lead, too. Maybe not as good as Delacroix. But you never know."

"Who?" I asked.

"Johnny Chambers," he said.

I looked up at him, astonished. "He's talked to you?" I said.

"Not yet, but he's going to."

"Why? He wouldn't talk to me."

"Tammy Dieter-White wouldn't let him," Carl said. "And the more I thought about that, the more I realized somebody needed to get to him. You couldn't do it. So I've been working on it."

"How did you get him to agree to talk?"

"I appealed to his self-interest," Carl responded.

"Meaning?"

"I just happened to mention the words *accessory to murder after the fact*."

*   *   *

After the screening I stopped at Camellia Grill just a couple of blocks from my house and ate a chili cheese omelet. Sitting beside me on the diner stools were people in costume. It was Lundi Gras, the last Monday of Carnival, by tradition a day for recuperation from a hard-partying weekend before the rigors to follow on Mardi Gras Day. In recent years, though, Rex had revived an ancient ritual of arriving at the city's riverfront on Lundi Gras night aboard a royal barge. And there'd been an effort to follow the Carnival King's arrival with a celebration in Spanish Plaza. One of the season's oldest parading Krewes, Proteus, rolled along the Napoleon-to-St. Charles-to-Canal route Lundi Gras night. My fellow Camellia Grill diners were no doubt about to catch an early streetcar so as to stake out a good spot to view Proteus before following the parade on downtown for the additional festivities. Not wanting to face a long night at home alone, I abruptly decided to join them.

When a Mardi Gras parade rolls in New Orleans, any activity not associated with the parade simply ceases in that part of town. The parade route becomes a gigantic block party. People use the street as a promenade and a dance floor. Streets surrounding the route gradually turn into parking lots, as parade-goers, desperate not to miss a single band or float, simply lock and abandon their cars.

Like any kid who was raised in this city, I grew up loving Mardi Gras. It was a time, as one of the city's slogans goes "that care forgot." When I returned to the city after graduate school, however, my fondness for Mardi Gras began to wane. I became ever more concerned about the pressing problems facing our city, and ever more convinced that the whole town had surrendered to a party-till-you-drop mentality. Let the problems wait until tomorrow, until next week, until next year, until the next generation. Let the problems wait until after Mardi Gras. Only, in New Orleans, Mardi Gras is a year-round proposition, a life-long state of mind.

It is said that even ambulances are forced to wait for the passing of a Mardi Gras parade. And so I warn our residents and visitors to our city to arrange their heart attacks and their strokes and their life-threatening accidents so as not to interfere with the urgency of a parade on the roll. And every year at Mardi Gras, scrambling for a doubloon, a worthless aluminum coin thrown from riding maskers to the howling crowds by the thousands, some child is crushed beneath the wheels of a float. But the parades go on. Every year some teenaged member of a school marching band is attacked by a drunk or a lunatic, stabbed or even shot. But the parades go on. Every year our public schools graduate students who cannot read and cannot add, for Christ's sake who cannot even spell their own names correctly. Every year hundreds, thousands of children are born to unwed teenaged mothers who haven't yet learned even the basics of birth control. But the parades go on.

This city spends untold millions of dollars on balls and on costumes and on floats, on gasoline to power the tractors that pull the floats, on policemen to marshal the parade routes. We spend millions of dollars on trinkets, beads that no one would wear, plastic cups that no one drinks from, doubloons that can't be used to purchase a newspaper much less a loaf of bread, millions of dollars on *trash* that maskers can throw to the crowds. And meanwhile our school children aren't allowed to take their textbooks home because we lack the resources to replace them should they become lost or damaged. People are growing up in this city without even rudimentary hopes for achieving the American Dream of middle-class comfort. But the parades go on.

What in the fuck are we parading about?

But lest I wax too superior, I hasten to admit that all my life I have been a parade goer. Joan loved the pageantry, and I loved the sense of festival. We always went to the Carrollton Parade, to Endymion and Mid-City and Bacchus. We always made ourselves costumes and spent Mardi Gras Day on the streets. I may object to the waste of Mardi Gras, in other words, but I have stood in the crowds with all my fellow New Orleanians, and I have slipped my flask of Black and White into my hip pocket and raised my arms to the passing floats. And I have strained my voice along with all the others, screaming, "Throw me something, mister, throw me something." And I have wrestled with children for the thrill of catching a pair of beads or a doubloon. For me, as for so many others, Mardi Gras has been a time of abandon. But I speak from experience and with identification when I judge that for our city, Mardi Gras has become what a quart bottle of Black and White has become to me, not a friend to be relished, but an enemy to be feared.

*   *   *

And there I was on Lundi Gras, watching Proteus, gathering for the arrival of Rex. My mood was not what it was in other, better, earlier years. But I was in the crowd again, my arms raised to catch a trinket, my mind desperate to forget my cares, my heart urgent for the solace of abandon.

I got home around midnight. On my answering machine was a message from Wilson. We hadn't seen or spoken to each other since she'd left. She said something about the annual Mardi Gras Day party at Amy Stuart's and maybe we could meet there. But she really needed to talk to me tonight, she said, and she asked that I call her. It was important, and she'd be up late, so I shouldn't worry about calling her whenever I got in.

I wanted to call her, but I felt awkward and embarrassed about what had happened between us. I didn't blame her for leaving. Some part of me was even relieved that she had. But another part wanted to ask her to please reconsider. Another part missed her and wanted to be comforted in her arms, wanted to hide against her bosom.

But immediately I lacked the emotional energy to dress Wilson's wounds. And so I dreaded talking to her. My psychic plate was full. Joan's death. Retif's corruption. Judge Delacroix's collaboration. The whole mess of the judge's story and his promise to help me identify my wife's killer. Carl's complicated role. I hadn't the strength to sort things out with Wilson when so much else seemed pending. So instead of calling her, I poured myself a Black and White and began providing myself with excuses. I told myself that it was too late to be making social calls. I told myself that, really, Wilson wasn't the right person for me anyway. That she was too young for me. That our sensibilities were too different. That we were both better off just letting the brief weeks of our affair settle into a bittersweet memory. That there wasn't a single hope that things might work out between us and that I'd be foolish and arguably even cruel not to just cut them off now. And I told myself that Wilson's feelings wouldn't be hurt if I didn't call her tonight. That I could just tell her that I got in late and didn't want to bother her. And that she'd be satisfied with that excuse.

That's what I told myself as I got out my bottle of Black and White and poured my first drink. But I knew even as I poured my fifth drink, and my seventh, that most everything I told myself was a lie.

*　　　*　　　*

Mardi Gras Day dawned cold and gray. I'd managed to go to bed with enough Scotch left in my bottle that I awoke without a hangover. When you consume as much alcohol as I do, it takes a lot to make you drunk. And more to make you regret the fleeting oblivion you achieved the night before.

But my mood on Mardi Gras morning was as gray as the day anyway. The first Mardi Gras after Joan died, I had been lucky enough to be in New York for piggy-backed junkets on John Huston's *The Dead*, Mike Nichols' *Biloxi Blues* and Alan Alda's *A New Life*. So this was going to be the first Mardi Gras I was going to have to spend without her. I wasn't sure I could bear it.

I always enjoyed the festivity of Mardi Gras Day. But Joan, I think, actively looked forward to it. She connected with the celebration in a way I didn't quite. Her need to get out on the streets on Mardi Gras was great enough that once she even climbed out of a sick bed to do it. It was chilly that year, too. She had a bad cold and a little fever. So we didn't stay out long after Rex had rolled past us. But on the way home from the parade she was beaming.

"I'm so glad we went," she said, snuffling and then blowing her nose, but smiling all the while. "I would have felt miserable all year long if we'd missed it."

I suspect that I'm the kind of man who would never have donned a costume even once. But at Joan's instigation and insistence, I went out masked on Mardi Gras Day every year that we were together. We never worried about costumes ahead of time, usually putting them together at the last minute on Sunday night after Bacchus or even on Monday night during Proteus. We absolutely never bought or rented costumes, a practice Joan thought utterly contrary to the spirit of the Carnival season. We bought masks, perhaps, and certainly accessories of all sorts. But the costumes were our own inventions and designs.

One year Joan made us mouse costumes out of old gray sweat suits onto which she sewed ears and tails. We painted our faces with whiskers and wore black gloves. She went as Mickey Mouse. I wore a Richard Nixon mask and went as Tricky Dickie Mouse. Another year I dressed up in a farmer's outfit and a black burglar's mask. I was the Lone Granger. Joan tied forks, knives and spoons all over her clothes. She was Silver. And all day long when I was the only one who might hear, she would rumble her throat and whinny, "Bridle me, saddle me and ride me like no tomorrow Kemosabe." The week before Joan's last Mardi Gras, we went to donate some old clothes to the Salvation Army Store on Jefferson Highway. While we were there, she found an old marching-band jacket she thought looked like the current costume of Michael Jackson. So we went as the Jacksons. She painted her face black, wore a long black wig and went about singing "Nasty Boys." She was Janet. Carl went with us that year making impassioned speeches that he *was* somebody. He was Jesse. I had an old Yankee uniform from the year I went as one of the Baseball

Furies from Walter Hill's *The Warriors*. So I thought of going as Reggie. But at the last minute Joan designed me a costume in the shape of our neighboring state. It featured a large star to represent the state capital. And so I went as Jackson, Mississippi.

But there was no Joan to costume me in 1989, no Joan to appreciate some silly idea for a costume I might produce upon my own. We almost never wore the same costume twice, but we carefully saved all our creations. It would have been plenty easy for me to just get down the costume box and put on something I'd worn previously. But I didn't have the heart for it.

I did, however, have the heart for another of our Mardi Gras rituals. Joan was never that big a drinker. She was a great, sexy, companionable and silly drunk, though, on those occasions when she had more than a couple of drinks. Mardi Gras Day was an occasion when she thought imbibing was practically required. We always mixed up a batch of Bloody Marys and a batch of Screwdrivers promptly on rising. We drank the Bloody Marys steadily while we ate breakfast and helped each other into our costumes and could both usually feel the effects by the time we were dressed. The Screwdrivers we funneled into wine skins and carried with us.

This year I didn't bother with finding a costume. But I didn't miss the opportunity to start getting loaded before nine a.m. By nine forty-five, I had drunk my share of Bloody Marys and Joan's as well. And I was depressed enough that I thought of just staying home, finishing off the Screwdrivers and going to bed.

That would have been a happier course of action.

But I thought about the fact that Wilson had proposed our meeting at Amy's, and I thought about the comfort I would derive from seeing her. It would have made more sense, of course, to have called her as she asked and to have made concrete plans. But I had some vague notion that our meeting almost by accident would be nicer. So I dressed in a long-sleeved flannel shirt and a couple of sweaters and a wind breaker to ward off the cold. I even remembered to wear a pair of gloves. I put two pint bottles of Black and White in a backpack, along with the wine skin of Screwdrivers. As I was locking the burglar door on the front of my house, I heard the phone ring and started to return to answer it. But fuck it, I thought, that's why I had an answering machine, wasn't it? I walked over to Carrollton Avenue and caught the streetcar heading downtown. I wasn't the only uncostumed rider, but I was in a distinct minority. And I was surely the sole person aboard without a smile.

On Mardi Gras Day the streetcar doesn't run past Napoleon until late afternoon. It was after ten o'clock when I disembarked with the other riders at Cadiz Street. The Rex Parade is supposed to roll at ten, but it never does. The streets were jammed. As always, the corner of St. Charles and Napoleon was a sea of partying humanity.

Amy Stuart lived in an apartment house on Napoleon behind the First Baptist Church. I crossed over and went up to her second story flat. There was a cheery purple and green sign on the door that said:

COME IN!

BEER IN THE FRIDGE

BOOZE ON THE TABLE

BATHROOM DOWN THE HALL

HAPPY CARNIVAL!

The door was open, but no one was inside. I had missed them. They were already out on the street.

I went looking for faces I knew, Wilson's in particular, but I had no luck finding anyone. I didn't know how any of my friends and colleagues might be costumed. I didn't know where they might have decided to station themselves this year. And I knew they weren't looking for me. I hadn't called Wilson back. I hadn't told Amy I was coming. About ten-forty the front end of Rex reached the turn onto St. Charles. I watched it from the neutral ground. I caught a couple of pairs of beads which I snapped into place around my neck. My heart wasn't into hollering, "Hey, throw me something, mister," however. And I mostly contented myself with transferring Screwdrivers from my wine bag to my stomach. If I could have bypassed the later, I'm sure I would have poured the vodka directly into my brain. I was beginning to get seriously drunk by the end of Rex. And it wasn't yet quite noon.

As the second parade began to make the turn onto St. Charles, people made their ways back to Amy's. Amy had put out sandwich materials, a pot of red beans and rice, potato salad and various other things to eat. People were eating and drinking and resting up to go back on the street. There were several faces in the apartment I didn't know. But there were also people from the paper, and I made small talk with them briefly. They hadn't seen Wilson, they said. Amy herself reported that Wilson had called to say she wasn't coming, would probably just go down to the Quarter if she went out today at all. Amy encouraged me to eat. Unwisely, I opted not to. The swirl of Bloody Marys and Screwdrivers in my brain led me instead to remark that I guessed I'd catch the Magazine Street bus to the Quarter and meet up with Wilson there.

Amy looked at me strangely because such an idea, of course, was purely preposterous.

I remember terrifyingly little of what happened to me after I left Amy Stuart's apartment. I remember becoming suddenly concerned that I was almost out of Screwdrivers and wouldn't be able to survive if I didn't replenish my supply. And I remember going into the K & B at Napoleon and St. Charles where I bought a half-gallon can of orange juice and a bottle of rot gut vodka.

"Who cares what it tastes like at this point," I told the young black cashier. "You know what I mean."

She knew what I meant, she said. And I felt a warmth for my fellow citizens that I hadn't in ages. If you only explained things to them, people knew what you meant. There was hope for New Orleans after all.

I remember sitting on the curb at Magazine and Louisiana where I'd walked when I discovered that no buses were leaving from Magazine and Napoleon. Sitting with my legs crossed, I tried to pour the contents of the vodka bottle into the wine skin and poured at least as much on my jeans leg and more into the gutter. And I remember realizing that I didn't have a way to open the orange juice and thinking that I'd probably just make a sticky mess if I did. And I remember deciding that I'd just leave the orange juice can on the street when the bus finally arrived.

I don't remember riding the bus down to the Quarter. I don't remember drinking the first of my pint bottles of Black and White. But I do remember discovering that I was down to but one. And I do remember feeling thirsty and standing in line for a cup of beer at a bar that was open on Canal Street. And I do remember going into the bathroom at that bar and looking at myself in the mirror and saying aloud to my own image, "I don't know who you are."

And I do remember turning from that mirror to a man standing at the sink next to me and saying, pointing to myself in the mirror, "I don't know who the fuck he is. What do you think of that?"

But I don't remember what the man thought of that. And I don't remember it getting dark. But I do remember standing on Canal Street screaming over and over again at the maskers of Comus, "Throw me something, mister. Throw me something." And I remember people in the crowd making conversation with me. And I remember discovering that all I could say in return was, "Throw me something, mister," a fact that I found absolutely hysterical and impossibly sad all at the same instant.

I don't remember what happened to my backpack or my wine skin or my gloves. Nor do I remember riding the bus back home. But I do remember standing on my porch trying to fit my key into the lock on the front door of the house. And I remember stirring through drawers in my bedroom. And I remember standing again on my front porch and cheering the sound of Mardi Gras fireworks. With every boom I lectured the red bud tree in my front yard and the houses across the street and the rest of the neighborhood and the whole world, "Throw me something, mister." Boom! "Throw me something."

"Throw me something, mister." Boom! "Throw me something."

*   *   *

Meanwhile, locked away from me on the desk in my study, was the message from the call I'd failed to answer that morning as I was leaving. The caller was again Wilson Malt and her message had to do with the serial-murder case she'd been covering for the last several months. The Gay Stalker had indeed struck again, or at least someone using his M.O. Ballistics tests were still being conducted to see if the gun was the same one used in the earlier killings. Still again, the victim's relatives denied that he was gay. The latest had gone with his wife to Sunday night's Bacchus Ball. The wife had grown tired and taken a taxi home shortly after midnight. The husband had never arrived. His nude body had been discovered floating near the seawall off Lakeshore Drive late Monday morning. He'd been identified early Monday evening.

"Somebody has put a bullet in Sheldon Retif's brain," Wilson informed the blankness of my phone recorder. "There appeared to be fresh semen in his mouth."

"And some of the cops think they've got a prime suspect, Mike," she added. "They think it was you."

CHAPTER TWENTY-FIVE

I awoke Ash Wednesday morning lying in a pool of frozen vomit on the side lawn of my house. I was lucky to be alive.

*   *   *

Normally when I'm crippled with the kind of hangover I had the morning after Mardi Gras, the new day comes at me in a glare of slow motion. This day, though, it rushed at me with the roar and blur of a jet engine. I listened to Wilson's latest message on my answering machine and instantly began throwing up again.

I had barely managed to shower and wash down a fistful of aspirins with two cups of black coffee when I had to deal with Lt. Giannetti and Sgt. Rideau who showed up at my front door to talk to me about Sheldon Retif's death. They made a pretense of casualness, of course. They were just "following up," they said, on the "unfortunate" drunk and disorderly incident at Retif's house. But even in my sick haze, I knew they were looking to catch me in some lie that would give them cause to arrest me immediately. They wanted to know my whereabouts on Sunday night. I told them I'd had an early evening meeting with Judge Delacroix about a story I was working on and that afterwards I'd gone over to Preacher Martin's house.

"And what time did you leave this Preacher Martin's place?" Giannetti inquired.

"I don't really remember," I said.

The two cops looked at each other.

"It wasn't late," I added. "And I came straight home." N.O.P.D. was conducting a murder investigation, and I was giving answers like a skittish teenager afraid of getting grounded.

"What time would that have been?" Rideau wanted to know. "When you got home. Before midnight? Or after?"

"Before," I said. "Definitely before. More like eleven I'd say."

"Then what'd you do?" Giannetti asked.

"I went to bed," I said. "Had a drink. Read a while. Went to bed. I needed to get to work early Monday morning. Which I did."

This routine accounting for my movements on Sunday night completed, the two policemen made their preparations to leave. As they were rising, Rideau said, "Do yourself a favor in the future, Mr. Barnett. Don't make public threats against people who end up dead a few days later."

The gravity of his advice was obvious, and I didn't respond.

Just before they stepped onto my front porch, Giannetti said, "You don't by any chance happen to own a thirty-eight-caliber pistol do you, Mr. Barnett."

I said, "No," automatically, and the policemen nodded and made their way down my front step to their unmarked car on the street. I didn't tell them, of course, that I had possession of Wilson's .38 caliber service revolver. I hadn't lied. But I hadn't been exactly expansive with the truth either. The whole idea of being a murder suspect utterly panicked me. I didn't know how to behave to best protect myself. In the future, though, I resolved to be as truthful as possible and to trust that the truth was my best defense.

Sheldon Retif was dead. For forty years he had been a cancer eating away at the vital organs of my home city. I hated Sheldon Retif and everything he and his kind of man stood for, the influence peddling, the inside connections, the manipulation of the popular will, the syphoning off the public trough. And now he was dead. I had fantasized about killing him with my own hands. And now some mad man had put a bullet in his brain. I should perhaps have felt a sense of triumph, of chickens having come home to roost. Or best, I should have felt a sense of guilt in recognizing that the violence in our society, which I so abhorred, was mirrored in my own soul. But actually, all I felt was fear, fear that the police didn't believe I'd come home and gone to bed on Sunday night, fear that they could somehow convince a jury it was I who'd killed Retif and dumped his body into Lake Pontchartrain.

*   *   *

When I finally got to work at noon, Carl had put a story in my box. There was a hand-written note paper-clipped to the top. It read:

> Mike,
>
> Chambers talked to me on Monday night. I've included what he told me in the attached. You're a better stylist than I am. And you'll probably want to rewrite it in your own language. But I've put the story together the way I think it should go. Now that Carnival is behind us, I think we should run it almost immediately.
>
> Carl

I looked at the hard copy underneath the note. Carl's proposed head read: "Prominent Local Attorney Murdered?" The story's byline read: "Michael Barnett." His lead read:

> Evidence suggests that the 1987 death of prominent local attorney Joan Barnett was a contract murder.
>
> Barnett died in the summer of 1987 when she was struck by a car while jogging on the neutral ground along the St. Charles Avenue streetcar line. In the early eighties, Barnett had achieved notoriety when she represented contractor Thomas Grieve in Grieve's attempt to win the Orleans Parish School Board's Certificate 34 to build Thomas Jefferson Magnet High School.
>
> The driver of the automobile which killed Barnett, unemployed sanitation worker Jackson Smith, was subsequently identified as a corpse found floating in the Industrial Canal.

New Orleans Police investigators ruled Barnett's death an accident. But new evidence uncovered by the *States-Tribune* suggests that Barnett may have been killed to silence her efforts to prove that Judge Leon Delacroix's decision against Grieve was tainted.

I had gotten no further in Carl's story when Wilson came into my office and closed the door behind her. She was very somber. She could tell at a glance that I was sick and commented about it tersely. It wasn't the time, she said, for my incessant self-pity to crowd out my need to protect myself. She asked if I'd gotten her message. I told her yes, but when I tried to get her to elaborate, she said there was no time.

"Where were you last night?" she asked.

"At Comus," I said.

"And afterwards?"

I shrugged. "I went home."

"Can anyone attest to your whereabouts?"

"Not that I know of," I said.

I couldn't even attest to them myself, I thought bitterly.

"Why?" I asked.

"I just got a call from my father," she replied. "Leon Delacroix was just found by his houseman, lying in his garden. There's a bullet hole in his right temple."

Wilson was going out to cover the story now. She knew very few other details except that Horace the houseman had reported witnessing an argument between me and Judge Delacroix on Sunday night and that now I was a suspect in two killings, the judge's murder as well as Sheldon Retif's.

*   *   *

Leon Delacroix was dead. First Retif, now Delacroix too. I sat at my desk and moved papers from one stack to another. I tried with flagging concentration to digest Carl's interview with Johnnie Chambers. I could imagine having killed Sheldon Retif, but never Leon Delacroix who was going to give me Joan's killer. But Delacroix hadn't lived long enough. Now, perhaps I was lost. At one time the judge had been a hero of mine, an example of rectitude and principle and conscience, among the best men the South had produced. And then the judge had been a man I detested, an example of unearned privilege, reflexive self-protectiveness and moral cowardice. I had admired him, and I had hated him, and in the end I had relied on him. And now he was dead, and I was a suspect in his murder. The world was mad.

I expected to see Gianetti and Rideau at my door momentarily.

Then Wilson called. She'd been at Delacroix's mansion watching the investigators pick over the crime scene and listening to their speculative conclusions about what had happened. She had new things to report. First of all, ballistic tests were continuing, police believed Sheldon Retif had been killed with a different gun than had been used in several other Gay Stalker murders. Second, whoever had killed Judge Delacroix had also killed his wife.

The killer, Wilson said, had evidently slipped into Jessica Delacroix's bedroom while she was sleeping late on Carnival night after she and the judge had returned from the Comus Ball. A pillow was placed over her face, presumably to muffle the firing of the pistol that killed her. But Jessica had awakened, it seemed. Her legs and arms were twisted in the bedsheets as if she had struggled, and two shots were fired through the pillow. The first, presumably, missed entirely. The slug passed clear through the mattress and the box springs and was found lying on the floor underneath the bed. The second passed through Jessica's forehead and lodged in the back of her skull.

The judge's body was found lying on the patio, Wilson said, his head in the flower bed. First appearances suggested suicide.

"Suicide!" I exclaimed. "His head was in the rose bush bed?"

"Yes," she said. "He was holding a gun in his right hand. And it appeared to be the gun that killed both the judge and his wife. It had been recently fired. Three chambers were empty."

But the police were skeptical that the killings were actually a murder-suicide, no matter the appearances.

"Why?" I asked.

"A host of reasons," she responded. "First, there was no note. Second, the judge had fresh semen traces in his mouth. Third, Horace says that the gun in the judge's hand wasn't the judge's because the judge didn't own a gun."

And what that made me now, Wilson explained, was the prime suspect in three murders. The way the police were figuring it, I had copy-catted my murder of Retif, hoping to hide it in the series of killings by the Gay Stalker. And now this.

"Jesus Christ," I said. "They think I killed Delacroix and his wife and tried to make it look like a murder-suicide?"

"That's the idea. Horace says the gun in the judge's hand looks like the one you were carrying."

"Oh Jesus," I said.

"Did you take my revolver with you when you went to see Delacroix?" Wilson asked.

"Yes," I admitted.

"And where is it now?"

"It's in the nightstand drawer where I always keep it. I put it back there when I got home Sunday night."

I could hear Wilson sigh through the phone line. "It's not there, Mike."

"How do you know?"

"I'm at your house right now. And I just looked."

*   *   *

Bewildered and terrified, I fled the office immediately, taking with me only my computer backpack and Carl's story on Johnny Chambers. I was afraid that Giannetti and Rideau would appear to arrest me before I made it to my car. I didn't know what to do. I drove around the city for a while but then became paranoid that I'd be identified from my automobile license plate number. Finally, I drove out to Metairie and sat on a stool at Morning Call, drinking one cup of café au lait after another. As I sat, to keep from hyperventilating, I made my way slowly through Carl's piece on Johnny Chambers, searching desperately for information that would serve to exonerate me. But though the information Carl had gotten from Chambers clarified certain things, the story as a whole made things for me seem worse yet.

After Chambers failed to make partner at Herbst, Gilman, he was hired as an associate by Tammy Dieter-White at Wallace and Jones. Almost from the beginning of his employment at Wallace, Dieter-White tried to extract information from him about his involvement with *Grieve versus Retif*. At first he'd joked that he wouldn't want to violate any legal ethics, now that he'd changed sides, so to speak. But he did let slip to Dieter-White that Joan was still poking around in the case, that he'd personally heard Joan say she thought Judge Delacroix's decision reeked and wasn't ever going to rest until she figured out what made him rule as he had. Chambers remembered saying to Dieter-White while holding his thumb and index finger three inches apart, "Joan's got a file this thick just on stuff she's dug up since the case settled."

Chambers reported that he felt uncomfortable making such revelations to Dieter-White. He'd always liked Joan, he said, though he kind of thought that her kamikaze work habits made things difficult for guys like himself who preferred to take life a little easier. But he never blamed her for his failing to make partner at Herbst. Really he didn't. He saw her around after he went over to Wallace, and they always had a laugh about something. Still, he pretty much felt that his position at Wallace depended to some important degree on his willingness to share with Tammy Dieter-White whatever information he had or could generate about the Certificate 34 case. That's why he told Dieter-White about the phone call he received from Joan the week before she died. Joan wanted to know what all he'd learned from Cheney Hickman and why he'd never reported any of it to her. Johnny'd worked with Joan some on the *Retif* case, but hell, as a firm associate he'd been everybody's lackey. He frankly couldn't even remember a Cheney Hickman and told her so. Anyway, she made mention she thought she had evidence that Delacroix had been blackmailed. He asked her for details, but all she'd say was that if she was right it was going to make a nasty mess for a whole lot of people. Chambers said he reported the essentials of his conversation with Joan to Dieter-White that night before he left the office.

After Joan's death, Chambers remembered Dieter-White's persistent curiosity about the contents of Joan's file. She inquired of Chambers more than once and in more than one way if he knew what was in it. Then a month or so after Joan died, Dieter-White requested that he go to the Place St. Charles offices of Herbst, Gilman and see if he could find that file. Dieter-White avoided making the request directly, Chambers admitted. But she alluded to it in a purportedly joking fashion on many occasions, and she so often spoke to Chambers about the importance at Wallace and Jones of being a team player, of being willing to sacrifice for the good of the team, that Chambers began to get the idea that his position at the new firm might depend on his willingness to perform this act of larceny for her. Having already failed to make partner at one firm, Chambers feared that his legal career might be over if he failed to deliver what his boss was asking of him.

Both Chambers and Dieter-White were careful never to speak of the matter directly. But finally, scared absolutely white, Chambers went to Herbst to do Dieter-White's bidding. The whole episode shook him badly. But his plan went off without a hitch. Carrying a large, empty briefcase, he walked into Herbst's 55th floor offices precisely at six o'clock so he could catch the receptionist as she was preparing to leave but before she had locked the front door. He strolled in, greeted her and said he had a meeting with Jason Roux.

"I think Mr. Roux has already gone for the day," she told him.

But he bluffed his way right past her with the breezy comment, "He may be out. But he isn't gone. Anyway, I'll go check. This is a meeting the man wants to keep."

In a smaller firm, and under other circumstances such an approach would surely have failed. But Chambers was known to the receptionist. The offices of the firm occupied two entire floors and housed so many people that not all were known to each other. Furthermore, there were strangers in the form of clients and other attorneys in the area all the time. Since Chambers was still practicing law in town, it wouldn't be at all remarkable for him to be on the 55th floor at Herbst. He could very well be there to work with a Herbst attorney on some case they had in common. Still, being spotted by someone who knew him could have been dangerous. So as soon as he walked behind the partition that separated the reception area from the corridor of attorneys' offices, he went directly to the men's bathroom, entered a toilet stall, dropped his trousers, sat down and waited two hours. When he finally came out, even the associates bucking for the firm's bottom tier of partnership had gone home. He then made his way directly to the file storage area and located the file cabinet in which the voluminous documents on *Retif* were stored. Presuming that Joan's current files contained whatever Tammy Dieter-White was looking for, he removed everything from the drawer labeled 1987 and carried it out in his briefcase.

But Dieter-White wasn't satisfied by any of those materials, of course, because the file she was looking for was lying inside a suitcase in our dining room closet. Dieter-White communicated her dissatisfaction in her indirect but nonetheless pointed fashion.

Chambers quoted her as saying, "Teamwork here at Wallace, Johnny, is the most essential quality we ask of people who aspire to join us as partners. Partnership stems from teamwork, all working together to achieve the common good. And to use a football analogy, it doesn't do any good if ten men on the team do their jobs but the eleventh man doesn't. A missed block by only one player results in a sack of the quarterback when he otherwise would have thrown a touchdown pass."

Tammy Dieter-White clearly ascribed to the school of ethics that believed breaking the rules wasn't something to be ashamed of unless you got caught. And Johnny Chambers came to believe that more was required of him than his failure to locate Joan's operational Delacroix file at her old office. He was certain of it some time later when Dieter-White told him one day, apropos of nothing they had been talking about, "You know, when I've got a case I'm really working on hard, I carry files home with me. I've even got filing cabinets at home that I keep materials stored in. How about you, Johnny? Do you ever take files home? I bet you do. Because I know how hard you're trying to make the team here at Wallace and Jones. And I know how much you're willing to do for us after regular working hours."

And so Johnny Chambers, Attorney at Law, became a burglar. It took him some time to work up his nerve. But when he was up for review and Tammy Dieter-White once again treated him to a homily about teamwork and files maintained at home, he decided he'd either have to do her bidding or get out of law practice. And the only thing else he could think of to do was deal drugs. Steal or deal, he said. Those were his options. He selected the former.

His own Uptown apartment had been burgled when he was on vacation once. And so he knew a standard M.O. He simply went to a nearby hardware store and bought a sledge hammer and gardening gloves. Then he called the *States-Tribune*. It had been his intent to try to fish out information about movie screenings by pretending he understood that he could get movie passes by calling the paper. His real purpose, of course, was to learn a time when I wouldn't be home. The switchboard operator at the paper, however, hadn't a clue as to what he was talking about and transferred him to editorial. Somebody there said he'd have to talk to me, but that I was in Los Angeles and wouldn't be back until Monday morning. That was the weekend of the *Cocktail/Rescue* junket.

The rest was easy. Late on Saturday night, twenty-four hours before I returned, he simply walked around the side of the house, splintered open the back gate with one blow of the sledge hammer, walked up on the back deck and hammered in the dead bolt on the back door. In my office, it took him a while to find anything of Joan's, during which time he made a mess out of my movie files. But when he finally found a single manila folder labeled *Retif* he was overjoyed and bolted from my house immediately.

The next day, though, he became extremely nervous about having left the house as he had. It didn't look like a standard burglary at all, he decided. It wouldn't take me or the police minutes to figure out what had happened. And even if such evidence didn't necessarily point at him as the burglar, it could lead to him. So on Sunday night, he returned to the house and worked his way from room to room, messing up something in each. It was his intent to steal a TV and stereo. But I surprised him coming in the front door. And he fled with only the camera he said he found on a shelf in the armoire in the dining room.

For weeks Chambers was terrified that he was going to be caught. When I tried to call him, he was sure I was on to him and demanded point blank that Dieter-White somehow keep me away from him. And the whole enterprise, he told Carl, was so pointless. The file he had stolen wasn't worth the effort. There was almost nothing in it and nothing at all even remotely illuminating. Still, he'd placed it in a plain manila envelope and left it on Dieter-White's desk when she was out to lunch. And she had dropped by his office later to remark, "You know, sometimes we work and work on a project. But we just don't get anywhere." Because they spoke to each other so cryptically, Chambers wasn't sure that she wasn't rebuking him for bringing her something worthless. Her manner, though, suggested a pleased conclusion that Joan hadn't seemingly gotten very far in her investigation of Delacroix after all.

Johnny Chambers had assured Carl during their interview that he had had nothing to do with Joan Barnett's death, had always presumed that Joan's death was the accident it had been reported to be in the paper. Carl quoted Chambers to this effect. And Carl's account made the reader tend to believe Chambers' innocence in this regard. For he revealed something else. Tammy Dieter-White and the firm of Wallace and Jones not only represented Retif Realty. For all the time that Chambers had been associated with her, at least, Tammy Dieter-White had also represented Mrs. Jessica Mason Delacroix.

*   *   *

Sitting on my stool at Morning Call, I looked into the light-bulb-framed mirror in front of me and saw there a vision of imminent ruin. My face was cadaverous white with fatigue smudges of blue black in the hollow under each eye. As best I could reason, things had come to such a twisted pass this Ash Wednesday evening that Johnny Chambers' revelations to Carl corroborated almost beyond dispute my motives for murder. Surely, I tried to comfort myself, I wasn't really in jeopardy from the current police investigation. No witness had yet come forward placing me at the murder scenes. But then, inevitably, I recalled Randall Adams from *The Thin Blue Line*. The police were never even able to establish a motive for the murder with which Adams was accused, and he not only was convicted and spent a decade in prison, he came within days of execution.

*   *   *

Finally, inevitably, I left Morning Call to go home. The police might well be waiting for me there, I recognized. But whatever lay in store for me, I could only make things worse by becoming a fugitive. I'd go home, call Jason Roux and ask him to represent me.

On my dark porch that Ash Wednesday night, I fiddled with my door keys and wondered if I'd manage to stay out of jail for one last night. It was still cold, somewhere in the low thirties, and the wind was howling. It whistled through the branches of the redbud tree in my front yard and rustled the brick-weighted sheets of plastic hanging from the sills of my house. My fingers were thick with cold and clumsy with anguish and exhaustion. I couldn't seem to flick the burglar door key loose from its neighbors on my key ring. Car lights illuminated the street behind me, and I shivered in fear that they belonged to a police car.

And suddenly Jackson Smith was standing on the sidewalk to my left.

It was as if he'd appeared from nowhere. The space in which he stood was empty. And then without sound or sense of movement he was there. He motioned at me with this chin.

"Psst," he seemed to say.

I turned to look at him, and he grinned. I could feel my heart pounding in my ears. I craned my head around to the street, yearning for the appearance of the very police car I'd been fearing. But the street was dark and empty.

"I need to talk to you," Jackson Smith said, almost whispering. "Come on down here and less us get out of the wind."

"What do you want?" I rasped. I could barely breathe. I considered and rejected a dozen different courses of action in a second, to run, to try to hit him with my computer backpack, to try to kick out at his head, which reached about halfway to my knees."

"Come on down here." He showed me his gun gripped in a gloved hand.

"What do you want?" I repeated, though I full well knew what he wanted.

"Come on," he said. "And put that pack thing down on the porch. We won't be needin' that."

I came slowly down the brick steps of my porch, contemplating again my chances of bolting away from him. I had always wondered why people followed the orders of those who were about to kill them.

The answer is that no alternative course of action seems viable until it's too late.

"Put that pack down now," he said, backing away from me. "And come on around here."

I set the backpack on the ground and moved around the side of the porch. He stepped back onto the grass, waving me past him with his pistol.

"Thass good," he said. "Less get on back here where you and me can talk."

As I moved past him, he laid the cold barrel of his pistol against my neck. I jerked when he did so, and he said, "Steady now. You don't want to be makin' no sudden moves. Now go on back there by that side porch where you and me can have ourselves some privacy."

I walked slowly back to the side porch which jutted out from the side of the house at a door to my dining room. When I got there, I stopped, and he touched me with the pistol again, this time in the center of my back. We were in a deep shadow caused by the roof line over the front bathroom.

"Now turn around here real slow like," he said.

As I turned, I stubbed my foot on a brick holding down a sheet of insulating plastic and stumbled. I lurched forward, and he hit me with his gun across my left shoulder.

"Thass it," he said as I fell, "down on your knees there where we can do some business."

He transferred the pistol to his left hand and then used the barrel tip under my chin to bring my head up. He unzipped himself, stepped closer to me and thrust his penis at my face. The gun was back in his right hand now, its barrel against my left temple. He twined the gloved fingers of his left hand in the hair on the back of my head and pulled me toward him.

His tone changed now and he dropped the false politeness. "Now you suck me good enough white boy," he hissed, "and I might let you live to suck me some other time. You touch me with your teeth even one time and I'm gonna stick your own dick in your mouth before I waste you."

His legs planted wide, he began to piston his penis in and out of my mouth. "Lick it, white boy. I want to feel your tongue workin'." His penis seemed to fill my entire mouth, and when the head jabbed at the back of my throat, I thought I was going to gag. His hand in my hair kept pulling me forward, but when I tried to shift my weight, the rough concrete of the porch apron bit painfully into my knees. I put my hands on the ground to try to steady myself.

My fingers found the brick when he began to grunt. As he rammed himself in and out of my mouth with greater and greater speed, I fought for grasp of the brick. And then I had it. And just as he spurted into my mouth I slammed the brick straight up between his legs. He uttered only a single yelp of pain, but he staggered back away from me, and the shot he squeezed off went into my house instead of my head. I came forward, rising to my feet and hit him between the legs with the brick again. I had the full leverage of my weight behind me this time, and the second blow was deadly; it knocked him down on his back. I fell immediately on top of him. I pinned his gun hand under my knee and hit him in the face this time. And again. It was too dark to see, but I could feel the brick tearing skin and cracking bone. And I hit him again.

The struggle went out of his arms and legs now. He was motionless beneath my body. But I hit him again.

In the blackness of night's shadow, I couldn't see what damage I had done, couldn't see the broken teeth, the crushed eye socket and the nose nearly torn away from his face. But I could feel the blood, slippery on my brick. And I could feel the rushing tide of my unspent fury.

And I hit him again.

And I spit in his dark, ruined face, my sputum and his semen mingled together.

And I hit him again.

I might have gone on hitting him until I had pounded his head to jelly, but suddenly I heard the squeak of my front gate, and I froze.

Footsteps on my front porch.

I wrenched the pistol from Jackson Smith's dead hand and rolled into deepest shadow against my house.

Footsteps down the porch and around the side. Stopping. Shoes sliding on concrete. Turning. The back of a black head looking into the street. Turning again. A black hand in the moonlight. A glint of metal.

Another one. Another one after me.

I fired. I fired again. Explosions ringing in my ear. Streaks of white light in the night. The new one clutched his chest and fell backwards without a sound.

I got to my feet. Wary now. Wary. There could be more.

I crept forward toward the body under my redbud tree. The gun was ready, gripped in my hand dripping with the blood of Jackson Smith.

But there was nothing more to fear. There were no more. Jackson Smith was dead. And both my shots had found their mark. Only my second assailant was carrying a piece of aluminum weather stripping rather than a gun. For my bullets had lodged themselves in the chest of my neighbor, Larwood Dupre.

CHAPTER TWENTY-SIX

When the police arrived after I bludgeoned Jackson Smith to death, they arrested me and charged me with a series of murders. The police had no records tracing to Jackson Smith the pistol I had used to shoot Larwood Dupre. Furthermore, Jackson Smith's gloved hands had left no fingerprints on the gun, whereas it was covered with my bloody prints. The Gay Stalker murders had been committed with a pair of .38 revolvers. And now the police had possession of the gun used to commit all but two of those killings. In the minds of the investigators, the Ash Wednesday blood bath was the final episode in my vengeful murder spree.

My life had now stopped spinning out of control and seemingly had blown entirely apart.

CHAPTER TWENTY-SEVEN

I was saved from beyond the grave by Judge Leon Delacroix. My salvation arrived via a letter received for me at the paper on the Friday after Mardi Gras. The letter bore an Ash Wednesday postmark, but was no doubt mailed sometime late on Mardi Gras night. It was Judge Delacroix's suicide note. A copy was brought to me in my cell at Central Lockup as Jason Roux made the arrangements for my release.

Dear Mr. Barnett:

I acknowledge that I have deceived you one last time. At our meeting on Sunday I promised you information about your wife's death by the end of Mardi Gras. And though I am technically keeping my end of the bargain, I realize, now, that this will not reach you until sometime later in the week. I hope that the delay will make no difference. And if it does, I apologize that I will not be here for you to chide.

Before I provide you the answer you have been searching for, I want to relate something else to you. You asked me during our conversation on Sunday how a man could rule as I did on the civil rights issues of the sixties and allow himself to be blackmailed in the eighties. I answered by crediting my eyesight. That was only a half truth.

You will forgive me, Mr. Barnett, for indulging myself some amateur philosophizing. But I conclude by looking backward at my life that Man is a most complicated beast. I have valued principled behavior above all. And I have lived a most unprincipled life. Early in my public life, I knew that the men with whom I was most closely associated were tolerant of, were even on the payroll of, illegal gambling operations in our city. I did nothing to expose them.

I rationalized that I took no payoffs myself, either directly or through contributions to my political campaigns. But I married the daughter of one of the city's gambling chiefs. And I lived a life of additional ease through money of hers I knew was soiled.

What has lingered with me longest, though, is the way I spent the Second World War. I was a prosecutor in the Judge Advocate General Corps. And it was there that I discovered the cowardly, treacherous nature that will be the legacy of this life I will shortly surrender. As other men faced the enemy, risked their lives and died for their country, it fell my lot to prosecute sailors who were accused of homosexual acts. I suffered under this bitterly ironic chore. But I prosecuted these unfortunate men to the best of my ability. And I ruined the lives of several score.

I tried to convince myself that I was different from the men I brought to humiliation, dishonorable discharge and imprisonment by arguing to myself that I had never engaged in a homosexual act while a commissioned officer in the Navy. I was separated from the young man who was my lover at that time for the duration of the war. And I was faithful to him. My celibacy during that period was, of course, pure happenstance. But I maintained my superiority to those I ruined based on that happenstance.

The hour draws late, Mr. Barnett, and I fear that I must hurry. What I am trying to tell you is that my seeming courage during the sixties, (And how courageous was I really? Were not my brethren members of the federal judiciary handing down decision after decision similar to mine?) was a belated act of penance. I had cooperated in pointlessly punishing one minority. So I tried to save my soul by helping another.

How foolish I was! The demanding God who made me a Navy prosecutor can obviously not be assuaged by so little.

For some long but altogether fleeting years, I thought I had bought my salvation. When the Jefferson High School affair forced itself into my life, I realized I had not. I acted, then, selfishly. I told myself that I was protecting my current lover. I even told myself that I was protecting Jessica. But, of course, as forty years earlier, in the military courts of the south Pacific, I was only protecting myself.

Your wife, Mr. Barnett, was murdered by mine. Jessica and I long since had lost even a semblance of affection for each other. Had it not been for Maria, we no doubt would have divorced long ago. The sixties were hard years on Jessica. For during that time, she was closed off from the society into which her alliance with me had purchased her entree. She became then, I fear, bitter and resentful. She hardly endorsed the decisions I made that rendered us social pariahs for nearly a decade. But she stood by me, determined, I understand now, not to be further humiliated by abandoning me.

Our reemergence into social acceptability in the seventies was a great victory for Jessica. She relished the fact that people who had snubbed her were forced once again to pay her court. She was not about to let me fall into disgrace a second time.

I made the mistake of confiding in Jessica when Sheldon Retif first brought up the issue of my racial parentage. He had misjudged me rather seriously on that point. For my boasts to you that I would have stood up to him were true. It would not bother me if my great-grandmother were black, though, as I have told you, she was not. I think I would rather have enjoyed the publicity associated with such charges. And that's exactly what I told Jessica.

I had not considered that she might react somewhat differently. In fact, she was determined that our lives not once again be stained with scandal. And you must understand that to Jessica Mason Delacroix being married for over a quarter of a century to a man of mixed racial ancestry was scandal indeed. Worse, being deemed the mother and grandmother of racially mixed off-spring was intolerable for her even to contemplate. She told me quite plainly at the time that I had no choice but to bow to Retif's demands in exchange for his silence. I refused. And I thought the matter was settled. But then Retif confronted me with his knowledge of my current relationship. And I capitulated.

Though I desperately hoped otherwise, I suspected Jessica's hand in this from the beginning. But until I learned of the circumstances of your wife's death a week ago. I had never confronted her. Her treachery was unforgivable. But her stance was consistent. It was I, on the other hand, who stood for principle and behaved only for self. And until I realized that your wife had been killed to protect my name and the names of my off-spring, I contented myself with mere self-loathing.

What I did not expect was the brazenness with which Jessica admitted her crime. When I stood up to Retif, she simply brought him the evidence that would insure my cooperation. As I understand it, she provided Ms. Tammy Dieter-White at the law firm of Wallace and Jones with the details of my relationship with my lover. Dieter-White gave the details to Retif and my cooperation in *Grieve versus Retif* was compelled.

Jessica placed Ms. Dieter-White on retainer after that. I did not know this, though I probably would not have done anything if I had. And from that point forward Ms. Dieter-White kept Jessica apprised of all developments in the case. When Dieter-White learned of your wife's continuing investigations, she told Jessica. And Jessica acted. She did not supply me with the details, of course. But I presume her father's old connections with the underworld provided her access to an assassin.

I found Jessica's indifference to your wife's fate quite outraging, Mr. Barnett. Scoundrel that I have been in my life, I was not a murderer. That is the final irony of this affair. For now I am that also.

On this Mardi Gras Night, 1989, I have dealt with one of the guilty and shall shortly deal with another: myself. I surrender these facts into your care in the trust that you will deal justly with those who deserve the glare of public scrutiny and those who deserve the opportunity to continue to stand in shadow.

Shadow beckons to me now, and I must go. It is my wish that I had resided there all my days.

May God Have Mercy on My Soul,
Leon Delacroix

*   *   *

What followed the judge's signing and mailing of his letter to me I have pieced together from examining the police photographs and assembling other details Wilson provided me about the murder scene. The judge's body was found dressed in a tuxedo. He had taken his wife to the Comus Ball on Mardi Gras night and hadn't undressed afterwards. He was lying on his stomach, one arm trapped under himself when he fell. In his right hand the judge gripped the pistol that had been used to end his life. A single blossom adorned the judge's beloved rose bushes. Before the fatal shot was fired, he had removed his boutonniere and placed it atop the bushes.

Leon Delacroix's decision to kill himself had been neither sudden nor rash. It was meticulously planned. The rose bushes had been pruned. The soil beneath them had been weeded and fertilized. There were no tools about, no mud on the patio. So all of this gardening had been performed before the judge and Mrs. Delacroix went out to the ball, perhaps as early as Monday. There was a brandy snifter on the wire table next to the chair where the judge had sat when we had talked during Bacchus on Sunday night. Sometime that night, perhaps as he wrote his letter to me, he had sat with his drink for a last hour and beheld the garden that was his treasure and his refuge. When the letter was mailed and he was returned home, he had come again into the garden, walked to the edge of the patio in front of his rose bushes and removed the flower from his lapel, replacing it in his hand with a .38 caliber pistol. Then he had knelt, a last genuflection to the Beauty he had let slip from his life. He had leaned forward, steadying himself with his left arm so that his final, symbolic position would be correct. And with his right hand he had raised the gun to his temple and watered his roses with his blood.

*   *   *

At N.O.P.D. Lieutenant Frank Giannetti reacted to Judge Delacroix's letter much as Carl had predicted so many would. At our final interview before I was allowed to go home, after begrudgingly admitting that he had no choice but to release me, he waved the sheets of the judge's letter back and forth in front of his face and said, "Some effing poetry this is huh? I always suspected he was a little faggot."

As I left the police station I witnessed Giannetti sharing the note with another officer. "How you like this end, huh?" I overheard him say. "Judge hopes God is a bleeding heart liberal just like he was." There was more, but it was drowned out in gales of laughter.

*   *   *

Judge Delacroix's note cleared up many of the mysteries associated with my life. Ballistic tests and police forensics resolved most of the others. In the final analysis, police concluded that Jackson Smith was the Gay Stalker, the creator of an elaborate serial murder subterfuge. Jessica Delacroix hired him to kill Joan and later, to insure the safety of her secret, to murder Sheldon Retif and me as well. The other victims were slain as part of his bloody camouflage scheme. To cover his trail after Joan's death, Smith feigned his own by drowning, placing I.D. in the clothing of the derelict he had thrown into the Industrial Canal, confident, evidently, that the death of another black man would hardly stir authorities enough to unveil his deception. The gun that he brought to my house was the one used to kill all but two of his victims. The gun used to kill Sheldon Retif and one earlier victim was never found, but given the lakeshore site of the murder, police assumed Smith had simply slung the pistol out into the water where it lay forever unfindable on the murky Pontchartrain floor. Forensic tests for semen on Retif's water-logged body were inconclusive. But critically, my semen did not match that taken from the mouths of the other Gay Stalker victims, whereas that of Jackson Smith on my face and clothes and on Smith's trousers did.

The source of the semen trace in the Judge Delacroix's mouth was not Jackson Smith, of course. That semen came from Arthur Adams.

He told me so in so many words when I visited him on the Saturday following Mardi Gras. And he told me that if for some reason I remained a suspect and such testimony would help, he would come forward to state that he and the judge had been together in the hours of Mardi Gras Night after the Comus Ball and that the judge had admitted he'd already killed his wife. But if his testimony was unneeded, Arthur Adams begged me not to reveal his identity. It would mean his job, he said. It would mean all the life he had left now that the judge was dead.

Arthur Adams acquainted me with another fact that Saturday, one that has provided me with much greater relief than his offer to testify in my behalf if need be. He told me that he had talked to Joan the week she died, that he had confirmed his relationship with the judge to her, and that he had implored her too not to make her knowledge public. And she didn't, of course. She died within days, but she wouldn't have had she lived. Joan had struggled on with the case of *Grieve versus Retif* for years. But Tom Grieve was dead. And confronted with another innocent to protect, a living innocent who could have been harmed by her actions, she had decided to let the whole matter drop. Just as Carl had before her.

I may have been disoriented and dismayed when I first thought about the surprise $100,000 in Joan's savings account. But I never really considered that she too had been bribed. Not really. And I'm sure that I could ascertain the origin of that money through a simple record search at Joan's bank. But I haven't done that, and I'm not going to. I presume her innocence as a matter of faith. She was going to let the whole matter drop. That's what she was going to talk to me about on the day that she died. And that was the ultimate irony in this tragedy. Jessica Delacroix had hired Jackson Smith to murder Joan for nothing.

*   *   *

The decision to keep Arthur Adams identity secret was out of my hands now, though. Despite Carl's penitent attempt to write his account of Johnny Chamber's involvement in this nightmare under my byline, the Old Man had predictably and understandably taken me out of the writing of any of this story in which I had become so centrally involved. That story had emerged piece meal on a daily basis since the details of Sheldon Retif's death first appeared on Mardi Gras morning. To tie the thousand threads of the story together, the Old Man had scheduled a massive front-page piece for Sunday. Carl Shaney was writing it. And with everything else he had to reveal, he was planning on identifying Arthur Adams as Delacroix's lover.

Nearing deadline at six p.m. on Saturday, I entered Carl's office and asked him to protect Adams now as he had two years earlier. Carl told me that was impossible. He'd made that mistake once, he said, and he wasn't going to make it again. And so I retreated to my office and waited until I saw Carl leave his office and deposit the hard copy of his story in the copy edit box. As soon as he left the building, I took his story from copy edit back to my own office. I punched up Carl's I.D. code and called his story file up to my own terminal. The piece was 225 inches long, but the search command made the surgery easy. I deleted all references to Arthur Adams. Wherever his name was mentioned, I substituted the phrase "male lover." I cut the entire section where Carl detailed his own interview with Adams and inserted the simple observation that Judge Delacroix's sexual partner had not yet been identified. Joan had died protecting Arthur Adams. The least I could do was protect him too, if only for one day longer. But this was a costly decision. When I entered the piece for Carl in the following year's Pulitzer competition, one of the judges complained that "the reporter's failure to identify and interview Judge Delacroix's lover seriously limits the scope of this story's impact. We need to know what this man knew and what light he may have been able to shed on the events the story narrates."

I made one other change in the copy I found in Carl's file. I deleted the sidebar he'd written detailing his own failure to go public with what he knew of the case in the year before Joan died.

I had finished my changes and saved them into the typeset system by eight o'clock. I felt contractions in my gut as I printed out new hard copy. Like a child to be put up for adoption, the story was not to bear my name, but I felt the labor pains of birth all the same. Bathed in the amniotic fluid of my grief, it had been gestating inside me so long that now the process of its final emergence seemed an excruciating rapture. I broke into a sweat as my printer squeezed out page after page. When finally it was out, I felt a sense of dazed relief as I tore the last page away. I cradled the story against my chest as I walked it to the copy box where I swaddled it among other late-breaking items, secure that as a front-page piece it would be, as always, attended to last.

*   *   *

The Mardi Gras cold front had snapped, and the city was invigorated with sudden spring. But the heaters were still running in the offices at the paper. As I prepared to go home I noticed for the first time how the stuffy inside air seemed to aggravate my fatigue. I felt slack, as if my skin had sagged all over my body. Slinging my Zenith onto the shoulder which still ached from the blow Jackson Smith had delivered with the butt of his pistol, I got up from my desk and walked through Editorial to the men's room. In a mirror above one of the sinks, I studied my image.

My hair was thinning. I wondered how long it would be before I would have to consider myself bald. I looked at the barrel of flesh around my chest and stomach and recalled a time that seemed not so long ago when I thought I could conceal my bulging middle by standing more erect and sucking in my gut. I told myself such lies no longer.

"You are more than halfway gone," I said now to myself in the mirror.

"But you've got nearly halfway yet to go," I responded.

"You're going bald," I said. "You're fat and out of shape."

"I can't do anything about the former," I replied. "But I can endure it. And I can go on a diet and start getting exercise. It's not too late."

"You're a drunk," I said.

"I can stop drinking," I answered.

"You don't know who you are," I reminded.

"But I know who I want to be," I contended.

"You're covering up for them, man," I accused. "What are you doing?"

"I'm doing what I do, *man.* I worked on a story. I've gotten to the end of it. I've looked at what I've got. And I've made a judgment."

I spoke aloud Carl's argument. "Somebody else may get hurt. Truth is your only refuge from responsibility."

And I echoed my own response. "Somebody has got to be responsible. And there are values which surpass even truth. Mercy is greater than truth."

"You are a fool," I told my image. "You can't save Arthur Adams or Carl Shaney either. Truth will out. And somebody else will write the truth of their stories."

"Or maybe somebody else will be merciful."

"No, as always you are naïve. You will never save them."

"Maybe I will fail to save them," I said, countering with the conclusion Joan had obviously drawn before me. "But maybe I can succeed in saving myself. For in the end, the only coin with which you may purchase mercy for yourself is the mercy you have shown to others."

CHAPTER TWENTY-EIGHT

Our softball season started the next afternoon. I was the first to arrive at the City Park diamond on the corner of Harrison and Marconi where we were to play. And as I sat waiting for my teammates, I thought again, as I always did when I came to this spot in the city, of the countless afternoons I spent on this square of grass practicing baseball when I was in high school. Like so many New Orleans high schools, mine lacked a grassy space as part of its campus, so we were bused to and from City Park each day to practice.

Among those hundreds of afternoons, one is fixed in my memory like a corner stone and reconstructs itself repeatedly in the protean landscapes of my dreams. I was terribly skinny my first year in high school. And although I made pretty good contact with the ball and hit for an adequate average, I lacked either power at the plate or a strong throwing arm. Our coach criticized me on more than one occasion for lacking a properly aggressive attitude. By my junior year, however, I had filled out to a stage I'd term rawboned. I was hitting the ball harder, and my arm had improved.

But our coach was a stickler for aggressive play, something he wasn't sure I possessed enough instinct for until our final intrasquad game before the season began. It was as utterly meaningless an exercise as its outcome was predictable. With two outs in the third inning, the starting team, of which I was a member, was already leading five to nothing over the back-ups. I was on second with a double. The batter behind me looped a single to left, and I was off with the swing of the bat. I rounded third with one of my teammates windmilling his arm. There shouldn't have been a play at the plate. I had the weak-armed left fielder's throw beaten by four strides. But the second string catcher came out to block the plate. He was a short, frail sophomore who had made the team primarily because of his willingness to perform the unpleasant duties of catching batting practice. Tommy Robbins was his name. I have not forgotten.

I could have slid. Better yet, I could have stepped around Tommy and scored standing up. But he had come out to block the plate. He was showing our coach his aggressiveness. He was challenging me. And I had to answer. I lowered my shoulder and ran him down. Knocked out, Tommy Robbins crumpled under me like a garbage can might were it set in front of a speeding freight train. When he hit the ground, his head twisted around into the dirt. A gush of air rushed from his mouth and stirred up a cloud of dust in the bare spot behind home plate. I'd knocked the wind out of him and given him a concussion.

I remember that event with the vividness of something that happened yesterday. And I have remembered it for some years with deepening embarrassment. I am ashamed that even in the midst of fearing I'd seriously injured someone, I was secretly joyous to have pleased our coach so much with my display of unrestrained aggressiveness. I am more ashamed of how much I relished the power I felt over Tommy Robbins and all those who were smaller and less capable than I.

But my embarrassment stems from a slightly different source than my shame. It emanates from the blind exuberance of my vanished youth. For running down Tommy Robbins made me feel invincible, made me feel as if the world was at my fingertips. It made me feel as if I was going to live forever. And that event was only yesterday, it seems. But already I am past my prime. And the future beckons only with the crooked finger of old age.

Since the horrors of Ash Wednesday night, I have had my dream about this event twice. It has taken on a new dimension, one I suspect it will never lose. There is nothing I can do but accept its scarring presence in my subconscious. For as I grow older, I know that when this scene runs nightly through the projector of my dreams, Tommy Robbins will now forever wear the startled, stricken visage of Larwood Dupre.

*   *   *

As I began to stretch in preparation for our game, I noted the signs of our city coming to life again after the dormancy of winter. I filled my lungs with the perfume of sweet olives beginning to bloom along the lagoon which curled through the park thirty paces beyond the left field foul line. The day was sunny and clear; the temperature was mild. The humidity was so low the city felt like a community in California.

As game time neared, I was troubled that Carl hadn't yet arrived. He had no doubt seen the paper by now, had figured out what had been done to his story and by whom. I had expected him to call me even before I left home. I couldn't imagine that he wouldn't show up to play this game, no matter what he might want to do to me afterwards.

Like me Carl loved the game of baseball, even the debased, slow-pitch version which was all that we could any longer play. He and I were our team's most devoted players. A decade ago, when we were younger and slimmer, we rated ourselves the best left side in the league, Carl at short, me at third. We'd lost a step or so since then, though, and had conceded our original positions to younger men on staff. I had shifted over to first base; Carl had moved behind the plate. But though our talent had atrophied, our competitive instincts burned as hotly as ever. We yelled the loudest, played the hardest. We savored each victory the most, and suffered the longest over each loss.

But as the game began, Carl had not shown, and Preacher Martin, our pitcher and captain, penciled in the name of Amy Stuart to catch. We missed his bat in our line-up and were down two runs when he finally showed up in the fifth.

He had brought Wilson out with him. They explained that the Old Man had called both in for a strategy meeting about the response to the front-page story in the paper that morning. Wilson was involved because of her role in reporting many of the story's breaking events. Retif's wife, Tammy Dieter-White and the widow of Hastings Moon were all already threatening to sue.

This was not in the least surprising. Carl seldom filed a piece that didn't result in a threatened lawsuit. In fact, he'd asserted on more than one occasion that in his area of journalism a story that didn't elicit the threat of a lawsuit was a story not worth writing. Still, the Old Man called a strategy session every time and always blustered that in his next life he was going to edit an advertiser.

After I flied out in the bottom of the fifth, our guys staged a rally to take a 14-12 lead. As we watched, I approached Carl and asked him if wanted to talk. At first he answered me only with a glare.

Finally, he blurted out, "Who in the fuck gave you the right to touch my stuff?"

"I tried to convince you," I responded. "But you wouldn't listen. And I figured it's what you really wanted to do."

"So you know better what I want than I know."

I didn't respond.

"The white man always thinks he knows what the black man wants. But he never wants to listen to what the black man says."

"This isn't about race, Carl, and you know it."

"You tell me what it's about then."

"It's about doing the right thing," I said.

Carl laughed derisively. "I do the right thing, Mike, and maybe I report this to the Old Man. Then you're on the street." He looked at me pointedly. "You know."

"I know."

"Is that what I should do, Mike? You tell me?"

"You should do what you have to do," I said.

Our ninth batter of the inning grounded to second for the third out, and I had to go out for the top of the sixth, during which our opponents scored four runs to retake the lead.

Carl briefly resumed our conversation while our side batted in the sixth. "I gotta ask you a question about what happened at your house on Wednesday," he said. "Would you have shot Larwood Dupre if he'd been a white man coming through your gate?"

I didn't answer for a long moment. Finally, I said, "I don't even know what the right answer to that question is. I wish I had never fired that gun at all."

"If it had been a white man," Carl insisted, "Would you have shot him?"

"I don't know. Maybe not. It's hard to say. Probably not, I guess."

"See it is about race, Mike. Man was your neighbor. Your friend. And you shot him because he was black. How you gonna live with that?"

"Day by day," I said. "Praying for forgiveness."

Amy Stuart popped to short to end our inning. We were still down 16-14. As we were about to take the field for the last inning, Preacher said to Carl and to Wilson, who had left us alone to talk by ourselves, "I didn't want to have to use you guys, disloyal teammates that you are, getting here with the game almost over like you did and making up this bullshit excuse that working was somehow more important than the American pastime. But it looks like I'm gonna have to put you in there if we're gonna pull this thing out. Carl, I want you behind the plate. And Wilson, you take over for me on the mound."

Preacher was chewing tobacco as he always did at the games and stopped to spit into the dirt.

"A new battery to charge things up," he said.

Both Carl and Wilson maintained that they didn't want to play, but Preacher refused to take no for an answer. I interjected that if Carl wanted to bat he had better go in for me at first because Amy had just made the last out and her spot wasn't likely to come up again.

Afterwards, Preacher asserted with his usual humility that he was obviously the John Wooden of softball. Wilson held the opposition without a run in the top of the seventh. Then, in our last at-bats, our first guy singled. The next batter doubled. With runners on second and third, Wilson, batting in Preacher's slot, was intentionally walked to create a force play at every base. And then Carl, in his first at-bat of the season, hit the ball so far the center fielder stopped running for it after about two steps. Wilson scored the winning run. And we won 18-16.

I felt that ephemeral surge of triumph I get whenever I prevail in an athletic contest or finish a column of which I am particularly proud. Life suddenly, if only briefly, feels so much worth living after all.

Hoping to sustain it, I said to my friends, "Let's go to The Columns for a victory drink. I'll buy."

"Nope," Preacher said. "Drinks are on the John Wooden of softball."

Some of the guys said they'd meet us there. Others said they couldn't make it. Carl was notably muted, despite being the hour's hero. He said he and Wilson had another meeting with the paper's attorney later in the afternoon, but he'd stop by afterwards to see if we were still there. Wilson said she'd do the same.

There were seven of us, altogether, who started out on the porch at The Columns, Preacher and me and five others. It was a glorious afternoon. Azaleas were beginning to bloom on the front lawn of the apartment house across the way. A redbud tree was a blaze of purple in the neutral ground. The soothing air was redolent with the hopefulness of spring.

Gradually, our five colleagues slipped away, and Preacher and I were left to ourselves. Carl and Wilson had promised to come, and we were determined to wait for them, though the meeting at the paper, we realized, might take hours. Afternoon gave way to evening, and they did not appear.

At six o'clock, we agreed to wait another hour. As the sun went down, a bite of chill crept into the air, and I wished I had a windbreaker with me or at least a long-sleeved shirt I could slip on. I shivered and suddenly I felt profoundly depressed.

I poured half a glass of tea back into the empty iced tea pitcher I'd been drinking from and placed my hand around the handle of Preacher's pitcher of beer. Before I could lift it, though, Preacher dropped his hand down over the top.

"You been good so far, son," he said. "Give yourself a break."

I looked out to the sidewalk where a man walked by clutching the hand of the little girl toddling along by his side.

Abruptly I said, "You know Joan and I couldn't have children."

"Yes," Preacher said quietly. "I knew that."

"Joan hid her disappointment in all the energy she invested in this *Retif* case. That's why losing it was so brutal for her."

"And that's why you wanted so much to solve the riddle she was working on when she died."

"I owed her," I said. "Everything I ever did was really her idea or her inspiration. After she went to the Supreme Court, I was so proud of her. And I told her I was going to do something someday that would make her just as proud of me. But I never did."

I shrugged my shoulders and wiped the back of my hand across my lips. "I've never told you this," I said, looking at Preacher intently for a second and then away. "Joan got pregnant when we were young. But we weren't ready, yet, and she had an abortion. That was especially rough on us later when we tried so hard to have children and couldn't. It never changed our attitude about abortion as a basic right, but it was hard personally. You know what I mean. We could have had a child this one time and we didn't." I paused and looked again at Preacher who sipped his beer without commenting. "But see, here's the bottom line. If the choice had been hers alone, she'd have carried the first pregnancy to term. I'm the one who insisted on the abortion. Mr. Logic. I had it all worked out. 'You see, honey, this isn't the time. It'll be so much better later.' Only later, of course, never came."

I tried to swallow down the lump of regret which had formed in my throat. I rubbed both eyes with the heels of my hands. And when I tried to talk again, my voice kept cracking.

"But you know what, Preacher?" I said. "She was so amazing. She was so goddamn amazing. During all that time, to the day she died, Joan never, never blamed me. She could have. It was my fault. But she never blamed me even one time. But if I hadn't insisted on that abortion. If she'd had that first baby. Then maybe she wouldn't have become so obsessed with *Retif*. Maybe she could have walked away from it."

I looked out at the avenue again. It was empty. And the air was still.

"Maybe she'd still be alive," I said.

"So she didn't need to blame you," Preacher said quietly. "Because you blamed yourself."

Preacher lifted a finger toward me and made the sign of the cross.

"In the name of the Father and the Son and the Holy Ghost," he said. "You are forgiven. Go and sin no more."

"Urging Joan to have an abortion wasn't a sin, Preacher. I've committed serious sins, but that wasn't one of them."

"I think it was a sin," Preacher said. "You know that, but I didn't say so. I said, 'Go and sin no more.' But rather than our quibbling over what is sin and what isn't, let's just agree that all of us are in need of forgiveness. You don't need God's forgiveness because you always have it. But you do need some forgiveness, Mike. Right now, you need your own."

I rubbed at my eyes again which were stinging. Preacher poured himself another glass of beer.

"I'm a man who always believed in the sanctity of human life, Preacher. And now in my forty-first year I find that I'm a killer. I'm a fucking mass murderer. I'm responsible for Joan's death, you know. In more ways than one. For the whole last week of her life she wrestled with whether or not to go public with the details she learned about her case. But I had practically forbidden her ever to talk to me again about the whole *Retif* business. And so she didn't confide in me, because I wouldn't let her, and worse, because she knew how rigid I could be, how dogmatic I always was about what was right and what was wrong."

"You gotta stop this, Mike."

"How can I stop it? I'm out of jail. But that doesn't mean I'm innocent. Christ, Preacher, I shot a man. And I beat another man to death with a brick. And I killed Joan, too. And Larwood, Jesus Christ Larwood. Don't try telling me I'm not responsible."

"I won't," Preacher said. "I'm gonna tell you that you are. We're all responsible for one another's deaths. We're lousy, selfish bastards and most everything we do makes somebody miserable, makes somebody sick, makes somebody die. We foul the air. We ravage the land. We make sewers of our rivers and cesspools of our seas. We fuck up by the merest act of being alive. Nothing we do is worth a damn and nothing could be. But one of these days the sun is gonna go out and this orb on which we sit is gonna slide into eternal freezing darkness. And at that point it won't matter shit what even the very best of us has done, not Shakespeare or Gandhi or Thomas Edison or Jonas Salk."

I put my head in my hands. "How can you think like that and believe in a God who cares for us?"

Preacher snorted. "I don't think I've once told you, son, that I *believe* in such a thing as a God who cares for us. But I sure as hell *hope* there's such a thing as God who cares for us. That's the only chance we've got. That's where *faith* comes from. Faith being different from belief, don't you see. I *hope* there's such a thing as a God who cares for us. And I hope such a thing so damn much I find the faith to live as if I really believed it."

"But what do you really *believe*, then?" I asked.

"I don't believe a goddamn thing," he said. "I'm a fucking anarchist. Except I don't believe in anarchy either. I call myself a Christian. But I mainly like doing that because it pisses off so many other people who call themselves Christians."

Preacher lit up one of his unfiltered Luckies. "If I'm a Christian," he said with a laugh, "it's only because Jesus was such a crazy fucker he'd let any manner of man follow after him."

"So you believe in Jesus," I said.

"Fuck no," Preacher replied. "I may have faith in Jesus. But I don't believe in him because my head won't let me. But I tell you three things I do believe. I believe that if we all lived like Jesus, we'd make the world a more hospitable place before the sun blinks off. The other two things I believe right this second have to do with you. I believe you need to forgive yourself about Joan. And about Larwood. And I believe you need to do something about Wilson before it's too late."

I shook my head.

"Wilson and I aren't right for each other," I said. "We come from different places. We look at things in different ways."

"You are surely the stupidest fucker I know," Preacher responded.

I checked my watch. The additional hour we had agreed to wait had passed. Preacher took a large swallow from his glass of beer.

"You tell me that Wilson has a cold heart," he said. "That's one thing. But you just tell me y'all look at things in different ways, that's something else altogether. Something that sounds pretty stupid to me."

I looked at my watch again.

"The main thing right now is that she's not coming. I don't blame her. But I had hoped she would come. I had hoped that she and Carl would both come today. We would celebrate our victory. And we would start over."

"You don't want to keep me company for one more pitcher?" he inquired.

"Nah," I said. "They're not coming. Anyway, I've got things to do."

Preacher drained his last glass and we stood.

As we started down the steps into the spring night, Preacher put his arm around my shoulders and squeezed me briefly to him. "Don't look at it as if Carl and Wilson didn't come, son," he said. "Look at it instead that we just didn't wait long enough."

*   *   *

When I left The Columns, I went to the hospital where Larwood Dupre still lay in intensive care. Only family were actually allowed inside to see him, and even they were restricted to just ten minutes every four hours. My hour-long visits each day to the ICU waiting room were a kind of meditation, an action not for Larwood's benefit, but for mine.

Larwood was still listed as in critical condition. He had technically regained consciousness, but spent most of the time resting in deep sedation. My bullets had injured ribs and severely damaged his right lung. But despite his age, his doctor had told me, he was strong, and there was a decent chance he was going to make it.

Delinda was there when I arrived. I nodded as I walked past her but didn't stop to speak. She studied the glass-walled chamber where Larwood lay and provided me no sign of recognition. I took a chair out of Delinda's line of vision and began my vigil as if I were alone.

Delinda had talked awhile with me when I came the first time after being released from jail on Friday. I had told her how desperately sorry I was.

She responded at the time, "I don't doubts that, Mr. Mike. Larwood say he know you didn't mean it. And I know thass right too. But I ain't forgived you yet, Mr. Mike. Maybe I won't never be able to."

Delinda was supposed to work for me tomorrow. I was sure she wouldn't come. I suspected that she might never be able to bring herself into my house again. And I hardly blamed her. But she needed the income, of course, and that would remain my responsibility whether she worked or not. I would have to slip cash into her mail box if necessary, so as to deny her the excuse to return or destroy a check with my name on it. But I knew there was no sum of money with which I could purchase expiation for what I had done.

*   *   *

As I walked up the steps to my house, I was shocked by an instance of sudden recollection, a drunkard's lost passage rising to the conscious memory like the surfacing of a drowned body. I opened my front door and flipped on the outside light. Then I went back down the steps and around to the side of my house.

Crawling on my hands and knees underneath the porch, I found what I had buried under a pile of leaves in an intoxicated strategy to foil discovery by the police: Wilson's revolver. I carried it back to the light and cracked open the magazine. All five chambers had been fired. I took the gun and placed it once again in my bedside nighttable drawer.

I showered slowly and afterwards, still naked, I stood for a time to examine myself before the full length mirror Joan had had me nail on the inside of a closet door. My shoulders still looked good. I had never had a weight-lifter's upper-body physique, but my arms and chest had good definition they somehow hadn't lost. My legs, too, were acceptable. My calves looked strong. And though my thighs were going soft on the inside, my quadriceps still stood out solid and hard.

From pelvic bone to sternum, though, I was a disgrace. My waist was encased from ribcage to navel with a handful of flab. I was disgusting to myself. But I forced myself to look. I had lost five pounds since Mardi Gras but I couldn't yet see the difference.

I looked over at the phone, willing it to ring. I wanted Carl to call to tell me that we could be friends again the way we had been in the past, if not tomorrow, then sometime soon. And I wanted Wilson to call, call to say that she was ready to begin again, to take some first step, however tenuous, however uncertain, back down the road we had traveled before Mardi Gras. But the phone remained silent.

*   *   *

In bed I lay for a long time in the dark, eyes open, turning this way and that, seeking a physical and emotional restfulness altogether elusive. Sleep, when it came, slipped into the spaces of my unbidden ruminations like a rat darting behind walls. The vision arrived in the dead hours of early morning and played through my mind like spinning frames of celluloid.

Brian DePalma's *Dressed to Kill* flickers unwatched across the screen of a late-night cable station while I attempt to anesthetize myself with Scotch. When I have consumed enough to bind my conscience, I switch off the television and quickly dress in a new pair of jeans, dark running shoes, a navy T-shirt and a black sweater. I slide my hands into a pair of black leather driving gloves. I put Wilson's loaded pistol in my belt and pull my sweater down to cover it. At my front door I make sure the street is empty before I slip out of my front yard and into my car.

Across town, parked in front of the house next door, I spot the Mercedes as it pulls into the dark driveway. I am behind him the moment he steps onto his carport.

"Come on down here," I whisper. And I show him the gun gripped in a gloved hand.

"What do you want?" he asks.

"Come on," I say. I step back onto the grass and wave him past me with the pistol. "Let's get on back here where you and me can talk."

I take him through the backyard, up the levee which borders the rear, down across the grassy stretch of park and across Lakeshore Drive to the seawall. It's a windless night and Pontchartrain is as smooth as glass. And Sheldon Retif and I are as alone and as unreachable as two people in a framed painting. I strike him a blow with the pistol across his shoulder and knock him to his knees.

"Now turn around here real slow like," I order.

When he's facing me, I unzip myself and jab my penis at his face. "Now you suck me good enough fat boy," I hiss, "and I might let you live long enough to suck me some other time."

When I come, my sperm seems to explode through the back of his head, and he tumbles backward down the steps of the seawall and splashes face first into the water.

*   *   *

My therapist would explain that this nightmare, which would plague me in the months to come, was the product of my having been raped. It was a psychic manifestation of my rage at Sheldon Retif for his role in Joan's death and at Jackson Smith for what he did to me. Akin to the phenomenon of a prisoner who identifies with his guard, it was a transliteration of the guilt a victim feels for having suffered humiliation into a violent fantasy of seemingly righteous aggression.

With time I would come to understand this. But on the first night when I awoke at two a.m. terrified by this dream, I lay in my bed breathless with fear that in an act of blind alcoholic fury I had actually murdered Sheldon Retif. I hadn't, of course. Retif was killed with a bullet from a gun used to murder another of Jackson's Smith's camouflaged Gay Stalker victims and that victim had traces of Smith's semen in his mouth. The mystery of the spent bullets in Wilson's gun, I am able to resolve through assembled fragments of memory. On Mardi Gras Night, in the dim translucence of an alcoholic daze, I stood on my porch and like those of my neighbors I have always excoriated, I fired Wilson's pistol as a deranged man's celebration of care forgot. And then afterwards, like a naughty child hiding from his parents the crayons with which he's written on the wall, I concealed the pistol under the porch.

But assuaged as I was by the advent of reality and sober reason, the horror and the shock of the dream that first night was powerful enough to leave me wide awake and catapult me into a state of profound loneliness and depression. In search of solace I rose, put on a bathrobe, went into the living room and took out the album into which Joan had placed the photos of our trip to Alaska the month before she died. I looked through the pictures slowly, recalling the moment each snapshot had frozen in time. There was Joan in her overcoat on the mountain trail above Skagway, the two of us together outside the bus overlooking Polychrome Mountain, Joan shivering at the face of Mendenhall Glacier outside of Juneau. There were a dozen pictures of a mother bear and her two frolicking cubs. On the last page was my favorite photo. It showed Joan in the batting cage aboard the Noordam. She was wearing a black sweater and khaki slacks, and she had tied her hair back in a blue bandana to keep it from whipping into her eyes. She was bent over in a batter's crouch, her bat, which was too long and heavy for her, held back and high, awaiting the next pitch. Before she had gone into the cage she told me that she had never learned to hit, but that she was going to practice so that one day she could knock a ball out of the Superdome. And so she stood waiting, bat cocked, tense and ready. Forever unable to swing.

*   *   *

I put away the album, went to the pantry and took down a quart bottle of Black and White. I filled a plastic Carnival cup with ice. I took the bottle and the cup back to my study and sat down at my desk.

For a long time, surrounded by the darkness elsewhere in my house and the black night outside, I sat doing nothing. The only sound in the room was the rustle of my indecisive breathing and the pop of the ice as it melted and settled in my cup.

Finally, I flipped up the lid of my Zenith lap-top, flicked the computer to life and opened a new file. Joan was dead. Larwood was critically wounded. Wilson and Carl hadn't come. Delinda wasn't coming. The bottle and the computer were before me. I could either drink or write. One or the other, not both.

For the moment, I chose to write.

This is what I wrote:

Near the beginning of Phil Alden Robinson's Field of Dreams, *a contemporary Iowa farmer wanders through his shoulder-high cornfield, inspecting the sturdy green stalks which provide his livelihood. Behind him, on the porch of their white frame farm house, his wife and young daughter take the pleasant air of a sunny summer afternoon. Suddenly, as if from heaven, he hears a whispering voice that insists, "If you build it, he will come." The farmer asks his wife if she has heard the voice, but she hasn't. And anyway, she wants to know, "If you build what, who will come?" There is not a lone answer to her joking query. But a subsequent cornfield vision provides farmer Ray Kinsella (Kevin Costner) the first in a series of answers to his wife's question. If he plows his corn under and replaces it with a baseball diamond, the shade of banned Black Sox legend "Shoeless" Joe Jackson (Ray Liotta) will come to the grassy expanse of left field to break at the crack of the bat with the grace of a startled deer and snatch fly balls from the Iowa sky. What kind of crazy movie is this, we ask ourselves. It's a movie the likes of which we have never before encountered.*

Based on the novel Shoeless Joe *by W.P. Kinsella,* Field of Dreams *is the story of a former Berkeley hippie's struggle to adjust to life at the dawn of middle age. Ray married his college sweetheart, Annie (Amy Madigan), and, much to Ray's surprise, they've settled near Annie's Iowa* home to try their hands at farming. They've achieved at least middling success. The farm is stable; there's a little money in the bank. They have an adorable daughter, Karin (Gaby Hoffman), whom they both cherish. But when Ray begins to hear the whispering in his cornfield, he admits to Annie that he's afraid of becoming like his father. "My father never did one spontaneous thing in his whole life," Ray explains to Annie. "He may have had visions, too, for all I know, but he certainly never did anything about them."

In rebellion against his father's example of growing old without ever heeding the voice of magic one hears in daydreams, Ray decides to build his baseball field. And wearing the disgraced white linens of the 1919 White Sox, Joe Jackson does come. Ray takes inexpressible pleasure in knocking flies to Joe or in throwing pitches the slugger clubs into the forest of corn that stands like a green wall behind the left field grass. He feels a unique sense of accomplishment in providing an opportunity for Joe to play again the game he loved so much. But the coming of Joe Jackson is not the end of Ray Kinsella's story; it is only the end of the first chapter. For the whisperer speaks again: "Ease his pain." And a vision clarifies that Ray is to seek out a disaffected black writer from the sixties named Terence Mann (James Earl Jones) and accompany him to a Red Sox game at Boston's Fenway Park. Destroying such a substantial part of his corn crop has sent Ray's financial profile plummeting. His avaricious brother-in-law has bought the mortgage on his farm and is threatening to foreclose. But with Annie's encouragement, Ray heads off to Boston. And once he's snared Mann with the net of his magical vision, the two of them journey to Chisolm, Minnesota, and back into time to meet a small-town doctor, Archie Graham (Burt Lancaster), who once played a single inning of major league baseball but never touched the ball and never got a chance to bat. Finally, Ray and Terence return to Iowa where the culmination of Ray's willingness to act on the impulse of his dreams results in an opportunity for reconciliation with his father who died when Ray was in college.

Field of Dreams *is such an unusual story, and it dares such a heavy measure of sentiment, that it will no doubt strike some viewers as irksomely fantastic on the one hand and noxiously treacly on the other. The New Yorker's Pauline Kael has already staked out a biting claim in this critical territory. "Field of Dreams is a crock," she says. She chides director Robinson for treating his audience "as if their brains were mush," for providing such "doggerel emotion" and "corn-fed epiphanies." In the end Kael sees the movie as a treatise on the importance of social conformity. "The movie is pretty close to saying," she argues, "don't challenge your parents' values, because if you do you'll be sorry."*

In short, I don't think Ms. Kael could be more wrong about a movie.

There's no quibbling about the fact that Field of Dreams *is a whimsy. It's a movie set in the Iowa and America of W.P. Kinsella's imagination. But there's a message in Kinsella and Robinson's homage to the magic of dreams. For possibilities reside there. In dreams, Joe Jackson can be forgiven his role in throwing the 1919 World Series and be allowed to run and throw and bat again, can enjoy once more the sensory thrills of smelling a ballfield's aroma of mown grass, raked dirt, parched peanuts and boiled hot dogs, of feeling a ballglove's oiled leather and a bat's polished ash, of hearing the thwok of a flyball lifted into the sun. In dreams, one can redo the past, and an aging man who craved but a single opportunity to bat in the major leagues can be a boy again and set his spikes and lift his Louisville Slugger to receive a pitch from fabled Eddie Cicotte. In dreams, a son who rebelled against his father shortly before the father's death can be afforded the chance for reconciliation. In sum, Time is an enemy that eventually defeats us all. But if we can dare to dream, if only for a fleeting second, we can hold the inevitability of Time's victory at bay.*

But does it all have to be so teary, you can hear a Pauline Kael demand. Does it have to try to stir you so? The answer is a resounding "yes." Field of Dreams *is a picture about magic. And magic can't be found on the path of logic. For it dwells in the realm of emotion.*

I was struck several years ago when I first read W.P. Kinsella's novel how much Shoeless Joe *was an allegory about the creative process, particularly the risk and investment of writing a novel (or maybe also that of making a film). Having seen the movie now, I'm all the more convinced of the story's allegorical intentions. And in this allegory resides the story's defense against Ms. Kael's accusation that it affirms conformity. The artist must always defy conformity as the initial act of creation. Thus, it's no accident that Kinsella gave his dreamer protagonist his own last name. Ray Kinsella is a man who hears a private voice that tells him to do something utterly impractical, something that will bring the dead back to life. Doing it occupies an immense amount of time and can be accomplished only at considerable psychological and financial risk. Ray's friends think he's gone crazy. They can't see what he's trying to do; once he's done it, they are slow either to comprehend or appreciate. As is true of a writer, Ray doesn't even know where he's heading at the outset of his creative quest. But he implicitly trusts the voice that whispers to him alone.*

In the end, when the creation is completed, a new temptation intervenes, in Field of Dreams *in the form of a brother-in-law who wants to convince Ray to sell out. But like the writer who must believe in the face of all evidence to the contrary that he has something to say worth hearing, Ray must listen to Terence, who counsels that Ray's problems will be solved by the arrival of those who appreciate what he has sought to accomplish. "Don't sell out, Ray," Terence advises. "People will come."*

Field of Dreams *is not a film that directly addresses issues of race. But in these troubled times of racial disharmony, I am struck that the abiding principle of this picture emerges as an agreement between two friends, one black, the other white. The absolutes of logical blacks and whites merge into the misty grays of the spirit. People will come.*

That was surely W.P. Kinsella's mantra as he wrote Shoeless Joe. *And it should be embraced by all who dare to dream of a better world.*

*   *   *

People will come. It may not be true, but we must believe it nonetheless. We must act on it nonetheless. If we build it, people will come. If we don't sell out, people will come. If we are remorseful, if we are willing to forgive, those around us and ourselves as well, people will come.

If we wait long enough, people will come.

ABOUT THE AUTHOR

In addition to *With Extreme Prejudice* Fredrick Barton is the author of the novels *In the Wake of the Flagship*, *The El Cholo Feeling Passes*, *Courting Pandemonium*, and *A House Divided*, which won the William Faulkner Prize in fiction. He is also the author of the collection of essays *Rowing to Sweden* and the jazz opera *Ash Wednesday*. He is co-editor of the collection of short stories *Monday Nights*. From 1980-2008, he served as the film critic for the New Orleans weekly, *Gambit*. His many awards include a Louisiana Arts Prize; the New Orleans Press Club's annual criticism prize 11 times and its highest honor, the Alex Waller Memorial Award; the Stephen T. Victory Award, the Louisiana Bar Association's prize for writing about legal issues; and the Award of Excellence from the Associated Church Press for his feature essay "Breaches of Faith" about recovery efforts in New Orleans after Hurricane Katrina. Rick received his B.A. from Valparaiso University and earned graduate degrees at UCLA and the Writers' Workshop at the University of Iowa. Valparaiso honored his lifetime achievements with an honorary Ph.D. in Humane Letters. Rick has been on the English faculty of the University of New Orleans since 1979 where he has served as Dean of Liberal Arts and as Provost and Vice Chancellor for Academic and Student Affairs. He is currently Research Professor Emeritus and Writer in Residence in the Creative Writing Workshop, UNO's MFA program in imaginative writing, which, with his colleagues, he founded in 1990.